MELT

A TimeBend Novel

Ann Denton

Le Rue Publishing

Le Rue Publishing
320 South Boston Avenue, Suite 1030
Tulsa, OK 74103
www.LeRuePublishing.com

Ordering Information:
Quantity sales. Special discounts are available on quantity purchases by corporations, associations, and others. For details, contact the publisher at the address above.
Orders by U.S. trade bookstores and wholesalers. Please contact Le Rue Publishing at: Tel: (918) 216-0180; or visit www.LeRuePublishing.com.

Printed in the United States of America

ISBN 978-0-9985437-1-0

First Edition

For Rob.

Table of Contents

CHAPTER ONE

"Don't look. Don't-look-don't-look-don't-look," Mala muttered under her breath. Her eyes were fixed on her mother across the entryway. Erinne had her shotgun slung over her shoulder as she bent and dug through a trunk full of moth-eaten quilts, pulling out something that resembled a colorful spiderweb more than a blanket.

She's not gonna look, Mala chided herself. *The light's too dim anyway.* It was true. Other than the window they'd crawled through, there was no light to speak of. The foyer of the mansion resembled a tomb more than anything. The bones of a rotted couch cast eerie shadows on the wall. And her mother dug deeper into the trunk, intent on scavenging. *She's not gonna look. Just do it.* But Mala's heart didn't trust her head. It beat out a worried rhythm on her ribs.

Slowly, Mala crouched down and slid her hand between two jagged panes of glass that threatened to bite her wrist. She held her breath as she twisted a little knob. Luckily, it fell off without a fight. She risked a glance down. A pitted, abused face stared back up at her. Jewels pried out of the center, numerals pried off the cheeks—someone had smashed this poor grandfather clock to pieces a long time ago. When gold had been worth something.

You are so stupid, Mala scolded herself. *This isn't gonna work. Just leave—* But her mother made a noise, and before Mala could argue with herself, she'd slipped the hour hand off the clock and into her frayed pocket.

Erinne led the way down a dim hall; Mala followed like a younger, suppler shadow. A cracked mirror gaped at the two women in threadbare brown trousers and collared shirts, the images of their untamed brown curls, sun-kissed skin, and chocolate eyes refracted back in slivers until the mirror saw only a shadowy, many-eyed monster. The women peered in every direction as they both stepped over a marble column—a fallen soldier among the many guarding this vast house. Erinne held the shotgun ready; Mala, a trident dagger that had been her father's.

Erinne jerked her brown curls toward a bedroom. Mala followed, and while her mother checked the closet, the seventeen-year-old peered out a broken window at the forest. Her eyes flickered over the trees, searching, seeking. An eerie feeling crept up her spine. *Calm down. It's just another supply run. No one's here. Scouts said the last Erlender boat was thirty kilometers upriver.* But a breeze caused the trees to shiver, and Mala couldn't help joining them.

She glanced back into the room to see her mother pocketing some rusted safety pins.

Mala returned to her mother. "We should hurry." She tried to sound calm, simply cautious. She tried not to let the fear trickle into her voice. The house had looked deserted, but this far north it was hard to tell. This far north, it was dangerous.

When Erinne was ready to move on, she grunted and Mala followed her into the hall. They went through room after room, quickly eliminating most. But Erinne stopped short in the master bedroom. A series of paintings stacked near the bed caught her eye. The first painting showed a girl swimming underneath the crusty hull of a ship. Mala barely glanced at it as she walked the perimeter of the room.

Crash.

Mala whirled around, prepared to throw the dagger. Her mother stood frozen, a hand to her mouth, the painting of the little girl forgotten on the floor. Mala followed her mother's gaze and saw the second painting. A ship aflame on the water. Her mother began to tremble.

Quickly, Mala crossed the room and turned the canvas around. She reached for her mother's hand but Erinne waved her off.

"Momma, I'm just trying to help—"

Erinne gave her *the look.*

"Fine," Mala muttered. "I'm going to check the kitchen. You stay here. When I get back, we're leaving." Her mother nodded absently, arms clutching her torso.

Mala sighed and walked purposefully down the hall to a vast kitchen. There was nothing to do but give her mother space when she was rattled like this.

The forest had already reclaimed a good portion of the kitchen. Ferns and stubby trees huddled in the shafts of sunlight filtering through the tattered roof. Mala yanked on a warped cabinet drawer. It wouldn't budge. Neither would its neighbor.

The top cabinets hadn't sealed themselves shut, and a quick glance told Mala they'd been raided long ago. But as she moved to close the last one, a glint from the top shelf caught her eye. She set down her knife and hoisted herself carefully onto the old stone countertop.

The lower cabinets groaned but held as Mala peered inside. She saw a single gleaming jam jar. It was full of bullets. *Flooding hell. I knew it.* Her heart raced as she reached for the jar. Behind it, well-polished and oiled, was a gun. Mala nearly fell off the countertop.

"Sludge!" she cursed and clung to the shelves. She tied a knot in her shirt and shoved the jam jar inside. She took the gun in her shaking hands and checked it. The magazine was fully loaded.

Mala wanted to yell for her mother, to run screaming down the hall and grab her. Instead, she counted internally. *One, two, three* ... her pulse started to calm. And then she slithered silently to the floor. Gun in one hand and knife in the other, she crept back to the master suite to collect her mother. But Erinne was nowhere to be seen.

"Mom!" she whispered, panicked. "Momma?" She ran across the room to a door on the other side. The breath fled from her body and cold flooded her. She grabbed the door handle for support.

Oh God—they've taken her.

The door smashed Mala in the face. She groaned.

Erinne peered around the edge apologetically. Mala clasped her jaw, but didn't feel the throbbing. She only felt relief. Her mother held out a long white plastic bag as a peace offering.

"We have to leave now! Forget that stuff, whatever it is. We have to go. Someone's been here. Someone's staying here. I found this." Mala held up the gun. Erinne's eyes widened in alarm.

"Come on!" Mala tucked the knife in her waistband and pushed at Erinne, but her mother wouldn't relinquish her hold on the plastic bag. "Then bring it—I don't care, but we've got to be out of here before they get—"

An explosion rattled their teeth. Mala grabbed her mother's hand and the two exchanged a long look. Then they raced down the hall, back toward the broken window that had served as their entry point.

Mala peered out the window before launching through it and dropping to the ground. Her mother landed softly beside her.

A sudden crash made the women freeze. Mala grabbed her weapons and flattened herself against the wall of the house. "Erlenders," she croaked weakly to her mother. Erinne shuddered in fear next to her, turning her head rapidly like a bird. Mala tightened her grip on the gun. She swallowed. *If I have to shoot someone, I have to. I have to protect mom. If I have to shoot someone... oh, please don't let that happen.* The gun quivered in her hand. The seconds dragged slowly, agonizingly, and each breath Mala took felt like a deafening roar, sure to give away their location. She held her breath.

But it did no good. A second explosion rang through the forest. Before Erinne could fully lift her shotgun or Mala could recover from her shock, a thick bull of a man barreled through the trees right in front of them.

Smack!

Pain radiated all the way from Mala's spine to her fingertips. It sang in her head like a bell. It reverberated through her body, shaking every last ounce of flesh.

Mala fought her body and forced her eyes to focus on the man in front of her. To her shock, she recognized him. He wasn't an Erlender. Deep brown skin, screws piercing his ears, snub nose, a black fish tattoo covering his chin and half his neck - he was one of the best soldiers in Bara's guard.

"Sorgen?" she whimpered.

"Mala!" Blood gushed down his forehead, into his eyes. "Help me."

CHAPTER TWO

Years later, decades later, eons later, they reached the safety of the river. Or so it seemed to Mala's aching back. She'd had to carry Sorgen; the explosion had taken a huge chunk out of his right leg; it was a miracle he'd collapsed onto her. The wide belt of water had never looked so inviting. Mala longed to dive in. But she knew she wouldn't be able to keep herself afloat. Only her swimmer's strength had let her stumble along with Sorgen this far.

As she'd struggled through the undergrowth, Mala had tried to ask Sorgen what had happened. She wanted to ask why he was off in this tributary instead of on the main patrol route, but the blood loss had shut him up and a glare from Erinne had shut her up.

She navigated carefully down the sloping bank. *So I guess this is what the frontlines feel like ...* Mala's thoughts fizzled as she focused on making it through the undergrowth without pitching face-first into a fallen tree with a grown man wrapped around her neck. Finally she was close enough to the water that she could set Sorgen down in the mud. Her body singing in relief, Mala didn't take a moment to relax. She slid down the riverbank.

Erinne's old speedboat, a rusting green pill with Bara's black fish painted on its deck, floated serenely on the water. Hopping aboard, Mala cleared the cabin and stood watch while her mother floated Sorgen to the ladder. With a lot of grunting, heaving, and near misses, they managed to get the unconscious Senebal warrior aboard.

"No more raiding," Mala said earnestly, as she gunned the engine and they sped away, heading south to safety. "We didn't find anything useful in that place. Wasted trip."

Erinne shook her head and slowly unwound the plastic bag she'd tied over her shoulder. A brilliant blue dress cascaded to the floor. It looked like the night sky, a deep navy encrusted with sparkling stars. The skirt fell out in a bell. Mala couldn't believe her eyes. But she swallowed her awe.

"Really, Mom? A dress? Are you going to rip that up for bandages? Because I don't see how it's gonna help Sorgen."

Her mother rolled her eyes and went into the cabin to get their meager supply chest. It held the few medicines sent from DasWort, ripped cloth strips that had been boiled to serve as bandages, and jars of roots and herbs gathered from the banks of the Gottermund River. *Hopefully it's enough,* Mala thought as the river swayed to the left. She didn't look down, but she knew her frayed khakis were soaked in blood. She hadn't looked closely, but she knew Sorgen's wounds were bad.

Mom's dealt with bad before. It will be enough. It has to be enough. Because the few jars were all they had. And because Mala couldn't stand the thought of losing another member of their guard. Couldn't stand the thought of another funeral.

But Erinne was a miracle worker. Everyone in Bara's contingent said she was the best medic they'd ever had. *And this is Sorgen,* Mala's brain scoffed. He was one of the best soldiers Bara had, probably one of the best soldiers in the entire Senebal nation. *He's lived through four major battles and an alligator attack.* Some people joked that Sorgen's ferocious determination kept him alive, that he was too bloodthirsty to die. Of course, he always said it was his lucky coin, a pre-bomb relic he wore on a chain around his neck. And he'd walked out of the smoking battle grounds more than once with it gleaming on his chest.

She'll fix him. Mala turned her attention back to steering, feeling more confident as Erinne settled to work on the deck behind her. The thrum of the engine was lulling and Mala's thoughts began to wander. Her eyes slid back to the dress. She'd never seen anything like it. Most of the clothing factories had gone up with the bomb. She only knew of one left in the capital city DasWort, and it only produced the most pedestrian necessities. There was no telling how old this dress was.

Someone really left it behind all those years? Mala grimaced internally as she realized the reason her mom had taken the dress. *She's gonna make me wear it at the celebration tonight.* But then she heard something that drove the celebration from her mind entirely.

Sorgen howled ferociously. Mala glanced back just in time to see him retch onto Erinne's lap.

Navigating to a bend sheltered by cyprus trees where they wouldn't be easily seen, Mala cut the engine, tossed an anchor, and crouched to help her mother.

"Sorgen," Mala touched his scarred arm. His eyelids fluttered, his eyes rolled ... and then he stilled. Mala took his pulse. *Thank goodness.* She gave a sigh of relief. It would be easier if he was unconscious.

She took stock of his injuries. His facial wounds were shallow: a bullet had grazed his forehead, another his lip and lower jaw. A lump formed in Mala's throat. His necklace was gone. *It's just a necklace,* she scolded herself. But she didn't really believe that.

She glanced down where her mother worked on the ragged leg wound, the shredded muscle and exposed bone.

"Is that—from the explosion?" Mala asked.

Erinne gave a brief nod and sifted through her supplies, selecting those she would need. She made an absentminded gesture, but Mala knew exactly what her mother was thinking.

We need a better tourniquet. Mala scanned the deck. She settled on a gnarled old piece of rope from a canopy pole. She offered it to her mother and gritted her teeth as they tightened it around his thigh.

A low moan escaped Sorgen's lips. Mala turned slowly to find his eyes on her. She froze, panicked. *But he—he was passed out.* She looked at her mother, but Erinne was bent over the leg. Mala backed up. *Just look away. Look away.* She tried to focus on her breathing. She stared at the blood coating the deck planks.

"Sorgen. My mom's fixing you. You're gonna be okay," Mala prayed her words proved true.

"Verrat …" he murmured his wife's name.

Mala shifted her eyes to her mother's hands.

"Do you want me to radio her—"

Erinne cut her off with a sharp jab and a shake of the head.

"I'm sorry—we're not in safe radio distance I guess. But ..."

Sorgen's lips moved, but Mala couldn't hear. She risked a quick glance at his face. Tears soaked his cheeks and carved little paths into the congealed blood.

"I could go get Verrat," Mala volunteered, but Erinne whipped her head up and flashed her eyes.

"He's conscious," she mouthed at her mom. "That could be a problem. I could—you know ..."

Erinne simply gave her *the look.*

I hate it when you do that! Mala wanted to yell, but she sighed. Her instincts were screaming but instead of leaving she unrolled some bandages and began to apply them to his face. *Stay calm,* she berated herself. *Or you'll bring on an episode.*

"They ... tell Bara ... they ... noooo," Sorgen's words came out in a ragged hiss as she tightened a bandage around his forehead.

"They what, Sorgen?" Mala asked, in a polite attempt to distract him from the pain rather than any attempt to listen.

"Noooo." He spit out blood that had trickled into his mouth. "Mala. You … don't go!"

"I'm not going anywhere," Mala tried to soothe him. But pain was making him frantic.

"They, they ... nooo!" His words ended in a mangled scream. "Verrat ... she ..." He grabbed Mala's arm and pulled her close. They were nearly nose to nose. His fiery expression set Mala's teeth on edge. Her stomach clenched. She started to feel uncomfortably warm.

"Can't we give him something?" Mala breathed, praying her mother would hurry.

Erinne checked her collection of sedatives. Most jars were nearly empty. Injuries were common in Bara's northern river guard. Erinne spent a good deal of her time walking the banks and replenishing or raiding like they had been today. As her mother pulled up a jar of skullcap, Mala saw that the leaves barely coated the bottom of the jar. There wasn't enough left to numb his pain. The thought made Mala tremble. One by one, she pried Sorgen's fingers off her arm. She slid back and stared hard at her mom. She willed the woman to let her go. But Erinne was stone.

Mala read the set, determined look on Erinne's face. *Muck. She's going to have to take the leg.* She avoided eye contact with Sorgen, whose brown orbs flickered frantically between Mala and her mother, silently asking why they were so still. *I've got to tell him.* She swallowed.

"Sorgen—" Before she could get anything out, his jaw dropped. Mala turned to see her mother holding a large, vicious-looking axe.

Sorgen spluttered and thrashed, and finally got a coherent phrase out. "No! Please, no!" Though the plea was for Erinne, he directed his face towards Mala. "Please. I … just wanted to be Kreis," he whispered. Mala tried to swallow the knot in her throat, and looked at her mother pleadingly.

Since he'd been eight, all Sorgen had ever dreamt about, all he'd ever talked about, was joining the elite guard. He wanted to wear the brand, be counted among the best Senebal warriors. He and his wife, Verrat, had trained every day, volunteered for the most dangerous assignments, both hoping one day they'd be chosen. Of all the soldiers in Bara's guard, Sorgen had worked hardest for that honor.

Mala felt ill. She had to count to three to calm herself before she could respond. "Sorgen, I'm sorry. It's the only way." She looked away, as his dream drowned in a messy pool of blood, spittle, and tears. *Don't think*, she told herself firmly. *Just do as you're told.*

At Erinne's gesture, Mala crawled forward and sat squarely on Sorgen's chest, knees pinning the man's arms to the deck. He was weak from the blood loss; she could feel the limpness in his limbs.

Mala made the mistake of glancing at Sorgen's dark brown eyes; they were full of anguish. She ripped her gaze away. *Count. Now.* She fought to keep her thoughts neutral. Fought the onslaught of another episode.

Mala had known Sorgen since she and her mother had joined the guard three years ago. She knew him as she knew everyone else in Bara's guard. But she had avoided him. She avoided everyone. Mala the Ghost, they called her. They all knew something was wrong with her. That she was off. They had no idea how far. Mala made sure they didn't. She figured loneliness was better than insanity. No one knew how much Mala feared seeing their faces contorted in grief. Because that kind of pain made her stomach burn and her insides turn to ash. It made her eyes feel like they would melt in their sockets. It made her hallucinate—feel as though she were burning alive. And sometimes, if she couldn't get away fast enough, she saw things.

Only her mother knew. Mala made sure it stayed that way. Because people hated a loner, but they'd lynch a psychopath. She and Erinne had had to leave guards before this. People didn't understand what it was like. How her ribs contracted. How it felt like a cigarette burn and morphed into a house fire in her chest.

Mala brawled with that burn now. She squeezed her eyes shut as Sorgen writhed beneath her. "Mom, please, can you do something?" she begged.

Erinne came and knelt beside Mala, staring for one second at Sorgen's face. Then she gave a swift backhanded chop to his neck. His eyes rolled back in his head. He was out. Erinne stood and pushed back her graying hair. She returned to the leg.

Mala felt a surge of relief. *And now he won't feel it,* she thought to herself. *Will he?* Without warning, there was a sickening thud. Mala bit her lip. Sorgen's face drained of color. So did hers. But she held fast to her position.

Erinne set to work, quickly tying off the stump and packing the wound with gauze and bandages. Mala climbed off Sorgen. She tried to breathe through her mouth to avoid the rancid scent of blood. *It's almost over. You did it. You got through it and didn't freak out or hallucinate ... and he's going to be fine.*

But then her mother gave a gasp. Mala looked over and felt panic flare in her stomach. Erinne was never surprised.

A torrent of blood was issuing from Sorgen's leg. Everything

Erinne had done to stop it had failed. The older woman sat back with a look of shock on her face, and Mala crept over to her. She touched her mother's shoulder. When Erinne lifted her head, there was a haunted, dead look in her eyes. It was a look Mala had seen before. Seen surrounding her, in every face on the night her father died ... Mala tried to count, to focus elsewhere, to block out the memories. But her mother's eyes locked her in, dragged her under.

The burning started. Mala could feel her face begin to melt and her stomach begin to twist in the heat. She felt the skin on her cheek bubble. She was on fire. Her vision blurred.

It was night. A man with a striped blue nose and a bullet hanging from his ear stalked across the deck toward her—

She felt rather than saw her mother push her to the edge of the boat. She was only half-conscious of her surroundings as she stripped to her underwear and climbed the rail. A blowtorch was ripping apart her stomach. She heard Sorgen moaning, but didn't look back. She didn't want to answer the question his eyes would ask.

Her mother pushed her, and she splashed feet first into the icy water. It froze the fire in its tracks. Mala dove deep into the river, desperate to escape her mother and Sorgen's dead eyes.

CHAPTER THREE

The sunset cast a dulled rainbow on the Gottermund's surface. Underneath the water, a shadow separated from the depths. Mala's head broke through orange waves. She stared forlornly at the gathering patrol boats. She saw some people rowing, others trying to catch the light breeze in their improvised sails. Few boats were allocated gas anymore. Only those going on patrol or to battle. Or her mother's. To save the wounded.

Ach, don't think about that. Sorgen's face appeared in her mind and shame filled her. She'd left her mother alone. Again. Her thoughts flickered back to the hour hand buttoned tight in the pocket of the pants she'd shed. *Maybe ...* she shook off hope before it could fully form. *You really are crazy, if you think something that mudding dumb could work,* she scolded herself.

She swam on. She was calm now. It had taken several hours, but she was herself again. She was not looking forward to the night's party; she shuddered at the thought of all those people, the entire guard coming together. The thought of weaving through that crowd, with all their joy at the celebration mingled with sadness at Sorgen's death, nearly made her ill. *I'll have to be careful. Stick to the shadows.*

She swam over to one of her regular lines. It was empty. She took off the hook, changing it for one of the many she wore strung around her neck. *Maybe one with a red lure will attract more attention.*

A raft floated past and Mala dove underneath it, heading for a small trap she'd tossed into the shallows yesterday. She crossed her fingers that she'd snagged a catfish or two. Otherwise, she and her mother would head to the celebration with empty stomachs. Not a good prospect for a night sure to be full of alcohol.

Luckily, Mala found a fat whiskered fish floating in her trap. She grabbed it by the gills and used her biggest hook to gut the wriggling fish. She used its innards to bait the trap. *Hopefully that'll tempt an even better dinner in tomorrow.* She swam briskly back to her mother's boat.

"Momma, I got a fish," she called out, tossing it onto the counter in the cabin.

Her mother emerged from the single bedroom, dressed to the nines in a patchwork lilac gown. She grabbed Mala's arm and stared at her face intently.

"Ohhay?" Erinne asked.

"I'm fine. I'm ... sorry. I know you needed my help. I just couldn't ..." Mala began, but her mother swept her into a deep, wordless hug. Sorgen was the third soul lost this month. Life in northern Senebal territory wasn't particularly kind.

Squeezing her once more, Erinne stepped back and tried to lighten the mood. She swept into a deep curtsey, and pirouetted with her hands above her head to show off her dress. It had gathers and poufs in odd places to hide the rips and rot of time. But it was a lovely shade of purple still and she knew exactly how to twist up her hair to compliment the dress. After thirty years wearing it, that was no surprise. The dress had belonged to Erinne's grandmother—a relic from before the bomb. It was her mother's treasure. And as Erinne wore it, she glowed. Her excitement filled the room until Mala could almost smell it. It was cloyingly sweet, almost childlike excitement, irresistible as a peach.

"Why didn't you wear the new dress?" Mala asked. "You found it."

At that, Erinne put her hands on her hips and gave Mala a no-nonsense look.

Mala bit her lip. No one else in the guard had had a new dress for as long as Mala could remember. The last thing she wanted was to garner extra attention from drunk, emotional soldiers.

But Erinne raised a single finger and pushed it against Mala's lips. Mala sighed. It was impossible to argue with her mother. "Fine. Can you cook while I get dressed?"

Mala squeezed into the bedroom. She wiped her hands and face down with a towel to remove any last trace of fish before carefully slipping on the midnight-blue gown. As she ran her hands over the fabric and wondered at the way it felt like water, Mala debated the evening. A niggling little thought entered her mind. She reached for the pants her mother had put in their dirty laundry. She undid the button. She pulled out the thin black piece of metal and traced the intricate paisley pattern that made up the arrow of the hour hand. What if she didn't have to dread every moment of celebrations like this? *What would that be like?* she wondered. Before she could snicker at herself, she undid her necklace and slid the little hand onto her line full of hooks.

She rolled her eyes at herself. *Idiot.* Impulsively, she grabbed the trident dagger that had once been her father's. She used a length of cord to tie it to her thigh. One of Bara's rules: always have a weapon on you. Always. As Mala finished her knot, she weighed her chances of being able to sneak off to a secluded bit of shore and go frog gigging. If she could ensure her mother was distracted, chances were pretty good. *There. An escape plan.*

The night proved muggy, though summer had lost her grip on the land. A cluster of blazing tamaracks spit bright yellow leaves onto a hidden lake, onto a little island, onto the hair of dancers galloping across a large floating platform anchored near the shore. The leaves glowed brighter than the stars, lit by bonfires lining the island.

A very drunk middle-aged man with no shirt and a red belly shouted, "Burn the heathens down!" The crowd took up the chant and stomped their feet.

On a shadowed bit of shore, Mala sat alone atop a keg, the dress helping her fade into the night. Her long locks tangled in the breeze and she swung her bare feet to keep the mosquitoes at bay. She held an empty cup as she watched the dancers. Really, she watched her mother. Erinne waved her shawl in the air like a lasso. Mala gave a disapproving shake of her head. *She always gets out of hand.*

Erinne celebrated the fifteen-year-old victory against the Erlenders with a vengeful joy. It was something Mala couldn't understand. Whenever she thought of the Erlenders herself, she only felt a slow panic seep into her stomach. The rest of the guard felt differently. They came together each year to renew their fiery hatred of the northerners—the river stealers.

A joyous gurgle escaped her mother's throat and Mala cringed. Her eyes scanned the crowd. But no one else seemed to notice the choked yowl. Mala sighed in relief. Even if she wasn't accepted, she was glad everyone seemed to embrace her mother.

Mala glanced to her right as a giggling couple stumbled through the brush to a private setting. Her heart sank a little more than usual, probably because it was weighed down by three cups of moonshine. She glanced back at her mother, who was being twirled in circles by the Barde, the red-bellied ringleader of the rowdy. Her hand slid up to her necklace. She traced the hour hand.

Oh what the hell. What can it hurt? Mala turned her back on the party and retreated farther into the trees. She ducked under the legs of a giggling little boy perched on a branch; he threw an acorn at her. She ignored him and trudged deeper. Only when it was black and silent, when she was sure that no one would stumble upon her and see what she was doing, only then did Mala stop.

She took a moment to gather her thoughts and her courage. And then, haltingly, she began the ritual. She'd only seen it once before, so as she used the tip of the hour hand to prick her palm, she searched her memory to ensure she was doing everything right.

She recalled that the girls had huddled together under a tent, but they'd brought a lantern and their silhouettes made it easy to distinguish who was who. Sari, of course, was wearing the bridal hat. Giggles floated up to the fireflies and to Mala, who sat in the gnarled old oak high above. The girls hadn't seen her, of course—she'd made sure they hadn't. She didn't want to scare them. It was just that she'd never seen a betrothal ceremony before and she was interested. *Or indulging in a bit of twist-the-knife self pity,* her conscience berated her, *since it'll never happen for you.* Nevertheless, Mala remained perched in the tree, listening to the gossip only teenage girls can share until she'd almost dozed off. She was startled awake when the knot of girls left the tent and one of them tripped over a tree root.

"Ah!" the girl cried as her friends shushed her.

"Come on," Sari whispered. "Don't want to get caught." Like little white ducklings, the girls in their shifts traipsed after the bride-to-be. Beautiful, with an elegant mane of black hair and crystalline skin, Sari flitted through the trees with an impish grin. "Tonight, girls, you'll see what magic can really do!"

Gasps of shock and laughter at her daring fluttered through the air.

"But that's illegal!" one gasped. "We could be hanged."

The other girls only shushed their friend, until she was shamed into silence.

Magic? Mala had climbed down slowly behind them, careful not to make a sound. She followed at a distance until she saw Sari stop at a small cluster of boulders. Mala slid behind a tree.

"Okay now, circle up," Sari commanded. "Grasp each other's elbows…" She waited until the girls were arranged to her liking, then Sari climbed up on one of the boulders. The blue-grey light of the stars and a waxing moon washed the color from her face. She looked like a statue as she surveyed them.

"We're told magic is evil, stupid, illegal. We're told it's the pathetic fantasy of Erlenders after the bomb. That's a lie. My grandmother told me. Magic is real." She glared at Rasen as the other girl stifled a giggle.

"For four generations, the women in my family have all cast the same spell. And it's kept us safe for two hundred years. My grandmother wasn't even scratched during the bomb. Their house was blown to pieces. My great grandfather died. Her baby brother died. But my grandmother and her mom walked away, not a scratch on them. Tonight ladies, I'm going to show you that spell. And you can perform it on yourselves—if you dare."

Mala could see Rasen and another girl rolling their eyes. But when Sari bade them bow their heads, every girl complied. And as the wind whipped around them, a few of the girls exchanged glances, clearly spooked.

Sari took a ring off of her finger. "This was my great grandmother's ring. It was a clock!" Several of the girls gasped at the revelation. Mala lost her grip on the tree. She had to scramble to stay upright, as Sari displayed the gears on the innards of the broken ring. The clock face and glass were long gone, the hinge warped into a twisted spike. All the girls were riveted in silence, awed by her audacity to touch something so utterly forbidden.

Sari held her left hand up toward the moon. "Divine Spirit, split me open. Take what you need. In return, protect me, that no harm may look upon my face." With a howl, Sari used the mangled hinge to slash open her left palm along the lifeline. She held it toward the moon. And as she unfurled her fingers, the breeze suddenly died. Blood dripped from her hand. And a moonbeam encased Sari like a spotlight, making her gleam amid the shadows.

Mala thought back to that night, the nervous titters and refusals of the other girls when Sari had offered them the ring. She recalled the admiration gleaming in their eyes as they'd followed Sari back to the tent. They might not have believed her. But they believed *in* her. *No one has ever looked at me that way*, Mala thought. Like she was brave or scandalous or special. Self-pity rose like vomit in her throat. After the awful, burning alcohol she'd drunk, she couldn't be entirely sure it wasn't really vomit. She swallowed. And she dug the hour hand deeper into her palm.

"Divine Spirit, split me open. Take what you need," Mala held out her bleeding hand to the darkness. "In return protect me. Please. Protect me from myself. That no harm may look upon my face."

She waited for a moment. The breeze didn't stir. The moonlight didn't break through the darkness of the trees. The trickle of blood running down her wrist attracted a mosquito, who began an intimate kiss—until she smacked him, smearing his dark body onto her arm.

Mala, you're an idiot.

CHAPTER FOUR

The brisk stink of sludge was her only warning. "Hey mumbler's daughter," a whisper came from just behind her ear. A hand at her back shoved her roughly to the ground. Her ankle twisted on a root and the tendon gave a painful snap. She turned to glare up at a big-shouldered, dark-eyed young man. He laughed, then took a drink from a bottle in his hand.

"What are you doing out here?" she grumbled.

"Searching for virgins stupid enough to wander to a secluded spot ..." he trailed off and smiled down at her viciously.

Mala rolled her eyes and reached for her necklace, hoping he wouldn't notice the hour hand as she slipped it back onto the line. "Sludge!" she used the pretense of putting the necklace on to act as though she'd just cut her hand.

Garon leaned in close, smiling viciously. "Did you understand me little girl?"

Mala ignored him. Garon was a brute to everyone.

"Oh. Of course not. Youth unlee uthedtu mumblublin ithnt youth?"

At that, Mala turned red and Garon took a moment to revel in his success. He loved pushing buttons. He took another swig of moonshine; from his blotchy complexion, it was clear that this was not Garon's first drink, probably not his fourth. "Wait, I can do better. That was too—here!" He set down his cup and made a series of low horrific moans and staggered towards her. "That sounds more like 'er, huh? Jus' like mommy?" A slow smile crept across his face. "Come here. Give mother a kiss," he leered.

Mala stared at the ground, shaking in fury. She tried to count, to dull her feelings. But her hands acted of their own accord. They grabbed his abandoned cup hurled it straight at him. She saw Garon's look of surprise as a small trickle of blood formed on his lip. She ran.

Through the trees, back to the party. Mala was panting when she reached the shore. She splashed through the warm shallows. She ignored the sting in her ankle and tried not to stumble over the slime-covered rocks. *Sludge! Why did you do that? And to him, of all people.* She climbed onto the platform of dancers.

A hand on her shoulder made Mala whirl in panic; she thought she'd been faster than Garon. Instead, she came face-to-face with Verrat, Sorgen's widow. The woman had coated her neck in ashes, as was appropriate for mourning, and tear tracks lined her beautiful face. Garon was just visible, grinning, as he waded toward them.

"I'm sorry Verrat, but I have to—"

Verrat interrupted, "That's a beautiful dress. Where'd you get it?" Her tone was tense.

She's cried herself hoarse. "My mother found it." She tried to back away politely, but Verrat grabbed her shoulders, stroking the silky material.

"Your mother found this … did he say anything about me?" The violet-eyed woman stared at her intensely, desperately. Her fingers dug into Mala's skin.

She wants comfort, Mala's brain whispered. But her eyes could focus only on Garon. *Only ten steps away.*

"No, I'm sorry. There was no time. It was quick," she lied. She didn't want to repeat the man's crazed mumbling to his wife. Better to let Verrat think he had died a quick warrior's death. Verrat gazed at her appraisingly. Mala tried to look innocent and shrugged her shoulders.

"Thank you for everything you did for him," Verrat said.

Mala didn't meet her eyes, just in case. "Don't thank me—" she tried to duck away but the widow grasped her hand.

"Mala, I want to give you something. I need to give you something to show my appreciation—" Verrat reached her hand into the patched pocket of her yellow dress.

"Look, it's really my mother you need to thank. I'm sorry—I have to go." She avoided Verrat's offended glare and pulled away just as Garon reached them.

Pushing people aside, Mala struggled toward the one person who might be able to still Garon's wrath. *Get to Bara,* she thought. *Get to Bara in the middle of the crowd, where there are too many people to see.*

"Hi Bara," Mala attempted to change her wince into a smile as she stopped suddenly in front of the hulking woman who led the northern river guard. Bara might have passed her enormous size to Garon, but his grandmother was known for her discipline and honor. If anyone could stop his sadism in its tracks, his fire-tongued grandmother could.

Bara eyed her suspiciously. "Hello Mala. I haven't seen you out here."

"I was just watching onshore." Her ankle screamed and Mala lifted her right foot.

Bara looked curiously at Mala's one-legged stance, but politely chose to ignore it. "I understand you had a hard day. Thank you for what you and your mother did for Sorgen. He ... was a good man. A great warrior ... never understood why the Kreis didn't come and take him away. I find it hard to believe the Erlenders got him. I saw the wounds. I've already told Verrat we'll avenge him. Fire for fire. Blood for blood." She recited the old line with fervor. Then great woman cleared her throat to quell any further emotion.

Mala shifted uncomfortably.

"I thought you and your mother would be out together tonigh—" Bara started.

Garon skidded to a halt just behind Mala, nearly bowling her over.

"Watch out, boy!" Bara exclaimed. "Why are you running?"

"Grandmother, I ... Mala ... Mala promised to dance with me!" he spit out, triumph in his eyes.

"Did she now?" Bara looked suspicious.

"No!" Mala gasped. *That swampy bastard!*

"You can't back out now! You promised when you kissed

me!" Garon exclaimed, loud enough for the adults nearby to hear. Some of nearby women peered around their partners to watch the scene. Garon laid it on thick for them, letting his lower lip tremble a bit.

"I never!" Her face grew hot under the disdainful stares surrounding her. Most of the women in the guard didn't trust a girl who kept to herself. One who bolted at blood. Ran from screaming faces. Not worthy to be a warrior. Not even able to be a medic. Mala avoided their eyes but stared desperately at Bara for help. The older woman was now regarding her with some suspicion.

"A deal is a deal, Mala." Garon used Bara's favorite saying and smiled at Mala with a glint in his eye. Mala's face flushed in frustration.

Bara must have seen something else, because she smiled kindly down at Mala. "Be a gentleman," Bara warned him. She clasped his right hand briefly, as if to impress her message. Then she walked away.

"Of course." Garon smiled and bowed to Mala. No one else could see the cruel gleam in his gaze. He loved the game of cat and mouse, no matter the mouse. His hands clamped down on her, pulling her slender form tight into his barrel chest. The alcohol seemed to form a haze around him; Mala found herself in a cloud of stench. The crowds pressed in close and the nearby dancers were too drunk to notice the way Garon leered.

"What were you talking to my grandmother about?" he asked. Mala didn't respond but kept alert for any possibility of escape from his vice-like grip.

"I asked a question," he growled, crushing her ribs.

"Sorgen," she sputtered. "She was talking about Sorgen and how he would have been a great Kreis—"

"Ha! Him? He'd never be able to hack it. Kreis are brutal. You have to be willing to do anything. *Anything.*"

"How would you know?"

"Trust me," Garon laughed and his putrid breath swept over her face. "Now, weren't you supposed to give me a kiss?" He grabbed Mala's hair and wrenched her head backward before she could blink. Her necklace of hooks dug into his hand and he yelped.

"Muck!" He sucked an injured finger. "You know, that necklace doesn't suit you at all. I think it's time—" He grasped her neck. Tighter. Tighter. The starry sky blurred red.

He's going to kill me. She knew she should try to get away. But her body could only focus on breathing.

"Excuse me," a cool male voice interrupted. Garon looked over, annoyed.

"What?" He glared down at the speaker. Mala's head was still firmly controlled by his hand; she couldn't turn to look at her savior, but a swell of gratitude filled her and her knees went weak in relief.

"Bara's watching you," the voice said levelly. "And I believe she told you to be a gentleman." The last word was a snarl.

Garon's lips curled and he released Mala to reach for the speaker. Mala slid straight to the deck. There was no room for her to crawl away; the kicking feet of the crowd left no path. She curled herself into a protective ball and waited for the blows overhead to begin. But there was nothing. And suddenly Garon's feet were shuffling away. She watched him retreat. He didn't look back.

Dumbfounded, Mala glanced up to see what the newcomer had possibly done to dispel Garon. He stood calmly, straightening his collar. It took Mala a second to recognize the face in front of her as the shock faded from her system. A tall lean young man with ebony curls and brilliant blue eyes gazed down at her curiously. She stared back, astonished.

People called him Lowe. He'd floated into their territory one day in midsummer on a homemade raft. His clothing had been shredded and his hair a frayed dandelion fuzz. Bara had instructed the guard to search him, question him, hold him. So they had. But, one day, not two months past, Lowe had escaped the confines of the guard ship and shown up on Bara's boat with a dead alligator. It must have been six feet long, not a hook or knife mark on it. Rumor was he'd wrestled it with his bare hands, reached down its throat, and pulled out the heart. Lowe had asked to speak with Bara alone when he'd presented her the trophy. He'd gone down into the cabin of her ship and remained there until dark. No one knew what had been said. Though people whispered.

"He's from the capital. Doing inspections for the government."

"No way. I heard he's an outlaw. Hiding out here."

But by far the most popular and far-fetched theory was that he was Kreis. No one from Bara's guard had been recruited in fifty years, and most of the soldiers were itching to be chosen.

But no matter what they guessed or what they asked, no one

knew where Lowe came from, or what had happened to him. He refused to talk. He also refused to settle into a natural place in the guard. He would disappear for days at a time and return to Bara's boat without any explanation. He would go with the guard on patrols or stay behind, as he wished. No matter what he did, Bara let him stay. It didn't make sense. And when things didn't make sense, people asked questions. Of course, Lowe shot down every question he was asked. Asked about his past, he'd simply respond, "They stole it." Asked about his life, he'd say, "They stole it."

"They stole it" was a common phrase among Mala's people. It was a phrase that summarized everything about the Erlenders, the northern tribe that plundered Senebal waters. Like locusts, they'd descended after the bomb. They'd tried to claim the Gottermund River, the only water source left untainted by the blast. They'd tried to cut off the life force that had nourished Senebal crops for centuries. It was unforgivable. Erlenders had tried, still tried, to steal the Gottermund.

Erlenders were the reason Bara's children and grandchildren had barely known land. Every waking thought of those in Bara's regiment was of water, of protecting the river from the two-legged demons that sought to leave the Senebal people nothing but empty husks and desiccated bellies. And Bara's group was the far north guard, closest to the enemy. Their righteous anger—Mala's mother's anger—held more potency than most. Tonight's antics were the glorification of a night fifteen years past when they'd put an entire Erlender encampment to the torch. But Mala didn't think of torches. Wouldn't think of them. She bit her lip.

Lowe held out a hand to her.

"I'm fine," Mala mumbled, aware that she had gazed at his eyes for far too long. She dropped her face to the floor, embarrassed. He didn't leave.

"Are you really alright?" Lowe asked.

"Yes. Thank you. I ... thank you." She didn't understand why he wouldn't just walk away.

"Falling!" A young bride with a tattered wedding hat tripped over Mala and smashed into Lowe. Sari stared up at him, her alabaster skin glowing with a gorgeous blush. "You can catch me anytime," she giggled drunkenly. She trailed a hand along his collar. "Oh!" she exclaimed. Lowe quickly backed away.

Sari smiled. "So you know?"

"Know what?" His tone was guarded.

Sari threw her arms in the air and spun. "Tonight's the end! Good-bye world! We're moving up! Everyone is …" She lost her balance and landed on Mala's bad ankle. "Oops."

Her groom hurried over and scooped up the raven-haired girl. "Honey!" He barely spared half a glance for Mala. "Sorry," he muttered, turning back to Sari. "Are you alright?"

Mala grabbed her throbbing ankle. *Muck and shit!*

"Are you gonna stand up?" Lowe asked, a hint of amusement in his tone. "Or are you waiting around for the next drunkard to trip?"

Mala flushed. "I can get up." She used her good leg and her hands to push herself up, but balance became tricky at the halfway point. Her hands flailed and Lowe caught them. His hands were strong and steady, and he helped her slowly upright. She chewed her lip, unsure how to react. He was awfully close.

"No worries," he smiled easily at her. "I don't think floating platforms and broken ankles mix well."

"Do you think it's broken?" A sudden twist of panic flared in her stomach.

"I think you'd better let me check. And I think we better get off this platform before you are trampled to death."

"Har har." She rolled her eyes, but he was right. The drunken milieu seemed as oblivious as ever. Even now, she felt someone's elbow jab her back.

Lowe kept her hand and guided her to the edge of the platform. People seemed to part for him warily. It made Mala wonder. Outsiders were rare, and Lowe was always quiet—at least he had been every time Mala had seen him—but what was it about him that cowed people so? Even people like Garon? *Maybe he* is *the president's man.*

At the edge of the platform, she made to jump to shore, but Lowe caught her as she crouched to leap. "Um, excuse me!" he demanded. "What are you doing?"

"How else am I supposed to get off the platform?"

"Let me lift you, like any sane injured person would," he retorted. And before she could mutter a protest, she was scooped up in his arms.

"I'm not a child!"

"Trust me. I am aware of that." His tone grew husky. Mala's face grew red as a beet until he laughed aloud. "Calm down.

I'm going to check your ankle. Not carry you off into the trees, though I don't know … if you asked, I might oblige," he winked.

Mala hopped down prematurely when they reached the shore. *He's mocking me.* She grimaced at him. But a slight thrill rushed up her spine as he smiled. She limped to a nearby boulder and tried to change the topic. "Where did you come from, anyway? You showed up out of nowhere."

"You aren't the only one who avoids crowds," he muttered, kneeling to check on her ankle. He tossed up the filmy layers of her skirt and for a second, the trident on her thigh was visible. She quickly covered up the knife, biting her lip. Lowe raised his eyebrows, but failed to comment.

"Where were you when I was on shore? I didn't see you. Ouch!" she exclaimed as he twisted her foot in a direction it wasn't willing to go.

"I didn't want to be seen."

Something about the way he said that made Mala's shiver. She felt very certain that there was a dark undertone to Lowe's words. She was also just as certain, from the faraway look in his eyes, that he wouldn't be sharing anything further on the topic.

"So am I broken? Do I need to hire you to carry me around?" she asked, trying to lighten the mood and ease the eerie tension.

Lowe gave a small half smile. "Just twisted. But I wouldn't recommend swimming for a day or two."

Mala was a little dismayed. She typically spent a few hours a day sequestered in the water, gliding underneath like a mermaid, coming up only when her lungs were fit to burst. It was one of the few pastimes where she didn't notice how everyone else looked at her, where she couldn't hear the whispered taunts, where she could forget that she was the mumbler's useless—and possibly psychotic—daughter.

"I'll figure something out. I'll swim somehow," She started to test the limits of her own foot. "Thanks. I'm fine now."

He ignored the hint. "That's completely illogical, you know. Why would you injure yourself more just to go swimming?"

"Swimming's the only way to get away when you live on a boat." She stared at the water.

Lowe looked amused and leaned back against the boulder, facing her. "And you swim a lot."

"What's that mean?"

"Clearly, you're a misanthrope."

"What?"

"You hate other people."

"I do not!" Mala was slightly offended, but with her ankle in its current state, she could hardly storm off.

"Then why are you always swimming alone? Why were you avoiding everyone tonight? Why'd you sneak off into the woods? I'm guessing it wasn't to meet Garon." Lowe's blue eyes swirled with expectation.

Mala's face heated up. *He's been watching me?* The thought made her chest clench slightly in panic. The only person to ever track her movements before had been Garon. And Garon's only motivation was cruelty. *What does Lowe want? Why is he watching me? And what else has he seen?* She recalled the spell in the woods and clenched her fist defensively.

"I don't swim alone," she scoffed.

"Yes you do. Every day you bait and check sixteen traps. Today you caught a catfish."

She tried not to gasp. "How do you know that?"

"I'm a very observant person."

"So fishing makes me a misanthrope? Because if that's the case, you need to let just about everyone on that platform know."

"No. There's more than that. I've asked around. For as long as anyone can remember, you've been quiet, elusive. A ghost. You avoid everyone."

A long moment of silence passed as Mala tried to determine if he was insane, dangerous, or just insatiably curious. She met his eyes and his gaze held hers. There was a gentleness in it that melted her stomach. It made her utterly uncomfortable. *No one looks that way. He is definitely manipulating me. Why?* She didn't know, but it didn't matter. There was no way she was going to share her problems with a stranger. No way she was going to mention her hallucinations or the fact that she wasn't sure whether she needed to be locked up. No way she was going to mention that despite everything, even tonight's pathetic disaster, some small part of her still believed in Erlender magic. In Erlender curses. She broke eye contact and stood despite the pain.

"You know, you're right. I avoid everyone but my mother. You included." She turned to go, but he grabbed her shoulder and turned her back. His face was far too near.

"Why?" He didn't let go, though she pulled. Instead he put another arm gently around her back and sent her heart into a flurried panic. *He's playing with me, like Garon, but using gentleness instead of force. He's* ... she was flustered; she couldn't even decide *what* he was.

She said the first thing that came into her mind. "Have you ever tried to speak with my mother?"

"No."

"Never asked anyone about her or our past, in your stalkerish curiosity?"

He grinned. "I haven't had *that* much time to ask questions. I just discovered you haunted these boats, Misanthrope."

"You're so funny."

"It's a side effect of being incredibly handsome." He tossed his hair.

At that, she couldn't help herself. She let out a deep roaring laugh, one that set her shoulders shaking. Before she had finished, he let go and stepped back.

"That's kind of offensive you know," he commented as he crossed his arms.

"What?" she asked, wiping a tear from her eye.

"That you find my looks so laughable."

"Well, I am a misanthrope, after all. I hate everything about you," she said with a grin.

Just then a loud alarm sounded, reverberating off the water. A dull clanging gong. Mala's entire body tensed. Only one thing set off the alarm: Erlenders.

CHAPTER FIVE

Bells trilled discordantly over one another, a chorus rising up from all sides of the island. *They're attacking.* Panic started to seep into Mala's stomach. A flurry of images came unbidden to her mind. Men dressed in black, long guns, torches, boats aflame. She pushed them back.

"Mom!" she yelled. Everyone was abandoning the platform and stumbling towards the boats. Children wailed and everyone was calling out for someone else. The warriors had all but abandoned the party, crashing through the trees toward the threat.

She could hear Bara shouting orders. "Arm up! Barde, you take a ship south—warn Kita's guard. Verrat—find them! Bring me a head!" In the cacophony, Mala knew her mother would never hear her. She tried to cut through the crowd, but like a river the current of people was flowing past her, forcing her farther up the shore.

She ignored the yells of those she passed, though something Barde said caught her ear. He asked his companion, "How did they find this place?" as both checked their semiautomatics and headed out. It was a good question. The island was well hidden. But Mala didn't have time to think about Erlender scouts and she pushed onward, eyes scanning for her mother.

Finally, she was able to edge sideways to where the crowd thinned and limp toward the right side of the platform, where she had last seen Erinne dancing. The older woman stood frozen, stoic, her thin lips stretched in a ragged line, eyes dull. The alarm had made a statue of her, as if she couldn't bear to face what followed in its wake.

"Mom!" Mala splashed through the shallows, adrenaline overcoming the pain in her ankle. "Mother. Come on! We have to go! We need to get to our boat now!" Her commands brought no response. When she grabbed her mother's hand and pulled, it was like trying to move an anchored buoy. Erinne swayed but wouldn't take a step.

"Please. Please Mom." Mala tried to stay focused on her mother. She pushed back thoughts of Erlenders, tried to ignore the sounds of war cries and gunfire in the distance. Suddenly someone was beside her. Without a word, Lowe swept her mother up over his shoulder. He looked at Mala. "Which way?"

She pointed. Left, through the trees, on the far side of the island, she had tethered their little craft, originally thinking she wanted to sleep as far from the revelers as possible. Less chance of a drunk peeing on her deck that way. Now the trees formed a formidable barrier, a dark black mass that would block out the moonlight and leave them wandering blind. But ships were their only option. Staying on the tiny island to face Erlender guns—that wasn't a choice.

They broke through a thicket and wove through tree trunks as silently as they could. Most of the crowd had gone in the opposite direction, so other than startling a few small families, they didn't see anyone. Mala tried to breathe evenly, stay calm, but her inhalations were ragged knives in her chest. She could hear her mother's panting and the sound nearly broke her heart.

"We'll get away, Momma. Don't worry. We'll get away."

Lowe didn't speak, but his eyes swept steadily from side to side as they moved.

The little green craft bobbed into sight in front of them and Mala sped up. Lowe yanked on her arm. He crouched down and shifted Erinne so she was cradled on his knees. He peered through the brush. Mala stood, uncertain whether to stay with him, or to take her mother's arm and drag her to the boat. Then she heard it: the scuff of a boot on the deck.

She crouched, trembling. She tried not to remember the last time Erlenders had been aboard their boat.

Lowe freed an arm and grabbed her hand. Shell-shocked, she turned to face him. "We have to go," he mouthed.

She nodded. He turned to her mother.

"Can you walk? I need to guard the rear."

Mala grasped her mother's hand. "She'll walk. She'll be fine." Erinne was unresponsive.

Lowe stared hard. "If I'm going to protect you, I need to know you're both running. I need to know she wants to run."

Mala hissed. "She wants to run."

"I need to hear her say it. Her voice."

"*They* stole her voice," Mala's pitch rose though she fought it. She could see his skepticism. “Show him, Momma.”

At first, Erinne didn't respond. But Mala shook her, impatient at her woodenness. Now was not the time for her mother to mentally collapse. Erinne's eyes slid back into focus. “Show him what the Erlenders did.” She turned back to Lowe. “They stole my mother's voice, so she could never name them or what they did to her.”

Mala’s mother opened her mouth to reveal a gaping black hole. Her tongue had been severed far back in her throat.

Lowe pointed, and Mala set off into the blackest patch of trees, towing her mother. She cringed at every crack of a twig, every rustle of a leaf. She counted to one thousand in her head, pushing back any other thought that threatened to creep up. *Just keep moving.*

Light flickered in the distance. Mala slowed, gesturing for Lowe and her mother to stop. “Wait here,” she mouthed.

Lowe grabbed her arm in protest, but she stared him down. “I'm small and dead quiet. And ...” her eyes slid to her mother. *I need your help with her.* She didn't have to say it aloud. He let her go.

Mala wove through the trees, a shadow, creeping toward the silhouettes circled around a fire. She stopped short as one of the men turned toward her. He was tall and lean, his head shaved; his bald pate gleamed orange in the firelight. His nose was clear, unstriped. That was rare. Erlenders took pride in their kills. *What kind of Erlender is he?*

Mala's thoughts were interrupted by the crunch of leaves to her left. She held her breath. The bald man peered into the darkness.

"Did you find it?" he asked brusquely.

A brute of a man stepped out of the cover of the trees near Mala. She shivered, unnerved by the fact that such a huge warrior had been within two meters of her and she hadn't even noticed him. He moved toward the fire, blue stripes gleaming on his nose.

Wilde township Erlenders, Mala processed. *Raiders. Known for isolating boats and attacking ... like wolves. Why would they attack us? Most of the guard was drunk. But still ... there are so many of us.*

"Cherub," the mountain spoke. "I think I fauund it, sir." He tossed something that flashed gold across to the bald man, who held it up. A chain with a little trinket dangling from it.

Something pretty? Mala balled her fists.

"Glad to see you're not all completely useless," the bald man sneered, his blue eyes fixed on the necklace. "Let me see her."

The mountain shrugged a body off his shoulder. Mala hadn't even seen the girl because of his bulk. Her throat tightened and she clamped her teeth together so hard that she could feel the tension travel up her skull.

Black and blue, a trickle of blood running under her eye, and her wedding hat smashed to a flimsy pulp, Sari curled into a fetal position at the bald man's feet.

"Stand up," he said.

When she didn't respond, he nodded to one of the Erlenders

and they dragged her upright. She swayed in place, eyes on the carpet of leaves beneath her toes.

"Look at me darlin'." The man called Cherub caressed Sari's cheek. The poor girl sobbed helplessly. He leaned forward. "Don't cry." He placed a gentle, chaste kiss on her cracked lips.

Then, without warning, his left arm slashed through the air. At first, Mala thought he'd smacked Sari, but that was before she saw the knife ... or the blood. Half of Sari's cheek flapped open, her gums and teeth protruding from her ruined face.

Before anyone could react, the bald man grabbed Sari again and forced his face to her tattered lips.

What the mucking hell—a demonic ritual? Mala bit back bile. She looked down and saw the trident dagger in her hand. She didn't remember unsheathing it. Her fingers tightened on the handle.

When the bald man tossed Sari aside like a piece of garbage, Mala closed her eyes and let instinct take over. She let the knife fly.

But the bald man bent at the last second and the trident soared into the trees.

Shit! Idiot!

"What wuz dat?" A shifty buck-toothed Erlender asked. "Did you see dat?" He nudged a companion.

"What?"

"I think it wuz an arrow or sum'in."

"Where it come from?"

Mala's breath stopped. Her stomach dropped as the buck-toothed blue nose raised a finger and pointed right at her. The Erlenders squinted in her direction. She knew they couldn't see her, but she edged behind a large tree. She was just in time. Bullets buzzed through the air around her. Boots tromped through the bushes.

They'll be here any second. She scanned behind her. Most of the trees leading to the clearing were too thin to offer good cover. Not when they knew she was here. Not when they were shooting blindly into the blackness. She had no escape. *Mudding Muck.*

A horrid bellow rent the air behind her. Mala looked back to see her mother charging at the Erlenders, waving her arms. Behind her, Lowe held his stomach and sank to his knees.

Fury boiled in Mala. *How could he have let her get away—* but that thought sank into oblivion as she heard the Wildes take the bait. Boots and bullets flew toward Erinne.

The clearing emptied but for Sari's prone form. Mala should have been backing toward it. But her limbs were frozen. A scream scratched viciously at her throat, but her mouth wouldn't open, and it shriveled on her tongue. Mala couldn't rip her gaze from her mother; Erinne was too far away for Mala to see her face, but the older woman held up her hand, thumb extended away from her fingers in a victory sign as bullets devoured her flesh.

CHAPTER SIX

Mala couldn't tell if it was minutes or hours later when Lowe pulled her to her feet. He replaced her trident dagger. *Did he see me throw it? When did he have time to get it?* Vague, simple thoughts floated through Mala's head. He slung her over his shoulder, and she nearly giggled at the fact that she couldn't feel her legs. *Was I shot?* She didn't see any blood. *Am I hallucinating again?* She searched her fuzzy thoughts. It took her a few minutes to decide she must be in shock. She felt dizzy.

Mala asked Lowe to put her down as they came over a rise. Below was a nightmarish scene. In a clearing near the water, Bara's guard lay like dock planks. Stiff shoulder touched stiff shoulder in a line of bodies that stretched as far as the eye could see. The ground was laced with rivulets of blood.

Barde and his flaming red hair lay on the near side of the clearing. *So the south will have no warning.* The Erlenders' attack had been well-planned.

Three black-clad Wilde soldiers were lining and frisking the bodies, filling their pockets with bullets and whatever knickknacks they could find. Their tattooed noses nearly touched the corpses they plundered, inhaling the scent of their fresh kill. Their faces were marred by stark blue horizontal stripes; the tattoos were a body count of those they'd killed. After tonight, most of their noses would be solid blue.

Mala turned away, disgusted. *Heathens.*

“We have to get out of here,” Lowe whispered. Mala nodded. But then she saw the bald man again. Cherub. With him was the mountain. Another body dropped from the peak of his shoulder.

Mala stared at her mother's blank face. The air left her body. She felt hollow. Lowe saw what was happening and swung her over his shoulder. He turned. The bald man scanned the trees. And his eyes, a pair of blue flames, met Mala's as Lowe carried her back into the shadows. A furious heat spread throughout her body. It radiated out from the center of Mala's chest, a biting, horrid burn clawing at her heart. She couldn't even count to control it. It felt as though her chest might liquefy. For a split second, the trees faded and she saw a bright blue house. She ran into the wind and it resisted; she felt like she was flying.

Mala found herself dumped into the lake and startled back to reality. The heat was gone. She was wet and shivering instead. Her heart was racing. Lowe was shaking her. “Mala, swim. Swim to the nearest boat! We'll go to Sonne Pointe. Follow me, okay?”

Mala nodded dully. She began to count to clear her mind. *One, two, three, four, five, six.*

Lowe turned back to stare at Mala. He waved her forward and jerked his head toward the boats. She followed. *Eighteen, nineteen, twenty.* She stroked hard in time with her counting. She refused to think of anything other than the numbers.

Gunfire echoed over the waves. Mala automatically dove, survival instinct overcoming everything else.

She tried to stay under as long as possible, but her twisted ankle wouldn't allow it. So she surfaced and began plowing the water with her arms, kicking with her one good leg. She couldn't see Lowe. Bara's massive speedboat loomed in front of her and she angled herself in that direction. It would shield her from the barrage of bullets. But something brought her up short.

Through the shadows she could see a figurehead perched on the bow of the ship. Bara's boat had no figurehead.

A torch was lit on the deck; a blue-nosed Erlender carried it. He marched forward, knelt down, and set the torch to the figurehead. A scream rent the air. Bara's voice. Mala watched in horror as the figure tied to the bow struggled.

The Erlenders were burning her alive, to send a message. Mala had almost forgotten they did that. Not forgotten, but wouldn't remember. Wouldn't remember a tall laughing man tying her father up, discovering a young girl crouched beneath some benches. Wouldn't remember the words he whispered in her ear as he dropped her overboard. Wouldn't remember bobbing in the water as her father became a mass of shrieking flames ... Mala grabbed onto a rubber lifeboat and pulled herself out of the water to keep from sinking as her legs again refused to work.

She turned her head to look for Lowe and Bara's eyes locked on her. Anger and agony swirled in their depths. Mala's chest heated up for the second time that night. Her face melted and she felt the bones in her hands collapse. Her skin bubbled and popped like Bara's. She felt as if she were outside her own body. The hallucination took over. Mala sank into the vision. She was floating. She looked down. Not floating. Perched on the back of a giant man, whose face she couldn't see, but who had a beard on his chest cut like a swallowtail. And she was wearing shoes. *Shoes! Only soldiers get shoes ...* She looked up from her shoes to see an Erlender with a solid blue nose aiming a shotgun right at them.

As if through a mist, Mala heard splashing nearby and gunshots on the distant shore of the island. She could hear someone calling her name. But she couldn't respond.

"Mala," Lowe whispered as he swam. "Mala, where are you? Dammit, why can't you follow instructions?"

He edged closer and closer. She leaned her head on the patched rubber bumper and looked out at the water. It was all she could manage. She could hear him only a few feet away. She desperately needed him to jerk her out of this pain, like he had earlier. Mala tried to call out for him, but in her agony, all she could manage was a slow, foreign wail. It sounded wrong even to her ears.

Lowe edged closer and scanned all the bodies in the water. Mala met his eyes for just a second. But her limbs wouldn't work.

Lowe dove beneath the water. Mala waited. There was a splash as he kicked off. She waited. He didn't come back.

CHAPTER SEVEN

In the predawn light Mala awoke, shivering, her right hand a shriveled prune. It had slipped into the water as she slept. She gave a cursory glance around, checking for Lowe, checking for Erlenders, and trying very hard to ignore the bodies floating around her like debris; she didn't want to see glazed eyes, swollen faces, or Bara's blackened husk.

The water was still but for the rustle and swoop of carrion birds fighting over delicacies washed ashore. The boats were gone, save for Bara's. Raiders like the Wilders didn't leave good boats to waste.

With no alternatives, Mala decided to swim. *But where?* Based on the body count, Bara's guard had been eliminated. Her mother was dead. *She's dead,* Mala repeated to herself. The words had no effect. A strange numbness had settled over her. It made her limbs feel heavy. She had to force them to move. To swim. *Go. Just go, Mala.*

Sonne Pointe. The hidden cove Lowe had mentioned floated into her brain and settled there. At least there, she'd be hidden from the Erlenders. *Even if that coward made it there*, she thought bitterly. *He could have reached out a hand. He saw me, I know he did.*

She focused on her bitter thoughts as she propelled herself through icy water. They proved a good outlet. They lessened the numbness without opening her up to pain. Or guilt. So long as she didn't let the anger turn inward, so long as she didn't think about how if she had only resisted her stupid impulses ... *That mucking idiot! If it weren't for him, I might have been off frog gigging. I might have seen them coming. I could've warn her. I could've gotten her out of there. But he wouldn't let me go. He had to be all gallant and puppy dog eyes. If it weren't for him, we would have left already. We wouldn't even have been there. And that flooding jerk just left me in the water.*

Mala let herself work up a furious wrath during the hours it took her to swim back to the river and up to the Pointe. That might have been why she didn't notice the figure bobbing in the water behind her.

She dragged herself onshore just as the sun reached its peak in the sky, still muttering under her breath. The rocky bank was torture on her ankle as she limped to cover, but she made it, and collapsed under a group of trees to rest her weary limbs. But resting turned her mind toward her mother. So she vocalized her rant at Lowe to fill up the silence.

"Mucking coward. Couldn't stay around for a minute. And people call me a bullet dodger." She tossed aside her sopping blue skirt and rubbed her ankle to soothe it. "Don't know what I was thinking, following him. I should have hid Momma, swam to my boat. I could have come back for her myself. Never should have followed that idiot. He had no clue."

A twig cracked behind her. Mala jumped up, and the dagger tied to her leg stabbed her slightly. She quickly brandished it.

Lowe walked out of the trees. "I hope you weren't just calling me an idiot."

Him. She pressed a switch to release the trident points and her dagger suddenly brandished three deadly blades instead of one. "You left me!" She jabbed the knife in the air accusingly.

"I did not." He stole her seat under the tree, irritating her further by ignoring her dagger. "I couldn't find you."

"Then you must be blind, because I was right there in front of your face!"

"You weren't. I swam the whole perimeter."

"I was. You looked into my eyes. Then you were gone! You left me there for damn Erlender target practice," Mala raged. Lowe was struck silent and she took the opportunity to get in all the furious lines she'd come up with during her swim. "I mean, what the hell kind of stalker just leaves someone stranded like that? I'm in total shock, I can't move. I look right at you and you leave. You're a flooding coward! I mean, I know we just met—or I just met you, but you have got to be the world's most disappointing psychopath. You probably have a collection of my hair in your pocket or something, but you just left me?"

"Mala?" he asked very quietly.

"What?" she threw down the knife in frustration and pinned a beetle to the earth. He wasn't responding at all to her very justified rage and she really, really wanted to smack him.

"Where were you when you said you saw me?"

"On the lake, duh."

"But where? What side were you on, my right or left? What was behind you or around you?"

"I don't understand the point of this," Mala said, frustrated. "I was probably three whole feet away from you. In the lifeboat."

Lowe was silent for a few seconds. He waited for her to calm down. "Mala?" he asked.

"What?"

"I'm not sure I saw you. Just stick with me here ok?" He held up a palm, trying to calm her. "I saw someone in that boat, but I didn't see you …"

"That's ridiculous."

"No … hear me out. I saw a little girl—six, maybe seven years old."

"There was no one else in there." Mala sank down on the rocky ground in confusion. Maybe the chaos had made him hallucinate. She hadn't been able to move. *Maybe the Wildes used some kind of gas ...* Bara had told stories of the old days when soldiers had used mass poisons. *Maybe they'd put something in the lake. Maybe it had made him crazy.*

"Did you see things, too?" she asked in a small voice.

"See things?" Lowe gave a small grin. "I'm not crazy." Mala flinched.

"But I think I might know what happened to you."

A clatter of rocks down on the shore broke the awkward

silence. Lowe shot up, grabbing Mala's abandoned dagger. He edged behind a tree and peered around, squinting at a small shirtless figure making its way up the shore. He stiffened and sucked in a breath. “Mala,” he whispered.

“What?”

Lowe nearly jumped out of his skin. She had come up right behind him.

“We have to run. Now.”

She peered past him. Then she burst into laughter. He clamped a hand over her mouth and glared furiously at her, eyes flashing.

When he removed his hand, she muttered, “You can't be serious? Run from a kid? He can't be more than eleven.” She gestured at the boy onshore, who was clambering toward them, his downy blond hair and stick-thin arms nearly blown away by the breeze. “He's just—”

“Have you ever seen this before?” Lowe pulled aside his collar. On his chest, just below his collar bone, his skin had been burnt, branded in a perfect circle. Her eyes widened and she instinctively cringed.

“You're Kreis?” A quick series of images ran through her head. *Bara let him join the guard, no explanation. Garon backed off.* No Senebal denied a Kreis. The Kreis were honored, prized, worshipped. It was the Kreis who had saved DasWort from destruction. The Kreis had killed one Erlender king. They infiltrated enemy territory and picked off Erlender generals one by one. And for the first time in fifty years, a Kreis had come to Bara's guard.

She gaped at Lowe as he answered. “Yes. I'm Kreis. And that little boy you're laughing at *was* one of our best assassins. Blut. He's gone rogue.”

They heard hacking, as the boy tried to clear his throat of river water. Instantly, Lowe's arm was at her back and he was half-carrying Mala up the hill.

Mala think of Erlenders without hearing the bitter edge to Bara's voice or seeing the pallor had swept over her mother's face whenever they were mentioned. She couldn't imagine anything other than bile seeping into one's throat at the thought of them. She couldn't imagine anyone turning traitor. “But how?”

“Now is not a good time for this discussion. I'm trying to come up with a plan.”

“Well, you're Kreis. Why don't you just kill him?” It seemed simple enough to Mala.

“Oh! Really? Novel idea. You're a genius. Wish I had thought of it myself.”

“You're older. You're bigger. Shouldn't you be better than him? I mean, how good can a kid be?”

Lowe laughed gruffly, cruelly. “Mala. You have a lot to learn about being Kreis.”

“I don't understand. Can't you just throw the knife at him or something? Aren't Kreis the most deadly warriors out there?”

“We aren’t warriors the way you think. We’re either spies or assassins. And my specialty is poison.”

“Oh,” Mala suddenly felt self-conscious about her lack of

knowledge. “What's Blut's specialty?”

“Hand-to-hand combat,” Lowe said gruffly. “I’m serious,” he muttered when Mala snorted. “Appearances can be deceiving …” He glanced back. His eyes widened, and he doubled their pace. “We have to stay as far ahead of him as possible.”

Several minutes passed in silence as they tramped rapidly through the woods. The birds overhead seemed to have no idea of the danger they faced, and twittered loudly. Behind them, Mala could hear the steady crack of twigs as Blut came nearer; each crack made her heart jump. She hoped Lowe was coming up with a plan, because she'd never gone on the raids with Bara's team. Mala had never even gone to their practice sessions. She had avoided all of it, afraid that seeing someone die at her hands would turn her stomach turn into a raging inferno and bring on the hallucination that wouldn't end. It was out there. She knew it was. It loomed over her like a thunderhead. The only question was, when would it burst? When would she lose reality forever?

“Why do you have this thing anyway?” he twirled the dagger in his hand as he held aside a tree branch and pushed her ahead of him.

“I was going to go frogging.” Last night seemed like it was years away. The simple idea of frogging, juxtaposed with every gut-wrenching moment since then, seemed almost foreign.

“You throw this at frogs?”

“Yeah.”

“How good's your aim?” Lowe stopped walking suddenly and spun Mala around so he could stare her right in the face.

“I can usually catch two of five.”

“Forty percent? Our lives depend on a forty-percent chance? Well he's bigger than a frog, so maybe that'll make your aim a little better.” He tugged her wrist to get her moving again, craning his head to check on Blut.

This time it was Mala who stopped short. “Wait. I don't ... I don't think I can do that.” The very thought of watching the agony in some boy's eyes as he died made her stomach churn. She counted out loud to get it to recede.

“What are you doing? We have to move!” Lowe jerked her roughly. Reluctantly, she followed; this time his pace was nearly a run. “I don't want to *make* you kill anyone, but we don't really have a choice.”

“I don't think you understand!” Mala said, becoming frantic despite her breathing techniques. “I'm crazy. I see things. I'm ... I'm cursed.” The words came out despite her effort to say something else, anything else. *Damn it.* But she couldn't take them back.

“What?” The disbelief was clearly etched in his tone.

Mala cringed. *I never should have opened my mouth. Sludge, Mala, you know better than that.* She tried to think fast—to rationalize. She glanced back… away from Lowe. “I don't know what it was. Maybe it's just some stress reaction to the night my dad died ... It's probably just in my head ... but ever since that night, if I'm around people and they're hurt or angry or sad ... I start to burn …”

Blut was gaining. He leapt over a fallen tree trunk and grinned up at them. Mala could see the savage gleam in his eyes. It froze the blood in her veins.

Lowe tugged at her. This time she didn't resist. She pushed her sore ankle to its limits. And when Lowe said, “Faster!” she pushed harder.

Mala thought Lowe had moved on, but then out of the blue, he asked, “You *burn*?”

“Not literally. I burn. Inside. And then I ... see things ...” she trailed off.

With that admission, Lowe’s entire demeanor shifted from disdain to curiosity. “Does the heat start in the pit of your stomach and then reach out to your limbs?” he panted, glancing at her, and then back at Blut. They'd managed to gain some distance, so he paused for a second to catch his breath.

Confused, Mala nodded. *How could he know that? How the pain radiates?*

Lowe patiently helped her wade through some of the more stubborn brambles. Then he pulled her to a stop. “Mala, I don't think you have a curse. I understand why you might think so right now. But ...” Lowe said carefully. “I think ... you'll have to pass the test to be sure, but I think you're Kreis.”

“What?” Mala felt shock ripple through her. Her head swirled with possibilities. *Me, Kreis?* “How is that possible?”

Lowe responded with a curt, “Survival first. Explanations later. You can do this.” He shuffled around in his shirt pockets as they continued to battle the briars. He looked back. They had maybe two minutes. He pulled a small vial out of a hidden inner pocket.

“What's that?” Mala gasped.

“My specialty,” he replied gruffly, holding the powder downwind as he sprinkled it deftly over Mala’s blade. When he was finished, he slipped the vial back into his shirt and then glanced cursorily at their surroundings. They were blocked in by at least two meters of hedge on any given side. Mala could barely move as the thorny branches scraped against her legs.

He turned her around to face downhill. Blut was close enough that she could make out his sadistic expression, the wide hungry smile.

Lowe whispered in her ear. “He'll be on us soon.”

Mala's heart pounded in her ears, until she couldn't hear the birds or insects surrounding them anymore. Her hands started shaking, and Lowe put his arm around her, as much to keep her upright as to keep her calm. He uncurled her fingers, and slid the knife into her hand.

“Mala, he's not a person anymore. He's an Erlender now. If I'm right, he's the reason the Wildes attacked. Which means he's ultimately the reason your mom died.”

He saw her fingers clench the weapon, and he smiled. “Go for the gut so the knife can penetrate. You're in the thicket so once he gets close, just throw. It will take him a minute to wade through the thorns. Engel powder will do the rest. It kills on contact. If you can even nick him, it will do the job.” His tone was soothing, a stark contrast to the deadly instructions he gave.

Mala nodded. But as she looked at Blut, heat swept over her and the fear of her hallucinations, a fear that had driven her all her life, took hold. "I … I can't." Her whole body began to quake. "You do it."

"Mala, I haven't thrown a knife in ... I can't remember. You want to pin your hopes on me?"

"Yes," she said desperately. *Anything else. Any other option.* "Please. Don't ask me to do this." She begged with her eyes.

"You're from the tributaries. Far north guard. You had to have killed some people if you've survived this long."

Mala shook her head desperately. "No. My mom's a medic. They always held us back ... they didn't want her to get hurt. Last night. I threw my knife at that man. That was the first time I ever did anything like that. And I missed. And ..." she couldn't go any further. Couldn't let herself think any further.

"Then he'll kill us," Lowe said simply. And he let go of Mala's shoulders and began to wade back through the thicket, directly towards Blut.

"What are you doing?" Mala screamed.

"If you won't save us, I'm not going to drag it out. Because he will. He likes the kill. I've seen it," Lowe responded. He took out the vial again and opened it. He turned back to face her, ignoring Blut as the boy started running forward. His manic laughter carried up the hill. Slowly, Lowe turned a shaking palm face up. He began to tilt the vial over his palm.

"You're faking," Mala shrieked, desperately.

Lowe turned to her, his lip curled, disgusted. "I fight when there's a chance of winning. I cut my losses when there's not.

Apparently, you don't want to live," Lowe said simply.

After a pause, Mala whispered, "Well, what have I got to live for?"

She heard the clink of the vial as Lowe closed it and put it back in his shirt. The bushes rustled as he approached her again. He lifted her chin gently and used the back of one hand to brush away her tears. He stared into her eyes and she saw a deep, burning ferocity there, one that ignited a new kind of heat in her belly.

"Mala, you can live for revenge," he breathed. "You can make your mother's blood and your father's pain worth something. Fire for fire. Blood for blood." His eyes bored into hers and she felt a spark.

Blut came bursting out of a gap between two trees. Mala hurled the knife without thinking. It sank deep into the young boy's belly, and the thrill of the chase faded from his eyes. He fell to his knees at the edge of the bushes, gasping, hands on the knife handle. He stared at her in disbelief.

"You—" he couldn't finish as pain took over.

Blut's gaze drew her in. She couldn't resist, couldn't turn away; Mala felt her face melt. The world surrounding him blurred slightly until only he was in focus. She saw the blood drain from his cheeks. The freckle under his right eye. The soft rounded shape of his baby cheeks. No one else existed but Blut. His gaze was magnetic.

Entranced, she started walking toward him. Lowe tried to hold her back, but she shrugged him off easily. The trance lent her extra strength. As she walked, her bones felt like they were cracking, bursting, fizzling. Her eyes felt like they might pucker and explode from the heat. The hallucination started. A toddler Blut ran on a dirt road toward her, arms outstretched, tears running down his pink cheeks. She scooped him into her arms. Mala blinked, and she was back in the woods. It seemed darker, somewhat dimmer, but she could still see. And suddenly, mysteriously, the heat was gone.

She crouched beside the Blut's eleven-year-old body, stroked his yellow hair. He was weak. His gasps for air became shallow and she took his head into her lap. His eyes widened at the sight of her. He gripped her wrist, and though he was dying, the grip was like an iron manacle.

"Mama," Blut gasped, through the pain.

Mala felt tears slide down her face. *What did I do? He's crying out for his mother. What did I do?*

"Mama, it hurts." Blut squeezed her hand. "Make it stop. Mama, help me." He stared up at her desperately.

"I'm sorry. I had to," she mumbled, choked by tears. *I'm a murderer.*

His eyes shifted, seemed to come out of their daze. "Mama ..." he searched her face carefully, but she could only offer confusion.

Mala didn't know what to say. *It must be the poison—it's making him see things.* She looked up to Lowe to confirm—and in that moment, failed to see Blut pull the knife from his belly and swing his arm ...

With an inhuman growl, Lowe leapt from the thicket, hurling his entire body forward onto Blut. He grabbed the boy's feet and tugged him back just in time to prevent Blut from stabbing Mala in the chest.

"Demon!" the boy screamed, but the movement was too much for him, and he gave a shuddering gasp. His limbs relaxed. Mala thought it was over.

But as she swatted at her tears, she saw Blut's skin bubble. She blinked. The skin on the edge of his face was undulating. She blinked again. And before her lay the bald-headed man from last night.

That's not possible. I—he's not…

She gasped and looked down further. Her legs were long poles, stick thin and white as the moon against the shredded remnants of her midnight dress. Her bare feet had toes long as fingers. As she stared at her feet, a lock of hair fell forward. It was golden yellow.

CHAPTER EIGHT

It's happened. It's finally happened. Mala covered her eyes with her foreign arms and let out a wail.

"Mala?" Lowe reached toward her, his eyes wide.

"Stay back!" Mala growled, as much as she could growl with this stranger's high-pitched voice. *I don't even sound like myself. I'm so far gone, I'm not even me.*

"Mala, calm down," his hand barely brushed her shoulder before she backed away, stumbling out of the briars.

"I knew this would happen someday," she whispered. "I knew it. I just had this gut feeling. I was right." *I wish I wasn't.*

"What would happen?" he asked.

Lowe's image wavered before her, an abstract blur of colors behind her tears. She laughed, a cracked, choked sound. "That was it. Look at me? But you can't, right? Because I'm done. Insane. Completely. I killed that boy, and now ... I ... I'm ... this," She ran her hands through her hair, which was now too soft, too light, free of the river of tangles that always bound up her brown mane. She ran her hands down her long arms, the whitest skin she'd ever seen. *I'm cursed. Delusional. That was it. My breaking point. And that stupid spell didn't do a thing to stop it.*

Her hands fumbled with her necklace. She pulled the series of hooks into her lap and fumbled them with her unfamiliar knobby fingers. She grabbed the hour hand and ripped it roughly off. She threw it as far as she could into the trees before collapsing on the ground. She sobbed into the dirt.

Momma—I need you. I need you. Come back. I need you.

Lowe waited until her crying quieted. And then he said the last thing on earth she expected to hear. "You haven't gone crazy."

Mala laughed brokenly. "That's exactly what my delusions *would* say."

He grabbed one of her hands before she could pull away. "I'm not a hallucination. You're not crazy."

"I'm seeing things that aren't possible. I'm hearing things—my own voice doesn't even sound like me. What other definition of crazy do you want?" *Or cursed?* But she didn't say that word again.

Lowe put a hand on either side of her face. "I can see it, too."

Mala's stomach dropped. *Is he telling the truth? Or just trying to get me to calm down?* She clutched his arms. She studied his face. His blue eyes were soft and sincere. "What do you see, exactly?" A tremor of hope ran through her.

"Well you're blond, and really tall right now, probably taller than me—"

"And Blut?"

"What? Yeah. That he's bald? That's how he normally

looks," Lowe responded nonchalantly. He seemed to think of something and started muttering to himself, not realizing, Mala's world was shaken to the core.

He sees what I see. If he sees what I see, am I really crazy? Or... or is it magic? Was I right all along? Is it a curse?

"... maybe there's some kind of relic nearby or ... who knows? Fell would know. I wish ... well she'll have a better idea than me." Lowe was stroking her hair in absentminded fascination.

"What are you talking about?"

"Look at Blut," Lowe pointed to the crumpled body. "You saw him as a kid, right? But he was really thirty-four."

"That's not possible."

"Not for typical humans, but it is for a Kreis."

"You're lying."

"Mala, look at me." He held her gaze steadily, unwavering, until she felt her denial begin to waver, then topple. She glanced back at Blut. *Magic.*

Lowe cleared his throat, "I don't know how much you know. Most of this is protected intelligence. But there are people who talk. We know there are rumors ..."

Mala cocked her head, at a loss. "The government knows that there's magic?"

"What? No! Not at all. Let me explain ... when the bomb went off, it destroyed most of the planet. It did more damage than the Sich thought it would when they set it off in the Last War. It warped time itself." Lowe paused to let this idea seep in.

"That sounds like flooding magic to me!" Indignation felt

good after all the anxiety and sorrow that had been threatening to overwhelm her for the past twenty four hours. Mala clung to it.

Lowe sighed. “It is *not* magic. Erlenders believe in that junk ... magic and fortune telling. That's not real. It's a bunch of fairy dust and lies strung together for idiots.”

Mala stood, offended. “Excuse me? So I’m not crazy.” She gestured at her face. “This is not crazy, but I *am* an idiot?”

Lowe grabbed her hand before she could take two steps. “I'm sorry. I'm sorry. You're not an idiot. You don't know. It's just ... trying to explain this. It's so obvious to me because I've been Kreis for years. There are people who study the bomb’s effects and the Kreis mutation all day, every day. This is science. Those people would be far better at explaining. But I'll try.” He stared at her a moment to ensure he'd gotten her forgiveness—or at least, her attention.

“All Kreis can change their appearance. Using their own body, of course. It’s an adaptation, see? Blut wanted to appear unthreatening. He wanted to have energy and endurance. He wanted to take us by surprise. That's why he chased us as a kid. He adapted for the hunt. Last night—I doubt you saw him—but he was with the Erlenders by the river.”

Mala took a closer look at the bald man lying on the forest floor. She studied his profile, his clear, unmarked nose. Ice gripped her spine. It made its way through her insides and the air fled from her lungs. “He was the only man there without any tattoos.”

Lowe jerked his head toward her in surprise. “I didn't think you'd notice that. We only saw him for a second—”

“That was the man I tried to kill in the clearing last night.”

She tried to reconcile the fact that the evil man from the attack was somehow dead in front of her. *Was this Cherub? The man who'd sliced open Sari's cheek like it was a peach?* She took two steps forward and stared down into his face. Pity shriveled up, guilt evaporated. It *was* the same man. *It's too bad I killed him before I knew how much he deserved to die.*

Lowe watched her carefully, uncertain of her mood. When Mala finally turned to him, her face a mix of hesitance and curiosity, he looked relieved.

“You’re saying all Kreis can change their age?”

“Yes.”

“You're Kreis.” She challenged him with her eyes.

Lowe backed up through the briars until he was next to Blut's body. He stared down for a second, squeezing his eyes shut in concentration.

Mala blinked. His face wavered. And suddenly, before her, stood a four-year-old with messy black curls, his hands hidden in the folds of Lowe's shirt. He giggled. She gasped. Here was the giggling little acorn-thrower from the celebration. Her mind reeled. She felt dizzy.

“What the—”

“It's me, Mala,” the boy said, tilting his chubby face up to smile at her.

It’s true! Or are you just hallucinating? Her mind was skeptical. But her heart believed Lowe. It rattled like a tin can in her chest. Like it was trying to jump out. Her breath shortened to gasps and her hands shook in time.

"Oh, geez, don't have a heart attack. Give me a second and I'll melt back." Lowe rolled his eyes in an expression far too sarcastic for a toddler. A second later, he was back: a tall and lanky twenty-something, adjusting his clothes.

"What was that?" Mala spoke very slowly, trying to contain her fear. She took a step away from him, not quite sure whether she was in her right mind at the moment.

"I melted," Lowe shrugged. "Let's talk." He sank down to the ground and crossed his ankles nonchalantly, as though shape-shifting was an everyday occurrence. He shredded a fallen leaf. It was a minute before Mala could hear his voice over the blood pounding in her ears.

"Like I said before, you're probably Kreis. What does that mean? That's a hard one. There are some theories floating around. Exposure to radiation, exposure to bomb relics, time dilation ... The most popular theory is that the bomb caused some genetic mutations that make absolute time irrelevant for some people."

"Meaning what?"

Lowe tugged on her arm, and wouldn't relent until she sat down across from him. Mala watched as he slowly and deliberately dragged a finger through the sand between them.

"Most people live their lives in a line. Time runs straight and narrow and constant for them. They are born, they grow up, they grow old, they die." He waited for this to sink in. "Time isn't the same if you're Kreis. Your body doesn't necessarily age in a straight line. You have some degree of control. It's more like ... this." He drew a circle in the dirt above the line.

Mala stared, but it didn't make sense. "I don't understand."

Lowe bit his lip trying to explain. "Kreis can melt in and out of different stages in their lives, shift their body's—"

"What?" This was beyond anything Mala had ever heard. "So magic, that's stupid Mala! But I believe in shape-shifting? That's what you're saying?" She shot Lowe a scathing look.

There was silence as Lowe struggled. It was clear he had never had to explain the meaning of being Kreis before. "Kind of. We can shift within our own skin."

Mala looked at him blankly.

Lowe sighed. "I'm bad at this. Let's use the adaptation theory. Being Kreis is like having wings or scales. An aspect of ourselves we can learn to control and manipulate to our advantage."

"So you can transform to any age you want?"

"If you're trained."

"For as long as you want?"

"Yes."

"Whenever you want?"

"Yes."

"But you only look like yourself?"

"That's right."

"But I don't look like me."

"No. And I'm not sure why."

"And you're saying I'm not crazy?"

"If you are, then I am too," he winked.

"And you're saying it's not magic?"

“Definitely not.”

There was a long moment while Mala digested this information. She watched the wind tease the leaves from their branches. She listened to squirrels chirrup at each other and birds take flight nearby. These sounds were calming compared to the clamor in her head as she warred over whether to accept this revelation.

But ultimately, she had no choice: she’d seen Lowe perform something impossible. She was seeing things that were impossible. And whatever he called it, he thought she could do the same. Hope murmured sweetly in her ears. *Maybe I'm not crazy. Maybe it's not a curse. Maybe I'm ... powerful.*

She glanced at Blut. “Why’d he change back to his true age when he died?” she asked.

“He had a meltdown. That’s what we call it when you can’t control yourself. You get overwhelmed by emotion and you just … change.” He muttered and bent over Blut. He patted the body down, emptied out the pant pockets, tossing aside bits of trash, some hooks, and a small necklace.

“Souvenir?” He tossed it at her.

Mala nudged the etched golden charm away with her foot, disgusted, knowing how Blut had gotten it. She cleared her throat, eager to suppress her memories. “So how old are you really?”

Lowe grinned up at her. “As old as I want to be.”

Mala rolled her eyes. “I get it. Okay? But if you were a normal guy ...”

“I am normal.”

"No, you're annoying."

"Well, annoying is a step up from being hated, Misanthrope, so I'll take it."

"What are you doing?"

Lowe had started unbuttoning Blut's shirt, methodically running his hands over both the material and the body. "I'm checking for messages, intel. Just in case."

Mala closed her mouth, but couldn't fully hid her shock. *Bara's guard always broke Erlender noses and raided pockets for ammunition.* They had never been so meticulous. In fact, desecration had been more likely than a full-body search. Somehow the act elevated Lowe.

"How come I've never heard of any of this? If people really can just change their age at the drop of a hook, why doesn't anyone know? All I've ever heard are stories of great warriors, that Kreis are the fiercest—"

"How could we be good spies if we let everyone know our secrets? And besides, there's not that many of us. You've never met a Kreis before, right?"

Mala considered him for a moment. "Well, what about me?"

"I don't know," Lowe said, standing. He sighed. "We need to get you to the Center. Hopefully they'll have some answers." He pulled out her knife and carefully cleaned it with Blut's shirt.

"The Center?"

"Headquarters. And that's enough questions for now."

"That is not fair. I'm a murderer and a giant because of you and I don't get to know why?"

"Technically, you killed in self-defense because a traitor assassin was after you. And you're a blond beauty because of me," Lowe countered, a gleam coming into his eye. "Though you weren't too bad before, either." He gave her a crooked smile.

Mala blushed but scolded him. "Don't flirt to throw me off. Tell me how to change back."

"I can't."

"You've already told me this much, what will it hur—" Mala started but Lowe interrupted.

"I literally am unable to tell you how to change back. It's intuitive for most of us. You think about an age, you become it. But there are times, if you have a meltdown—if you've melted because of something really emotionally intense … you can get stuck for a while. You have to figure out how to get out of it yourself. There's no easy solution."

"Well, great. So now I'm stork-girl, no end in sight?"

"I think the Center will have some answers for you, once you've passed the test to prove you're Kreis." Lowe turned. "We should probably go, anyway. The Erlenders will be expecting Blut back. They'll come looking for him soon. And we won't want to be here."

He started tramping back down the way they'd come. When Mala made up her mind to follow, she had to run to keep up. But the ground was covered in leaves that slid every which way beneath her. Flailing her arms a bit to slow her downhill momentum on her long legs, Mala asked, "So, what's this test? At the Center? What are they going to make me do?"

That made Lowe pull up short. He watched her awkwardly fail to stop running and bit back a laugh as Mala tripped and slid on her butt in front of him. He held out a hand to help her up and a wicked grin bent his lips.

"Do you really want to know what the test is?" he asked, not letting go of her hand.

"Yes," she breathed. She waited expectantly, but he seemed to enjoy drawing out her anticipation. "It's terrible, isn't it? Am I going to have to kill someone else?"

"Worse," he said, and he leaned towards her. His eyes locked with hers. She could feel his breath on her cheek. Her stomach did a little flop and she felt a tingling in her palms. "The test," he whispered, "is a kiss."

Then suddenly he whirled and was running down the trail, laughing loudly and leaving Mala utterly breathless and confused.

CHAPTER NINE

When Mala finally made her way down to the rocky beach an hour later, she could see Lowe had already started on a homemade raft. Several mismatched driftwood logs had been bound together and were floating on the water. A few more waited on the beach.

"You made it," he said. "I thought the birds might have gotten you." He laughed and pulled severely on the makeshift twine, ensuring the logs were tightly lashed.

"Where are you going?" Mala asked.

"Um, *we* are going to the Center," Lowe responded.

Mala stood quietly for a moment. "I don't know if I can do that."

Lowe dropped the log he was binding and it fell with a thud onto his foot. "Ow!" He shoved it off and limped toward her. "What are you talking about?"

She knotted her fingers and stared at them. "I don't think I can ... kill people. I don't think I can walk away from my life and just—"

"What life?" Lowe exclaimed, his face incredulous.

Mala's voice trembled and she held back memories that

threatened to come forward. She swallowed before she spoke. "Bara's guard is the only—"

"They're all dead, Mala! Every last one of them."

"You don't know that!" Mala raged, but cringed internally. "We never checked! I just ... swam away. Like I always do." She could feel her throat getting tight from tears.

Lowe took a deep breath and seemed to regain his composure. "Mala, it was a massacre. You were lucky to get out."

She shook her head. "I can't." She stumbled along the rocky bank and headed toward the water, away from Lowe, away from the raft. "Look what it's done to me: I'm not even myself!" She looked down at her long arms in disgust. "I'm a monster."

"That's enough," Lowe said gruffly. "I know this is a lot. I know that everything is different. But stop running away. You have a talent. What exactly it is is still a mystery, but it's amazing. You have this ability. Don't run from it; come learn how to use it."

Mala heard his words, but chose to ignore them. She clambered clumsily across the rocks as Lowe called to her. She came to a large boulder that could serve as a diving board. "I have to go back," she repeated to herself.

"Who'd recognize you?" Lowe yelled. But it was too late. Mala closed her eyes and dove into the frigid water.

She'd misjudged the water's depth; with her new height, it was far too shallow. Her forehead smacked against a rock on the river bottom. But that was nothing compared to the pain she felt the instant water touched her skin.

Instead of fire, this was ice: her limbs immediately felt frozen and stiff, as though the river were full of snow. The cold pricked her toes and her fingers and spread its way up through her limbs in a painful wave. And then came the numbness; it took over her body and her mind and set her adrift. She couldn't feel anything and no longer cared ...

Suddenly, the numbness retreated. She felt herself being lifted from the water. She was placed—none too gently—on Lowe's makeshift raft. The stumps of branches bit into her back. Her lungs ached and she drew a ragged breath, spewing out muddy river water. When she opened her eyes, she saw Lowe's face smiling cheerily down at her. She couldn't help but be annoyed by his expression, even though he'd saved her.

"Do near-death experiences always make you this happy?" she muttered, turning her head to the side as she choked up even more water. "Because, I have to say, it's creepy."

His smile only widened. He didn't say anything, but reached out and grabbed a strand of her hair. He pulled it gently in front of her face.

She stared. Her knotted, gnarled, long brown curls were back. She sat up quickly and checked the rest of her body. Her arms and feet were back to their slender, tanned selves. Her right hand bore the scratch from the clock's hour hand. She looked back at Lowe's beaming face, and despite herself, she laughed.

"All those years, it seems like you unconsciously knew your own antidote," he stated.

A rush of relief filled her. And a sudden rush of unexplained joy. She was Mala again. Dull brown, comfortable, cowardly Mala.

She rubbed her hands down her arms, feeling their length. She touched her face to make sure her nose was the same small triangle she remembered. She looked at the sky and at Lowe's face and everything seemed much brighter than normal. She had never felt so ... euphoric.

"Quite the high, isn't it?" Lowe asked, pushing her hair gently back behind her shoulders.

"What?" she looked at him. His face seemed rosier than normal. The sun surrounded him with a halo of light.

"The rush when you return to yourself. Feels good, right?"

She giggled. "I don't know what it is, but it's amazing!"

He smiled at her. "I'm glad to have you back. This Mala happens to be my favorite."

She laughed again, giddiness rushing through her system. "That's only because this Mala isn't tall enough to squash you flat like a bug." She had trouble keeping herself upright. She was swooning from the ecstatic rush.

"That's true," Lowe laughed, as he put his arms around her to prevent her from falling. His touch sent an electric current through Mala's insides. She felt as if her entire chest was abuzz with energy. His eyes were flashing, glinting from sunlight—and something more. He leaned closer to her so their foreheads touched. "But you know what?" he whispered.

"What?" she tried to focus on his face, but found it difficult.

"I think I like this Mala's eyes more, and her nose is cuter." He nuzzled her nose with his own. "And her lips," he brought up a finger and traced the outline, pulling his head away just slightly so he could watch his finger swoop along the soft red curve. "Mala?" he breathed.

"What?"

"Can I *test* you?"

His words threw her, and her buzz fizzled slightly. "What?" she asked, for a third time. The confusion must have shown on her face. He pulled back a few more centimeters and stared solemnly into her eyes.

"To determine if you're Kreis, they test you with a kiss. I wasn't joking earlier, though I was giving you a hard time. Typically, if you're Kreis, you'll transform ... back to the moment you had your first kiss." He traced her lips once more, and though this still sent a thrill through her, an edge of fear eroded her high.

"But what if ..." Mala began, but she couldn't bring herself to finish. Her cheeks reddened.

"What if you've never been kissed?"

She nodded, nervously avoiding his eyes. But the corners of his mouth twitched up.

"I was hoping that was the case, Misanthrope." She looked back up, a little bewildered. He smiled. "Mala, there's an easy test to fix that." He put his hands behind her neck and slowly untied her necklace. "I'll kiss you, and while I kiss you I'll prick your finger with this." He held up a hook. "If you're Kreis, then when you transform afterward, the cut will be healed. Restored to the first moment of our kiss."

"But ..." she interjected and he cut her off with a simple finger to her lips.

"If I'm your first kiss, then whenever they test you at the Center—anytime in the future any Kreis kisses you for the first time—you'll be brought back to this moment," he stroked a gentle path along her jaw. "You'll remember my kiss forever." There was a warmth in his voice that liquefied her kneecaps.

Mala was almost swept up in the moment, but another fear—a deeper fear—held her back.

"What if ... I'm not really Kreis?" she whispered, in a voice so small she wasn't sure that any sound even came out.

"Then it will still be the best damn kiss you've ever had." And with that, Lowe stopped asking, and his lips crushed hers.

The euphoria of the transformation changed instantly into a sensation Mala had never known. Her heart fluttered like a hummingbird and she felt breathless and light. Joy swept through her and made her dizzy. She didn't even feel the hook prick her fingertip. She just felt an electric surge that ran all the way to her toes. Lowe's hand stroked the back of her hair and he gave a little sigh.

"Wow," he said, pulling back and opening his eyes.

"Yeah," she muttered, her cheeks flushed. She glanced up at him. And a terrible pain took hold.

CHAPTER TEN

"What the hell just happened?" Mala asked. Lowe had fallen backwards into the shallows.

"I have no idea." His voice came out as a rusty squeak. He stared at Mala with a pained expression, almost as if he were looking at the sun. Then he shifted his gaze to his own arms, which had become narrow and stick-thin. His grey shirt hung loose and baggy and his pant legs dragged in the mud; he'd shrunk quite a bit. His black hair was buzzed short, and he was long-limbed, as young teen boys often are.

"Why do you look like you're fourteen?"

Lowe didn't respond. He rubbed a nervous hand across a rough patch of acne coating his cheeks. He seemed dumbstruck.

"How come you changed?" Mala demanded. Her voice came out a gravelly purr and she tried to clear her throat to get rid of the scratch, but this body kept her voice low. She wasn't as shocked this time by melting; she'd been expecting something like this from what Lowe had told her about the test. But to watch him transform from the brawny sarcastic man she was used to into a gawky teen was very disconcerting. "Does the test always work like that? Where both people change?"

"No." He stared down at his hands, and out at the muddy currents of the river.

Mala waited. And her heart filled with longing and regret. The kiss had started so magically. She had still been buzzed on the high of reversing her transformation, and that had combined with the passion of Lowe's kiss. *I never imagined anything could feel that intense.* But then she had opened her eyes and met his. She'd seen a lot of emotions living in the northern guard. But she'd never seen someone that shade of horrified. He still couldn't look directly at her.

Eventually, Lowe broke the silence. "I think we need to get to the Center as soon as possible. I don't know enough ... I don't know what happened." He stayed quiet for a minute, fingers tracing a pattern in the water. "I think it would be best if we melt back." He stood and started to walk up the shore to the cover of the trees. He didn't look at her.

Mala sat aghast, hurt and frustrated. "Wait!" she turned and yelled after him. He stopped but didn't turn back. "What do I look like?"

"I need to melt ... it'll easier for me to do it in private." Lowe's non-answer only made Mala more uneasy. She touched her fingers to her face. The skin felt smooth. No scars. No missing nose. Her body looked normal. *I'm not disfigured. But clearly something about this girl freaks Lowe out.* Mala watched his retreating form. And the realization came to her as she slipped back into the water. *He knows this girl. He knows who I look like. Blut thought I looked like his mom ...* Mala's stomach dropped. She slid as far under the shallows as she could. She clasped her knees and tried to hold herself still against the current. But her stomach churned like the waves. *I turned into his mom.*

They didn't speak all afternoon. Mala didn't know what to say. How to bring up the awkward, awful thing that had ruined the perfect mood. Ruined the perfect kiss. *I was better off as a misanthrope,* she thought as she cooked fish for dinner.

She watched Lowe check the raft one last time before sunset. Mala sighed. Thinking about him had been her escape. And now the chasm inside her threatened to engulf her. Tears rushed down her face as she dutifully covered her neck in ashes. Even the thought that her mother was gone hurt too much. Her heart howled and clawed at her ribs. It hurt to breathe. She pulled at her hair just to relieve the tension in her throbbing chest. It took everything she had to keep from screaming. But finally, gradually, the pain ebbed a little.

She climbed aboard raft in silence. Lowe didn't comment on her grieving, and she was grateful. He poled them skillfully toward a tributary as fireflies and the mosquitoes buzzed around them. Mala's head was heavy, and her heart was sore beyond aching. She counted her breaths, refusing to allow sleep or more emotion to cloud her thoughts. But as the night wore on and Lowe remained focused on their destination, she found she was nodding in the muggy air.

And suddenly the air around her was full of screams. Her

mother danced and sang on the deck of a ship and a fountain of bullets poured from her mouth. Erinne reached her hands to her stomach and peeled away her dress and skin in a single layer and Mala could see her lungs move, her heart beating.

Then Mala was shaking, falling into the river. On the deck of her father's ship she saw an Erlender with a knife who cackled and said, "I know, I know." And there was her father tied up to the ship's bow. Her throat clenched ...

Mala screamed again and again. Lowe shook her awake with difficulty. "Hey, Mala, it's okay. It's okay."

I'm alone. They're gone. I'm alone. It was a minute before she realized Lowe's hands were still on her shoulders.

"Are you okay?" His eyes were gentle, and though the pain didn't leave her, it receded enough that she could speak.

"Sorry. I must have fallen asleep." The dream fell away from her as she felt the warmth of his hands on her shoulders. She didn't need to count to make the nightmare recede. *That's a first.*

"Was it Blut?" he asked softly, tucking her hair back.

"What? No." She shook her head to clear it. "I would have thought it would be. But it wasn't." She couldn't talk about what it was. The pain crouched, ready to spring forward and devour her.

Lowe let go of her. "Hey, don't worry. It's a good thing. Another sign you're probably Kreis."

"What do you mean?" His train of thought distracted her and she clutched at it.

His blue eyes gazed into the darkness for a moment before he said, "Most Kreis don't feel regret." He stood abruptly and started poling the raft forward once more. “How about we play a game? It will help me stay awake and we've got awhile to go.”

“Where are we going?”

“The Center.”

“Right. Where is it?” she started to ask, but cut herself off. “Oh. Secret. Right. Never mind.”

Lowe yawned loudly. “What about that game?” he asked again.

“What kind of game can you play in the dark?” she demanded.

“Oh,” he chuckled. “You *really* didn't mean to ask that question.” There was a sultry edge to his tone that brought her back to that afternoon, to their kiss. It made Mala nervous and she shifted self-consciously on the raft. They hadn't spoken about the kiss. Mala didn't really know what to say.

“How about the question game?” Lowe said. “Ever played?”

Mala would have chosen just about any distraction over falling back asleep. Over becoming vulnerable to the pain again. She knew the game, even if she'd only ever watched from the trees as it was played by the other kids below.

“If I haven't, are you going to teach me the rules?” she shot back. They passed under the shadow of a hill, which blocked the moon. She could just make out the grey shadow of his cheek as he smiled in the starlight.

“How old are you, Mala?”

“Would it matter to you if I was seventeen?” she arched an eyebrow.

He waited for a moment before responding. "Would I be a bad person if I said no?" he said.

"If I'm Kreis, isn't the rule that I get to be any age I want to be?" she said.

"Time-out. That's not really a question," he said. "That's really a statement with an *isn't* tossed in. And you know the consequence: losers have to take something off."

"It is too a question! I'm asking if that's the rule," Mala exclaimed. "And you never said this was going to be a stripping game!" Her voice trembled high and tense, but a little ribbon of excitement threaded through her.

"You never gave me a chance to explain. You started off with a question ... so I assumed you knew the rules."

Mala thought quickly as they slid past the hill and back into the moonlit night. Lowe's expectant grin made her bite her lip. Then she grudgingly unhooked her necklace and tossed it at his feet. "There. Ready to lose?" *'Cause you will,* she thought as she gritted her teeth, determined.

"Did you dream about me?"

"Do you think that's why I woke up screaming?"

"Nah, you would have been screaming my name." With a swoop, Lowe took off his shirt, tossing the tattered thing at her feet. Mala stared at his slim torso and abs, a lump forming in her throat. She caught him grinning at her with the same mischievous look he'd had earlier when he'd talked about games in the dark. "Like what you see?" he asked.

She was too tongue-tied to respond. Lowe grinned. His

tactic seemed to be working. He held up one hand and started folding down fingers, counting down to when Mala would have to take off her dress. *Cheater!* Her mind screamed at her, but it took a few seconds for Mala's mouth to catch up. He was folding down the last finger when she stuttered out a question. "Who—Who did I look like after we kissed?"

Instantly, Lowe's face collapsed. He stared off into the darkness.

Idiot Mala. He was stripping for you and you had to ruin it. You're a ruiner. Ruiner. Self-destructive—

"Why do you want to know?" Lowe's question was so quiet Mala could barely hear it over her internal rant.

"What?"

"Why do you want to know?" There was an edge to his voice. Mala wasn't sure what it was. She wasn't sure if he was still playing the game or not. She sat for a minute, trying to figure out the best way to approach him. But when he held up his fingers again, she gave a sigh of relief. *So he's not mad at me.*

"Did you know her?" Mala queried.

"Do we really know anyone?" he responded.

"Is that a yes or a no?"

"Why are you so insistent?" Lowe raised his eyebrows innocently, but something in his tone tipped Mala off. She was right.

"Was it ... your mom?"

Lowe's jaw dropped. "Why the hell would you think that?"

Mala felt her insides relax. *Not his mom. Oh, thank God. I did not turn into his mom.* “Was she important to you?”

It was a minute before Lowe responded, but Mala didn't count down with her fingers. She was far too eager to hear his response.

“How important is your first love?”

“No!” Mala gasped. *His first love.* Shock ran through her. *But he seemed so disgusted ... could it have been hurt?* She recalled his fourteen-year old-face as he'd backed away from her. *I turned into the girl who broke his heart.*

She glanced up at Lowe, apology in her eyes, and was instantly confused. *Why is he grinning?* It took a minute. She cringed as she realized what had happened: she had to lose the dress.

“You are a *cheater*!” she jumped up and nearly made the raft capsize. Lowe carefully steadied it.

“Manipulator—I’ll grant you that—but not a cheater. And ... a winner.” He chuckled and waggled his eyebrows.

“Was any of that even true?”

He laughed. “I'm trying to get you naked and you want to talk about other girls?”

He gestured at the dress. Mala's fingers trembled as she fumbled for the zipper. It was caught on some fabric. She couldn't get it down. *You swim in your underwear all the time, idiot. This is no big deal.* But then his hands were on her, and it was a big deal.

“If you want it off, you're gonna have to do it yourself.” She tried to sound sarcastic, but she only sounded scared.

“With pleasure.” Lowe took to the task with feather-light hands.

Mala's heart began a frantic dance. It leapt into her throat and left her breathless. Her blood was racing. She felt out of control. She sought distraction. “You could at least tell me if it was true. I think I deserve that much.” His warm breath, which had been befuddling her blood, suddenly vanished. Mala turned to look at him.

Lowe sat back on the raft, his hand still attached to her parted zipper. “Her name was Stelle. The Erlenders ... stole her.” He shook his head at her. “Has anyone ever told you how good you are at ruining a moment?”

“Sorry,” Mala breathed. “Misanthrope.”

Lowe smiled. But a sudden cracking twig onshore made him jerk his head. His eyes quickly scanned their surroundings. “Game over. We have to stop here.” He jumped off the raft and pulled it to the sandy bank. He grabbed his shirt and rifled through hidden pockets, bottles clinking under his fingers. “I’m really sorry about this Mala. But I can’t let you see anymore. You’re gonna have to sleep until we get there. And promise me one thing ...” He laid her back gently on the raft. He re-zipped her dress. He brushed back her hair. She stared up at him. His face was tender again. She nodded.

"Don't tell anyone about how you melt until I talk to you again. Promise?"

"But why—"

He shook his head. "Just promise."

"Okay."

He tipped a small vial to her lips and she swallowed.

CHAPTER ELEVEN

Mala awoke in the pitch dark. She squinted at her surroundings as the tranquilizer wore off. She could feel the water swaying gently beneath her. But this ... this was not the raft. She was on a lumpy mattress and another one lay on the planks beside her. She found herself staring at the reed walls of a windowless hut. A pile of clothing sat in a corner of the floor. She realized it was her dress. *Holy—* she clutched her hands to her chest. She had something on. But her necklace was gone. Her knife was gone. She sat up and saw she wore a long yellow wetsuit. Star-shaped cut outs in the sleeves revealed her tan arms, and as she examined herself she realized a huge cutout exposed most of her back. *What the muck is this? Were we captured?* The thought rose in her mind as bile rose in her throat. She had no time to gather her thoughts before a short door swung inward and a shadow, backlit by brilliant sun, towered over her.

"Oh! You're awake! Ha! Lowe was wrong, he thought you'd be out another couple hours," An elderly woman crouched to get through the door. She chuckled and plopped herself down next to Mala. "Ow, my hip," she groaned.

She knows Lowe. Mala's panic immediately receded. As her eyes adjusted, they drew out the features of the old woman. She had meticulously shaped eyebrows over drooping eyes. Her hair was glossy silver, pulled into a bouncy ponytail, and she was wearing an inappropriately short wetsuit that perfectly matched her lipstick—a garish shade of red. A fork was folded around the base of her left ear, the tines clinging to her earlobe.

"So tell me," the woman croaked, elbowing Mala playfully in the ribs, "What was it like to get recruited by Lowe?" She gave a lovesick sigh and leaned on Mala's shoulder. "He's so hot."

Mala shifted uncomfortably. "Um ... I'm sorry. Who are you?"

"Oh!" the old lady giggled. "Whoops. I'm Alberna. I know, don't say anything. My name is horrible. I can't believe my mother did that. You can call me Alba." Alba scooted over slightly on the pallet so she could face Mala. She tried to sit cross-legged but her knees wouldn't bend enough. "Damn! I can't wait until I find that trigger. Let me tell you, old age, not so great. Avoid melting to an age like this if at all possible."

Mala watched the silver-haired woman with interest. "You're Kreis?"

Alba nodded impatiently. "Tell me about it. Please. I'm dying here."

"About what?"

"Tell me about Lowe! He's so cute! It's so unfair you're his first recruit." Alba pouted a moment before her curiosity overwhelmed her again. "So, open the floodgates. Details. I want details."

"Um ..." Mala had never had anyone demand information within five seconds of meeting her before. *Maybe she's really a twelve-year-old.*

"Was it romantic? Did he sweep you off your feet?" Alba was practically bouncing up and down with excitement.

Better say something before she wets herself. "Um ... A guy I really don't like had forced me to dance and Lowe cut in," she said, thinking back to the first moment she'd seen his eyes and their shocking blue.

"Oh! That's so unfair! I would have died! Romance times ten! Ugh ... my recruiter showed up as this old git who had money. You know—mid-life-crisis kind-of-looking guy. I was working for this one ferry as a server; you know, I had to do something after my parents died. And he offered me a job. Totally unromantically BORING. I'll never forgive him for it," Alba crossed her arms in a pout and tossed her silver hair.

"Where is Lowe?" *Why isn't he here?*

Alba waved her hand nonchalantly. "Filling out reports. I didn't see my recruiter for two days after I showed up here. Supposedly newbies are tons of paperwork." She saw Mala's stricken face and tried to soften the blow. "But, look, for sure he'll be at your test ceremony. And they scheduled it for tomorrow, which is really early, in fact. You'll see him then. And I'm sure he'll make puppy eyes at you. Because you're his first. Recruiters always fall for their firsts. It's like a high for them. You know. To get to be a recruiter … it's like two ranks below an Ancient. Really rare. My recruiter said it's kinda like you just won a living trophy. And you're Lowe's!" she squealed.

Alba might have hit her across the head with a plank. *A high? Just some living trophy?*

"Oh my gosh, don't get all pouty. You'll never make it if you do. Look. Bright side: you are totally elite now, which means lots of guys will fall at your feet. And you're Kreis, which also means lots of Erlenders will fall at your feet, preferably dead." She giggled.

Mala shoved her self-pity aside. *She's right. If Lowe doesn't really like me, it doesn't matter*— her heart thumped hard in disagreement. Mala looked to Alba for an escape.

"So … what now?"

"Are you ready for the Grrrrand Tourrrrr?" Alba trilled her tongue.

"Um. A tour? Sure. Just let me grab my necklace."

"I wouldn't advise that."

"Why?"

"Well, there's always combat practice for one- something to grab makes you an easy target," Alba said. "And it's not so good to show too much of an emotional connection around here." Then she winked. "Kinda defeats the whole 'unfazed assassin' thing."

Mala retracted her hand. She could see Alba's point. But she didn't like it. She shifted the necklace and placed it under her pillow. But her stomach jumped a little at the thought of leaving it behind, so she shoved her hand back under, grabbed the hooks, and fixed the clasp behind her neck.

"Ok then. Don't say I didn't warn you. Let's get moving!" Alba tried to bounce up but her knees cracked and she jerked to a stop. "Little help, please?"

Mala stood, bumped her head on the low ceiling, and crouched to help the old woman to her feet. "Alba, um ... how old are you really?"

Alba laughed. "It's been so long since I've been my linear age, I almost don't know. But I'm sixteen, I think." She began to lead the way out of the dark room onto a floating platform that stretched across sparkling water as placid as blown glass.

Mala followed. They were smack in the middle of a vast lake. And high in the mountains. The edges of the lake were framed by jagged peaks; the entire thing looked like a giant mirror. She saw dozens of other low, windowless huts bobbing nearby. They were all woven out of reeds and shone pale gold in the sunshine. They weren't drifting so Mala assumed they must be anchored somehow. The back of each hut was covered in a rough collection of unwoven reeds, as tall as the huts themselves. At first, Mala found the mess confusing. But then she realized that from the distant shore, the huts must look like nothing more than a growth of weeds in a shallow part of the lake. It must keep outsiders from approaching. *Simple, but clever*. Each little hut had its own floating bridge leading to a platform lined with larger huts; the bridges formed spokes in a large floating wheel. It all was so primitive-looking, Mala had a hard time believing this was where the elite trained. She had an even harder time believing Alba was one of the elite as the old woman tried to skip.

“Where are we?” Mala asked as she gawked.

“Undisclosed location. You don’t really get to find out where until you’re through training and several missions. It’s completely hidden from the Erlenders, though.”

A nagging thought poked around in Mala’s head. *That’s what Bara had said about the island.* She shoved the thought away and followed Alba out onto a bridge.

Mala glanced down as she walked. A dark shadow rippled under the water and she saw massive steel posts disappearing into the depths. She gave a shiver and peered down. It was hard to see past the reflections on the surface of the water, but it looked as though the huts were simply a cap for a large metal structure lurking in the depths. Tilting her head, Mala could see the crossbeams and windows of an enormous skyscraper beneath her. Light poured from some of the windows, distorted by the underwater currents so that the building appeared surrounded by flecks of glitter. “Whoa. What's that?” she pointed.

Alba stopped short and glanced carelessly down. “That's the Center,” she said.

“But, what is it?”

“It used to be some kind of underwater hotel or something ... before the bomb,” Alba said, clearly disinterested in the topic. “Come on, there's so many people you have to meet! Including Verrukter. The hottest of the hot! But I've called him, so hands-off!”

Alba pulled Mala along, not letting her stay and count the stories that descended under the water. Even so, Mala had seen at least eight levels of windows before the shadows swallowed the building. The thought of being that far underwater sent fear tickling up her spine. But Alba was talking and Mala quickly refocused her thoughts.

"...and here's where we come for meditation," Alba pointed a gnarled finger towards a courtyard of woven reeds. "Boring. You have to go at least twice a week. And sit for hours! But at least you get combat lessons in between. Otherwise I think I would have died."

"How long have you been here?" Mala asked, thinking meditation wouldn't be so bad. The sun was warm and bright and she could imagine lying down out here and drifting off to sleep.

"About two years," Alba replied. "And I've gotten three kills in, which is awesome. Nobody's broken my record yet and you'd better not, either. Or we'll really have problems," she teased.

"Well," a deep voice rumbled behind them, "guess she better not count that kill she got on the way here, then."

Alba turned quickly. A warm blush rose on her cheeks. Mala guessed the teenager who joined them must be Verrukter from the nervous way Alba clenched her hands. "No!" Alba sounded scandalized. She poked Mala in the ribs. "Did Lowe tell you? You did *not* get a kill on your way here!"

Mala didn't know how to respond to an accusation that sounded insane. "I didn't realize there was a score ..."

Verrukter strolled closer and put a hand on Alba's shoulder. "Everything's a score. And he made sure his newbie came in with a scratch. Gonna put you out of business, sweetheart," he murmured in Alba's ear.

Tall and blond and incredibly muscular under his navy wetsuit, Mala could see why Alba found him attractive, but she couldn't help noticing he had a weak chin. Alba's doe-eyed grin made Mala wonder if the girl had even heard a word Verrukter had said. *Does she know she's drooling?*

Verrukter patted Alba. “You know though, you have an advantage over this newbie.”

“Oh?” Alba practically purred at the compliment. “And what's that?”

“Age!” Verrukter cracked up and Alba hit him playfully.

“When I get back to one of my younger forms, I will so pound your you-know-what!”

“When you get back to your younger form, I'll so pound *your* you-know-what.”

“I meant in combat!”

“I didn't,” he laughed and turned to Mala. “Do you know, she's been stuck like that for over a month? She had a meltdown during combat practice and now she can't melt back! I was giving it to her good. And I guess she couldn't handle it.”

Mala watched Alba carefully, and though the other girl laughed, it was a little too high- pitched, a little too reedy to be sincere. Alba was embarrassed.

Trying to change the subject, Mala said, “I'm guessing I don't really have to introduce myself since you seem to know all about my trip here. But I'm Mala.” She held out a hand.

“I'm guessing I don't have to introduce myself either,”

Verrukter hitched his eyebrow up and slid his eyes slyly over to Alba in a way that said he knew exactly the effect he had on her. Mala found his crudeness and smugness irritating, and she ground her teeth into a smile. She wasn't used to dealing with people—not people she liked and especially not people she didn't. But she feigned politeness and shook his hand. It looked like Verrukter saw the grimace through her smile because his grin changed and challenge flashed in his eyes.

“We're going on a tour. Want to join?” Alba had regained her composure.

“No, sorry. Gotta go. Chores,” he sighed dramatically, and strode off.

“Chores?” Mala asked. “That doesn’t sound very glamorous for a secret training camp of highly trained warriors.”

Alba shrugged. “They want us to learn a 'trade' so they say. It helps with cover on longer missions. But you have to go on several quickies first, so you’ll get the basics: combat, espionage, meditation, all that. You only get a trade after you’ve had several successful missions. I’m the youngest with a trade right now. Well, you know what I mean.” Alba waved a wrinkled hand.

“What trade have you got?”

“I cook,” Alba said, with a toss of her hair. “It's for my next mission. At least there are knives. And taste-testing. But I wish I had Verrukter's job. He gets to hunt onshore. That means guns. Which probably means a sniper assignment. Which probably means a high-level kill. I'm probably gonna get stuck with some dumb mid-level Blue Nose and be forced to make it look like an accident

..." She moaned as she led Mala over to a grass hut that looked dingier than the rest. "We're going down to the real Center. The surface is just where we sleep so we can defend if there's ever an attack. The real work is all below. And some of the stuff they salvaged from pre-bomb years is a-mazing!" She sang the last word as she pulled open the door. An eerie blue light flickered inside the darkened room from the floor, which was solid glass. The walls sparkled with yellow buttons, like thousands of beetle eyes. Through the floor, Mala could see the Center's roof, glowing windows with a metal steeple that pointed ominously towards their feet. A school of red fish swam around the building and flipped down to explore the depths. It was anything but normal.

In a corner of the hut behind Mala, Alba was checking some dials at a control station far more complex than any boat's. When she seemed satisfied, she turned back to Mala. "Ready?" she asked.

"Ready for what?"

"To go down," Alba sounded impatient. She didn't wait for an answer from the dumbstruck Mala. She hobbled over and slammed the door of the hut closed. Instead of the soft thump of grass, the door gave a heavy metallic clang as it shut. Alba turned her age-spotted hands on a wheel located on the back of the door to seal it, then returned to the control panel.

The entire hut began to descend. Mala watched in awe: the straw cover peeled away and collapsed on the surface of the water. The metal walls of the submarine became visible, like the meat under a thin layer of fish scales. Not sure what to think, Mala gave a nervous laugh.

"Pretty cool, huh? I remember when I first came. I thought this thing was awesome," Alba said as she carefully steered them toward a docking station several stories below the top floor of the glowing building.

"My grandma told me about these," Mala said. "I thought the submarines were all gone."

"Oh dearie," Alba wagged a finger at her playfully and played up her old lady croak. "You've gotta lot to learn. There's awesome stuff about being Kreis that you won't see anywhere else. And this is just the start."

Watching the glowing building loom in front of her like a radioactive missile, Mala felt a swell of hope. *If subs still exist ... if our assassins can melt ...* She closed her eyes and imagined grand houses lining the Gottermund River, kids with shoes playing in the yards. She imagined the president floating down the river on a barge, people crowding the banks with signs and banners and a rainbow of streamers. For the first time in a long time, Mala felt a flicker of optimism. Victory didn't seem so far away.

The girls docked roughly on a metal platform outside the Center, jarring Mala from her reverie. Alba moved lazily to open the door and Mala panicked. *We can't swim this far down.* But no sooner had that thought bubbled frantically in her mind than metal walls extended from the building like arms and wrapped around the sub on all sides. A giant whoosh nearly knocked Mala to the ground. Air was forced into the temporary docking room and the water was forced out in great gushes through vents in the floor. They exited the little sub just as two burly dockworkers came out a sliding door from the Center.

"Thanks, boys!" Alba gave a tinkling laugh and grabbed Mala's hand. "I can't wait to show you my favorite place!"

The girls passed through a set of sliding glass doors. They walked into what once must have been the lobby of the hotel. A magnificent tile mosaic spread across the floor. The mosaic was a map of local tributaries feeding the river, azure waterways edged in gold. Mala could see, at the far end of the room, the great mouth of the Gottermund, where the water spilled into blue ocean tiles, those fertile plains where the Senebal capital, DasWort, lay. And in a giant circle encapsulating the map the Senebal creed repeated: IT IS US. Mala couldn't read, but she knew the shapes of the letters well enough to know they were the creed Bara had flown on her flag.

The creed was a reminder of their purpose here, of what the Senebals had to protect. The only waterway uncontaminated by the bomb that blackened the world, the Gottermund proved that Mala's people, the Senebals, were the chosen. Those fit to live and repopulate the world. But the Erlenders and their deformed offspring had swarmed in, their jets like locusts, and eaten the entire northeast portion of the river. Most of the lakes and tributaries had had to be abandoned there; the Senebals hadn't been able to protect them. It was a moment of weakness in their history. A moment when they had thought they were the only survivors. The tribe had let their defenses slip. And they were still paying the price, seventy-three years later. Though Erlender jets had been destroyed, the scavenging band still tried to creep south into the rich farmland. They still tried to steal the Senebal homeland. And they took as many lives as possible in the process.

"These are the most revered Ancients." Alba gestured at a circle of giant bronze statues that ringed the mosaic, drawing Mala's attention away from the floor. "So, it's required that I give you a quick intro. Here you go. Um ... here. Tier is our current head of the Ancients. He's known for completely re-engineering our recruiting process. We have twice as many Kreis now as we've ever had, thanks to him. Los is known for his epic kills—over a hundred or something," she scoffed a little. "They don't have his annual numbers available, but who wants to bet he didn't have three in his first two years of training?" She flicked the statue on the elbow as she passed it. "Here's a good one: Sich was a seductress and she's the one who killed the Erlender king forty years back. She was on mission as a spy but turned assassin. Totally my idol. Forget who that is ... forget this guy ... well, you get the point. I'm gonna have one of those statues one day."

Mala gaped at the fierce features of the Kreis heroes. Their exploits had been bedtime stories for her. Seeing what they looked like, the lifelike poses and the strength in their faces ... it had both a haunting and an invigorating effect on her. But she spotted one statue that didn't look like the rest. "Who's this?" she asked, reaching toward the foot of a massive man.

"Don't touch it! It's bad luck," Alba exclaimed.

Mala drew her hand back but continued to stare up at the statue. It was covered in a series of pockmarks and scratches. She couldn't quite decide if it was old or if it had been deliberately ruined.

“That,” Alba said disparagingly, “is Klaren, the deranged. Fifteen years ago they found him killing another Kreis, crushing the guy’s throat. They say he went crazy, didn't know what he was doing. Tier killed him. As you can see, he's not very popular. I think they keep this up as, you know, a reminder.”

“Oh,” Mala shuddered and stepped back.

“Yeah, it's a warning, because you know, like two out of every ten Kreis go crazy.”

“What?” Mala turned to her, horrified.

Alba shrugged. “They can't hack it. But really—it's not that bad of odds—considering only half of us make it past the first mission anyway.”

Mala's throat constricted. “But ... you guys can melt. Walk in as one person and out as another.”

Alba raised an eyebrow. “That doesn't make us bulletproof, honey.”

Mala bit her lip and turned back to stare at the scratched and abused bronze statue of Klaren. She counted furiously to quell her fear.

“Hey, you've got a three in ten chance of coming out alright,” Alba put a hand on her shoulder and squeezed. “Not bad odds for getting to be elite. It could be worse. You could be typical.”

CHAPTER TWELVE

"Oh no," Alba whispered as a group of teens clad in multicolored wetsuits came toward them. "Watch out. Idiot patrol approaches."

"Albie!" A blond in her early twenties, whose features would make girl cringe in jealousy, called out across the room. She wore a blue wetsuit accented with swirling cutouts across her abdomen, cutouts that trailed dangerously low and left little to the imagination. "How are you? Killed anyone today?" She gushed but her eyes were hard as rock.

"Not yet. Volunteering?" Alba spit back.

"Heard you're bunking with the new girl!" She and her band of followers, a set of teen boys who trailed after her with slavish looks on their faces, came to a halt in front of Mala.

"Hi, I'm Neid." the blond held out her hand delicately, bent at the wrist. She eyed Mala and gave a derisive sniff. "So, where did he find you? Back of a tugboat? Or were you a street-crawler?"

"Neid," Alba's voice grew low and threatening.

"Sorry. But she does have 'tributary' written all over her face. I mean, look at the necklace. I bet she even believes in magic.

Are those your magic charms, honey?" She gestured at Mala's necklace.

Mala stiffened. *Did Lowe tell people? No. He wouldn't. Would he?* She studied Neid. The woman glared at Alba, shooting venom from her eyes. *Okay, no. I think this is just some personal thing. I think.*

Mala tried to break the tension with the truth. "I came from the northern guard—Bara's guard."

"See I knew it. Outskirts." Neid said *outskirts* as thought it was a dirty word.

"So?" Alba challenged.

"I've heard lots of those river guards out there like to get flooded. That they spend half their days dizzy drunk." Several boys with Neid nodded in agreement.

"Maybe it's easy to stay sober when you haven't actually killed someone," Alba hissed.

Neid opened her mouth to respond but Mala interrupted. "My entire guard was just massacred by Erlenders. So maybe you should shut up." She dug her nails into her palms.

One of Neid's companions gasped. He was a little younger than the rest of the group, maybe fourteen or fifteen. He was awkward and short and his face was covered in freckles. "I heard about that. The Kurz Erlender band attacked this big group a few days ago with a homemade grenade launcher, midday right in the middle of—"

Mala cocked her head at him. "No. We were attacked by the Wilde band. At night."

He looked confused. “Oh ...” He bit his lip and stared at his feet. “Sorry. I thought that it was something else.”

Neid gazed back and forth between the two of them, eyes growing wide. “Does this mean there have been two attacks in a week?”

The boy nodded his spiky-haired head. Mala felt her stomach drop at that news. If the other attack had been anything like hers, it must have been awful. All the hope she'd felt started to drain away in a little worried spiral. *Are the Erlenders winning?*

But the news seemed to have the opposite effect on Neid. Her face was positively glowing. “That means more missions!” she exclaimed. She turned to Alba. “For some of us, at least.”

“Maybe they'll have so many missions they'll finally *have* to give you one despite the fact that you can’t seem to pass your final trial.” Alba retorted.

Neid just grinned. Then she sprinted down a hallway, her hair and laughter trailing behind her. Without her, the knot of boys started to disperse.

Alba glared after Neid. Then she grabbed Mala's shoulder. “Come on. I have to take you on a tour.” Her voice sounded dull though her eyes still burned.

“You don't have to ...” Mala said, seeing her roommate was clearly preoccupied.

“No. I do.” Alba finally shifted her gaze. A soft smile lit her face a second later. “I can take you to the best place ever!”

“Excuse me,” the freckled boy still stood timidly in his spot. He shot Mala a small smile. “I believe I've been assigned as Mala's research assistant." He held out his hand. "Ges."

Mala went to shake it, but Alba slapped Ges's hand away. "No touching."

Um. That was rude. Mala raised her eyebrows, but Ges shrugged it off and ran a hand through his spiked hair.

"I just wanted to offer to come with you because if you'd like, I can show Mala the archives."

Alba looked torn. She clearly wanted to tell off Neid's little companion, but she was also tempted by his offer. It was almost comical to watch the wheels turning as she looked back and forth between Mala and Ges.

"Um … what's an archive?" Mala ventured.

"It's a compendium of—" Ges began, but Alba cut him off.

"It's a torture chamber. Fine, Kid. You can take Mala after I'm done- alright? But keep the conversation to work. Work only. Got it?"

"Yes ma'am." Ges rolled his eyes when Alba looked away.

Mala was utterly confused—even more so when Alba turned a stern face to her. "Ges is your assistant, not your friend. Got it? There's no such thing as a friend here." The air sizzled for a second with tension. And then, without warning, Alba slipped back into ditz mode. "Okay, let's go!"

Mala followed her, wondering all the while if her roommate was one of the Kreis who'd gone mad.

The trio climbed into a glass elevator and began to sink down several floors. Mala could see hundreds of people working at desks, walking the halls, even a floor full of machinery that must be an underwater factory. There were more people here than she'd seen her entire life. She asked, “How many Kreis are there?”

Alba smiled. “Two hundred, maybe? There's more than just Kreis here you know ... Kreis are rare. Like that whole group with Neid the Nimbo, none of them are Kreis but her, including this dodo,” she gestured at Ges, who stuck his tongue out at her when she wasn't looking.

Mala swallowed a smile. “But I thought that this place was top secret. Lowe wouldn't even let me know where it was because I haven't passed the first test—”

“Oh, it is! It's just, you know, Kreis families have built up and stayed here and the whole complex just grew.”

The freckled boy piped up. “My granddaddy was Kreis. He was a sniper. He helped take out the last Erlender jet more than fifty years—”

“Ok, Ges. What did I say about talking? Do you really want to push me?”

Ges closed his mouth and leaned back against the elevator walls, arms crossed resentfully.

Mala tried to ease the awkward tension. “So if you're Kreis, your kids and grandkids aren't Kreis?”

“Neid is, so she’s *special*,” Alba's voice dripped with disdain. “But most of us come from the outside.”

Ges piped up. “It’s not her fault if she’s—”

“Don’t defend the tramp just because you grew up with her,” Alba glared at him and turned back to Mala. “It’s all complicated. There’s a whole science wing that studies why and how and all that stuff. But it's easy enough to separate out the Typicals from the Kreis. They get a line branded into their hand."

Alba gestured at Ges and he obligingly lifted his left hand to display a raised red scar.

"But why would you want to separate—?"

"Yay! Our stop!" Alba's excitement overpowered Mala's question. Her wrinkled face was as giddy as a little girl's. "Wait 'till you see!" She clapped her hands together as the doors slid open and they stepped into a long hallway.

Alba pushed open the first door on their right and called out, "Hi!" Immediately she was accosted by a gaggle of wrinkled men who bowed and crooned over her. Some came with needles still stuck in their mouths, others wearing thimbles and dragging bolts of cloth. They crowded the doorway, all trying to get an arm around Alba. She laughed, enjoying the attention. "Okay gents, I want to introduce you to Mala. She's the newest recruit. Lowe just brought her in."

Immediately the white-haired crowd swarmed toward Mala and her eyes widened in alarm as a toothless man grabbed her around the middle and swung her up in the air. "Size four!" he yelled.

She skittered back as soon as he released her and said, "I don't really like to be touched."

The men drew back, but rather than looking embarrassed, they stared at her as though she was ill. She looked at the floor, avoiding their eyes.

"Don't worry, guys, she's new. She doesn't know

ANYTHING yet," Alba pushed through the crowd. "Show me what you've been working on."

The men quickly bustled around the room, babbling about colors and patterns. Mala followed hesitantly. The room she entered was a massive cave-like closet. Clothes hung from bars on the ceiling: skirts and pants floated a meter overhead, organized by color, pattern, size. Accessories were attached to outfits in bags tucked smartly onto the front of each hanger. The floor was covered in bolts of cloth and foot-powered sewing machines hummed a manic tune. Some of the men resumed their places, but one or two fought over who would get to show Alba their project first.

"Mala, come on!" Alba called, gleeful.

"Where are we?" Mala hung back with Ges in the doorway. She didn't want to be picked up again.

"This is the Costume Shop. It's the biggest collection of pre-bomb and Erlender clothing ever assembled," Ges narrated like a good host, as they watched Alba try on three different hats.

Alba called back to Mala, "Do you like? Our tailors are absolute geniuses. They are the entire reason my last kill went off! I had to dress as a dancer so that I could get backstage and take out this Lieutenant. Three-and-a-half hours, by the way. Almost broke the record. And they made me the most gorgeous dress ever! But of course, I mean, just look at this place—isn't it AMAZING?" She opened her arms and spun around, giggling all the while. This made her suit ride up until ...

"Is that ...?" Mala asked.

"Yup. I'd say avert your eyes, but I'm not allowed to say

anything that's not work related," Ges quipped.

Mala quickly shuttered her face with her hands and peered at Ges between her fingers. "Do you think she'd notice if we just ... continued the tour?"

He glanced over and grimaced. "Not a chance."

They headed out the door. As they reached the hallway, Ges took a sharp right. He led her to an inconspicuous door painted white to blend in with the wall. He pushed it open. Fog rolled eerily out of the dark stairwell before them. It curled around his legs. "You'll have to excuse the creep factor. We're gonna take the back way. It's ... less complicated. No other Kreis in here."

Mala lifted an eyebrow. *Complicated?* She was about to ask why, but behind her, she heard Alba shriek with delight.

"Oh my God! A-mazing! I have to try this dress on right now!" An old man's wolf whistle traveled down the hall.

With a dubious mental image looming, Mala hurried through the door.

"What is that?" Mala stopped so suddenly that Ges ran face-first into her back. She gazed upward—not at the spiraling metal staircase, but at the back wall, which was lined with a great set of enormous interlocking brass wheels, wheels that were churning as water cascaded down them. The din of the wheels and the waterfall was almost overpowering. And the fog and misty heat of the staircase seemed to swallow Mala up; she felt as though she'd just gone for a swim. She leaned close to Ges to hear his answer.

"It's how we generate power," Ges resumed in his narrator's voice once he'd finished rubbing his nose. "Something one of our top Typical scientists designed—"

"Wait, what?"

"HYDRO-ELECTRIC POWER," Ges shouted, thinking she couldn't hear.

Mala turned away from the machine-made waterfall. "No ... did you say typical scientist? What's typical mean? Alba said that word ..."

Ges gave her a disbelieving look and held up his left hand. A raised red scar marred the back of his hand. "You mean, Alberna didn't give you the high and mighty speech yet?"

"She said that being Kreis was better than being typical ... or something like that."

Ges sighed and shook his head. "Let's get out of here first." He turned and stomped up the stairwell, leaving her little choice but to follow.

When Ges opened the door, Mala was certain they'd come out into the medic's wing. She heard shouts and screams and yells coming from all sides. It made her shrink back into the shadow of the stairwell, trying not to think of all the screams she'd heard two nights ago.

But as her eyes adjusted, she saw the hallway was empty, save for a series of giant metallic doors that rolled upward. Some doors were propped partially open, some were closed. No medical equipment.

She ventured into the hall. Ges was already four doors down. Mala started to scamper after him when she heard a series of grunts. Curiosity got the best of her and she bent down to peer under one of the half-open doors.

She could see a black mat on the floor, and the lake through a massive window beyond. The room was dark, with no lighting, and she could only make out the hazy black outlines of objects. A fierce yell echoed inside the massive room, clanging off the metallic walls.

"This," Ges was suddenly beside her; his formal voice was back as he pulled her hand and helped her up, "is the combat wing. You'll be in here for practice pretty much every day. Every room is different. Learn to fight in all circumstances they say. We call that room the Shadow Room."

"Oh," Mala replied. She opened her mouth to ask again about Typicals, but at that moment, the garage door on their left rolled up and two men came strolling out of it. One was bald, age spots patterning his head. He carried a deerskin canvas and was furiously scribbling on it.

Behind him, out of the shadows, came a man in a long coat and top hat. At first, Mala could only see his silhouette. But as he strode into the hall, she realized he radiated power. He was one of those guys who had the self-assured confidence that sucked the mettle out of every other man in the room. He was a tall, intimidating presence. And while he was on the thin side, there was something about his steady gaze as he took in Mala and Ges standing in his path, something that made her step back a little.

He swept off the hat, and his brown hair fell immediately into his eyes. He pushed it back impatiently as he put two silver tools into the hatband, which already held several other gadgets in place. Then he plunked the hat back into place.

"We'll have to add that mess to the queue," he told the old man. "In the meantime, seal off that room. Tier has some other asinine high-priority project for me, so I've been pulled off this detail for a bit, though if this plumbing goes ... that shit's his fault."

The old man laughed. And suddenly so did Ges. High. Slightly manically.

Mala glanced over at him, concerned. But Ges only had eyes for the scientist. And his face was suddenly flushed.

Oh. Insight came to Mala at once. *Oh.* Unfortunately, she was too busy watching Ges to notice that the scientist was now looming right over her.

"You're new. Are you Mala?" His gravelly voice was commanding, demanding. She stared up at him.

He's young! Younger than I thought. Maybe twenty? His chin's not weak like Verrukter's. I guess I can see the appeal for Ges. And hazel eyes ... Is he glaring at me?

"Are you … mute?"

He could not have asked a worse question. Though his tone had been more curious than insulting, he immediately struck a nerve with Mala and her hackles rose. "Do you have a problem with mutes?" Mala retorted, her teeth on edge.

"I have a problem with being ignored," the scientist replied, crossing his arms. He turned away from her and addressed Ges.

"Is this her?"

Ges, still captivated, nodded.

"Why do you need to know?" Mala asked, her eyes icy. She refused to let this man intimidate her. Even if she had to tilt her head so far up to glare in his eyes that she felt like a three-year-old. *What am I d oing?* This wasn't like her. She normally avoided confrontation. She tried to blend into the background. *Maybe it was the mute comment.* But something about this guy's arrogance got to her. Got under her skin. It was different from Verrukter's self-absorbed arrogance or Neid's generic disdain for the outskirts. It was more pungent. She could taste it. It made her want to strip him down a peg. *Who is he to think he's so special?*

"Because you're the reason I just got pulled away from my research. To babysit a Kreis who doesn't know how to melt."

How would this guy know that? Is that what Lowe's telling people? Is that what Lowe thinks of me? The insecurities she'd been suppressing banged against her skull, desperate to be given voice. Only the smug stare of the man looming over her kept Mala together. "I know how—" Mala started to spit back, too late, but he cut her off.

"Right. That's why my ecoresearch and our sanitation issues have been given the shelf. My lab. Sunrise. Day after your test. Don't be late." He turned and strode off, his little old companion struggling to tail him and Ges's halfhearted wave dying before it had even begun.

Mala spun around to Ges, fury making her blood boil. "Who the hell was that?"

Ges was still wistfully watching the corner where the scientist had turned, as if he could wish him back.

"Ges ..." Mala snapped her fingers in front of his face. "Who was that?"

"Oh ... um. That was Ein. He's the head of the science department here. Remember the stairwell? He designed that when he was eleven. *Eleven.* He's pure genius."

"Did you say pure arrogance? Cause that's what I heard. Is there something weird in the water here? Because it seems like I've been in for an amazing amount of ego today. Other than you—of course."

"Mala- Ein's a total legend!"

"You are so love-struck you can't even see—" A hand over her mouth muffled Mala's voice. Ges's eyes were wide, scared.

He called out so the hall could hear, "Star-struck maybe. He's like the most famous Typical ever." But he bit his lip. His fingers on her mouth trembled a little.

Slowly, she pried them away. "I'm sorry. I'm so sorry. I didn't know that you weren't … telling people." *God, Mala! The one nice, normal-seeming person and you had to go and out him! Great job.*

Ges stepped up and whispered in her ear, "Do you think anyone heard?"

Mala glanced up and down the hall. No one had come out of their rooms to gawk. "Well—they're still all screaming and grunting at each other. So I would guess not. Look, I'm really sorry. If there's anything I can do to make it up to you—"

"Tell me your secret."

"What?" Mala took a step back.

"It's a trade. How do I know you won't go tell anyone else now that you know?"

"I wouldn't!"

"How can I trust you?" The vulnerability, the desperation in Ges's eyes made Mala's heart clench. It was exactly how she felt about the slip she'd made to Lowe. What guarantee did she have that he wouldn't let it slip? *I mean, he told people I couldn't melt, didn't he? He had to ... or that jerk Ein wouldn't be assigned to me. But did he* tell *them ...?*

She just had hope, hope that he felt the same way about her, that his feelings would keep him from revealing the belief she'd harbored since the day her father died. Since the day the burning started. But she wasn't sure Lowe did feel the same way about her. *If it's* some *recruiter side effect... some kind of pat-himself-on-the-back thing, it might not even be real. Or, I might have made it seem bigger than it is ... because I needed the distraction. Because I didn't want to think about what happened. Because I didn't want to think about Mom.* That self-doubt buzzed around in her stomach for a moment. And that terrible feeling, that worry that she might not be able to trust the person she most wanted to trust, made her decision easy. She had to trust someone.

"Okay," she breathed, glancing up and down the hall. "Okay." She took a step forward and bent to whisper into Ges's ear. "I believe."

CHAPTER THIRTEEN

"OH MY GOSH! ARE YOU KIDDING?" Ges's reaction startled Mala. He was practically yelling, his words bounding back to them in an echo. He grabbed Mala's hand. "This is the best thing ever. Follow me!"

Without another word, Ges scurried back to the mist and tugged Mala down three flights of stairs. When he stopped and opened a set of doors, Mala's hair was plastered to her face. She pushed a dripping curl out of her eyes as Ges hustled her into a massive empty room.

"Hurry up, we can't let moisture in here."

Ges's spiky head whipped past as he slammed the door behind her and pushed her toward a set of double doors two stories tall. The doors were glass, chiseled with a scene of fish and turtles and massive water creatures Mala had never seen.

"Drumroll." Ges pitched his voice low and dramatic. But just as he was about to grandly open the doors, a very large backside pushed them open from inside. An old woman with a cart full of books backed right into Ges, knocking him down.

"Whoop! Sorry, honey," the matronly woman apologized.

"Oh, you brought a friend …" her voice trailed off as she looked at Mala. She gave a stiff bow and turned to Ges. "Better be quick. We've got a new data set to get out tonight."

He nodded. With another bow in Mala's direction, the old woman hobbled away.

"Okay, what was that?"

Ges shrugged. "Data set? We've got to put together a battle analysis for Tier—"

"That's not what I mean. What was with the bow?"

"Nothing. It's just … you're Kreis."

Thanks for clearing that up.

Reading the sarcasm in her face, Ges explained, "You know how you asked what being Typical was? Well, basically everyone at the Center who's not Kreis is Typical. There are approximately two hundred Kreis. Of those, there are only eighty-four active Kreis and about half of them are gone on a mission at any given time. Typicals are usually families of Kreis who make Ancient. Or people with special skills. And we know the truth about melting, so … we're here."

Mala caught something more in his tone. "You mean, they don't let you leave?"

"Well … no. I mean, we do farm nearby and stuff. But not leave the way you mean. Think what a huge security risk that would be. Hey! Guess what? We've got a secret military trove of mutating assassins. Don't think that would go over so well. And if the Erlenders found out? They already blame us for the world ending. Think that's why we survived. Anyway, it's no big deal.

We're happy to serve and all that …"

"Serve? As in servants?" *Who would do that to their own family?*

"Don't *ever* let a Typical hear you say that," Ges's eyes grew wide. "But there are a lotta Kreis who think that. Usually the ones who don't last," he added, with a note of satisfaction.

"Anyway, that's so not important when I'm about to show you the most fabulous, amazing thing you've ever seen!"

Mala couldn't resist. She arched a brow and asked, "Is it anything like the Costume Shop?"

Ges smacked her arm and led her into the archive.

Mala's mind could only register one word as they stepped inside: *massive.* Six-meter stacks surrounded them on either side. Stored in towering metal racks were videos and books and maps, rows and rows of them. And the stacks moved on rails, stiff metal monsters with arms reaching as far as she could see. Mala saw one young girl turning a giant wheel to compress two sets of shelves in order to allow her to climb a third.

As they walked down the aisle, Mala realized that there was a circular opening in the center of the room, a giant hole in the floor and in the ceiling. She looked up: the opening continued to the floor above. It went down at least six floors below. The balconies at each floor had no rails, but were studded with ladders every meter, alternating up a floor and down a floor. Female archivists in hunter green wetsuits like Ges's climbed up and down the ladders with packs strapped to their backs. One woman carried a shelf full of books tied to her spine. A second climbed with two rolled paintings sheathed like swords. She jumped midfloor from the ladder she was on to the adjacent when someone started down the same route. Green suits bustled everywhere, swarming up and down the ladders, each with a purpose.

Ges watched Mala as he gestured to the room at large. "So this is where I live. The Anthill, we like to call it."

Mala nodded but didn't know what to say. She'd never seen anything like it. "There's so much … paper." She'd only kept a book on the boat for kindling when it was too wet to find good tinder outside. And here they had it stacked to the ceiling.

Ges smiled at her baffled face. "These are all the informative materials we've scavenged. Engineering, physics, chemistry … Instructions for how to build boats, bombs, airplanes …"

Mala's jaw dropped. She'd used maps before, seen a video feed from Das Wort once. But that was it. In front of her, above her, below her, were the instructions to rebuild the world.

Mala touched a shelf, letting her fingers skim the spines of several books. She wondered if there were any instructions in this room for a thing her grandmother had called an air conditioner. Mala recalled how her grandmother's voice had crackled, full of electric joy, as she'd described coming inside in the middle of summer only to feel to a cool fall breeze, lying down in the middle of the floor and fanning her hair out for the icy air. Mala had been young, four or five. She hadn't been able to picture a cold house, an ice cube resisting the sun. Mala had thought it was magic. *I wonder if it's real.*

Mala turned to ask Ges, but her question morphed into a

shriek as she saw a young girl in a green wetsuit somersault right off the edge of the balcony. Mala ran forward, and only Ges's arm kept her from toppling over. Two floors below, the girl calmly descended a ladder, eyes smirking up at Mala, as if she knew the panic she'd caused.

"Show-off," Ges shook his head.

Wide-eyed, Mala turned to him. "That's normal?" But even as her sentence ended, a body toppled upside down past their floor. Mala heard the thud as feet connected with a ladder a floor below.

Ges winked at her. "Don't worry. I won't be trying to get you to do it anytime soon."

"Or ever."

He shrugged. "It's efficient. And fun. So anyway … you were about to follow me past this boring data-mine and into the realm of awesomeness." He started steering her through the stacks, back to a dark, dim, rather shabby-looking section. After peering in both directions, he peeled an old map off the wall and revealed a small alcove behind it.

Mala followed him into the cramped cave. It was so full of piles of books and scrolls that she didn't have room for her feet, much less room to sit, until Ges shoved a whole stack of books right under her legs and plopped her down.

Ges lit a lantern. "No electricity back here," he explained, as he stacked his own seat below an aged photo of a man with a beard.

"Where are we?" Mala flipped open a few books to stare at their hazy black marks.

"We're in the autobiography section. Or, as I like to call it,

The Room of Possibilities. My grandfather," Ges gestured at the photo, "started collecting them when he went out on missions. Some Kreis have helped over the years. A lot of times, I luck out when they send a new shipment of scavenged books …"

"What do you mean by possibilities?"

"Well. All of these books have one thing in common. They describe the lives of people who had experiences they couldn't explain. Most of them are from right after the bomb."

A thrill raced through Mala's blood as he spoke. She stared at the books. *An entire roomful of people wrote down things, weird things ... unexplainable things.*

"Like being Kreis?"

"Exactly. But some are even beyond that."

"What do you mean?" The hairs on the ends of her arms rose.

"Well. Some believe—Erlenders believe… but some other people too—that there was no bomb. Some think it was a curse."

Mala inhaled. She'd heard mutters of curses. But, just like all of their charms for luck, it was something no one in the guard had ever openly discussed. And she'd never told anyone about how she thought she'd been cursed.

"Was it?" she breathed. *Do they exist?* That was the question she wanted to ask, but didn't.

"That's the extreme," Ges continued, oblivious to the chill radiating down Mala's spine. "Sometimes, there are things in life that don't make sense. Or don't mesh with what we're told. And people make up different explanations. That's just one. Like—example—there's one guy after the bomb who kept opening the door to his house and seeing a different place every day. That's a major one. Everyone called him delusional. But his daughter documented everything. And you know what Mala? The man was blind. The entire time. He was blind."

"Blind?"

"You see the paradox, right? And people who found out couldn't get past that. Both the reality of his blindness and his sight were something they couldn't reconcile. They'd grown up hearing that you could be one or the other. Both was not a possibility for them. That's not true in this room."

Is he saying what I think? Is he saying it's real? He hasn't used the word yet.

Ges was in his element. His speech sped up and his hands gesticulated furiously. "Or there's a diary from a woman who noticed that every day she wore her father's wedding ring on her necklace, she had a lucky day. More subtle, but far more relatable, right? Well, what about a woman who thought she was going crazy because her toddler kept disappearing on her? And shortly after that, she started seeing a man standing in the woods at night, at the edge of her yard—just watching her? Who would you group her with?"

"She probably had some kind of mental illness."

Ges's brown eyes blazed at that and he swung his freckled fist down onto a map, crushing it. "Really, Mala? You're Kreis!"

"I've seen a lot of people with battle syndrome. Or paranoia."

"Mala—you don't think it was possible, her baby might have been Kreis? That her missing baby and the man in the woods might be the same person?"

It took Mala a second to picture the scene, of the toddler screwing up his face to cry and suddenly growing taller. A few days ago, if anyone had asked her that question, she would have laughed. But, that was before her entire guard had been massacred at the whim of a bald man who had changed into a child and back again. Before she lost her mother. Mala stared fiercely at Ges. It was a minute before she had her grief under control and could ask him the question she wanted.

"Do Kreis normally melt when they're babies?"

"Is there anything normal about Kreis? No offense—but like you said earlier—they aren't normal. They're Rude-o with a capital R. But to answer your question—no. Puberty is a more typical onset. Some a little younger. Some later. But is it *possible*? To have a toddler transform?"

"Is it?"

"Did you?"

"I don't know ... my mother. She couldn't speak." The grief rushed back, quick and awful, punching the inside of her stomach black and blue.

Ges grabbed her hand and pulled her up. Her loss of balance pulled her back from the pit of despair but Ges's attempt to catch her only knocked both of them to the floor, legs splayed.

Ges ignored their compromising position, too intent on his discussion. "Well then it's possible, isn't it? That you are one of the only living Kreis to transform as a baby. That's what this room is all about. Asking that question. What's possible? And the crazier it is, the more I try to resist the urge to shut down the judge-o-meter. I try to stay open. To search for the tiniest possibility."

"But … why?"

"Because Mala. You said it yourself. You believe. Who else believes?" He stood too quickly, his feet slipping on a scroll. He grabbed Mala's arms for balance, but leaned in for emphasis. "There's a whole culture out there, fighting us day in and day out. And what do they believe in? Magic. Demons. Curses. Why? Are they all just crazy? The thousands of them? Or is there something else going on? What do they believe in, exactly? Everyone else here dismisses them out of hand. But is what they believe possible? … Is what you believe possible? I think it is." His eyes glowed like copper pennies in the dim lantern light.

His fervent intensity, his innocence, everything about Ges drew her in. *He believes.* It was like a weight had lifted. Despite her grief, despite the fact that the loss of her mother was still a gaping, bleeding wound, Mala felt as if a burden had been lifted from her shoulders. For as long as she could remember, she'd hidden her hallucinations from the guard. Her belief, she'd hidden even from her mother. Though people in the northern guard were known to have lucky rituals, and to play at magic, no one would ever admit to being a true believer. It was the ultimate betrayal. Only savages believed. Only Erlenders. But since the night she'd seen her father die, since the night that Erlender muttered an incantation over her before tossing her into the river, Mala had believed. For a long time, she'd believed that her hallucinations had stemmed from that moment. From what her four-year old self had imagined to be a curse. It was illogical, she knew—particularly in light of everything Lowe had told her, but a childish part of Mala still clung to that belief. *Maybe it's been so long that I just don't want to let it go.*

"Ges, does anyone write about being Kreis?"

"Oh yeah, I've got maybe fifteen different accounts here. Supposedly the Ancients have even more journals, but those are restricted."

"And what makes someone Kries? Are you born with it?"

"No one knows for sure. There are theories about genetic manipulation, about radiation—like poisoning of the blood. But that's the thing … Kreis didn't really develop immediately after the bomb. Or at least we don't have accounts of them. You'd think we would if they were survivors, right? Or that if it were genetic, maybe we'd be able to tell when someone was younger if they'd get it. Or that parents would pass it down to their kids. It's really controversial. Especially here. Everyone subscribes to a particular theory; bomb relic exposure is currently the most popular among Typicals, genetics among the Kreis. And are these theories plausible? Maybe. Possible? Of course. But there's another theory out there …" Ges stretched precariously and swiped a green cover with his fingertips. "This book here says that there's a blood rite involving relics. It says a sacrifice has to be made—"

"What?" Mala's sharp tone cut him off. Her mind spun. She stared at Ges but didn't see him. She was back in the forest, slicing her hand open like a letter, the hour hand a dull knife she'd had to press hard into her skin. She saw the red drops beading on her palm in the darkness. She smelled the crisp scent of dead leaves mixed with the salty tang of her blood. She started to tremble. "Do you think it's true?" *Did I do this to myself?*

Ges tilted his head to evaluate her reaction. "I think it's possible. But clearly you think it's true. What happened, Mala?"

"I—" She never finished her sentence. At that moment a shriek echoed through the archives.

"MALA! GET OUT HERE RIGHT NOW!" Alba's screech echoed throughout the seven floors of the archive.

"Sludge!" Ges cursed and pulled Mala out of the alcove through a twisting maze of shelves. He led her past a room filled with a series of paintings, and into a room where forty Typicals sat at tables, dutifully staring at screens and then turning to their pages, making quick black strokes with their pens.

Ges stepped a friendly distance away and assumed a bored narrator voice. "This is the transcription room. After the bomb, some Senebals thought to save box-book devices, known as computers. We've been able to transcribe the contents of over—"

"YOU LEFT ME!" The shriek Mala had heard earlier now reverberated painfully in her ears.

She turned to see Alba, one eyelid crusted in purple makeup and the other bare, shaking a veiny fist in fury.

"Um ..." *What do I say?* "I just really wanted to see these—" *What the hell are they called?* She gesticulated wildly at the boxes on the tables.

"Computers," Ges said. "Mala was fascinated by the idea of keyboards."

"Keyboards. Yes. Alba, it's amazing. Tons of keys. You

can unlock any lock you can think of!"

Alba arched an eyebrow and glanced at the scribes skeptically. "I don't see any keys."

"Figuratively. She meant figuratively," Ges interjected.

I hope I don't look as lost as Alba, because I don't have a mucking clue what he just said.

Alba shrugged him off. She turned to Mala, her quivering jowls undermining the serious and strained tone of her voice. “Mala, when I have orders to give you a tour, you go on my tour. You do not just leave. You cannot just leave." She took a step closer, so only Mala could hear the fear under the anger. "They'll think I just let you leave. You cannot do that to me. Those were my orders; I have to follow my orders.”

Mala immediately felt guilty. She could see the desperation in Alba's eyes. “Okay. Sorry—I didn't realize it was such a big deal. I didn't know they were orders. It won't happen again, I promise. Are you okay?”

“What?” Alba plastered a smile across her face. “I'm fine. We need to get out of here. It's creepy. Now we need to eat. I'll show you the cafeteria.”

“Um, okay.” Mala followed dutifully in Alba's wake, giving Ges a sad little shrug and a half wave good-bye.

CHAPTER FOURTEEN

The cafeteria was yet another big space with a giant window out to the lake. It must have been relatively close to the surface, because the water was laced with sunbeams. Alba filled Mala's plate with bread and fish then led the way to seats far from the window. Mala followed reluctantly. She would rather have stared out at the water and watched the fish than sit down at a table full of Kries, but she wasn't about to push Alba again. *Eighty-year-olds can have heart attacks.*

So, Mala sat down and ate, at a table surrounded by people, in a hall full of people. After hours of constant interaction, she was exhausted. She was used to the quiet solitude of the river, the gentle thrum of the boat's motor, the whisper of the water. She wanted nothing more than for Alba to take her back to the surface so she could throw herself into the lake and swim until the quiet soaked back into her eardrums.

But no such luck awaited her. Instead of peace, her heart jumped into her throat every time the blue cafeteria door swung open and someone with black hair walked in. Even though Alba had said she wouldn't see him, part of Mala longed for Lowe. In all this newness, she wanted the comfort of something known.

Known. Ha. You've known *him for less than forty-eight hours. And you don't even know if he really likes you. You don't even know if he's telling people you can't melt. Or that you believe—* But her heart petulantly plugged its ears and refused to listen, stubbornly staying on watch.

After the fourth or fifth time Mala merely grunted in response to her questions, Alba placed a hand on Mala's shoulder. "He's not coming, you know. It's protocol to stay away. And Lowe's like the perfect soldier, honey. It's how he rose so high in the ranks so fast. He is by-the-books all the way."

Mala nodded and gave a disappointed sigh.

Alba laughed and patted her hand. "You'll see him tomorrow. It's not forever. But I get that feels like it. Ok— distraction challenge. I'm supposed to teach you things about being Kreis. First thing. Every Kreis melts to different ages. Some ages are harder than others. Like this old. Lots of people can't melt this old."

"That's right, crone-face," a greasy-haired teenage Kries sitting a few seats down from them laughed and threw a balled-up napkin at Alba.

"Real mature, Witz," Alba tossed the napkin back at him and rolled her eyes for Mala's amusement.

"I'm glad I'm not as mature as you, *Grandma*," the guy shot back.

Mala saw Alba's face shiver for just a second before the girl sighed, turned her back on the rest of the table, and continued explaining in a voice that was sure to carry back to the nitwit and his friends, "So, there are some theories out there that people can melt ONLY to the age they'll actually live to linearly… meaning I, UNLIKE SOME PEOPLE, am good enough at being Kries that I'll actually survive to be eighty. Questions?"

Mala saw the guys down the table lose interest and turn back to their food. They didn't seem too worried by this theory. Alba watched her expectantly.

"Is that why the highest rank is Ancient?"

"Yup. They run the show because, no matter what they look like, they've survived at least forty missions and made it past the linear age of thirty."

"And they're the ones I have to do this test in front of tomorrow?"

"Yes—and I wish I could give you details about it but I can't, it's VERBODEN … other than the outfit you have to wear—it's hideous. Grey, with black leather armor that's so stiff you can hardly move. And the clasps? It's like they're buckling you into a bronze straitjacket." That comment launched Alba into a fifteen-minute description of all the uniforms she'd ever worn and her evaluation of each. Mala struggled to keep her eyes open and a smile plastered on her face.

Mala tried to interrupt Alba with questions about schedules, training, and expectations, but Alba always seemed to drift back to something shoe-related. "My last mission was in Prahlen, and I think they're only like twelve kilometers from Wilde—that group you said came after your guard. Anyway, when I was in Prahlen, I had to wear this nasty bearskin boot contraption—"

"What do you know about Wilde? I mean, do you know what kind of place it is?"

Alba gave her a look. "Boring research questions are why you have a research assistant, Mala. I know Wilde's small. I think it's in the freeze zone, so boats can't get through in winter. Other than that, you'll have to tell Ges to look it up if you want more info."

The freeze zone. Something about that fact scratched at Mala's skull like a dull itch. *It doesn't make sense.* She didn't know much more than rumors about the different Erlender bands, but she felt certain the Wildes were not typically prone to slaughter. *So why did they do it?*

Mala tuned Alba out. *If Wilde was in the freeze zone, it would make sense that Wildes were raiders like I thought... how else would they get through winter? But why would they have taken out the entire guard? Why wouldn't they have taken prisoners to trade or slaves to sell? Why would they have killed everyone?*

Mala wiped a stray tear with her napkin. Alba didn't notice, but Witz gave her a confused look. Embarrassed, she turned toward Alba and used her giant mane of curls as a curtain. *Was it just because Blut said so? Why would Blut have chosen us? We were a nothing guard—a small outpost. We manned the border. But that's it. Not like it was a great crossing or even a tributary that was really strategic. Bara was never given the option of bigger missions or more prestige. She wasn't a threat. We weren't a threat ... were we?*

A gong interrupted her thoughts. Mala grabbed the table.

The last time she'd heard a bell was when the Erlender alarm had sounded. *It's just the lunch bell, idiot.* It took her a moment to recover, releasing her fingers one by one. It took another minute before she was ready to follow Alba's bouncy grey ponytail out the door.

Alba shepherded Mala to another elevator, and to Mala's surprise, remained silent. The ride was almost serene. The doors opened into a hall that was pitch dark, save for a line of lanterns on a side table next to the elevator. Alba took one and silently gestured for Mala to take another.

They walked down a black corridor lined with closed doors. When they came to two open doors, Alba stopped and turned to Mala. "Last stop for today since Ges already took you by combat. These are memorial rooms. You can come down here whenever you have free time. Pick an open room. Inside, you can mourn your ancestors. You can mourn your fate. Hell, you can cry over a guy who dumped you. These rooms are your key to release. But when you leave these rooms, you leave grief inside. You cannot carry grief with you on your missions. You can carry vengeance. Justice. Hate. But grief will drown you."

Mala marveled at the poetics of the girl she'd deemed a ditz.

Alba continued, "Just understand this … in a memorial room, meltdowns are permitted. Outside, you will be punished for any unintentional melting. Severely punished."

With that, Alba stepped into one of the rooms and closed the door.

Tentatively, Mala stepped into her own room. She wasn't

sure she wanted an hour to mourn. Or a minute to mourn. She felt as if she might shred into a million tiny pieces and never be made whole again if she let herself feel the full extent of the pain she was keeping at bay. *I'd rather meltdown and take the punishment.*

But then she thought of the way Alba's lantern had shaken on the words 'severely punished' and wondered what had happened to the girl when she'd accidentally become an eighty-year-old during combat practice. Pondering that, Mala took the few steps into the room, shut the door, and turned around.

The room was a perfect dome, with walls of beaten steel. The floor was covered in a thin layer of ashes that suffused the space with a faint campfire scent. Mala saw a symbol half traced into the dust. A bird. It must have been the symbol for someone else's guard.

Mala carefully stepped over it as she made her way to the center of the room. She set her lantern on a spindly table there. As she did, blinding light filled the room: the angle of the lantern and the polished surface on the walls made for the perfect reflection. Mala was suddenly standing in the middle of a ball of light, of fire. A chill ran through her stomach, and the hair stood up on her arms. It was exactly the way she'd always felt when she thought of magic. The light felt like magic, filling her, strengthening her.

Mala focused on the light. Mentally she pulled it into herself, pictured herself the tiny blue flicker in a bright ball of flame. She let it seep into her consciousness. Let it fill her. She stared at the lantern glow, letting it burn her retinas, smolder in her brain until all thoughts burned away but one. *Fire for fire. Blood for blood.*

Eyes still on the lantern, Mala reached up and unhooked her necklace. She took one of her more vicious looking hooks off the line. She traced the half-healed scar from the sacrifice she'd made the other night. She wasn't sure how she felt about the scar just yet, or how she felt about being Kreis. But this moment wasn't about her, and she wiped selfish thoughts away.

This time, when Mala let metal bite into her flesh, she pictured her mother. She pictured Bara. She pictured Sari and the other foolish teenage girls who'd perished. She pictured Verrat and Sorgen and all the warriors in their motley little band. She even spared a moment for Garon. And instead of asking the spirits for anything, she made a promise.

It was an old promise, a poem her father had recited to her as a child. It was a promise she had never made before, because she could still imagine her father crouching beside her, shaking her for singing it as she cleaned the deck of their boat.

"Mala," he'd said, "Never say those words unless you mean them. Never." He'd grabbed her shoulders hard, his voice deep and gruff. She'd been scared and run to Erinne for comfort.

Her mother had scooped her up and held her close. "Darling, he's just trying to protect you."

"But why?" Mala had asked.

"Because once you make an oath, you cannot take it back. It's a promise, to the death. We always promise to the death."

That memory was one of Mala's last memories of her mother's voice. One of her last memories of her father. The Erlenders had burned their ship just days later. And she and Erinne had been set adrift, wandering guard to guard, leaving whenever Mala had an 'episode.' They'd stayed longest with Bara's group, partially because Mala had learned to keep a low profile, and partially because the massive woman had had a massive heart.

The piercing sound of Bara's final scream ripped through Mala, and she closed her eyes. But her lids betrayed her. She saw her mother, holding up her hand in a victorious V as her shirt bloomed red. Mala blinked, but the ghosts of the guard appeared before her, lining the room just as their bodies had lined the beach. A whirlpool started in her stomach. It grew to her chest, and she could feel herself being sucked in, sucked under. With her last bit of strength, Mala smacked her bleeding hand against the flaming wall and traced Bara's sign—the fish—in blood; the brackish paint became a black shadow swimming in the pulsing light. She gave her oath, "Revenge promised. Justice sworn. Death be my life. 'Til blood soak my knife."

And then pain opened its roaring jaws and she was swallowed whole.

CHAPTER FIFTEEN

She stood right next to him as the tailors in the Costume Shop pulled and pinned and chattered. But she didn't know what to say. Yesterday, he'd been an undercurrent in her thoughts, a worry swirling beneath the surface as she'd floated from one introduction to the next. Part of her had wished he'd show up and explain himself. Explain away the whole living-trophy business and tell her he actually liked her. But the other part of her didn't want to see him. The other part of her had hidden behind Alba every time a black-haired man turned the corner. That part of her, the misanthrope, thought Alba might be right.

Now he was here, looking like some dark god in a skintight steel-grey suit padded with body armor. Alba's despised bronze buckles lined the left side of his chest, his forearms, and the outsides of his boots. Her mouth went dry even as she looked at his reflection in the large mirror they both faced. She couldn't find the words she needed.

Lowe was all formality and courtesy, thanking the old man who brought him a tricorner hat. He stood stiff and rigid as his grey military uniform. He gave Mala instructions through the corner of his mouth as the tailors did their work; he wouldn't even look at her.

It made her want to scream. He was telling her about their entrance, about what she needed to say, about the test ... but all she wanted him to do was face her and answer the gut-wrenching questions that had kept her up all night. *Why am I here? Did you tell them I believe? And what the hell is wrong with me? Why are you telling people I can't melt? Why can't I tell people about my melting? What is going on?* And the worst question of all ... *Am I just some stupid recruiter high to you?* She wondered, trying to find an answer in his eyes. But his face was stoically reflected in the mirror, staring deftly at the brass buttons on his jacket, no trace of emotion visible.

When the tailors had finished buttoning up her stiff lace collar Mala turned to them and asked, “Can we have a minute, please?” She thought she might have even been able to toss a smile in there, though her insides were wriggling like snakes on the water, ripples of panic flowing out to her limbs. If he answered, she'd know. *But what if I don't like his answer?*

The old men bowed and backed away and she could hear one explaining to another, “First recruit.” The other man's eyes glowed and his hands clapped together, clearly anticipating a romantic interlude. *If only it were that easy.* She swallowed and turned to face Lowe. But her courage failed her. Instead of asking what she really wanted, she asked the first thing that came to mind.

“Um ... so how long until I get a mission?”

“What do you mean?” he asked.

“Well Alba didn't really explain ...” Mala trailed off. She

couldn't look at him. She was so disgusted with herself. Her hands were shaking. *You shouldn't be scared. You should be annoyed—angry even.*

“Typically, your first mission would come after you completed the first series of espionage lessons and combat lessons, once you've got a handle on melting,” Lowe explained blandly.

"But, what about my ... melting?" she whispered.

Lowe crossed to her quickly. He leaned down and breathed into her hair, so that anyone from a distance would think he was comforting and caressing her. But his whisper was a warning.

"Don't say anything. Until I kiss you during the ceremony, don't say anything. And after that—this is the first time it ever happened. We've never kissed. You did not melt into Blut's mother. You melted to a little girl on the raft. And that's it. Understand?"

"But, why?"

"Because, only one Kreis has ever melted the way you do."

That shocked Mala to her core. She blinked. Her heart picked up a bit. *So I'm not some freak of nature? There's someone else like me? Someone here can teach me, guide me.* "Who? Who is it?"

Lowe placed his hands carefully on her shoulders. His blue eyes were wide as he leaned in. "Klaren—the deranged," he whispered.

Mala sagged into him in shock. Her thoughts flashed back to the hall of statues, and the massive bronze figure that stood desecrated. Her heart fell. No mentor, only a man whose life stood as a pillar of shame in a room full of pride. "That's why you didn't want me to tell people about my melting. You didn't want them to compare me to him."

Lowe shook his head. "No. I didn't want them to kill you on sight."

"What?"

"They might have. You have no idea the reaction Klaren still evokes in most people, Mala. And given the theories out there, given what you do … some people would have thought—will think—you're his daughter. Some people will equate you with him. And he's evil incarnate in this place."

"I saw the statue."

"The statue doesn't even begin to cover it. The man was brilliant. One of the best Kreis in our history. And with good reason. What he could do—what you can do—you can literally put on the skin of any Erlender you want—"

"Fat chance of that. I have no idea what I'm doing."

"Once we figure it out, you will. I already talked to my recruiter about it. She's on board. She's gotten Tier to set up help for you. You'll be brilliant. Beyond. You'll be able to avenge your mother and your father and every other Senebal who lost their life to an Erlender cretin. You'll be able to do it single-handedly." He brushed her cheek and his tone was almost reverent. "I believe in you, Mala."

His look sent a tendril of heat racing down Mala's spine into her toes. She looked down, breaking the moment, worried that she might melt if she stared at him too much longer. And clearly, if she did, it might be the last time she ever got to stare at him.

"Thank you," she breathed, a little overwhelmed. *And here I was worried he was ashamed of me. Avoiding me. God, Mala—you're paranoid.*

"I think I need to explain one more thing," Lowe whispered. "I broke the rules for you Mala. And I never break the rules. Ever. I broke them again when we got here, going to my recruiter Fell instead of the head Ancient, to keep you safe. I need you to keep that secret. Keep your prior melts secret as long as you can. Don't let them judge you until we know more. Don't let them hurt you. And you know, it wouldn't be so bad if you didn't throw me under the boat."

"Of course," Mala promised in a rush. She grabbed Lowe's fingers and looked up at him. "I'll never tell anyone. I promise."

He gave the tiniest hint of a smile. It made her insides liquefy and slosh in her stomach. And it made her brave enough to bring up the one topic he hadn't touched on, the one thing he hadn't really addressed. He'd protected her. He'd lied for her. *But he might have done that because of what I could do ... not for me,* the little doubt in her head whispered.

"I ... um ... just have one more question." She took a deep breath. "About us. What is this?"

Lowe looked uncomfortable and glanced over the racks of clothing. He unlocked their fingers and brushed his hand over his jaw. "I don't know."

Mala waited for a second. But he didn't offer anything else. Her heart plunged through the floor beneath her feet, and through several floors beneath that. It buried itself in the dark mud of the lake bottom.

Mala wasn't sure where she found the breath to continue, because all the air had fled her lungs, but she did. “What do you mean you don't know? You know most recruiters end up with their firsts, right? At least for a while. Alba told me. You knew that this connection thing would happen. But you didn't tell me."

His cheeks flushed. *He did know.* She had a choice: anger or pain. Anger was easier, though she had to blink hard to keep the tears back.

"So, I'm some living trophy. Some grand prize. Maybe even the greatest prize ever, if things go according to your plan and I'm some amazing Kreis, right? You're the kingmaker? You let me think ..." she trailed off for a minute, anger and sadness swirling inside. *I knew it.*

Anger took over and she lashed out. “So I'm just something you can whip out in front of other Kreis to prove what a man you are?” There was a huge pressure in her chest, like someone had dropped a boulder there.

“No, Mala. It's complicated.” He reached for her but she jerked away. She was hyperventilating. Mala counted furiously to regain control.

“And what about how you made me kill Blut? Was that just for the stat? So your new recruit would come in on top?”

“He was trying to kill us!”

“And you refused to kill him,” Mala snarled.

“You had a better shot at finishing him safely from a distance.”

She gave him a derisive sneer. *Don't look at his eyes,* she told herself. He was a soldier. He was Kreis. *He is trained to lie and to kill*, she thought furiously. *He's trained to manipulate people. You don't want him anyway.* She lied, trying to convince herself, to lift the boulder in her ribs before it smashed her to pieces.

"I thought it wouldn't matter. That you being my first would only make a good thing better. But ..."

When Mala felt she was in control of her breath, she looked up. She saw tears form in the corner of Lowe's eyes. He blinked them away. She gritted her teeth, uncertainty shredding her insides. But the boulder lifted slightly.

Lowe traced a medallion on his cuffs. He searched for the words to explain. After several false starts, he said, "Mala, I don't know what makes our reactions to one another so intense. Am I proud you're my first recruit? Hell yes. You're beyond what I could have dreamed. As a recruit. And as more. God, you're beautiful ... You're witty. You're even funny in your own twisted little Misanthropic way. But I know that all of this is made more intense by my emotional deprivation. And that ... scares me."

Mala shrugged off the compliments, intent on keeping her wall up. "You knew it would be this way. And you didn't tell me. You used me."

"No! I've had to be dead inside for seven years. Seven years, Mala. Do you know what that's like? I couldn't feel anything. I've been undercover for months at a time, every possible emotion thrown at me and I couldn't feel a thing. Or I'd meltdown. Because, unlike whatever it is you do, if I feel something uncontrollable, I melt. And I can't stop it. Can't control it. I couldn't feel or I'd die.

You've been hungry before, right? Imagine starving. Imagine seven years of closing your eyes and telling your heart to shut up. That's been my life. That's what it means to be Kreis.

I'm sorry that I didn't tell you. It was selfish of me. To want to bask in it a little bit. I don't think you understand how amazing it is to actually feel something so good when I have to spend every other waking hour trying not to feel at all. But how could you think I faked that? Or used that?" He stepped in close and whispered in her ear. "You melted. And you saw me melt."

"In reaction to seeing her."

"No. In reaction to you." He stared at her a minute, waiting for this to sink in. As though Mala should understand the depth of what he said. She simply watched and waited.

"Mala, I've been Kreis for years. I don't just meltdown. I don't lose control. But when I kissed you … it was like lightning ..." He paused. Their eyes locked. Mala felt her heart skip and blood rush to her cheeks.

"Will I always melt like that?" she asked in a small voice. "Will you?"

Lowe smiled sadly. "That's the thing: I have no idea. Klaren kept his melting secret ... we don't have any idea how he did it. I wish I could tell you. All I do know is that unplanned melting is dangerous, deadly. If the Ancients knew what happened ... I don't know if either of us would be standing here right now. That's why you can never ever tell anyone about what happened out there. That's why today will be your first official melt. And that's why we'll spend every waking moment trying to figure out how to control your melts. Because I can't kiss you if you're gonna turn me into a gawky little boy. And I can't stand the thought of not kissing you." He reached out and stroked her lips briefly with his fingertips. He gave a half smile. Mala smiled weakly back at him. Then he straightened and moved aside.

Silently, the tailors came creeping back to their posts.

CHAPTER SIXTEEN

Mala stood before a pair of enormous black doors, her breathing shallow as she summoned the courage to push them apart and face the Ancients. She ran her stiff lace gloves over her grey suit one final time. Her right glove snagged on a buckle and she cursed. Sighing, Lowe leaned over and freed her. He smiled briefly, tensely, and nodded toward the doors. His mask of propriety had fallen back into place.

She could feel his tension. The energy between them was electric, even if half of it was nerves about the ceremony. Her insides were a frantic churning mess, but there was nothing she could do. Nowhere she could run. *Remember, Mala: just say the words. Go through the motions.*

But her feet wouldn't move. Not until her brain conjured up the image of the memorial room and Bara's symbol on the wall. *Death be my life.* Mala leaned into the doors, using her body weight to nudge them forward on their creaking hinges.

She slipped into a tall chamber. The entire room was painted black and the ceiling was lost in darkness. Incense gave the room a smoky flavor that lingered unpleasantly on her tongue. Only one harsh ring of neon-blue light circled the walls and curled lazily over the tendrils of smoke rising from the incense burners on the floor. The light was broken at irregular intervals by the silhouettes of the Ancients, all in black boots, black bodysuits covered in bulletproof armor, and black capes. The whites of their eyes shone aquamarine in the light as they stared at Mala. No one smiled, no one blinked.

Her throat dry, Mala had to swallow several times before she was able to get through her first line. "I come to preserve the Senebal nation." A moment of silence followed, and Mala wondered whether she had gotten it wrong.

"Why do you come?" A scratchy voice rang out and echoed in the chamber. Mala couldn't tell who it belonged to.

"I come because it is right. I come because we were chosen. I come because the only way to peace is to annihilate those who force war upon us. I come to end their persecution, humiliation, and destruction. I come to pay the blood debt we owe our ancestors. I come to preserve the Senebal nation. I come to preserve the Senebal nation."

Suddenly, the room around her took up the chant. Together all the Ancients repeated the line with her and Mala could feel her heart, which had been cringing in fear, unclench. A chill went through her spine. The room echoed with the words until she felt them pulsing in her chest.

Eventually, one of the Ancients put up a hand and the chant died to a hum. An old man with hanging jowls walked forward. "If you would join us, you must first pass the test," he stated, voice quivering.

Mala stepped forward and waited.

Lowe clicked his heels together and turned toward her. In the dim lighting, his face was little more than a mask. He did not meet her eyes as he leaned in and planted a soft, chaste kiss on her lips. She felt him prick her finger and squeeze out a single drop of blood. Lowe gave her a second kiss. This one was more intense than the first. She felt his teeth lightly, teasingly, bite her lip. He held up her bleeding hand. And stepped back.

Nothing happened. Mala glanced at Lowe. He stared straight ahead, his expression immobile but for a slight frown.

She glanced nervously at the row of Ancients. A lone chuckle rose up from among them, and a tall man, with steel grey hair and a scruffy beard, strode forward.

"Are you nervous, young lady?" he asked.

Mala bit her lip and nodded.

"Well now, you shouldn't be. You're one of us." He placed a comforting arm on her shoulder. "But you're Lowe's first recruit. And sometimes nerves get the best of all of us. So I'll forgive him for the fact that he didn't get you properly prepared for the occasion. And now, I get the pleasure of administering your test."

Alarmed, Mala glanced at Lowe. But his face remained as rigid as ever.

The Ancient leaned forward and Mala could smell the funk of his breath. She fought hard to keep from flinching. She felt his lips press hers and she waited for him to finish, to back away. But suddenly, his hand crushed her hair and his tongue invaded her mouth. She gasped at the intrusion and her eyes popped open.

She squeaked as this tall man held her in a death grip, tongue grappling with her own. She tried to gently nudge him back with her arms. The Ancient ignored her, and pulled her body closer. He grabbed one of her wrists, twisted it roughly, and Mala felt the prick of a second pin. Blood welled on her fingertip and he forced her hand upward, slowly drawing a line of blood along her cheek as he moaned in delight at their kiss.

It took all the willpower Mala had to stop herself from punching him, from fighting him off. She relaxed into the kiss, hoping that would end it.

Thankfully, the Ancient relented as soon as he realized she'd given up control. He leaned back, his gaze calm, smirking slightly as he stared into her face, waiting for the change to take over. And ... nothing.

Why isn't it working?

A whisper flew around the room. Both she and the Ancient turned to stare at Lowe, his eyes accusing while Mala's pled. *What did I do wrong?*

Lowe looked just as startled as anyone. Confusion flooded his features.

"Lowe," a woman's harsh voice came from the side of the room. "What have you done?"

"You've brought a Typical!" chimed another. The circle began to close in, accusations coming from every direction.

"Fool!"

Mala backed into Lowe, overwhelmed by the sudden hostility. "Am I the only person to ever fail the test?" she asked tremulously. She looked up at Lowe, and though his eyes were locked on the furious Ancients, he nodded.

"I don't know what I did," her voice broke. "I'm sorry. I'm sorry." She reached for his hand instinctively, but he was ripped away by the furious mob of elder Kreis. One of them smashed a fist into his jaw. She heard a sickening crack.

"No!" Mala cried. "It's me, not him. It's my fault!" She reached for Lowe as they dragged him back to the doors but the Ancients easily batted her away.

To Mala, it felt like the world had slowed, just as it had in the seconds before her mother died. *This is all my fault.* She met Lowe's eyes for a split second and that spurred her to action. *I have to prove I'm Kreis.*

She caught the eye of the Ancient who had kissed her. A vicious look lit his face. There was no doubt the violent end he saw in store. His rage at Lowe consumed him. His own cheek started to bubble. Mala grabbed him by the face, desperate impulse taking over. She locked her eyes on him, refusing to let him gaze around her, refusing to break the stare even when hands started to claw at her arms, at her neck. She ignored a knife that bit into her shoulder. She held his horrid veined eyes in her sight until she felt a flicker. Then she threw herself into flame.

Reality blurred and the world in front of her lost focus. Instead, Mala saw

a tall man, silhouetted in a darkened room, holding another man aloft by the throat while a little boy, hidden in the shadows, screamed. The vision flickered and faded.

Seconds later she stood, panting and triumphant, over six feet tall. Her broad chest had ripped apart the uniform she'd worn, and her gleaming pecs and muscled arms glowed blue. She reached a rough hand up to her square, stubbled jaw, then touched the knife wound. No one else moved. They seemed frozen in shock.

Lowe, who'd been dropped on the ground, scrambled to his feet and ran to block Mala from the others. "It's not him!" he exclaimed, as one of the Ancients brandished a sword.

The Ancient swung the sword upward, ignoring Lowe. The fear in his eyes tugged her back into the fire again. The vision was too fast for her brain to register this time. She emerged a tiny woman, with soft brown hair and a bump at her belly. That stopped the Ancient short. His expression turned to one of anguish and his own face began to bubble. He dropped the sword.

Lowe scooped the sword up, but did not brandish it.

From the back of the crowd a tall black woman strode forward. "Stop!" she bellowed to the room at large. She marched toward Mala.

Mala locked eyes with the woman. She was like the calm in the midst of a hurricane. All around her, faces were aflame with fury. Their expressions tugged at Mala. They fed the flame inside. Someone else caught Mala's eye. She felt her skin start to heat again and her body began to morph.

Another face came into view, and that was the last thing Mala remembered before a whirlwind of visions and a deep screaming pain took over.

When Mala awoke, she was naked, a cloak loosely draped

over her shoulders. Her hands were locked in rusted handcuffs. She blinked and blearily faced the room. She felt sick. She felt exhausted. And with the cold emotionless expressions of the Ancients greeting her, she felt scared. She heard a gavel slam onto a table.

“Let the judgment begin.” The Kreis who had kissed Mala sat at a small table directly in front of her. The remaining Kreis stood behind him. Lowe was at the far end of the room, also shackled, but loosely. Just his wrists were bound—not like Mala. Straps dug into her skin every few inches and she could already feel her left foot tingling, going numb.

She grimly faced the Ancient in charge. He cleared his throat. “I am Tier, chief of the Ancients. You, Mala, will explain yourself.”

“I don’t understand.”

“How do you melt?”

“I’m not sure.”

Tier raised his eyebrows skeptically, revealing a scar across his forehead.

“It only just started,” Mala looked at Lowe for reassurance, but he just jerked his head toward Tier.

“Tier. Is this really necessary?” The calm black Ancient came striding forward. She rested a hand on Tier’s shoulder. “She’s committed no crime other than melting … differently.”

"What if she's related to him? What if she's his daughter?" Tier's voice was harsh; he stood up to challenge Fell.

Daughter? Not yet. No.

Fell also took a step forward, standing nose to nose with Tier. "One, that assumes the only way to get this ability is from Klaren. We don't know that."

Mala's eyes went wide. *This wasn't supposed to happen yet. This is bad. So bad* ... She stared at a sea of unfriendly faces. *He's wrong!* Defiant words clamored in her head, but she didn't give them voice. Fell was arguing her point for her.

"Lowe said she's traveled between guards. There's no telling what kind of toxins or relics she was exposed to, what might have happened."

"That's speculation," Tier responded. "You've got no proof."

Fell stepped in front of Mala and squared off against Tier. "Neither do you. If she is his daughter ... she never knew him. Klaren was here. She wasn't tainted by him. You saw her. She has no control over herself. No idea what's going on. And I sure as hell am not gonna waste a shot at desecrating those blue-nosed bastards … just because of one mucked Kreis, once upon a time."

Fell moved to Mala's side, and put a hand on her uninjured shoulder. Fell turned away from Tier, and faced the group at large. "Imagine. If we can train her ... she could turn into anyone. The Erlender King, if we needed. If we can train her … she could well be the one who ends the war."

A deep and profound silence settled over the room. The only sound was the hum of electricity in the neon lights. Mala's heartbeat pounded in her ears as she waited for the Ancients to decide her fate. A huge part of her wanted to sink into the floor. Or become invisible.

Tier stared at Fell, who offered a wide smile. "Instead of a trial, I propose a vote. Who here believes we should attempt to train this girl?" she asked.

Two hands rose immediately—and slowly, a dozen more followed suit. Eight hands, including Tier's, remained down. Tier glared at Fell, then at Mala. His eyes roved over the other Ancients, some of whom kept their hands defiantly in the air as they stared back.

Tier finally spoke to Mala. His voice was a harsh, grating whisper. "Do you swear allegiance to all that is Kreis?" He waited until she nodded, then he continued. "Do you promise life and limb to the Senebal nation? Do you willingly enter the circle of blood and violence required to be a warrior?"

She nodded again. "I do."

"Do you vow to exterminate, to kill in order to protect the Senebal people? Do you promise duty and diligence in the execution of your orders? Do you swear to put your duty as Kreis above all else?"

"I swear it."

Tier stared for a moment, eyes slitted as he evaluated Mala. Then he muttered, "Release her. Bring out the brand."

Fell unlocked the cuffs and stripped off the cloak. Lowe appeared at her side. He rubbed her sore wrists and whispered, "Mala, keep your eyes on me." She looked up and saw his eyes shining. But he did not let a single tear fall. He moved his hands to gently cup her face. "You belong here. You will make a difference here. You will find revenge here. And if you want it, maybe something more."

A panel opened in the smooth wall and a young boy backed into the room. The boy turned and Mala could see a glowing red poker. On its tip was a circle that symbolized all she would become. She clenched her teeth.

As her flesh burned, Mala kept her eyes riveted on Lowe. *This is my future.*

CHAPTER SEVENTEEN

Word of her test traveled fast. Alba bounded into their hut at midnight and shook Mala awake, demanding to know if she really triggered into a bird when she'd been kissed. When she found out Mala had turned into a man instead, she laughed uproariously. "That beats my old maid for sure!" she'd giggled. That was, until she'd heard the full story. Then her face had grown serious and she'd asked a number of questions.

"You turned into Klaren ... the deranged?" Alba asked, her voice tiny in shock.

Mala thought back to the statue she'd seen and how disfigured it was from people dragging knives across its surface. She shivered, glad the rumor that she'd transformed into a bird was circulating instead. "Can you tell me more about what he did?"

Alba leaned forward conspiratorially, "He was one of the Ancients. He was giving Los a run for his money in number of kills. But on his last mission, the Kreis who went with him disappeared. Klaren said they'd gotten separated. No one thought anything of it. But a few nights later, they found Klaren in combat room two ... and he was holding another Kreis by the throat—crushing his windpipe, about to stab him in the stomach. Tier showed up. He killed Klaren himself. And then he noticed the other guy's five-year-old son had been in the room the entire time. Messed up, right? It freaked everyone here out. Still does."

Mala nodded. She tried not to picture the awful scene, but it ran on a loop in her head. The gasping struggle for air. A little boy crying as he watched his daddy slip away. The scene made her own haunted memories rise, her father's earth-shattering scream as gasoline splashed down his shoulders and a torch … Mala shook herself.

"Do all Kreis go that crazy?" she asked.

Alba gave her a sad smile. "Not like that. But our job is hard."

"Tier said Klaren might be my father."

At that Alba gave a barking laugh. "If that were true, wouldn't there be like twenty million Kreis babies running around this place? Even if this thing is genetic, Kreis don't have Kreis babies, Mala. He was freaked out, is all."

The pair sat in silence for a while. Alba picked at lint on her blankets. Mala tried think of a way to change the subject. But before one had formed on her tongue, Alba burst out, "It's so unfair!"

Mala looked up in surprise. "What is?"

"How come you can melt into Tier's worst nightmare and I can't even melt out of this damn old lady body!" She slammed her fist onto her knee. "Ow! See—look how totally useless I am. And Tier's already been to see me about this once." She fell back onto her mattress dramatically.

Mala couldn't help but be both amused and grateful for the interruption. “What does Tier have to do with anything?”

“He's elected head of the Ancients. He assigns all our missions—well, approves them anyway. And he’ll never let me out like this.”

“Oh.” The girls sat for a while in companionable misery, as their hut bobbed on gentle waves.

“What made you meltdown in the first place? I mean, if you don’t mind telling me.”

Alba was silent for a minute before she answered. “I just freaked out. I was in combat. Facing Verrukter. Which is distracting enough. Especially when he’s in gorgeous mode. And for no good reason, I kept picturing my grandma. The day before she died. She had all these regrets—you know? Stuff she’d never been able to do since the bomb. Stuff she’d taken for granted before. Like flying to another country or something—I can’t remember exactly. But like pre-bomb stuff. Anyway, I couldn’t stay focused. I just kept thinking, ‘What am I going to regret? When it’s my time, what am I going to regret?’ And for some reason—this totally sounds hokey—but that question scares me to death.”

Silence filled the hut. Mala didn’t know how to respond. But Alba didn’t seem to expect comfort.

“How can you do it? Melt into other people?” Alba asked. “I mean, how does that fit with all the crap theories?”

“No clue,” Mala responded. “Hopefully, that’s something they can figure out.”

"Do you think … maybe you could …"

"If they figure out how, you'll be the first person I tell."

"Pinky promise?" Alba solemnly held out her little finger.

Mala smiled into the darkness. "Promise." She linked pinkies with the other girl. It was the first time she'd ever made such a promise. Her heart swelled a little. *Lowe. Ges. Alba.* Though the ache in her chest remained, there was a glimmer in the darkness. A small glint of hope. *Maybe.* She almost didn't dare to think it. It felt so awful and selfish and horrible after everything that had happened. Everyone she'd lost. But the thought wouldn't let her resist. It pushed on her mind until she gave it voice. *Maybe I've finally found where I belong.*

After a while she sighed and rolled over. Mala stared at the reedy ceiling, until sleep stole over her.

The dream seeped in and she couldn't stop it. Mala moaned and turned restlessly, but the dream began to rise, flooding her mind. She saw her mother again, holding up an axe to chop off Sorgen's leg as he cried, "No!" Then Sorgen transformed into an Erlender and her mother was eating his face like a wolf, tearing out strips of flesh. A twig cracked and Erinne glanced up, alert. Women streaked like gazelles through the trees on shore.

She heard red-headed Nar yelling after them, "How did they find us?" before tripping over a pile of bodies. And Mala could see them all, the blue dead faces of the children. Blut's face was among them. They all had expressions of horror in their open, unblinking eyes.

Mala looked up to see Bara on her boat, shouting orders.

"Tie him up!" And a group of men came forward and tied up her father. A bronze statue clanked forward with a torch and held it to her father's hair until it was ablaze. And then Mala was in the ropes herself, twisting and turning and trying to get away.

She woke up with a start. She was sweating. She glanced around the hut for a moment, forgetting where she was, wondering why her mother wasn't curled up asleep beside her. Reality came crashing down like a thunderstorm.

Mala kicked off her covers and sidled toward the door, careful not to wake Alba. She dove into the water, seeking her old comfort, the familiarity of the waves. The cold water sent a chill up her spine, but Mala squeezed her eyes shut and dove into the depths.

The next morning, Mala trailed after Alba to the cafeteria in matching bright orange wetsuits. The circle cutouts along her backbone mercifully exposed her aching brand. Alba had helped her rub some ointment on it that morning, but it still prickled.

She spotted Ges as soon as she stepped inside. "Hey, I need to go request some research from Ges. I'll see you later," she called. She left a gape-jawed Alba in her wake as she scurried over to Ges's table full of Typicals.

"Morning," she said cheerily to them all. She pulled out a chair directly across from Ges and sat down. Immediately, the other four boys at the table scraped their chairs back, bowed politely and grabbed their trays, marching to a table on the far side of the room.

Mala raised an eyebrow at Ges.

"The rumor that you turned into a bird? That's dead. The

fact that you melted into Klaren? Tier and Fell's resulting face-off—that's the big gossip now." He grinned and rolled his eyes, "Of course you had to get yourself tangled up in the biggest political showdown we've had in years."

Mala stole an apple slice from his plate. "What do you mean?"

"Fell—that Ancient who stood up for you—is the head of the espionage unit. She oversees Lowe and a bunch of others. She also determines the final test before any Kreis goes on a first mission. She's angling to be the next Head. Elections are in high summer. Maybe eight months away."

Mala glanced around. Dozens of necks bent like straws as people strained to get a glimpse of her. "Muck. I just want to shove my head under the table and tell them to go away."

Ges laughed. "Try it. Let me know if that works for you." He swatted Mala's hand as she tried to steal another apple slice. "So, what are you here for? Other than to steal my food? I'm assuming you didn't make a public spectacle of sitting down with a Typical for no reason."

"I had something I wanted you to check out for me. I don't really know how this research assistant thing works. Bara's guard was all together when we were attacked. And everyone was drunk. But we were in a secret location. I mean, nobody even knew where the celebration was going to be until just before. Even then, only one of Bara's lieutenants could take you. So how did the Wilde group find us?"

Ges shook his head. "Mala, I don't need to research to tell

you what happened. Someone sold you guys out."

Mala's stomach dropped. Instinct told her Ges was right. "Who would do that?"

"Now *that* question will require some research." Ges handed her an apple slice, but his hand froze midway across the table.

A shadow fell across Mala.

"Come. With Me. Now."

Mala turned to see Ein, the tall scientist in his billowing silver cloak, looming over her. He glowered. "You're late."

Mala was about to give him a snarky retort, but Ges rushed in with a series of apologies. "Ein, I'm so sorry. I didn't realize she was supposed to be over at the lab right now or I would have taken her myself. I'm sorry."

Mala rolled her eyes at Ges and stood up. "Lead the way."

Ein turned and stomped off. Mala sighed as she followed him through the hall into a submarine.

As they rose in the water, Ein turned to address her again. "I told you to come to my lab at sunrise the day after your test. Why didn't you?"

"Excuse me. I forgot—what with the trial to determine whether I should become Kreis or be killed on sight. That sort of thing is a little distracting."

Ein's lip gave a little curl, and she couldn't decide whether he found her funny or was smirking at her. "Well, unfortunately for me, they decided to keep you. Which means we have a lot of work to do."

"Oh joyous day."

Ein ignored her and steered the ship to the docking port as he launched into a round of questions. "When did you first melt? How did it happen? What do you think caused it?"

True to her promise to Lowe, Mala only described the melt after she'd seen Bara. But it wasn't enough for Ein.

"That's the only time you've melted?"

"The only one."

"You're lying."

"No, I'm not."

Ein gave her a sidelong glance, before returning to steering. "Yes, you are. Your pulse is accelerating, you're breathing rapidly, and you won't make eye contact."

Mala crossed her arms. "Did they have to assign me the rudest possible person at the Center?"

"Defensiveness and changing the subject are also characteristic traits of liars." Ein docked the ship on the surface and turned toward her. He cocked his head with an expectant look. But Mala sealed her lips.

Ein stared at her for a bit and slowly a grin spread across his face. He took deliberately slow steps, stalking her. She backed up. He didn't stop until she hit the wall of the sub. And then he stood close enough that she could feel the heat radiating from his chest.

What's he doing? He made her feel childish and foolish and frightened all at once. *Mudding jerk.* Mala glared at his ribcage. She refused to look up at him.

Ein checked the lock on the door of the sub. Typicals repairing the floating platform turned to stare.

Ein put his arms on either side of her and leaned down, effectively trapping her. "Tell me the truth."

Mala pushed against his arm to no avail. She saw the crowd gathering outside. "You're making a spectacle—"

Ein slammed his hand into the wall right next to her head. The little vibrations in the metal rattled Mala's skull. "No. I'm giving you a chance to answer in a space where no video cameras are around to monitor your answer. The same won't be true anywhere else in the Center."

Mala glared up at him, trying to decide whether sincerity was possible in such an arrogant face. Ein cocked his head, evaluating her with a long, lingering stare. "You obviously don't want Tier to know. And there's only one Kreis you could logically be protecting. So tell me. I need to know."

"I've never—"

Ein leaned forward and whispered into her ear as one of his hands snaked around her neck. "Do NOT lie to me. If you don't tell me, I'll go to Tier. And let him question Lowe. Imagine how that little scene might play out."

Mala bit her lip. "You won't tell Tier?"

Ein released her neck and leaned back slightly, so they were eye-to-eye. His hazel orbs gleamed. "Your little trial yesterday? That was nothing. Lowe would be facing a lot worse. You promise not to waste my time with lies and I promise I won't tell the old bastard anything."

Mala took a deep breath. "I don't think I trust you."

Ein smiled dangerously. "I don't think you should." He

traced a finger along her collarbone.

Mala slapped it away. "What the hell do you think you're doing?" One of Ein's hands slid to her hip and held her in place, just as the thought to knee him flitted through her head. She was effectively pinned against the wall: his hand was so large it covered nearly half her stomach. She froze, but under the surface her heart pounded and her blood roared in her ears. *This isn't happening.*

Ein leaned in closer. She could feel his breath on her skin.

Ignore it.

He blew a gentle stream of air against the base of her neck.

Look away. This isn't happening. He's trying to get a rise out of you, idiot. Just count by threes. She started to count.

He blew up the nape of her neck and into her ear. "Mala…" he whispered. "I'm waiting."

She pushed him, but it was like pushing into a wall. He was solid and determined. And his hands … Mala was livid and confused and ungodly scared and she couldn't decide whether spitting in his face or blubbering out the entire truth was the better option.

When his teeth started skimming her chin, she yelled, "Fine! I give. I'll tell the truth. Just get back, okay? Back off! What is it with you people?" She shuddered as she remembered Tier's groping kiss.

Ein sighed and pushed away from the wall. "Finally! Mala, I don't really care if you trust me as long as you tell me the truth. I just want to get this sludge assignment over with as quickly as possible. I want to get back to my research."

"Which is?"

"Don't change the subject or I'll be happy to make you as uncomfortable as humanly possible. Again."

"That's what that was?"

Ein growled and stalked over to her. He slammed his body into hers, making her skull crack painfully on the sub's metallic wall. He lifted her until their hips ground together. "Lowe was happy enough to describe your shy little nature. Most Kreis melt from emotion. Did you know that? They're drawn to it. They love that little spike of adrenaline." He dropped her swiftly, and she fell to the floor. The fresh brand on her back screamed.

Ein continued, "We believe the amygdala is at the root of melting. Fear. Anger. Lust. The basic drives. Doesn't take much to activate the brainstem, as I've just shown you. It takes years for most Kreis to get their emotions under control so they can be effective little killing machines for Tier." He crouched down and Mala scooted away. He didn't seem to mind.

"But not you. Your pulse was elevated. Your pupils dilated. Traditional fear responses. But you didn't meltdown. I have to figure out if that's why you melt differently. I have to figure out what makes you tick." He walked his fingers across the floor toward her.

Mala kicked his hand. "That's what's going through your head as you feel me up?" She didn't know whether to laugh or cry. "Should I be offended?"

She looked up at Ein's smoldering green gaze and saw curiosity, frustration, theories. And then that damn annoying smirk crinkled the corners of his eyes. A long brown lock of hair fell across his forehead. Mala had to stifle her thoughts as they started to register that Ein was handsome. *No. Uh-uh. Stupid Ges. I wouldn't even think that if you hadn't swooned ... But this guy is all business. So he says.*

And Mala realized how she could get revenge. She leaned forward just enough to push back the lock of hair and let her fingers travel, feather-light, down the back of Ein's neck. He stiffened. Mala hid her smile, "So all you want is the truth? Just the truth? Nothing else?" She leaned forward and traced his lips with her free hand.

Startled, Ein leaned back.

Glad to see that smirk's gone. "What's the problem? Don't like a taste of your own medicine?"

Ein rolled his eyes at her. "Enough games, little girl. I'll just go to Tier. He's on the surface right now."

His hand was on the wheel to unseal the chamber when Mala sighed. "Fine. I melted into a little girl when I saw Bara tied to her boat and being burned alive … I melted into a blond woman when I killed Blut and he called me mother, and …"

"You killed Blut?"

"He was with the Erlenders. He sliced up one of our girls. I think he was leading them. He came after Lowe and me." And it clicked. *Blut. What if someone in the guard met Blut? What if they'd told Blut where we were? What if they thought they were talking to a Kreis soldier?*

Ein snapped his fingers at her. "Did you hear me? I *said,*

don't tell anybody else about Blut."

Mala nodded, but she was only half-listening. *I need to tell Lowe. Anyone in the guard would have told Blut anything. And they wouldn't even have known. They wouldn't have thought they were betraying us. How could they know? How could they?* "Why not?"

"You've already got enough hot-button issues. You don't need everyone knowing you killed a Kreis on top of it."

"So many secrets." *I thought coming here would be the end of that. No more hiding. Now I'm just hiding everything.*

Ein grabbed her face. She tried to focus. "Sorry. I'm here."

"Alright. Continue. Next melt?"

Mala felt a blush start to rise on her cheeks and she stared down at her feet. "I melted when Lowe kissed me."

Ein was silent. Mala glanced up, and saw a slight frown as he processed this information.

"Do you know who you melted into?"

Mala shook her head. "No. I'd never seen any of them before in my life. Lowe knew who I melted into, though."

That jerked Ein's head up. "Who?"

"A girl he used to date." She couldn't bring herself to say the word love.

Ein nodded and stroked his chin in thought. "Fear … lust …" Suddenly he popped upright and marched over to the door. "Okay. I think that's enough to get started. I'll see you tomorrow."

Mala tried to scramble up after him, but her knees were stiff. "Wait," she grumbled. "That's it?"

"For today. Tomorrow at sunrise, we'll start again." Ein

opened the door to the sub and fresh air rushed in.

"Ein," she called out. "Just out of curiosity, what important research project did I interrupt?"

Ein glanced back at her and grinned, revealing a dimple on his left cheek. "Weather patterns. I'm trying to find the perfect bunny-shaped cloud …"

"I thought we weren't allowed to lie!" Mala growled at him. He just laughed harder and waved a hand as he strolled off down the floating platform. He yelled over his shoulder, "If you thought today was uncomfortable … just wait for tomorrow!"

"That's a lie, right?" Mala yelled after him. But he didn't answer. *Oh God. I hope that's a lie.*

CHAPTER EIGHTEEN

Mala hadn't taken two steps out of the sub when a voice called her name. She squinted in the sunlight at a figure leaning against the side of the sub. It was Verrukter. He had one foot propped up on the metallic ribs, arms crossed to display his triceps.

Ridiculous, Mala thought to herself, mentally rolling her eyes. *I don't think he realizes not everyone is like Alba.*

He wore a wide grin on his face. "Guess what, newbie? Time for your first combat practice!"

Mala's stomach grumbled. She still hadn't eaten breakfast. But the stares in the cafeteria had turned her stomach sour. She sighed and stepped toward Verrukter. "Who's teaching?"

A slow and evil smile lit his face. "I'm teaching."

"You? But you're—" Mala stopped mid-sentence. "You're not really a teenager, are you?"

He nodded. Then he shook his head. Then he nodded again.

Mala grinned despite herself. "Ok, whatever. You are or you aren't. Irrelevant. What are we practicing today?"

His idea of combat practice turned out to be a million sit-ups and push-ups on a small floating platform away from the main submarine dock.

He's doing that on purpose, Mala thought as she scraped her chin against the boards for the millionth time. Verrukter was circling her, making the platform dip in the waves. "Will you stop moving?" she demanded.

"Sure," Verrukter stopped circling. He placed a foot on her back to add extra weight instead. "Keep going."

Mala gritted her teeth but didn't complain. Alba had mentioned that a lot of people would heckle her.

"It's totally a newbie thing. They'll try to get a rise out of you. Make you meltdown. They track it. There's gonna be some bets on it. So don't take it personally."

"I won't," Mala had assured her, as Alba had bandaged her brand. "You'd better bet I won't melt, though!"

Alba had laughed. "Oh honey! Wish I could. But after all the rumors about your melts and after your test … I had to bet you'd go down at least five times today."

Mala turned and swatted Alba. "How dare you! I thought meltdowns were punished?"

Alba turned serious. "They are. You get a week, that's it. Also why people giving you a hard time now isn't such a bad thing. You've gotta get control—fast."

Mala smiled as she remembered the little interchange. *Thank God Alba's my roommate.*

"Having fun are we? Then I think it's time we move on to the next phase of practice."

Verrukter turned and dove into the water. He swam the short

distance to the main platform and climbed up. For the first time in her life, Mala looked down at the water in dread. Her arms felt like limp reeds. *I hate this guy.* She jumped into the water and used her legs to power her to the platform. It took a couple tries, but she finally heaved her aching limbs up. She collapsed on the deck, letting her arms flop out.

"Not done yet. Come on," Verrukter headed to a sub and motioned her in. Mala would have protested, but a crowd of Typical workers on the platform had gathered to watch her. *Can't wimp out on my first day.* She shoved herself up.

Verrukter steered and docked, while Mala tried to rub some feeling back into her sore muscles. As soon as the sub door opened in the Center, he started off at a brisk jog. Mala trailed after him like a lone duckling as he bobbed through the crowd. They went upstairs and downstairs, through rooms upon rooms.

Alba's tour was totally insufficient, Mala thought as she followed Verrukter through the kitchens and snagged a roll. They jogged through empty meeting rooms and giant laundry facilities, even a classroom full of young Typicals. He went through so many rooms and past so many doors that she felt sure he was trying to confuse her.

Finally, they entered a strange warehouse-sized room. It was set up for people who lived onshore instead of on the water. Ancient storefronts and houses crowded together. Everything was made of stacked metal shipyard containers. The buildings towered over her, like a rusty layered cake. Gaping holes were patched with metal and wood panels. *But Senebals moved onto the water after the bomb.*

"What is this?" She had to shout to make herself heard over a steam vent in the floor that spewed foggy mist into the room.

"Heard your guard was attacked by the Wildes. This is a mock-up of the middle of their town."

An involuntary shiver crawled up her spine.

"We're almost done. All that's left for you today is … to win." He bowed with mock formality at her.

"Please define winning," Mala said irritably. She didn't like his smug expression. And she didn't know if she could win anything combat-related with legs and arms that felt like jelly.

"Let's say this for today: when you get back to the surface, you win."

Mala's jaw dropped. "But you've been taking me through this maze for at least half an hour! How am I ever supposed to remember—" she was cut off by a blow to her face. Verrukter knocked the wind out of her with an open-handed smack. Mala's eyes stung with tears and her cheeks turned red as blood rushed to her face.

"First lesson. Fights aren't fair," Verrukter's harsh military tone sounded like Bara's old command voice. "And details are important. You should never just blindly follow anyone. Now, you'll win when you find your way back to the surface."

Mala glared at him resentfully. Then she tossed her hair and went to side-step him. Big mistake. Before she knew what was happening, Verrukter's fist was in her face. She was staring up at the ceiling. The back of her head ached like it had been split in two. Her jaw felt twice its normal size. And her brand was on fire. She lay there for a moment and considered just staying on the cool concrete. But she saw a flicker of movement in one of the windows of the Wilde town. *Someone's watching.* Pride made Mala drag herself to her knees.

Verrukter leaned over her. "Oh, I forgot to mention—you have to get past me first." He grinned and offered her a hand up. She didn't take it.

"Does Alba know what a jerk you really are?" she asked stiffly, slowly rising to her feet.

He laughed. "Oh honey, Alba doesn't care about my personality. She's too busy staring at me slack-jawed to let a little thing like that get in the way."

Mala tried to roll her eyes in disgust but even that hurt. Her head throbbed horribly. She tried to think between the pulsing aches. *How am I going to do this?* "I think I need a medic."

"I think you're making excuses," Verrukter challenged. "Come on now, don't tell me a socially awkward freak show like yourself never got in a fight?"

"Never," Mala responded. "So are you gonna tell me what I need to—" her sentence was cut off as Verrukter swept her legs out from under her with a low kick. He caught her just before she hit the ground.

"Sweetheart," he shoved his face right up to hers. There was no mercy in his eyes. "Your daddy's dead. And you're not my princess. So don't expect me to coddle your pretty ass. Figure it out."

Mala's eyes flashed at his words. Adrenaline rushed through

her. Her pain receded as she focused entirely on him. In a split second, one arm wrapped behind his neck and her other fist was at his throat, pressed against his carotid artery. Shock sparked in his eyes. She pressed harder. She let all of her body weight go limp as she clung to his neck, so that he sunk into her fist.

Verrukter's eyes stayed locked on her. His shock transformed into panic. Mala felt her stomach heat. Her skin bubbled. She melted. Into a man whose arms gave her greater strength. Her earlier weariness vanished in her new body. She pushed harder. Verrukter's eyes started to dim. Mala struggled to regain her footing, but he fell forward on top of her, passed out. She shoved him off with a groan and then slowly got up.

She brushed off her torn wetsuit and said, "I never got a chance to be daddy's little princess. I was momma's little helper. And lucky for you, I've had to staunch more neck wounds than you could count. Otherwise you'd be dead right now. Bottom-feeder."

Mala heard a single clap. She glanced up sharply to see Fell step onto a balcony, out of the shadows. Her afro dipped as she gave Mala a nod of approval.

Mala turned and made her way out of the warehouse, biting back a smile.

CHAPTER NINETEEN

Mala dangled her feet off the platform in front of Lowe's hut. She peered up at the pink sunset, watching a V of geese flying south. She caught sight of Lowe as she twisted to follow the birds' path.

Lowe brushed a hand through his black curls. He sat down next to her and bumped her shoulder with his. "Hey."

"Hey you," Mala murmured back.

"Had your first combat practice?"

She nodded. They both watched the waves lap at their calves.

"Heard you had a meltdown."

"Only once."

His hand brushed hers and he dropped something into her palm. "Thought I'd share my winnings."

Mala looked down. "What is it?"

"Candy. They tap some maple trees nearby for syrup."

Mala popped it into her mouth and savored the flavor as it dissolved on her tongue. "Amazing! So … you bet on me?" She glanced sideways at him.

He turned to face her. "Of course. But I'm the only one who

thought you'd meltdown less than four times today."

Warmth flooded Mala's insides. Her cheeks flushed.

Lowe brushed his hand against hers again. But this time, he just let his fingers drift over hers. "So, what did you learn in combat?"

"That Verrukter is a sludge-mouth jerk."

He laughed softly. "Well, his job is to break you down."

"Why did you tell me to come see you after I fought him?"

"His job is to break you down. Mine's to build you up."

His hand was on her hair. Mala's spine sizzled. She tried to sound nonchalant as she asked, "And how, exactly, are you going to build me up?"

"Well, I have a few ideas." He leaned forward. His lips were against her ear. "But we can't try any of them here. Why don't you follow me?" He extended a hand.

Mala had to shove her heart back down; it had leapt into her throat. *Is he saying what I think he's saying?* She had to remind herself to breathe. She counted to three before she took his hand. She tried to hide her panic by keeping her eyes down, but her trembling gave her away.

Lowe pulled her up and stared at her until she tentatively glanced at him. Then, with a wicked grin he said, "Last one to the main platform's a rotten heathen!" And he darted back down the bridge.

When she caught up with him, she hit his shoulder. "That was just plain mean."

He laughed. "*What* was?"

"You know what," she grumbled, blushing.

He stepped closer. "Why don't you show me what I did that was so wrong?" His eyes glinted.

In a moment of daring, Mala stepped forward so that they were toe-to-toe. She leaned toward him. She breathed, "When you tell a girl you've got ideas … she thinks you mean *ideas*." She heard his breath catch.

"Why Misanthrope, is there a dirty mind hiding underneath all that innocence?" His chest was like a magnet, drawing her in. She pressed her cheek against his. The force between them was so intense it was almost painful. Her skin prickled.

You can't make him meltdown. The stupid little voice in her head ruined the moment. She pulled back and sighed. "I don't know if we can kiss yet. I don't know if it's safe."

"I think you're right. But if we can't kiss, we can always do the next best thing."

"What's that?"

"Fight," he smiled.

The main platform was empty but for the two of them, practicing in the fading glow of the sun. Lowe taught her a fighting stance, then tested her balance, pushing on one shoulder.

"Good. Now, I have some strategies I think will work for you. First, given your size, I think you should go for a surprise attack. Second, given the fact that you're new to hand-to-hand, I think you should go for a surprise attack."

"Geez, I don't know. That might be too much for me to remember. It's so complex," Mala teased.

"I always say, the best plan is the simplest one."

"Alright. So, what do I need to do?"

"Surprise is going to vary based on the individual you're facing. But I do think we can come up with some general strategies. Let's start with the easiest: kids."

Lowe turned his back for a moment. Before Mala could blink twice, she was facing a six-year-old. He had pudgy cheeks and his hair was just long enough to stick out in every direction.

Mala covered her mouth with her hand. "You were so … cute!"

In a high-pitched, lisping voice, Lowe responded, "Yes, I know. But let's stay focused. We've only got a little light left."

Mala stifled a giggle. "Yes sir."

He rolled his eyes. "Never underestimate a kid. They're fast, they're loud as alarm bells, and they have a better sense of intuition than most adults. They know when something's off."

"Okay. How do I surprise them, then?"

"Shiny things."

"You're joking, right?"

He put his arms on his hips. "Nope. You take an Erlender kid. You bring over some cool trinket that you've captured off a 'stupid Southerner' and they'll be so caught up in it, they won't see what's coming. Typically tech gadgets work best. And you can take them out of the equation fast. Quick knockout so you can get to your real target."

Mala balked. "I'm gonna have to punch kids out?"

"Mala, we do a lot of recon work as kids. Remember the

night of the celebration? I sat in a tree and threw a nut at you, and you didn't even look up."

Mala started. He nodded and continued, "Adults don't notice kids. But other kids do. So yeah, you're gonna have to suck it up and knock some out." Bossy Lowe grabbed a walkie-talkie out of a side pocket in his now-oversized navy wetsuit. "Here, use this and practice on me. Just do whatever your instincts tell you. I'll give you corrections in a minute."

Mala leaned forward and held out the walkie. "Hey kid. Look what I got off a dead Senebal. Want it?"

Lowe screamed, "*Demon!!!!*" and kicked Mala hard in the shins. As she fell, he yanked her hair and pulled her to the ground.

"Umpfff," Mala groaned. "I think I might like Verrukter better."

"No one offers kids cool stuff. Kids are inherently selfish. No kid offers another kid something awesome. They brag about it. And adults don't think kids can handle cool stuff. Try again."

Mala sighed. "If you pull my hair again, I'm pulling yours back."

A devilish grin lit Lowe's face. "You can try."

When the moon had evicted the sun from the sky, the pair made their way to a sub.

"I'm starving," Lowe said.

"Do you have the energy to answer a question?"

Lowe raised an eyebrow, "Only if it's an inappropriate one."

"Ha! No. I was thinking about what happened. The attack. How do you think the Wildes found us? Do you think it was because of Blut? I was thinking, he might have shown someone his brand, you know? And then anyone in Bara's guard would have told him everything he wanted to know."

Lowe sealed the sub and walked to the controls before answering. "Fell and I agree; Blut probably showed someone his brand. And the Wildes might have lost their heads. Massacres have been accidental before. The blood craze gets to some people. But that doesn't answer the bigger question. Why did Blut follow you?"

Ice slid down Mala's spine. *Me? That's right. He swam after me—not Lowe. Me.*

Lowe continued, "Was he doing recon on me? Did he see us together? You had time to see him, maybe he saw us. Did he think you'd lead him to me? What was his motivation? Why?"

Mala sucked in a breath. "Maybe he wanted to tie up loose ends? Finish the job?"

Lowe shook his head. "Maybe. I just don't think so …"

"Well, do you have any theories?" Mala prompted.

"I work mostly in intelligence, so I don't know why he'd target me, unless I have something he thinks is important ... But I've been poring over my files and I can't figure it out. Unless … he was on the water that night and saw you transform."

Mala's heart stopped. It was a minute before she could even process what Lowe had said. "So you think he was hunting me?"

Lowe turned a serious gaze on her as the water *whooshed* out of the loading dock. He came forward and gripped her hands. "Mala, if he saw what I've seen, I'm sure he was. Klaren was Blut's mentor, so he knows what that kind of melt looks like. He knows how powerful someone like that is."

Mala shivered involuntarily. Lowe ran his hands up and down her arms to comfort her. "Look, you got him—so he failed right? He didn't get to sweep you away and brainwash you into being an Erlender foot soldier. He didn't get to turn you over for some crazed religious sacrifice. But you need to understand how careful you need to be. How serious your training is. Because if you meltdown on a mission … you won't just be labeled a demon like the rest of us. They'll hunt you down like they're hunting the devil himself."

CHAPTER TWENTY

A month later Mala pulled open the door to her hut with a sigh. She was so exhausted it was a fight to shut the door against the chill fall air. After that, all she could do was fall into bed. She'd gotten to a point where her fatigue even outweighed the demands of her empty stomach. Combat practice and lessons with Lowe had worn her to the bone. After her initial victory over Verrukter—and his intense displeasure at the resulting gossip—he'd made sure she'd never won again. She had the bruises to prove it. And while practicing with Lowe was much more pleasant, it wasn't much easier.

At this point, Mala didn't think she could control her melts even if she knew how. Ein had nearly pulled out his hair at her zombie-like responses. The second day of his "melt experiment," he'd had her parade in her underwear for a group of teenage Typicals.

"I'm not doing that, you dirty mudbreather!" Mala had screamed when he'd proposed it.

"I don't think I was tapping into the right kind of fear yesterday," Ein had smirked and crossed his arms. "I have a feeling this fear might be more potent."

She had kicked and screamed and fought so much that it had taken Ein and three assistants to get her stripped down. But it had happened. And he'd shoved her into a room full of fourteen to twenty-year-old teenage boys, locking the door behind him.

Luckily, Ges had been in the group, and she'd focused all her attention on him. They'd talked and chatted and Ges had acted like nothing out of the ordinary was going on at all. Ein had been livid.

"Why are you making this harder than it has to be?"

In response, Mala had slapped him.

After that, Ein had brought Kreis after Kreis into the lab and had them stage arguments and get in her face to make her angry. No go. He'd tried bringing in crying Typical kids. After he found out how Mala had jumped ship as a kid, he'd wheeled in injured people, but by the time he'd dragged them into the lab, most of them were so confused that all Mala could do was shrug in pity. He'd even brought in Lowe and Tier for additional kisses. Trying to recreate those uncomfortable scenarios had left Mala cold. And in her own skin. She wasn't sure if she was relieved or sad each time Ein's experiments failed. She loved that it drove him mad, but she hated that she had to spend another day with him, and another day without understanding her melts. Or lack thereof.

After each botched experiment, Ein cursed and swore and shoved her against the wall, demanding that she tell him the truth. The entire truth.

"You're a damn liar! You're hiding something. That's why these experiments are failing!"

“Maybe you’re the failure,” she’d snapped back at first.

But lately, she’d adopted a new policy. Mala had noticed Ein’s lab was cluttered with half-built gadgets and unfinished projects. He was often tinkering when she arrived at sunrise, shadows under his eyes, the tell-tale mark of insomnia. If it had been anyone else, Mala might have suggested valerian root tea. But it was Ein.

He couldn’t seem to take a breath without insulting her. His superiority rankled some deep part of her and made her want to snap back. Tier had taken to casually dropping in on their experiments. This had increased the tension between them both exponentially. Ein barked at her over every tiny thing whenever Tier was around.

“No! Stand to the left! Hands up! Can’t you even follow basic instructions? Or did Verrukter beat the little bit of brains left out of you?”

You didn’t give me half a second to follow your instructions, you sludge head. But Mala bit her tongue. She had to fight to maintain her cool while Ein subjected her to wilder and wilder experiments. He’d plunged her into ice water to elicit a reaction. He’d locked her in the morgue, and forced her to stare at hollow-eyed dead bodies on metallic tables. He’d shocked her with low volts of electricity. Mala put up with all of it solely because Tier stood in the doorway, watching. He hovered like a shadow in the back of her thoughts. Because if Tier decided she’d failed … if he kicked her out of the Center … *What will I have left?* So she clenched her jaw and glared at Ein. To prove she wouldn’t break. To prove she belonged.

But Mala got her revenge. She started filching parts from Ein's constructions. First a gear, a couple bolts—small things. Her skintight wetsuits wouldn't let her hide much, but her hair was a wild thicket. And she used it to her advantage. She strung small trinkets into her curls when Ein's back was turned. She'd pull up her hair while Ein picked out her next torture device, and slide a screwdriver into her updo. It gave her a sense of satisfaction that carried her through all the hours she spent locked up with him.

And it was Mala's magpie habit that led her to find the clock.

Buried in the back of a drawer, it was a gorgeous, golden masterwork. The face depicted the phases of the moon. And the intricate golden hands looked like jewelry. Ein was clearly reconstructing the timepiece. *But clocks are forbidden.* They had been outlawed since the bomb.

Ges had often complained about the inaccuracy of hourglasses. "We don't have a glassblower here and so we've had to construct them out of whatever we can find. Time isn't something you can mess around with and those hourglasses are crap." Most people carried pillar candles that burned down by the hour.

One such candle had been burning on the table between them in the archive when Mala leaned over diagrams of the Wilde town and asked him, "Why? No one's ever told me why."

He knew what Mala was asking without her having to say the word 'clock' and turn heads. Ges always seemed to know. "Senebal law states that they were mechanisms tainted by the explosion. The radiation left behind somehow affects them. I mean, granted, there aren't that many labs left. And priorities after the bomb were more survival. Testing didn't happen right away. So skeptics wonder about their equipment, political motivations, all that. In any case, official word is that clocks are inaccurate—but more important, they're toxic. Highly dangerous. Unofficial versions …" he lowered his voice and glanced around to ensure no one nearby was listening, "talk about how the bomb destroyed our illusion of time. I have the diary of a woman who writes that everyone around her was frozen after the explosion. Just stopped, mid-motion—people jumping in the air, brushing their hair. Like statues. But she'd been fixing her grandfather clock at the very second the bomb hit. She walked away. What's the truth? Who knows? What's possible? Well … you cut into yourself with a piece of one. And look at what you think's possible."

Ges had been awed, scolding, and pensive when Mala had told him about her secret ceremony with the hour hand and the fact that she'd felt the burn but never fully melted before that night. He'd researched extensively after that, finally scrounging up a beat-up Erlender diary about blood sacrifice. Cross referencing it with a book he'd found earlier about Kreis and blood sacrifice had cemented his opinion.

"By the light of the moon, a blood sacrifice must be made. And the intended will be affected so that time will bend to their will."

Ges snapped the book shut, his eyes round as saucers. "Well, this guy definitely thinks your ceremony is it. If you don't automatically write off the Erlender belief system … I'd say it's possible."

"So, what do you think I should do?"

"Well, as Ein would say …"

"Do NOT quote that mudbreather at me." Several heads turned in their direction at Mala's outburst. She cleared her throat and mouthed, *Sorry.* The Kreis and their research assistants slowly turned back to their recon assignments.

"As Ein would say," Ges began again, grinning and ducking when Mala tossed a scroll at him. "I think we need to test your theory. Who do you know that's desperate enough to try magic?"

CHAPTER TWENTY-ONE

Mala shut the door to her hut, and Alba let out an excited squeak. "Did you get it?"

"Yup." Mala reached into her hair and slowly untied a delicate golden arrow. "Ein was busy setting up some suspension torture device for me. Didn't even notice me digging it out of the drawer." She tossed it to her roommate.

Alba caught it in a wrinkled hand. Her blue eyes gleamed with hope and desire. She held the minute hand up in the lantern light.

Staring at her roommate, Mala felt pity and hope swell simultaneously in her stomach.

At first, Alba had scoffed and refused Mala's suggestion to try the ceremony.

"Please. I'm not some newbie you can pull a prank like that on, Mala," she'd responded with a wave of her hand.

When she'd realized Mala was serious, she'd been distraught. "Are you mucked? Are you *crazy*? This is because of your stupid assistant, isn't it? He's a weird one. They all say he's …"

The ensuing fight hadn't helped matters. Alba had stormed

off. And days had gone by, the girls hardly acknowledging one another. Until the night Alba had seen Verrukter kissing Neid.

Alba had been more angry than tearful, throwing things around their hut. Mala had delicately moved over to sit on her knife, glad she still wore her hook necklace, so it turned into a projectile. "That stupid blond nimbo! The one I hate more than anyone? She's not even a *real* Kreis, Mala! She's never passed her final trial. She refuses. Won't go on a mission! He picked *her*?"

Alba had shattered their lantern and Mala had rushed to stomp out the flames. When Mala had turned around, Alba had been sitting woodenly on her bed, tracing the spider veins on the back of her wrinkled hand.

Her eyes were brimming when she finally glanced at Mala, "Who can blame him, right? Look at me: I can't melt. I'm worthless." She shook her head pitifully. Mala had sat down beside her, wrapping an arm around her roommate.

"Fine. You win. You want me to try magic? I'm in."

"What do you think?" Alba asked, glancing surreptitiously from the minute hand to Mala.

"Tonight's the night," Mala replied solemnly. She and Ges had been researching magical rituals. She'd spent more time on that recently than on her assigned project to study the layout of Wilde township. "Full moon's the best, so they say. And that's tonight."

Alba bit her lip and nodded, turning back to stare at the tiny dagger. "Am I crazy for hoping it works?"

"Not as crazy as I am for thinking it will," Mala replied,

flopping down onto her mattress. "We need full exposure to the moon, but if we get caught …"

Alba laughed bitterly. "Court martial can't be worse than this. Mala, I haven't melted—not even a meltdown—for over two months. But maybe you shouldn't come with me. In case—"

Mala shook her head. "I need to know if this works just as much as you do." She didn't say, *Because I think the alternative might be that the most despised man in history might just be my father.* After all of the failed testing, the thought that Klaren might really be her father kept haunting her dreams.

The girls waited in silence until the pillar candle in the corner indicated it was nearly midnight. Then they stood, dressed in grey wetsuits, and walked slowly out of their hut. The first hints of winter made them shiver. Crisp air bit at their skin, and the lake water that dampened the boards beneath their feet was ice cold. But excitement outweighed the weather.

Alba stopped in the very center of the hub platform, and Mala stayed back, near one of the sub huts that sheltered her from the wind. The wind began to howl as Alba raised the minute hand. It whipped her white hair out like a flag behind her.

"Divine Spirit, split me open. Take what you need. In return, protect me. That—"

"WHAT THE HELL?" The bellow froze Alba in her tracks.

Ein shoved Mala roughly aside and grabbed the minute hand from Alba's shocked grasp. "Get out of here *now*," he seethed. "Before I get Tier."

Alba tried to sneer but Ein stopped her short. "So you *want* Tier to know you're performing demonic magic rituals?"

Alba crouched into a fighting stance and kicked Ein. But her eighty-year-old legs had no power, and he swatted her easily to the ground.

Mala ran forward and threw herself protectively between the two of them. "Ein, you'll break her hip! Stop!" She helped Alba upright.

The old woman's face was full of fury. Her skin bubbled, and Mala watched as Alba struggled to focus on her anger—to hold onto it, to melt. But wracking shivers got the best of her, and her skin settled back into its familiar crisscrossed crevices.

"I hate you." Alba's teeth chattered as she glared up at Ein.

"I'm heartbroken."

Mala slung Alba's arm over her shoulder and began to walk away, but Ein grabbed her.

Alba looked at her questioningly, but Mala waved her roommate away. Alba didn't look like she could stand five more minutes of cold, much less whatever Ein had in store. Alba gave her a pitying backward glance before scurrying back to their hut.

A rough shove sent Mala marching toward the nearest submarine. She stepped inside and Ein followed, closing the door against the wind. Her momentary relief from the cold was quickly shattered by Ein's voice.

"What the mucking hell were you thinking?" he shouted. "*Magic?* Was that a suicide attempt right there? Because if it wasn't, it was the stupidest thing I've ever seen. We're in the middle of an all-out political war here. If Tier had seen you … Do you want to be shot as a traitor?" Ein towered over Mala, and she was reminded of their first meeting. Only now, he wasn't smiling. He was nearly purple with rage. Mala opened her mouth to respond, but his eyes burned into her before she had the chance.

And she saw a tall man with grey hair screaming at her, swinging a book into her ribs. The painful *crack* brought her back to reality. Mala emerged from the vision and realized she and Ein were standing eye-to-eye. But his rage was gone. Instead, for the first time since she'd known him, Ein was speechless.

"Who am I?" Mala demanded, taking advantage of his confusion.

"My father," Ein responded automatically. He stared at her a moment more, then looked away and started muttering, his brain working rapid-fire.

"I …you … then I …" Ein prattled on under his breath. Mala sat down and rested her massive head against the wall of the submarine. She waited. When Ein got like this, she knew better than to say anything. And this melt had taken them both by surprise.

When his muttering slowed, she glanced up, "Figure it out yet?" her voice boomed in the compact room. She wasn't used to such deep vocal chords.

"Can you melt back?" Ein asked. He avoided looking directly at her. Mala stored that little fact away for later.

"I need water," Mala responded. Ein nodded and turned the wheel to open the door of the sub. He disappeared for a moment into the frigid night and returned with a handful of lake water.

"Pour it over my head, then give me your coat. And close your eyes," Mala said, as Ein dumped the water unceremoniously over her. A glacial melt ran through her hair and her skin bubbled in response. Euphoria stole over her and despite the cold, a smile caught hold of her lips. *I forgot how good this feels.* Her entire body tingled, as if butterflies were landing on her skin. She sighed in pleasure.

When she finally opened her own eyes, Ein was staring down at her. His gaze was smoldering, but not with anger.

That's when Mala realized he hadn't handed her his coat.

"Turn around! Turn around!" Mala's hands flew to cover herself. She tugged at the shredded remains of her wetsuit. When Ein didn't respond, she turned around herself. "I told you to give me your coat! What the hell's wrong with you?"

Ein's hands were at her waist and he slammed her into the wall of the sub before she could breathe. The glacial metal stole the heat from her cheeks and chest.

Ein's fingers traced her sides and when she slapped at him, he simply gathered her hands and pinned them with one of his own.

"I have a new theory," Ein said into her ear.

The heat of his breath on her ear made her tremble. She tried to ignore it. And the heat of his body up against hers was a stark contrast to the frigid metal side of the sub. *He's done this before. Just get him into preachy theory mode and he'll drop you.* Mala eyed the sub door, trying to judge if she could make it. *Too far.*

"Ein, your theories are always pathetically wrong," she scoffed.

Instead of bristling, as she'd hoped he would, he laughed. "You're right. They were always wrong. Because I made them under the false assumption that you operate at a basic level like other Kreis. I was trying to shock you, scare you, entice you into melting. But now that I've seen it for myself, I don't think you're like other Kreis at all."

He skimmed his teeth along her shoulder and she struggled to get free.

He chuckled breathily. "Mala, I think you're special. And not just because your mother dropped your head on the boat deck. I think you melt in a way that's unique."

He flipped her around on the wall so she faced him. "And I'm about to prove it."

She tried to kick him, but he used his long arm to capture her leg and pin it around his waist. He leaned forward and Mala turned her head to the side, desperate to escape him.

"Mala, look at me," he crooned.

"No." It was the only resistance she had left.

"Look at me and I'll tell you my theory," he whispered.

What other choice do I have? Slowly, Mala inched her gaze back in his direction. His hazel eyes were blazing with lust and triumph.

"I think," he said, tracing his fingers along her thigh, "that your melts are in reaction to what *other* people feel. It's not *your* amygdala that's triggered, but theirs. I think you reflect back their emotions … by turning into the very person they associate with that emotion."

His hand traveled dangerously high on her thigh and Mala used her heel to kick him in the butt.

"Did you want me closer?" he teased, pressing his body into hers.

Part of her body responded to him. But her mind kicked that part into submission. *Gross.* "Ugh! No. Back off!"

He took a step back so he could lean down and look at her.

Mala engaged warily. *Keep him talking. Until daylight. Until someone comes to use this damn sub.* "So you're saying I'm doomed to become everyone's worst nightmare?"

He cocked his head as he contemplated her question. "Mostly, yes. But, as part of that theory, I think there might be an exception. An exception that lets you melt into whomever you want. And I want to prove that part of my theory right."

Without warning he leaned in and kissed her. Roughly. Deeply. He lifted her up the side of the sub and kissed her until they were both breathless. Mala's thoughts shattered and fell away. Only sensation was left. The cold wall, his warmth, and his furious, controlling kiss.

Ein opened his eyes and whispered. "Mala. Look at me."

She melted without a second thought. It was easy. It was fast. No vision clouded her senses. Heat stole over her body and in the blink of an eye she was standing before him, a muscular, heavyset older woman.

Ein gave a whoop of delight. He jumped and smacked the ceiling of the sub with his hands. He started to do a victory dance. But Mala's punch knocked him to the floor.

"What the hell was that?" he grabbed his cheek.

"When are you going to realize that half-raping people in the name of science is not okay?" Mala shot at him.

"You stupid ingrate! Didn't I just tell you that you melt based on other people's emotions?" He climbed to his feet and marched toward her.

"So, what? You lust after old women?" Mala stumbled. She wasn't used to the bulk of this older woman's body; all of her training with Lowe had been focused on retreat and small quick movements best suited to her petite stature. She had no idea what to do.

"Did you listen at all? Do your ears even *work*?" he taunted. "This is the exception. *I'm* the exception. I didn't choose who you melted into, you did."

"What?" She turned and looked at her reflection. She was heavily muscled. And her hair had streaks of grey. But her face was still beautiful. Lavender eyes stared back at Mala.

"I didn't choose Verrat!"

"Whoever this is, you subconsciously chose … probably because you wanted to punch me. So you picked a she-man."

Sludge. It makes sense. He doesn't know her. How could he? I hate when he makes sense. But wait—he's focusing on my part. Not on his. "So the only way you can feel anything is by holding a half-naked woman against her will? What does that say about you? Why does that make you an exception?"

"It says I have to choke back the vomit before I can feel something for a half-wit like you!" Ein snarled.

Mala's foot slipped in the puddle of lake water. She melted back to her body before she hit the floor. And she was out.

Ein was cradling her head when she came to, his fingers delicately taking her pulse. And the look on his face was … concerned. Until he realized she'd opened her eyes. Then he shoved her back down.

"You'll be happy to know brain damage isn't possible for mouth breathers like you. So other than the bump on your head—"

He didn't get to finish his sentence. Mala jumped up on him, wrapped her arms around his neck, and kissed him furiously. At first, he tried to peel her off, but when she let out a low moan, he relented. His arms snaked up around her. She let him cop a feel.

"Ein." She pulled back for a breath.

"Yeah?" his eyes were cloudy with lust.

"I heard you have a sister," she replied. "How do you feel about making out with her?" She cackled as the melt took over.

Ein stormed from the sub, slamming the door behind him. Mala remained inside, laughing on the floor until her ribs hurt. But as the laughter died, she sat back on her elbows and sighed.

"Why does he have to be the damn exception? Why is he an exception? He never explained that." Mulling that over, she stood and prepared to walk back to her hut and put Alba out of her worried misery. As she covered herself with the scraps of her wetsuit (destroyed after three melts) she caught a glimpse of her reflection. "No way!" She hurried up to the glass. Pouty lips, full blond hair, and a gorgeous figure that guys would trail after. That Typical boys *did* trail after. *Ein's sister is Neid! The only Typical to every become*

Kreis ... Ein's sister is the Verrukter-stealer Alba hates so much? Ein's sister? How the hell did that happen?

CHAPTER TWENTY-TWO

Mala eyelids cracked open before she was quite sure why. Then she heard it: someone was pounding on her door. She rolled over. Alba's mattress was empty, just like it had been when she'd gotten home last night. Mala groaned.

"I'm coming." She sat up, and when she did, she realized the hut didn't sway beneath her. She looked around again. No light drifted through the crack under the door. She couldn't smell the water. *Where am I?* She scuttled quickly to the pile of clothes in the corner and sifted through until she found her trident dagger. Wherever she was, someone had gone to great lengths to disorient her. *Ein?* But they'd left her a weapon. *Ein wouldn't be stupid enough to do that. Was it Verrukter? Is this another combat practice? Thank God I melted back into my own skin or I'd be mucked.* Grimly, she slid behind the front door, her heart beating quickly.

She pulled open the latch and let the door fall open, raising the knife and squaring her feet. But no one stepped inside. Instead, she heard a distorted female voice say, "Welcome to your first espionage lesson. You can put down the knife. No one is going to attack you."

Mala didn't lower the knife.

The voice continued. "In these lessons, you will learn several skills: to listen, to find, to steal, and to escape. Today, you will learn to listen. It's a skill you will use on reconnaissance missions and even on assassinations in order to verify intel. Your goal is to determine what is said. When you can fit your words to the video, you will be free to go." Mala heard a metallic click, and she tensed. Eerie silence filled the room.

Cautiously, she edged around the door, her arm tensed and ready to throw the knife. No one was there. Only the sound of her own breathing echoed throughout the black chamber. It looked as though her hut had been placed in the center of a large windowless hall. A very dim green light came from a series of neon tubes far above. Another thin line of light snuck in underneath a door at the far end of the room. Mala tried the handle cautiously. It was locked. She gave a sigh.

Another click. Mala threw herself to the floor. But soon she regretted her skittishness. The click had turned on a projector overhead and a silent movie played on the wall in front of her. For a minute, she stared. Bara's guard had lived on the periphery of Senebal territory. And the guards she and her mother had been with before Bara's hadn't been much more advanced. She'd only seen one video before, of the president making a speech. It took a second for her to shake off her awe at the miniature people moving in front of her.

It was foggy and a boat drifted up to a dock. A pair of

leather-clad men clambered down. It was only as they grew closer that Mala saw their striped blue noses. Her lip automatically curled. The Wilde Erlenders walked casually past, chatting and laughing, though she couldn't hear what they said. Behind them, a second group unloaded the boat. The heathens rolled out large pieces of scrap metal and bags stuffed with stolen treasures. A giant brute climbed over the side of the boat and jumped onto the dock. He tugged at a long thick chain and yelled. That's when Mala saw them: six survivors. Her breath caught in her throat and she reached a hand to trace the moving images on the wall. Six left ... out of well over a hundred. She swiped at her eyes.

Three young boys emerged. Mala didn't know their names. *They're so little! How old's that biggest one? Six maybe?* Bile rose in her throat. Garon followed, hulking, sullen, and silent behind them. For all that she'd hated him, Mala hadn't wished this future on him.

Sari, the drunken bride, shuffled forward, a nightmare to behold. Her eye makeup ran down her face in black tear tracks. Her ruined cheek was attached to her face with safety pins.

Last came Sorgen's violet-eyed widow, Verrat. She stared at her feet, unlike the other prisoners, who glanced nervously around. *She was always so proud. So strong. And now she looks ... broken.*

They were all connected to each other by short lengths of chain. When a little boy fell, the entire group stumbled. Mala's heart swelled like a bruise at the thought that she should have gone back. *I might have saved them. I should have done something.*

An Erlender general stomped into view. Someone else might

have thought he was just a poor man in patched rags, but Ges had taught her the marks of Erlender rank. In addition to his blue nose, a series of dotted lines were inked on his left cheek.

The general evaluated his prisoners like one might check an animal. He lifted and dropped their arms. He forced their mouths open and peered inside. When he was satisfied, he snapped his fingers. Several blue-nosed lackeys ran up. He gave them each directions. Mala tried desperately to watch his mouth. She thought he whispered "fields" when he sent Garon off. She thought she saw his lips form the word "observation" for the little boys. But she had no idea what he mumbled about Sari or Verrat.

The screen flickered and the image died. Mala was left in darkness for a moment, before she heard a click. The video sprang back to life, beginning again.

It took several viewings before Mala could tamp down her self-loathing and focus on the task at hand. She really only felt calm after she'd insulted herself. *What would you have done, idiot? It's not like you were combat-trained. You didn't have a gun. And they had lots of them.* She heard Lowe's voice in her head once more. *You will make a difference here. You will find revenge here. And if you want it, maybe something more.*

Mala sharpened her focus. Still, it felt like days before she had a handle on what was being said. Erlenders elongated their words and that made it difficult for her to understand them. In the dark room it was impossible to have any true concept of time. Her throat was raw and parched. Her eyes became sore from staring at the screen. But finally, she thought she had it. She called out into the ether. "I think I know! I think I know what was said."

Immediately, the video rewound to the beginning. Mala mouthed the words as the two men walked up the deck. "Haw many sorrows didja' earn?" one asked the other.

"Twelve," his skinny friend replied. "More dan I ever gotten."

"Me too," the Erlender sighed. "And it wuz a waste. No gurl ..."

"Dat's whaat we git for trustin' a witch," Skinny said.

His husky friend groaned. "Yer right. But now we hav'a tell da' general and tha' chiara."

"That's yer job. No way I'm tellin' her she wuz wrong."

Mala recited these lines blandly, glossing over them because she understood the words but not the meaning. *I'll have to check with Ges about sorrows.*

The men walked out of the frame and Mala focused her attention on the prisoners. The general performed his inspection, and she said his lines through her teeth. Ges's descriptions of General Keptiker had been accurate. His evaluation of the prisoners was so cold, so scientific. And unlike Ein's arrogance, which aggravated her, General Keptiker gave off no emotion whatsoever. He could have been sorting plants or boat parts.

Mala repeated his lines directing Garron to the fields. She had to breathe deeply as she repeated his command to send the boys "out to tha' house fer observation." She didn't even want to think what that might mean. When he turned to the women, Mala swallowed hard and forced herself to continue. "Dis one, he can be my errand boy." He gestured to Sari's scarred cheek. "'er face ain't no good. But dis one," he gestured at Verrat, whose neck was still covered in ashes. "Take 'er to my office. Chain 'er up. Tell the guards … free reign." He winked.

Mala hadn't been a warrior, but she had heard about the evil things Erlenders did to prisoners. Slaves like Garon or Sari were made useful, beaten only as deemed necessary. *But to give guards free reign. Verrat will just be breathing bag of body parts.* It was the worst kind of death sentence. Mala bit back tears. Verrat merely bowed her head, accepting her fate.

Mala couldn't decide if she wanted to yell at the woman to resist, or if she admired her for not showing fear in the face of such a future. She turned to watch the Wilde general walk off screen, memorizing his face, his gold hair and green eyes. He would have been handsome if his face hadn't been covered in tattoos. *Or if he wasn't the epitome of evil.*

I will help them. I won't turn my back on them again. And I'll make him wish he'd never seen a black fish banner. I will find him and repay Bara's death with fire.

The film shut off, the lights came up, and she heard the solid *click* as the lock on the hall door released. Mala was freed with no outlet for her anger.

CHAPTER TWENTY-THREE

Mala marched to the cafeteria. She secretly wished for a combat session with Verrukter. She wanted to punch someone. Watching that video for hours had dredged up so many memories that she thought her head might explode. Her stomach twisted in pity for the survivors. The little boys with no parents and no future. Sari, who'd once given Mala a ribbon because she'd been crying. Verrat, who used to sing to the children. She even felt sorry for Garon. *Even a bottomfeeder like him doesn't deserve to die under the Erlender whip.*

She grabbed a cup of water and drained it in under a minute. She was gulping a second when a hand clamped down on her shoulder.

"Can I talk to you?"

Startled, she spilt the entire glass. Water soaked her face and chest. Mala grimaced and turned to see Lowe. He was striking in a navy wetsuit: the color emphasized his eyes and the cling emphasized his muscular torso. *And I look like a three-year-old,* she groaned internally, mopping up her chin.

"Sorry," he apologized and handed her a cloth napkin. "I've

been looking for you all day. Where have you been?"

"Espionage lesson," Mala replied shortly. "You didn't tell me that training includes random lockups."

Lowe's eyes glinted with amusement. "Well, I think Fell thought you'd earned some special treatment. Not to mention caution on her part. I mean, you did take out Verrukter in your first lesson."

"That was a fluke. Obviously. Fell's my instructor? I thought she was the head of all the espionage instructors."

"I didn't say that. You never heard that." Lowe muttered. "You aren't supposed to know. That lady will kick my you-know-what if she finds out you know."

"Okay, okay! I don't know," Mala reassured him. She finished mopping herself up. *You need to tell him about Ein,* her brain nagged. *Now is better than later.* She took a deep breath.

But before she could speak, Lowe grabbed her hand and whisked her out of the cafeteria. He pulled her into a secluded hallway and turned to face her. He took her hands gently, and a soft grin lit his face. "So … I wanted to see you because I've thought up a solution to our little problem. I got something for you—us. Here." He reached into his back pocket and pulled out a strip of black cloth.

"A rag?" Mala looked at him quizzically.

"Close your eyes." His tone was commanding. It reminded her of Ein's orders the night before. The memory of Ein pushing her against the wall flashed through her head for a second. *Damnit.*

"Wait. I need to tell you—"

"In a minute," Lowe turned her around. "Keep your eyes

closed."

If only Ein had kept his eyes closed last night.

"Lowe I have a problem."

"I've been waiting all day to show you Mala. Just two seconds."

Resigned, Mala closed her eyes. He slid the black piece of cloth over her eyes and tied it securely behind her head. Then he spun her around to face him.

"It's a blindfold," he said, as if that explained everything.

"Okay?"

She felt his arms caress her forearms and slide gently up to hold her shoulders. A sensitive little shiver ran up her spine. One hand slid to cup her chin. "Now I can kiss you without meltdowns. It's perfect!" And his lips were on hers.

A million thoughts rushed through Mala's head. Not one of them was romantic. *Should we be doing this? I didn't brush my teeth! I need to tell him. Why isn't this kiss as hot as the one Ein gave me? Oh, sludge—I did not just think that. Lowe beats Ein on so many levels it's not even funny.*

She pulled away but left the blindfold on. She wasn't sure how he'd react. *Coward.* "Lowe, Ein figured out my melts last night. He figured out what starts them and he figured out a way for me to control who I melt into. Kind of."

"That's great! That's awesome! So we don't need this thing," he whipped the blindfold off her head and kissed her full on the mouth. His joy and giddiness washed over her.

A minute later, a gangly and confused fourteen-year-old

Lowe stared at her. "But I thought you said …"

Mala pulled a strand of red hair nervously, shifting her eyes to look for water. The lake beyond the windows mocked her. She stared at her reflection for a second, memorizing the features of the girl Lowe had once loved. She bit her lip and turned away. Lowe wouldn't look at her. She sighed. "Ein figured it out, kind of, I said. Not everything. Emphasis on HE forcefully figured it out. But the only way I can control who I melt into … is if he kisses me"

Lowe straightened. "I see." He stared down the hall. Mala gave him a moment to compose himself. He used that moment to melt, shifting calmly back into the smooth, confident adult Lowe.

"Lowe, I did NOT kiss him. He just shoved his face into mine and said he knew what would happen. And he was right. I hate it. But he was."

Lowe looked back at her, then quickly away. "Where does that leave us?"

She put a hand on his. "With a blindfold and a couple months of pent-up frustration to release."

A crooked smile stole over his face. "But … why does it have to be a kiss? When you melted with Tier—there was no kiss. Blut—no kiss. Bara—no kiss."

Mala cocked her head, "He said … something about how it didn't matter what I felt. That I reflect back what other people feel."

Lowe's grin died instantly. "So he feels something for you."

Mala started, "What? No! We fight all the time. We hate each other. He basically told me he had to swallow vomit in order to kiss me."

Lowe shook his head sadly. "Mala … Ein loves to argue. And I don't know what's been going on in your lab sessions. I didn't think that was something I needed to worry about. Honestly, I was more concerned about Verrukter."

"Gag me. Please! They are both equally disgusting. In their own awful ways."

Lowe glanced at her, then away. "Sorry—I still have trouble focusing when you look like that."

"Do you want me to go get some water?" Mala offered.

Lowe sighed and rubbed his chin. "No. I'd rather figure out how you can melt without Ein so that I don't have to add that to the list of things—"

"Answer to your prayers right here," Ein bounded up the hallway, smirking. Behind him trailed a line of hesitant Typical boys. "Line up, guys. Kissing booth is about to open." He turned to Mala. "You look better like that. Maybe you should just stay that way permanently."

Mala narrowed her eyes and Lowe took a step forward.

Ein held up his hands. "Calm down. Joking. Kind of. But I am here to verify that Mala's melts are uniquely controlled by my impressive abilities." He winked at Mala. "So, pucker up, little princess. Let's see what these poor souls willing to sacrifice their lips to herpes can do."

Mala punched him. But even the vision of Ein gasping for breath didn't satisfy her. She turned to Lowe. "You see what you were worried about? Mud-breathing jerkface."

"I agree. But I also think he's right. To test to see if anyone else can make you melt at will. The more people, the better for you. Safer."

Mala's stomach sank to her feet. *Kissing a lineup of strange guys sounds as appealing as licking a raw fish.* But if Lowe agreed with Ein, then she wasn't going to have a choice. *Sludge.* She braced herself as the first, pimple faced Typical approached.

She melted.

Melted again.

And again.

Each time was the same. Once the guy got really into the kiss, she'd back off and stare. The melt would take over. And she'd have no choice. She'd melt into a random girl. Of course, Ein could never be merciful. Several of the men in the lineup were nearly as crusty-looking as Tier. Mala's black wetsuit ripped as her body expanded. After a particularly bad rip across the stomach, she tried to call off the experiment.

As Ein opened his mouth to argue, a door burst open at the far end of the hall. A hulking man hurtled towards the group. He skidded to a stop and turned to Lowe, bowing respectfully. Mala noticed the straight line burned into his hand.

"Sir," he panted. "It's the Erlenders. They just stole four boats."

"When?"

"About an hour ago. Eight Senebals killed. Verloren guard is evacuating their territory. Firefight is too rough. Tier's getting together a meeting right now to discuss our response."

"Response?"

“Classified, sir.”

“Where’s the meeting?” Lowe asked.

“Combat four.”

Without a backward glance, Lowe sprinted down the hall and slammed through a door. Mala and Ein were left with a line of shuffling Typicals.

Mala turned to Ein. “Okay, point proven, muck brain. No one else can help me control my melts. I’ll see you tomorrow.”

“There’s still six more guys in line.”

“We’re done,” Mala didn’t wait for a response. She tied up the sagging remains of her wetsuit so they settled on her hips and marched off. *Well, that could have gone worse. Marginally.* She made her way back to the cafeteria.

She grabbed a cup of water and dunked her hand in. She smiled at the slack jawed serving boy after she’d melted. Then she headed for the food.

Ges entered just as Mala sat down at an empty table. He spotted her and her heaping plate, smiled, and walked over. With a perfunctory bow for the watching eyes, he said, “Wow. You know obese assassins can't really make a quick getaway, right?”

“Ha ha. I haven't eaten all day,” Mala grumbled between mouthfuls of pasta. “What time is it, anyway? I've been locked up in espionage.”

“Oh,” Ges nodded knowingly and sunk down into a chair. “Nine-ish. But it feels like midnight. I swear—they run us ragged.”

Mala gave a sarcastic grunt as she thought, *You, ragged? Ha.*

"Why was today so awful?" she asked before slurping up some pumpkin sauce.

Ges made a face at her table manners. "Well, you know we keep all the data on Kreis—historical, current missions, video feeds, right? So, we also run the stats. And Tier had ordered up this huge project on missions over the past twelve months and we were just finishing up under deadline when video feed of all these attacks came in. Chaos!"

"I heard about those attacks. Four boats, right? But they run raids all the time. So do we. What's the big deal?"

Ges leaned forward. "You can't tell anyone, okay?" His eyes were piercing, intense. He ran a hand through his spiky hair. "I mean it."

"I won't." Mala put down her fork and leaned toward him.

"All four boats were in different places. Far beyond typical radio communication. But they all occurred simultaneously. In one attack, they stole almost a ton of milled flour. They stole felled timber another place. That was quite a feat because we were in the middle of loading it. Stole a ship. But in the last attack, they slaughtered the adults and took the kids with them."

Mala felt like someone had taken a sledgehammer to her stomach. The hair stood up on her arms. She'd just gotten through hours on end of watching this evil. *Now this?* "How? Why?"

Ges shrugged. "We don't know. But their coordination, their strategy, taking the kids ... my guess is they took the kids so we'd focus on getting them back, instead of going after the other supplies. But something's changed. In the past six months, Mala, only twenty-four percent of our missions have been successful. Twenty-four percent. They're killing us. Literally. And we've got no mucking idea."

A shiver ran down Mala's spine. *The Center has the most advanced technology I've ever seen. Even if Ein has to beat its brains in to get it to work.* These gadgets were far superior to the rusted handheld walkie-talkies Bara's guard had used. She'd seen giant guns here that had stands and fired faster than she could blink. Lowe and one of those guns alone could have taken out half of Bara's guard.

The Erlenders were just a group of superstitious heathens. They didn't believe in science, they prayed for miracles. They didn't have this tech. They stole everything they had, from land to water to ships. *How can they be winning? Unless I'm right. Unless their stupid superstitions actually mean something. Damnit, Ein! If that stupid mudbreather hadn't barged in, we'd know. Alba would have melted.* She leaned forward on her elbow. "What do you think is going on?"

"Well—" Ges's answer died and Mala saw him staring fearfully behind her. She turned to see Alba. "I better go," Ges mumbled. He scrambled out of his seat, bowed, and left the cafeteria without even grabbing something to eat.

Mala watched him in astonishment and then turned to Alba, more than a little upset. "Why did you do that?"

"Mala, I ... I think I probably need to explain better. I've seen you with him a lot and I thought you were totally into the research, which is good. And then, with, you know … the other stuff. I knew he was helping you with that, too. But, I just should have explained that Kreis and Typicals don't usually hang out."

Immediately Mala stiffened. "You didn't seem to have a problem with that yesterday, when he was helping me research the ceremony."

Alba bit her lip. "I was desperate. It was wrong. I shouldn't have done that. I think I confused you. And that's dangerous."

"How? What is so wrong about me and Ges being friends?"

Alba looked uncomfortable. "Well yeah but ... I can't …we're like the elite. They're ... more like servants. I mean, assistants. They help us ... they aren't, maybe I should put it another way: we're active-duty Kreis. We're supposed to focus on training. We aren't supposed to get attached. So you shouldn't be gossiping with him. And he should know better."

"What is this really about?" Mala couldn't believe what she was hearing. *What's the matter with her?* "Neid hangs around a whole group of them."

"Yeah well, Neid's a little boyfriend-stealing tramp with bad habits. Habits she's gonna have to break if she ever wants—" Alba stopped herself from getting into a bitter tirade. "Nevermind. Off topic. Honey, look. I'm just saying this because I'm supposed to tell you what I can." She stared intently at Mala.

"Well thanks," Mala said. "Great advice. Excuse me if I don't take it."

"Whoa! Don't get mad at me. Go ahead and hang out. Whatever. It's not my funeral. But I hadn't ever told you and like I said it's kinda my job. But clearly I stink at my job because everything I do just turns to sludge, so hey, get mad at me. Not like you're the first today or yesterday or every damn day I'm stuck in this mucked up old body!" Alba's tone got progressively louder and more incomprehensible as tears welled up. Finally she could hold it in no longer and a sob burst out. She rushed away from Mala towards the door.

Mala sighed. She sat uncertainly for a moment, torn between guilt and gnawing hunger. *Well, I won't be able to help her if I pass out*, she rationalized, and finished her meal before heading down to the Costume Shop.

She knocked hesitantly at the door, shifting her feet and second-guessing whether Alba would have gone back to their hut. But before she could turn to leave, one of the tailors opened the door. He looked at Mala for a moment, weighed her expression, and then he slid aside and allowed her into the cave of clothes.

Alba's sobbing made her easy to find. She was perched in the jewelry section in front of a small circular mirror, trying on earrings even as tears dripped down the rivulets of her wrinkled cheeks. She saw Mala's reflection and stiffened. She didn't turn around.

"I'm sorry I got upset with you," Mala said. "I am not very good at ... well at much. And Ges's been really nice to me and you have, too and I just ... I'm sorry." She stopped awkwardly, not knowing if she should say anything about melting, or if that would just make Alba cry more. Part of her wished someone else would come along and break the tension. But all the old men vanished.

Alba tried on a pair of thirty-four caliber bullet studs before replying. “It’s alright.”

Mala stood for a second, shifting from foot to foot then decided her nervous energy was making things more awkward. She sat on a stepstool nearby. “So, wanna tell me what’s going on with you?” Once she’d said it, she didn’t know if she’d gone too far. “Of course, you don’t have to. I can tell you all about my day in lockup without anything to eat trying to figure out how to lip-read silent film and not pass out from starvation because no one in this place seems to prioritize food ...”

Alba just smiled sadly and picked up a box of necklaces. She started to untangle them one by one. “I’ve always been the best. Literally. My recruiter is like my mentor and he’s always helped me with everything ... he gave me tricks and tips and he was there for my first mission, my first kill ... now he’s on this mission and he’s been gone for months. Then *this* happens and I can’t fix it. Nothing can fix it. And I’m useless. And so now it’s like, was I ever really any good? Or was it all him? And now, they want me to try shock therapy. These medics came today while I was working in the cafeteria. They think they need to jolt my brain or something.” She tugged at a knot of gold chain futilely, her eyes too full of tears to focus.

Mala took a deep breath. “As in, electricity?”

Alba nodded. “They think my brain patterns have shifted or something ... depression they said. And they want to try and reverse it.”

Mala didn't say what she wanted to say. *Wouldn't it kill you?* Instead she asked, “What’s the success rate?”

"Seventy percent," Alba replied gloomily. "Probably not high enough. And if they do it, I could get amnesia. Like, I could literally not even remember Verrukter's name. Maybe that's not such a bad thing. But if I don't ... a guy like that will never look at me again. I'm broken."

Mala inhaled and attempted her first motivational speech. "Alba, you are not broken. You got three kills, right? I think you just have a mental block going, that's all. You know, I used to jump in the water and swim away whenever my mom was operating? My mom would be stitching someone up and need my help and I couldn't stand to see them scream so I would just jump off the boat. And now supposedly they're teaching me to stand there and kill someone instead. Who looks like the worst possible Kreis candidate ever? You or me?"

Reluctantly, Alba grinned. "Did you really jump off the boat?"

Mala nodded. "They all thought I was psychotic or something. I thought I was. I'd be standing there, handing bandages to my mom and I would just hit this wall. Then splash. I was gone."

Alba's fingers fumbled with the necklaces and Mala held out a hand to take them. She took a breath before tackling the tangled gold wire. "The people in the guard hated me. But I didn't know what this melt thing was. And I couldn't stand it—the feeling right before you melt. So I'd go swimming for a couple hours and just hope the person didn't die."

Alba rubbed her cheeks and swiped at her eyes. "When I used to melt—before I was recruited, back home—I'd run and hide in the woods. My auntie thought I was trying to avoid chores." Alba half-smiled at the memory. "She made me scrub all the fish guts off the boat deck every time it happened."

Mala smiled and gazed down at the ball of knotted necklaces. She was about to respond to Alba when one of the tokens caught her eye. It was a small square of gold, hammered with a series of Xs. She stared at it. Then her fingers started working it loose. Soon she had separated the tiny chain and pendant. She stared, her thoughts abuzz.

This looks so familiar—why? Nobody wears gold anymore. Where have I seen this? Her skin grew cold. She wasn't sure why. Mala freed the caged memories buzzing in the back of her head and a series of scattered images flashed in her mind's eye. Her mother and the dresses. Sorgen looking to her as he died. Bara's fire. Blut lunging at her with the knife. But nothing tied those images to the necklace. Yet she couldn't shake the feeling she had seen it ...

"Hello, are you there? Come back, Mala. Come back!" Alba called, waving her hand in Mala's face.

Mala turned to her, voice laced with urgency. "Have you ever seen this necklace before?"

"No idea. They have so many, I don't even know ... want me to get someone? " Alba asked, confused by the sudden fixation.

"Yes, please." She stared at the little golden Xs, burning their image into her head, unable to shake the haunted mist swirling in the pit of her stomach.

Soon Alba reappeared with a short little man who wore spectacles that made his eyes appear twice their normal size. "This is Gilden. He makes most of the jewelry in here."

Silently, Mala held the necklace out for him. He took it and held it above his face, close to his eyes. "Ah, yes. This is a marker."

"What's that?" Alba tilted her head so she could see the pattern better.

"It's an Erlender piece. They used to use it about twenty years back. To mark their targets," the last word came out with a spray of spit. Gilden looked disgusted at the thought. Alba just looked shocked. Her expression reminded Mala of something ...

Slowly, Mala reached for the piece. She stared at the little square as it twisted in midair before her ...

She saw Blut's body. And she remembered Lowe rifling through his pockets, throwing things aside. Throwing a necklace at her. She stared again at the little charm. *Could it be the same thing?* She reviewed the memory. Her jaw clenched.

"I need to go see Lowe." She stood, reached for the necklace and tucked it safely into her palm.

He wasn't after Lowe. And he didn't just see me melt on the water. This was the necklace he pulled off Sari. Before that. Blut cut into her face. Kiss, cut, kiss. Blut was there that night hunting Kreis.

CHAPTER TWENTY-FOUR

"Focus!" Verrukter bellowed in her face. He'd managed to land three punches in a row. Mala couldn't control herself in her gangly new body, which she'd acquired courtesy of a smirking, chap-lipped Ein, who stood on the sidelines during her latest combat practice. Having Ein there was distracting enough. Trying to fight in different bodies was nearly impossible. But, to top everything off, Lowe hadn't said a word when she'd found him at his hut last night and handed him the necklace.

He'd listened to her. But he hadn't said a word. *Did he believe me?* Lowe had simply covered her eyes, kissed her gently, and strode off to a sub, disappearing down into the lake. Mala had waited for him on the platform outside his hut, shivering despite the black bear cloak she'd been issued for winter. She'd watched the ice on the far side of the lake crack, and frost flowers bloom in the winter air. They'd looked like the hands of some lake monster rising from the depths.

Lowe hadn't come back. She hadn't seen him this morning. *Where did he go? Did he bring it to the Ancients? Why was Blut looking for Kreis? Why did he think that Sari was Kreis? Was he there to recruit them to the Erlender side*—Ouch!

A kick to her kidney brought Mala back to the present. She fell to her knees. Her vision blurred. She felt like she might vomit.

"Get up," Verrukter demanded.

Mala held up a hand in protest.

"Pathetic, isn't she?" Ein quipped to Verrukter. "Tier and I are always discussing how she can't make the cut. Would be better to put her out of her misery and—"

Mala swallowed the pain. She let out a howl as she tried to bowl Ein over. But Verrukter was too fast. He intercepted her and pinned her hands behind her back. She kicked him, and her male body (Mala couldn't even remember who she looked like at the moment) proved effective for once. Verrukter swallowed a yelp. Mala pressed her advantage and stomped his instep. Once he'd released one of her hands she smashed the flat of her palm furiously into his nose.

Verrukter let go. And she stepped around him. She did not let herself wince despite the fact that she felt like a hook was yanking her insides out through her spine. Instead she marched over to Ein, angry to find he was still taller than her.

"You do NOT get to decide if I make the cut," she growled. "Your job is over. You're just a pair of lips. That's all."

"Oh really?" Ein smirked. He pointed at Verrukter, who stood to one side of the practice mat, holding his nose. "Did I not just motivate you to kick his ass?"

Mala glared at him as the realization clicked into place. *He pushed my buttons.* "I hate you."

"Your clever remarks really cut deep, Mala," Ein laughed and stepped back as she swiped at him. Before she could move again, she felt ice-cold water splash her face.

She melted. And for the fifth time that day, she felt eternal gratitude toward the little old men at the Costume Shop. Alba had managed to smuggle her a pair of holey spandex shorts, a bra, and a very large t-shirt. The spandex was pushing its limits after all of her melts, but she had yet to flash anyone today.

"You know, I'm getting tired of this," Mala sighed. "You don't have to splash my face—"

Ein shut her up with a kiss. Jerk though he was, he'd at least badgered the cook for mint leaves so that his kisses were not completely unpleasant. Mala hated that he'd thought to do that. Because when he grabbed her and held her up against him, cradled her with his arms, all that rage she felt turned suddenly into a different kind of smolder. Worse, a tiny part of her felt safe in his massive arms. *Which is not the case, idiot. Clearly he's going behind your back to get you thrown out of here.* Her heart scoffed at her head's logic. *If that was really the case, how could he still make me melt? No, deep down, he feels something. Braniac's just never gotten past the pull-the-pigtails phase.* When her head and heart warred like that Mala often found herself lost. In this case, lost in the kiss.

A male voice jolted her back to reality. "That's enough, Ein." Lowe's command boomed across the room.

Mala dropped her hands from Ein's brown hair, and didn't even look into Ein's eyes to finish the melt. She swiveled immediately to look at Lowe, pressing on Ein's arms so that he'd drop her.

"Now you've made her miss a melt," Ein groaned. "I'm gonna have to kiss her again." And though Ein's tone was horrified, his grin was wider than the river's mouth.

Lowe's expression was dark. He approached Mala and grabbed her hand. She leaned into him.

"So, you don't kiss him back, huh?" Lowe raised an eyebrow.

Mala wasn't sure what the right answer was. She wasn't sure if there was an answer that wouldn't get her in trouble. Her eyes searched Lowe's face for a hint of compassion. "I … We've been at this all day, fighting and melting. I'm sorry." She sighed. "I wish you'd walked in five seconds earlier, when I'd told him I hated his guts."

"Five seconds?" Verrukter quipped. "Try five minutes! You were making out so long I thought I might go grab something to eat."

Mala stuck her tongue out at him. He winked. "Anytime you want to stick that in my mouth you're welcome to."

Mala turned back to Lowe. "Do you see what I've been dealing with all day? The two of them … it's insane. And then they're beating me to death on top of it. Help me." She jutted out her lower lip.

Lowe rolled his eyes, but he grinned and pulled her into him. Mala noticed Ein stiffen slightly. "That," Lowe smiled, "is exactly what I'm here to do." He turned Mala to face the doorway.

Haloed in light from the hallway, Fell pushed away from the doorjamb and made her way toward Mala. Her chocolate skin contrasted beautifully against a violet wetsuit. She glanced at Verrukter, then jerked her head once toward the door. It didn't take a second gesture; Verrukter scurried off like an ant avoiding a shoe.

Fell stopped a few feet away, calmly appraising Ein. "You know the rumors, I suppose?" Ein bit his lip. For the first time since Mala had known him, he looked slightly cowed. But Mala didn't have more than a second to gloat before Fell continued. "Tier's saying she's useless. Shackled to a Typical who can't transform. Who can't fight. All it's going to take is one Erlender to recognize you and she's blown. Tier's saying I backed a loser, that my judgement's bad."

Fell took a step closer to Ein. "You are going to correct that inaccurate opinion." Her gaze pummeled him. The only sound in the room was wheeze of the air vents.

"How?" Ein breathed.

"You have two options. Teach her how to control her melts with different people … or you get to sign up for combat and the Costume Shop."

Mala's eyes flicked between the two of them as Ein weighed his options.

"Can I speak with you privately?" he finally choked out.

Fell jerked her head toward the door. Lowe grabbed Mala's arm and marched her out.

"But, why can't I stay in there? Why don't I get a say in this? This is about *my* melts!" Mala exclaimed. *Why does Ein get the choice? What if I don't want him to do the combat-and-disguises sludge?*

Lowe leaned against the wall. "Mala… you need to understand. From now on nothing is solely about you."

Mala shut her mouth. *Don't be a baby,* she scolded internally. *Of course it's not just about me. But it is my life. And what if I don't want …* she couldn't finish the thought. She wasn't sure what she wanted. Did she want Ein out in the field with her? *Sure, he's a technological god here, bu t…* she tried to picture him on her mother's boat. *Would he survive in the wild? Do I care?* Her confusion was interrupted.

Fell stood in the doorway. Ein hung back, eyes downcast. Mala felt a moment of panic. Her eyes flickered between the two of them. Fell watched her, only the slightest tilt of her head indicating interest in Mala's reaction. "I have come to a decision."

Lowe straightened. Mala followed suit, and tried to keep her eyes from straying to Ein, trying to figure out what the decision was.

"Ein will begin combat practice immediately," Fell said. "Lowe, you will train him. This will all be classified as confidential."

Lowe couldn't keep the shock off his face. "Is that safest for Mala?"

Fell just raised her eyebrow.

Lowe stuttered, "I mean, yes ma'am." And though his tone remained flat and professional, a wild glint came into his eyes as he suggested to Ein, "Why don't we get started?"

Ein scrambled backward. His face went as white as a kid

fallen overboard. "What? Right now? Are we sure this is …" he trailed off at the look on Fell's face. "Like I said—I can just help Mala melt and then stay hidden while she does her thing."

Lowe cocked his head. "And what if Mala's out 'doing her thing' and someone's crying their eyes out? What if she bumps into someone who happens to be pissed? *Anyone* could make her melt. No, I think you're going to need to be by her side every step of the way—just in case." Lowe cracked his knuckles deliberately, one by one. "I'm happy to help get you ready for such an experience."

Ein skittered across the practice mat. Lowe smiled, but didn't pursue him. Instead, he turned to Mala and caressed her cheek. "Why don't you take rest of the morning off? Your partner has a lot of training to catch up on."

"Are you sure you don't need my help?" *I really want to see this,* her eyes begged.

"Next time."

Mala gave Ein a little wink. "Don't be so scared. I'm sure your big brain will keep you safe."

Fell pulled a chain and the garage door to the combat room rolled shut with a clang. She turned to Mala. "I know he's put you through the wringer. But I wouldn't be too hard on him. You and Ein are partners now, for better or worse." She swept away, a purple wave gliding down the hall.

Bursting with news, Mala made her way to the archive. It had rapidly become her favorite retreat since she'd started at the Center. Not only because Ges was there, but because all of the archive workers had grown more friendly as she'd spent time there. It was a great place to catch up on gossip, and she couldn't wait to tell Ges everything.

But when she got to the archive, her smile dimmed. She sensed tension in the air. Everyone was working, green wetsuits moving methodically from shelf to desk and back, but they were plodding. They were slow. No one was catapulting off the sides of the balcony. No one was smiling.

Mala made her way to Ges's usual haunt, over by the computers. He wasn't there. One of the archivists told her she needed to look for him in the painting room.

She climbed a ladder and found Ges alone on a rare open stretch of floor, one not crowded by books or tables or scrolls. He was crouching in front of a series of canvases unrolled on the floor in a circle around his feet. Mala waved, and while he smiled to see her, the smile quickly gave way to a frown.

"Hey, what's going on? Why's everyone so upset?"

Ges stared at her a long moment. He opened his mouth, closed it again, and sighed. "There's a funeral today. One of the archivists, Gluck, died yesterday."

"I'm so sorry," Mala touched his hand. "Is there anything I can do? Do you want me to go with you?"

Ges's face flushed, making his freckles pop more than usual. "Oh, no. You better not. I mean, I'll be alright."

"What? Why not? I mean, I didn't know Gluck, but I know what it's like to lose someone." She swallowed a lump in her throat as her mom's face came to mind. "I'm happy to go support you."

"Thanks. But … it's a Typical thing."

"Oh, got it." Mala still didn't fully understand the Kreis-Typical divide, but she stepped back to give Ges some space. "Do you want me to go?"

"No don't go. I'm sorry. The funeral's not for an hour," Ges responded. "Want to help me try to categorize these pictures?"

Mala turned back. "Sure, I guess. I don't know if I'll be much help."

"Well, you've seen more of the river than I have," Ges joked. "Maybe you can at least help me identify locations."

"Ok," Mala agreed, and she stepped over a painting, into the ring Ges had made for himself. He picked up a notebook and a pen. "Am I allowed to know what these are?"

"King Troe commissions them. Erlenders don't have as much access to video or old tech as we do, since one of our raids destroyed their bunker about thirty years ago. And because they don't have your favorite person, Ein, on their side. Troe uses these for reconnaissance. Planning. Some advisors called chiaras are sent out. They paint or draw different locales. You can see how many of them are quick - brush strokes sloppy and stuff. And they're not beautiful or anything. Sometimes they have people. Sometimes they don't. But, it's always good to get into your enemy's head. So we try and think of it that way. Seeing what he sees. Documenting the areas he's interested in so we can be sure to defend them adequately."

Mala looked at each painting in turn. Most were simply of bends in the river, strategic positions that she could see the king would want. But the last one was a beautifully detailed painting.

Tiny daubs of yellow paint kissed the canvas, imitating the falling leaves of tamarack trees. Quick brush strokes showed a solitary boat on the lake. Mala couldn't be sure if she was projecting, but she swore the profile looked exactly like Bara's boat.

Tears gathered in her eyes, despite herself. She bit her lip and pointed at the painting, that looked like nothing more than a study of fall leaves. "There. That one's off the Vers tributary. Northeast of Sonne Pointe. Maybe five kilometers. I'm not exactly sure."

"Awesome! Nobody knew that one here," Ges bent his spiky head of hair and scribbled into his notebook.

Mala turned to stare at another painting, not wanting the wound to open up any further. She swiped at a tear.

Ges glanced up. "What is it?"

"That's where, you know … the attack," Mala couldn't finish her sentence. She took a deep calming breath.

"Hey, I'm sorry. Do you want to go somewhere else?" Ges asked.

Mala shook her head. "No. I'm good. Just have to distract myself. I actually came to tell you some good news. Lowe's giving Ein his first combat practice as we speak."

Ges's jaw dropped. He looked scandalized. "No!"

Mala smiled. *That was exactly the reaction I needed.* "Oh yes. Since Ein has to help me melt, he has to be prepared for the consequences of the real world."

"More like the consequences of a jealous boyfriend."

Mala shrugged. "Maybe both."

"I can't believe you'd let Lowe do that. Now who am I gonna stare at? You've seen the other guys here. Hideous. Mala, couldn't you have held him off? Why didn't you think of me for once?"

"Sorry. With Ein, I only ever think about revenge." *And kissing,* a snickering little voice in the back of her mind said.

"Oh my gosh!" Ges dropped his notebook and grabbed her arms. He stared into her face. "No. Oh my gosh! You do—you like him!"

Mala shrugged him off. "Ew. Not even close. We hate each other. He tries to make my life as miserable as possible. So when the opportunity comes to retaliate—I take it."

Ges raised an eyebrow.

Mala held up her hands in protest. "I don't. Ein's a big smelly fish-head." *Even if his kissing is semi-adequate, the rest of him most definitely is not. And I don't know why Fell is making us partner up.* Seeing that Ges wasn't going to drop the topic, she decided to change it. And a flash of inspiration came to her.

"Hey, so I don't know how important these paintings are or anything. I don't even know if the ones I saw are still there. But there was this abandoned mansion near the merge of the Vers trib and the Gottermund. West bank side. Anyway, there was a whole stack of paintings there if you want it. Found a gun there, too, so that would make sense. I mean, if the Erlender King is sending out scouts for attacks."

"You're trying to change the subject."

"Yes."

"Because you're uncomfortable."

"No," Mala scoffed.

"Because it's true!" Ges crowed.

"You know what? I better go check on Alba. I think she and I were supposed to meet up for a mediation session," she lied. "Good luck with this," she gestured at the paintings.

"Good luck with your little love triangle!" Ges called out as she descended the ladder.

Mala almost fell. *Sludge! Did he have to announce that to the world?* She flipped him off before her head disappeared beneath the ledge.

CHAPTER TWENTY-FIVE

Mala made her way to the Costume Shop. To her surprise, the door was locked and it looked like the lights were off. *Maybe they closed for the funeral?* Mala wandered back to the elevator.

Not quite sure where else in the vast complex to look for Alba, Mala decided to head for the surface and take a quick nap in her cold hut, before heading to a lecture on explosives. *It'll be like icing these bruises.* She tried to convince herself that would be a good thing.

When she'd successfully docked the sub after her third try, she walked onto the floating platform only to run smack into her roommate.

"Alba!" Mala grabbed the tall old lady, who was wearing a rumpled fuchsia wetsuit and smeared lipstick. "Sorry! Are you okay?"

Alba gave her a glazed glance, then pitched forward and puked right next to Mala's feet.

"Ew! Alba! Over the water, please!" Witz, a pock-faced teenage Kreis called out. His friends snickered.

A large cluster of Kreis sat in a circle on the main platform.

They were wrapped in fur cloaks and a rainbow of blankets. Two empty jugs sat nearby.

"Want to join the party?" Witz grinned at Mala.

"Party for what?"

"Beispiel passed his final test. He is now mission-bound and should be back with a kill in thirty-six hours."

"If he comes back," Alba muttered as she curled up in a ball on the icy platform.

"What's that supposed to mean?" Witz responded. He looked too drunk to be truly offended. He seemed more the chatty, philosophical type.

"Durch's recruits only have like a thirty-percent success rate. He's not a good picker. Teacher. Whatever." Alba draped an arm dramatically over her face to block out the sun.

"Do you want me to take you back to the hut?" Mala offered. *I hope she's done puking. She's lying awfully close to the puke. One big wave and ...* "Here, let me help you up." She grabbed Alba's arm but the girl whined in protest.

"No!"

"You know Alba, it's not like people get to pick their recruiter. Why can't you just wish him the best?" Hecken, a Kreis girl Mala had sparred with a few times, called out.

"I'm just being realistic," Alba hiccupped from the platform.

"You're just being negative." Hecken flipped her hair and turned away.

But another drunk Kreis took up the argument before Mala could haul Alba away. Mala didn't know this guy's name, she'd never done more than nod at him in the halls.

"Not all of us could have the best recruiter at the Center holding our hand during our first mission, Alba."

"He didn't hold my hand."

"Not what I heard." The Kreis crossed his arms. "I heard he practically pulled the trigger for you, you were so scared."

Alba balled her hands into fists and weakly shook one at him. "You're lucky I'm drunk."

"What would you do?" he scoffed. "Besides, your recruiter isn't here. In fact, he hasn't come home from his own mission. How long's it been? Five months? That's a long time. I wonder if they've started looking for a body."

This brought Alba to her knees, which was as close as she could get to standing, with the pitch and sway of the platform. "Shut UP!" Spit sprayed from her mouth as she faced her attacker. "Don't say that. Don't—don't don't say that!" A tear dropped onto her cheek.

Mala grabbed Alba's arm to support her. She saw the old woman's face start to ripple. But Alba took a deep breath and the moment passed.

After so many years of practice, does it become second nature to stop a melt? I wonder if she even knows she's doing it. Why didn't she push it more? Try to melt? Maybe she's too drunk to realize ...

Mala had lost the flow of the conversation and had to tune back into the argument.

"You don't know anything!" another Kreis yelled at Alba.

"Look at you—without him, you're nothing."

"I know he's the best recruiter the Center ever had!" Alba shouted back.

One of her debaters decided to stand and raise the stakes. Before things could get drunkenly physical on a swaying platform in the middle of an ice-cold lake, Mala hauled Alba to her feet.

"Ok, time to go for a rest," Mala stated. "We're leaving." She draped Alba's arm over her shoulder and walked toward the narrow gangway that led to their hut. It was a challenge to drag Alba's semi limp form over the slick planks. But she managed.

"I love you Mala," Alba slurred as Mala helped her into her pallet. Alba grabbed her hand. "I mean it. I love you. You're the best roommate ever."

"Thanks," Mala patted her arm and tried to scoot back. The scent of vomit still radiated from Alba's mouth. "I love you too."

"They're stupid!" Alba muttered.

"Yup," Mala tried to appease the girl as she eased her stiff muscles onto her own pallet.

"You're not."

"Nope."

"They shoulda never said those things about Blut."

Cold flooded Mala's heart. "What?" *No. You heard wrong. You're hearing things. That's not what's going on. This is an episode. This is craziness. You're making things up. She's drunk. She didn't say that name.*

Alba muttered into her pillow, "He's the best recruiter. He always has been. They're just jealous. Did you know, he even gave me this two-way radio after my first mission? So we could talk you know. When we're apart. We used to talk every night. But he hasn't been on in a long time. And now they're gonna electroshock me. Tier came by. They're gonna fry my brain to fix it. I wish he was here. He'd fix me. I wish …"

"Alba," Mala breathed. "Who did you say your recruiter was?"

But a loud snore was her only answer.

CHAPTER TWENTY-SIX

Mala stood in a hallway at the end of the line waiting to be admitted to the explosives lecture. Instead of watching the fish go by or watching the subs rise and fall in the water like silver balloons, she stared at the floor. She twisted her hands together as her mind ran over Alba's revelation. *Do I tell her?*

A tap on her shoulder interrupted her train of thought as she weighed the pros and cons for the millionth time. She looked up to see a freshly showered Lowe smiling down at her.

"Hi."

His grin was magnetic; she couldn't help smiling in response. "Finish the combat lesson?" She raised her eyebrows.

"Yup."

"How was it?"

"Almost satisfying."

"Almost?"

"Well, a victory dance wouldn't have been professional."

Mala laughed. "You can do one now."

He swept her into his arms. "I was hoping you'd say that." He spun her out and back in for a dip. And then Lowe started doing the most ridiculous chicken-like kick-and-karate-chop dance moves Mala had ever seen. She doubled up in laughter.

"Feel better?"

"Fully satisfied," Lowe winked.

"Good." She sighed. "Because my ribs hurt. I don't know how much more dancing I could stand."

"None," a solemn voice replied from behind her.

Mala stiffened and turned. There, like a shadow materializing out of thin air, was Fell, her afro haloing her head like a crown. The queue shifted; so that those nearest them shuffled into a semi-circle of onlookers.

Mala was speechless. Since her first combat practice, the only time she'd seen Fell was this morning. And now she'd appeared twice within one day. *What does this mean?*

Fell didn't answer her unspoken question. "Come with me. Both of you." Her glance flicked toward Lowe as she turned and strode solemnly down the hall. People scattered like fish before her, ducking into the safety of alcoves and halls.

Mala swallowed the lump in her throat and followed. Lowe trailed at her heels.

Fell pushed on a wall panel, and it slid away to reveal a brass elevator. She stepped inside and Mala and Lowe had no choice but to follow. In the middle of the elevator were several ropes on pulleys.

"We need to go up four floors," Fell said as she pulled the elevator grille shut. "I'll tell you when we get there." She didn't look directly at either of them, but Mala could feel anger rolling off of her in waves.

Mala bit her lip and looked at Lowe. *I've got no clue how to work this thing,* she tried to communicate with her gaze. She didn't want to make Fell even more angry.

Luckily, Lowe didn't seem too lost. He gestured to one of the ropes and grabbed its neighbor. They pulled. It was hard work. Mala had to throw her entire body weight into it. She was cursing Verrukter and his punches by the time Fell gestured for them to stop. Mala secured her rope and turned to face the door.

The grate opened with a metallic screech that sent shivers down Mala's spine. They emerged in a hallway that was padded with deep blue carpet. Mala's feet were in awe as she walked down the hall. *I've never felt anything this soft. I could sleep on this.*

They came to a tall wooden door. Fell stopped just outside and turned to face them.

"Once we step in here, everything you see, hear, touch … is classified. You will never speak of it again to anyone who is not in this room. You will never speak of it to anyone in this room without being one-hundred-percent certain no one else can hear you. Understood?"

Mala's heart thrummed excitedly. She swallowed hard, and nodded. Fell took out a key and unlocked the door.

The room was nothing short of opulent. A chandelier cascaded from the ceiling, giving the appearance of water droplets frozen and suspended in midair. A rich mahogany table and tall velvet-backed chairs took up the majority of the floor space. As Lowe pulled out a chair for her Mala noticed the red velvet had molted with age, leaving bald pink patches. He sat next to her, in the chair closest to the door, while Fell walked to the head of the table.

Mala glanced around. She bit back shock when she realized Ein was there, with a tissue tucked into his bruised nose. Neid sat next to him. His blond sister shot glares at Mala and Lowe. Mala turned her head away. That's when she saw Tier.

Dressed in Erlender leather from head to toe, including a skullcap, he'd melted to a younger age—he looked around thirty. Dusty brown hair peeked out from under his cap. Mala only recognized him from his expression: the sour look he wore when he watched her work with Ein was marring his features.

"You have been selected for a mission."

Neid gave an excited squeak and quickly smashed her lips shut in an attempt to recover her composure.

Unlike Neid, Mala's blood stopped at the thought. *He can't be serious? I've only been here a couple months. I'm not ready for this. He knows I'm not. Ein literally just started training two hours ago ... Oh.* She turned to evaluate his face. *Maybe that's why I'm here: Tier wants me out of the picture.*

She couldn't read anything in Tier's expression. So she turned to Fell.

Fell wouldn't let him just throw me to the wolves, right? She's my champion—or whatever. It would look bad for her. But she's pissed. So what does that mean? Mala had never really interacted with Fell. She didn't know the woman's true intentions. *And what choice do I have, anyway?* she grumbled internally. *It's not like I'm going to refuse to go.*

Only Ein looked as shocked as she did. For the second time that day, his face drained of color. This time, Mala's stomach twisted in pity, not delight. *He's not ready.* He hadn't asked for this. *He's never even left the Center.*

Tier unrolled a scroll. It was a map of the Gottermund River. Red dots marred the map in a multitude of places.

"This is a map of recent attacks. Most of them have been made well inside our territory, meaning the Erlenders have figured out how to slither past our border guards." Tier ran his finger to each of the red dots in turn. "I'm sure you've heard unauthorized rumors that the Erlenders are beating us. This is true. And this is where you come in: the President wants intelligence. He wants action. He wants something done now. You all are going to find out what the Erlenders are doing, how they keep getting ahead of us."

Mala's stomach dropped. *This does not sound like a quick in-and-out assignment. I thought a first mission was supposed to be quick.* She glanced at the others. Now Neid's face mirrored Ein's; she looked sick. Mala had to count her breaths to get the panic to recede.

"Oh now, no need to vomit," Fell interjected, seeing the dread on every face but Lowe's. "The President has decided we need to use Mala's skills to our advantage." Fell's glare at Tier told everyone in the room exactly how the President had learned about and decided to use Mala.

"You have two objectives: first, see what the Erlenders are up to. They aren't going on more raids for no reason. But we haven't been able to find out why. What's their goal? What's their next target? How are they getting past us?

King Troe is a shut in. Paranoid—and for good reason, after Sich seduced and assassinated his father. We need Mala to go in looking like someone he trusts. We need you guys to find out his next move."

Reconnaissance, Mala thought. *We can do that. Right?* Her heart wasn't sure. It tried to run out of her chest, thumping hard against her ribs, like a prisoner held against its will. Mala looked back at Fell.

"We think …" Fell glanced at Tier and then back at the group before continuing. "We think there must be a mole here. Someone feeding the Erlenders information. Helping them. Lowe, this is assigned to you. Find out who the mole is. Whatever it takes, figure out who they're working with. Figure out which Erlender is coordinating this. Find the web. Trace it to the source. And kill them. All."

Mala's heart constricted. But Lowe only nodded solemnly, his face an unreadable mask.

Fell turned to the opposite side of the table. "It's nearly time to pay the piper. Each year, every Erlender town's General visits the King. Tax and tribute time." She tossed a scroll at Mala, who unrolled it to find a series of illegible scribbles dancing across the page. "That's the tax list issued by King Troe, typically paid in the form of food, weapons, and slaves. Mala, you will pay the taxes for Wilde this year, posing as Wilde's General Keptiker. I know that after what they did to your guard, revenge is going to be the first thing that comes to mind. But Keptiker is the King's cousin. More likely to be trusted." Fell leaned forward and her gaze speared Mala. "You will resist the temptation to give in to revenge. We need you to find out Troe's next move—moves if possible. Ein will pose as one of your guards so you have access to him. Lowe—you'll be a cupbearer; gain access to the kitchens, servant quarters, gossip. Neid, you're a slave paid for taxes; see what whispers are alive in the dungeons."

Tier took up the explanation. "Lowe, you also need to prepare to distract Troe from Mala in case she has any trouble in Keptiker's role."

So much for the vote of confidence. He obviously thinks I'm not ready for this. Why the muck toss me in, then?

Tier continued. "Neid, we'll have an extraction team ready for you if the old mud-breather decides on sacrifice. But our intel says Troe is currently showing a penchant for breaking slaves, particularly the pretty ones. The last human sacrifice was four years ago."

Mala glanced at Neid's face. The other girl raised her eyebrows but kept her mouth shut. Her expression clearly stated she didn't like idea of human sacrifice. *I wouldn't, either.*

"Ein," Tier grinned, "to quote your charge here, 'You're just a pair of lips.' Don't get in the way." He stood, causing everyone else to rise and stand at attention. "Okay, that about sums it up. You have two weeks to research and prep. Mala, you are to melt into General Keptiker and stay in his form. Any other questions?"

Mala had a million questions buzzing in her head, battling with the butterflies flittering through her stomach. But it was Lowe who spoke.

"What's the expected timeframe at the King's bunker?"

Tier raised an eyebrow. "Once you arrive, three days. But you'll have to infiltrate Wilde, kill Keptiker, and replace him with Mala before that. We estimate a week total. So get moving." He gestured to Fell. The two of them left the room without another sound.

Silently, everyone sank back into their seats.

Neid was the first to speak. "Did that really just happen?"

Lowe nodded. "Well, let's talk assignments. Ein, I want you get ahold of any maps or videos of the King's compound. Figure out at least forty exit strategies. It's complicated because of the rubble moat he built, blowing up all those buildings around his compound. There are mountains of rubble outside that place. There's no way we're depending on an extraction team alone. Neid, you'd better research the King's … preferences. For slaves and their training. Figure out his weaknesses, figure out how to stroke his ego. You'll need both." He didn't say "to survive," but those words hung in the air, unspoken and sour.

Lowe turned his blue eyes solemnly to Mala. His face was stern, jaw tight. Mala could read the fear in his expression. "Mala, you need to melt. You have four days with Ges, getting in the General's head. Then Verrukter will take over. And you will learn to fight like him."

Mala sat back in her chair and ran her fingers through her hair, overwhelmed. "I still don't understand why they're giving us this assignment. No offense Neid, but you and I don't rank high enough for this."

There was a moment of silence. It was Ein, rather than Lowe who responded. "The President's desperate. Too many high-visibility raids. That one with the kids that nobody wants to mention. It's pretty public. And Tier, though he'd love to get rid of us, is also somewhat practical. Of the Kreis available, most have gone on over four missions. That gives them a forty-eight-percent chance of being recognized by someone the moment they step into Troe's compound because he rotates his staff through different villages. Paranoia—doesn't want anyone there too long. Tier and Fell want better odds."

Everyone turned to stare. Ein steepled his fingers, relaxing into lecture mode. "Neid's highly trained, even if she hasn't been on a mission. She's got years of combat, weapons, and espionage to support her. And a new face. Even it breaks protocol. They've been itching to use Mala since she stepped onto a sub. I'm included by default here obviously. And Lowe … I'm guessing Fell chose you because you'll do anything to ensure Mala survives."

"Not that I happen to be good at what I do or anything," Lowe smirked.

Ein cocked his head. "If you were as good of a spy as you think you are, you would have already recognized the most likely possible mole."

Lowe's eyes blazed. "Oh really? Who?"

"It's obvious. Which Kreis has managed to stay here for months on end, creating the perfect situation for ferreting out information? No guesses? Ok, this Kreis has a very special relationship with a Kreis who's officially gone missing."

"There are like six of those," Lowe shot back.

Ein rolled his eyes. "Ok. This Kreis used to be the very pinnacle of training but recently has *withered …*"

A warning buzz sounded in the back of Mala's brain. Something Ein said triggered a realization, but she was still too overwhelmed by the thought of impending death to sort through his words.

"Oh come on, that clue was obvious. Remind me never to pick any of you as partners on game night. *If* we survive long enough to see one."

It was Neid who ultimately answered. Her rosy lips dropped in surprise when she connected the dots. "Are you saying it's Alba?"

Holy mucking shit. Mala's brain clicked into overdrive. *All those times she almost melted. She wasn't trying to melt. She was trying not to.*

But Lowe scoffed. "Okay, genius. How has she been communicating to him all this time?"

Ein didn't have an answer for that. But Mala did. She took a deep breath and turned to Lowe. "This morning, on the surface … Alba was drunk. When I put her to bed, she told me her recruiter *Blut* had given her a two-way radio. They used to talk all the time."

Lowe's eyes widened. "That's against protocol."

"Yeah and traitors who turn Erlender are really stuck on protocol," Ein sneered.

Silence spread through the room like fog across the surface

of water. It hung thick in the air.

Lowe stood, breaking the tension. "You all have your assignments. We'll meet daily at 6:00 p.m. for dinner and status updates."

"You're welcome," Ein called as Lowe walked to the door. His voice took on a slightly manic tone. "Glad I could do your thinking for you. I'll just stay here and make out with your girlfriend while you go get your suspect."

Lowe didn't respond. His back didn't even tense. He simply walked through the door and didn't look back.

Ein turned to the girls and clapped his hands with mock cheerfulness. "Alright. Who's ready to get this death sentence started?"

CHAPTER TWENTY-SEVEN

Mala sat with Ges, rubbing her eyes as they watched the millionth video of the day. *Another whole day of this tomorrow? I'm going to die of boredom before we even go.* It turned out, most of the video cameras planted by their spy operations captured endless footage of the dull grey squabbling of Erlender peasants.

She watched Keptiker solve another petty dispute between two villagers whose legs were wrapped in scraps of cloth, the poorest of the poor. They'd been fighting over a pair of scissors. He took out the screw, and handed half back to each, telling them they'd have to make do with a knife. "First one ta stab de other, gets tha' scissors." The villagers glanced at each other, bowed, and quickly retreated. "Too bad," Keptiker sighed.

Another petitioner stepped forward. The general leaned on his hand, stroking the scar that ran just under his left eye. Mala mirrored him.

"No!" Ges cried out, grabbing at her hand. "Look at your wrist. It's way too girly. See how he keeps his stiffer?" He molded her wrist to his liking. "He might play for my team, but he's not girly."

"What?"

Ges winked. "Didn't they tell you? Should at least make recovery from your meltdowns easier—on you. Maybe not on Ein." He laughed and paused the video. "Okay, now repeat what he said."

Mala sighed. "First one ta stab de other, gets tha' scissors." The Erlenders spoke the same language as Senebals, but had a drawl. It took practice. Mala hadn't grown up talking to them, she'd grown up watching their corpses grow cold as she and her mother had picked their way through battlefields to help injured Senebals. Talking like them was completely unnatural. As was the THING.

The THING was what she'd come to call it, and though she didn't mention it to Ges, it really bothered her. She had to sit differently. She had to walk funny. And she'd avoided going to the bathroom if at all possible. She'd been ordered to stay in the General's form, and everyone knew it, so it wasn't like she could easily melt back. *Ein would only laugh if I asked him for help,* she thought bitterly. *But the stupid THING itches! And it gets in the way. Not to mention the other problem ... I'll have to tell somebody. I'll have to talk to Lowe, I guess.* Mala sighed. *I wish someone else could do this. I wish it wasn't me.*

She shook herself mentally. *Shut up. You don't mean that. You made a vow. Now focus.* She tried to ignore the THING. She tried to ignore the scratchy Erlender wool shirt that had been rubbing her skin raw for days now. She tried to ignore the fact that the General's left-hand dominance kept confusing her. Mala delivered the lines for Ges and then turned her attention back to the video. She saw the General slouch a bit and spread his legs wide. She imitated that.

"Okay, let's take a break, I think you're starting to glaze over," Ges pressed the stop button. "Let's talk about the general and King Troe's relationship again."

"First cousins," Mala recited. "General Keptiker was born to the old King's sister. They grew up together. Same tutors. But Keptiker left to take over his father's village and assume the role of general—aka mayor—there. They see each other once a year for tax delivery. Not close, because Keptiker isn't as idiotic and superstitious as Troe."

"You think he's idiotic?" Ges interrupted.

"Based on what you told me. You said the guy eats jewels when he's sick. I don't know everything my mother knew, but eating rocks? Not because he thinks they're magic either—he thinks that somehow, scratching up his organs internally is going to help," Mala scoffed. "And he's a shut-in, not a warrior. He's into a ton of rituals. He puts dead rats in the window to ward off evil spirits. He keeps his own hair and burns it so other people can't use it against him. Bizarre things. I mean, I really get why people here scoff at magic so much. I don't get why Keptiker hasn't made a play for the throne. Why does everyone follow this guy? The paranoid recluse?"

"You think this is boring?" Ges motioned to the paused video. "Imagine instead of a thousand peasants, you oversaw forty thousand. And they all expect to be fed. Not everyone's into management."

Mala stuck out her tongue. Ges laughed. "I definitely think you're gonna have to cut down on the tongue thing at the Erlender compound. Unless you want it to get cut off."

He pulled out a different video clip. Mala sighed.

"I saved this one for last today. I thought it might keep you interested after hours of work." Ges pressed play.

Verrat appeared on the screen. Her face was battered but still recognizable. *No.* Mala leaned forward, her heart pumping hard in shock. "She's still alive? She's tougher than I thought." It was a minute before Mala could focus on anything other than the violet-eyed warrior woman. When she did look around, she realized Verrat had been chained in a corner of the General's office. She knelt on the concrete floor, gravel spread beneath her knees to ensure that every moment was torture. Her hands were chained to a ring in the floor. It looked like her shoulder had been dislocated.

Mala watched Keptiker enter his makeshift office, noticing the puff of his chest, and the direct line of his gaze as he marched a set of files over to the desk. He dropped them there and turned, reclining against the battered desktop, to regard his prisoner.

"So disappointin'," he said aloud. "You had so much potential. Straighten up now."

"Yes sir," Verrat kept her eyes downcast but straightened so that her weight pushed forward onto her knees, forcing the gravel farther into her skin. The pain registered on her face, but she remained silent.

"I hate this guy," Mala said.

"Actually, Mala, he's pretty merciful. Most other generals would have sliced and diced her by now, to see what intel they could have gotten." Ges commented.

Mala cocked her head at this. "Why hasn't he?"

"Keptiker's known for the long game. Rumors are he once waited seven years to get back at a general who'd stolen a slave-girl from him. When the guy's village was attacked, Wilde was called in to reinforce. Keptiker followed orders. He reinforced, but in the village—not at the general's compound. One of the President's regular divisions took out that general in under three hours. Couldn't take the town, though."

"So he's got a reputation as dangerous." *That's good for me, right? People won't mess with me.*

"You mucking idiot!" A bellow echoed behind them. Mala turned to see what the drama was all about. Unfortunately, it appeared to be all about her. Ein stood in the doorway, quivering in rage, his gaze scorching.

"Ges, excuse us, but I have to take this ingrate she-man up to her hut immediately. Turns out she's a thief."

Mala's blood ran cold. *Crap.* Her mind flashed to all the items she'd ferreted away. It was all sitting in a nice little pile, tucked into the corner of her hut, like a squirrel's stash of nuts. *But I didn't take anything important* ... her mind scrolled through the list of the things she'd taken while Ein dragged her by the scruff of her neck to the sub docks. Even when she was a man, he towered over her.

Ein shoved her into the first waiting submarine and started the ascent without speaking another word. She could feel the anger rolling off of him. She decided not to break the silence. *Better give him time to calm down.*

When they'd almost reached the surface, he finally spoke. "Why would you do it *again*? I told you last time it was suicide."

"What?" But Mala barely had time to sputter the question before Ein shoved her. The shove didn't have as big an impact on her Keptiker's body as it would have on her own. She didn't fly across the sub. But she got the point: the question had been rhetorical. Ein didn't want her to speak.

Ein docked the sub and pointed at the hatch. Mala opened it and led the way to her hut, deciding that crying wouldn't evoke any pity while she was stuck in this man's body. She pulled open the door to her hut and ducked inside.

Ein lit the lantern near the door. As soon as his eyes adjusted, he spotted Mala's pile. "What the sludge is that?" He shuffled through the trinkets, glancing once back at Mala. "You've been stealing all this stuff from me?" His anger subsided, shock and bemusement taking its place.

Mala shrugged. "It's not like I could do anything else to get back at you with Tier around all the time."

"How'd you get it out?"

"Hid it in my hair."

Ein chuckled. Mala breathed a sigh of relief. Then he picked up a strange silver gear. "Ah, muck. You had to take this, huh?"

Mala peered at it. "I'm sorry if that's what got you all riled up. I literally just took whatever I could. I don't even know what half this stuff is."

Ein turned to her. "Just a part of the fix for the plumbing I recently implemented. Kind of a key component in my design.

Which now I'll have to fix again, if there's time before we ...." He pocketed it. "But that's not what I was looking for. I don't see it here. Which means it must be on you." He sighed. "It would be so much more fun if I could make you melt back. But since I can't: strip."

"What?" Mala was indignant. No way was she stripping down in front of him. Especially since the THING had decided Ein's chuckle was cute. *Go away,* she mentally scolded it, all while backing away from Ein.

"I haven't been to your lab for days. This is my third day of research with Ges. I'm sure he has video footage of me and I've got about a hundred witnesses to prove that whatever you're mad about, I didn't do it."

"You are the only one who's dumb enough to steal something as dangerous as a clock for a prank—"

"It wasn't a prank!" Mala yelled before she could help herself. She bit her lip. *Idiot. I shouldn't have said that.*

After a very deliberate silence, during which she guessed Ein was calming himself down, he asked, "What do you mean? If it wasn't a prank, what was it?" His hazel eyes zeroed in on her and she felt small. Tiny. Insignificant. Stupid.

Mala sank to the floor. *Do I lie? He knew when I lied before.* She chewed her lip and wished she still had her hook necklace. She wanted to trace the lines of the hooks as she searched for the right answer.

Ein sat down cross-legged in front of her. He waited without saying a word, which was odd. *He's always so demanding.* But he just sat, waiting, his face expressionless. Maybe it was his unexpected patience, or the fact that she really wanted to validate her theory, or the fact that she was so uncomfortable in this stupid man body that she couldn't think straight, but something inside prompted Mala to tell him.

"We were performing a ritual. It was something I did the night I first melted."

Ein's intake of breath was loud and sudden. She saw him clench his jaw to hold back the volley of insults she knew he wanted to launch.

"You melted the night your mother died, correct?" Ein put on his neutral scientist's voice.

"Yes," Mala cringed as memories poked at her like sharpened sticks.

"You melted the night after you'd seen a massacre."

"Yes."

"You melted the night after you'd been through some of the most traumatic and fear-inducing moments of your life, moments that would have triggered your amygdala. Moments that would have triggered the amygdala of nearly every person around you. And yet, you still think that some silly—excuse me—some ritual that you dug up from who-knows-where caused your melts?" He arched an eyebrow, superiority seeping from every pore in his body.

Part of Mala's brain understood his argument. But another, baser part of her growled. "You have no idea what you're talking about either," she spat back. "Just because you read something in one of your books, does that make it more true than what I've done or seen? What's more real?"

"Those books are scientific works resulting from experiments—"

She cut Ein off. "So they say. Have you replicated all those experiments? How do you know they're true? Yeah—Ges told me all about your scientific theory and how it works. You believe in those books."

"Those books are mucking logical!" Ein shouted.

Good, I'm glad he's at least as mad as I am. "I'm not some stupid tributary idiot mud-breather," Mala shot at him. "I had episodes for years, but I never melted before I did that ritual. And yes, all that stuff happened in between. But that's why I took that damn minute hand. So I could do an experiment—you damned muck head! So I could see if that ritual actually caused me to melt differently than everyone else. If you think the amygdala is the key—then everyone Kreis here's been through something traumatic. But why are my melts different? You're so mucking arrogant, sometimes I just want to—"

"I'm arrogant because I'm right. I'm right because I don't just believe anything that comes out of someone's mouth."

"Well, guess what? I found the ritual about blood sacrifice in a book, too. Or Ges did. Does that make it more real for you?"

"That shit's barbaric. Some Erlender book by some guy who thinks spit and shit will heal you. Would you take medical advice from someone like that? Come on Mala! That's crazy."

He'd said it. The word she hated above all others. The word she'd feared for years. *I'M NOT CRAZY.* Her hand swung of its own accord. Ein blocked it, but she launched herself at him and soon they were grappling on the floor, making the hut roll as each of them kicked and punched and pinched.

Mala was biting down on Ein's hand when he suddenly went deathly still. She froze, alarmed.

"Did you hear that?" he whispered.

There was a faint growling sound. And then a subtle *gloop*: the sound of a sub slipping under the surface.

"Muck!" Ein bolted out the door, knocking Mala down as he barreled for the main platform.

She followed, confused. "What's going on?" she asked as she reached him.

Ein was staring forlornly at the spot their sub had occupied. "She must have hidden in there. She's been waiting for someone to take the sub so she wouldn't be seen driving it off to nowhere from the Center."

"Who? What? Ein, what are you talking about?"

He turned soberly to her. "Mala, I came after you because the hour hand's now missing from my clock. I thought you'd taken it."

"I already said I didn't."

"I know." He turned back toward the water, watching the silver sub race away. "Alba did. She's making a break for it."

CHAPTER TWENTY-EIGHT

Mala's jaw dropped. "We have to tell someone. Do something."

Ein walked away across the platform. "Well, we took the first sub up here. Everyone else is down in the Center … it's almost dinner."

Mala took long strides to catch up with him. "But we can't just let her run off to the Erlenders … we have to try and stop her."

Ein rolled his eyes. "No. We do? Really? Stand back." He waved her away and pulled up a trapdoor in the middle of the platform. Beneath it bobbed a small canoe. Ein explained as he hauled it up and carried it to the edge of the platform. "We use them to maintain the huts… sometimes to haul in supplies."

"I was kind of hoping for some kind of alarm. I mean, we can't be the first people ever to get stranded on the platform, right?"

Ein sighed and walked back toward the trapdoor. With nothing better to do, Mala trailed after him like a lost duckling.

Ein grabbed some oars, tossed them aside, and tugged a rope that had been coiled beneath the canoe. "Little help?" he grunted.

"What is that?"

"This is your alarm," he muttered. "Pull it taut and we ring a bell down below. Supposed to be used for outsiders, really. But it will work."

Mala put her burly body to work. They pulled on the rope, backing across the platform. It was slippery and heavy with water. It made Mala melt back into her own skin, so she was little help as they struggled. The fibers cross-hatched Mala's hands with tiny stinging cuts. Finally they met what seemed like resistance.

"Got it," Ein panted. He immediately dropped the rope and ran for the oars. He scooped them up and was back at the canoe, sliding it into the water before Mala could fully register what he was doing.

"What's this?"

"We have to try to figure out which direction she's going," Ein grunted.

Mala looked dubiously down at the canoe. She shucked off her boots and pants, which would only weigh her down if they flipped. Better to freeze in the air that in the water.

Three seconds later, she and Ein were rowing furiously in the direction they'd seen Alba disappear, into the pink sunset. *We'll never catch her,* Mala thought. *But if we can get everyone pointed in the right direction at least ...*

Mala heard the *gloop* of the sub surfacing. She shouted to Ein and pointed. They turned their little canoe and rowed furiously. *Smack.* The sub crashed into a rocky bit of shoreline. Mala stared as she rowed. Alba forced open the hatch and stumbled through the shallows to the shore. She carried a backpack that looked nearly as big as her eighty-year-old frame.

As they rowed close, Mala caught her breath. Alba's silhouette limping painfully toward the trees. Her old body clearly hadn't handled the wreck well.

"Alba!" Mala shouted.

The silhouette turned. Alba's stooped figure peered at them. "Mala?"

"Yeah. Don't do this!" Mala called.

"I can't let them shock me!" Alba's reply echoed across the water. She hiked a travelling bag further up her bony shoulder and turned to leave.

Instinct fizzled in Mala's mind. *I have to slow her down. Keep her here.* As they had before, her hands acted of their own accord. She found herself staring down at a silver gear. She stood, balancing carefully in the canoe, took aim, and threw as hard as she could.

A dull thwack confirmed she'd hit her target, though on the shoulder and not the head. Alba dropped her pack and turned. She pulled a gun from her belt.

"Back off, Mala," she threatened. "I have to find Blut. He said he'd help me."

"Blut's dead," Mala shouted. "I killed him. You know that kill I got on the way here? It was him. He'd gone rogue."

"Liar!" Alba screamed.

"Ask Lowe," Mala replied.

Alba's face twisted and her limbs started to contort. Her skin bubbled. And suddenly, Alba didn't look like herself anymore—at least, not the self Mala had grown to know. She became tall and muscular. Her waves of strawberry blond hair glinted in the final rays of the sunset. She looked every bit the warrior when she trained the gun on Mala. She fired.

Ein yanked Mala sideways and flipped the canoe. Ice water flooded her nose and lungs. Mala surface spluttering and shivering. Ein pulled her behind the canoe as bullets peppered the water around them. She treaded water while he stood easily on the lake bottom.

"What was that?" he asked.

"I'm trying to delay her."

"Oh. Thought it was another suicide attempt. You seem fond of those."

"Shu-u-u-ut it," Mala's teeth chattered.

"Think you can last another minute in this water?" he asked, peering around the edge of the canoe. Another bullet. He hissed as he ducked back, clutching his shoulder.

"I think you might have ticked her off," his light tone belied the blood streaking down his wetsuit.

Mala's shivers prevented her reply. The cold was so intense she felt as if her bones might splinter, like she might turn to glass and shatter. She was about to swim for the shore, bullets or no, when she heard it. The soft *creshhh* sound of a sub breaking the surface. And then another. And another. And another.

Mala peered around the edge of the canoe. Alba had disappeared.

It was nearly an hour later, after she and Ein had been dried, warmed, checked by the medics, and recited their story to Tier, Fell,

Neid, and Lowe, when Mala finally felt she could relax. Wrapped in a blanket, her feet curled around a lantern to absorb every tiny bit of heat, she sat back in a velvet chair in a meeting room at the Center as she watched her companions debate possibilities.

Ein, for once, was silent. Mala wasn't sure if it was blood loss or hypothermia that was making him quiet. His shoulder had been grazed by Alba's bullet. And while the wound wasn't life threatening, Neid kept glaring at Mala in a way that made her feel as if it was.

"They'll find her," Tier reassured the group.

Fell seemed more doubtful. "I don't know. She melted back to her younger form. She always passed every test I threw at her with flying colors. I don't doubt she'll be able to hole up somewhere and hide."

"When you find her, what will you do?" Mala asked the question, even though she wasn't sure she wanted to hear the answer.

"She's a traitor," Tier replied.

"Suspected traitor," Mala responded, not sure where her audacity was coming from. *Maybe it's the near-death experience.* "We don't have proof."

"She was in secret communication with Blut."

"We don't know if she was aware he was a traitor. She didn't know he was dead; that meltdown was from shock. She said she left because she didn't want you to fry her brain."

Tier's jowls quivered angrily. "A deserter is still a traitor."

"Completely different kind," Mala replied.

Lowe interrupted their standoff. "At least she dropped this. It could be our way in." He fingered a hand-held radio. He'd been fiddling with it ever since one of the sub teams had returned to report after scouring the shoreline and towing back the battered sub.

"Blut's dead," Mala looked at him. "What good's that gonna do?"

"But she told you he was going to help her." Lowe glanced up, fire dancing in his eyes. "That means someone's been using this thing. Someone's pretending to be Blut. And whoever that is, they most definitely know Blut was a traitor." He turned the radio over in his hands once more, and started fiddling with the dials. Staccato static filled Mala's ears.

After several minutes Fell said, "Well, I do think this accelerates our timeline." Every eye in the room locked onto her. "With a potential spy on the loose, and no idea what knowledge she may or may not have about this mission, we need to get it under way before she has a chance to report. We're about three hundred kilometers from the nearest human inhabitance, Erlender or Senebal. And she's injured. But still. I'd say we need to move out in two days, to be safe."

Tier nodded. "Agreed." He stood and stretched. "The cover story will be that Wilde has a suspected traitor. Close enough to your reality that it should work. Keptiker will tell the King he's set a trap for the traitor but needed to leave to give it time to work. Lowe, you can fill in the details. If you can take out one of Keptiker's confidantes with this, that's a bonus. Okay, everyone: dismissed." He strode toward the door. He pulled it open and turned back. "And

Mala?"

"Yes?" she asked.

"Watch your mouth." The door slammed shut behind him.

CHAPTER TWENTY-NINE

They stayed up through the night, working in the meeting room. Reviewing endlessly. After a kiss from Ein that made Lowe frown, Mala was back in Keptiker's body.

The table was shoved aside and Mala, Lowe, and Neid reviewed Erlender combat positions. They reviewed Keptiker's specific techniques as a lefty, making her punch southpaw until her shoulder burned like someone had set a torch to it.

When Lowe noticed Mala couldn't lift her arm any longer, he switched tactics. He had Mala and Neid review interactions between slave and master, and for the first time in her life, Mala had to fasten a rope around someone's neck and lead them as if they were a pack mule. It took an hour before Lowe was satisfied with her confidence and dominion over Neid. It was longer until he believed Neid's submissiveness. The blond had a hard time keeping expressions off her face, particularly disgust.

At least that attitude will work when we're in disguise, Mala sighed internally. She'd given up hope of the blond ever easing up on her. *After all, she's Ein's sister.* And little though she knew Neid, she knew Ein's boiling-hot temper very well. *If they're at all the same, we'll be enemies for life.* She tugged on Neid's rope, forcing the girl to crawl. *Who knows how long that will be, though.*

And for the first time since she'd had that thought—and she'd had it often recently—Mala wasn't scared. She was set on a path, her feet firmly leading her in one direction. She'd never felt so confident in her life. She felt drawn to this mission, like it was right somehow. Like it fit. *The tug of destiny,* she thought, then smiled at her own corniness.

Lowe barked at her for smiling and she got back to business.

In the meantime, in a corner away from all of the activity, Ein scribbled furiously on a roll of parchment. Well after midnight, when he sensed a lull in their activity, he called out. "I have forty-three different escape routes. I think we should review them, since we'll probably need one."

Mala propped the general's head on his hand and tried not to doze as Ein pointed out their options using the rough map of the King's compound he'd sketched. He'd thought of different scenarios, from Lowe somehow tipping off the servants to Mala botching it in front of the King. And he had backup plans for backup plans. *Which is all really good, but ... how am I supposed to remember this?* Mala yawned mentally. Lowe saw her fading, and punched her hard in the burning arm. She sat up straighter, rueful.

Neid had a more pressing question: "We're all going to be in different parts of the compound. How can we know when we need to use an escape route?"

Ein sat back. "I've been working on fixing some pre-bomb communication earpieces. But with our new timeline, there's no way they'll be ready. So, in short, you'll only know when you need it."

Lowe stepped in. "As the servant, I'll be going between all of you throughout the day. I'm responsible for keeping everyone in the party fed. So there's that."

"That could be hours!" Neid exclaimed. "What if something happens in between?"

Lowe shrugged. "Better memorize your escape routes, then. Because it's the best we've got."

Mala leaned forward, suddenly quite a bit more awake than she'd been before. She and Neid leaned over the map and started pummeling Ein with questions about the routes he'd just described.

Mala felt confident she'd committed about fifteen of the escape scenarios to memory when Ein brought up a new scenario that made her jolt.

"I think," he said, "that if something goes wrong directly with the King and Keptiker here, our best bet is magic. If Mala melts into his father, I think the panic that sets off would be enough to get us out. Troe's stupidly superstitious." Ein raised an eyebrow at Mala as he said that, indicating his insult wasn't only for the king.

Lowe held up a hand of caution. "If she melts into his father, Keptiker is going to be labeled a demon. They skin demons alive. If Mala melts while in Keptiker's body, she can't melt back into him to escape. Everyone will be after her."

Ein grinned. "I know. But imagine the dead king striding through the halls, calling for his boat—the shock. I don't know how much footage any of you watched on the Troe, but he has a shrine.

He talks to his father daily. And long ago, when he was growing up, he used to have episodes, panic attacks. If his father were to condemn him, tell him he's a disappointment … I think we might be able to give the mucking bastard a heart attack."

Lowe shook his head. "Not part of our mission."

"Nope, just an added bonus," Ein replied, putting his hands behind his head and leaning back.

"You may be a genius, but if we give him a heart attack, that undermines the entire purpose of our mission," Lowe's blue eyes glinted with superiority. "If we kill the King, who's going to put all his attack plans into place? Our intel goes to crap if there's a fight for the throne because his sons are too young to take over."

"Sons? I thought he only had one," Neid furrowed her brow.

Lowe rubbed his face, exasperated and exhausted. "Is everyone in the Archive useless? Didn't they go over the King's paranoia? He only has one true son. But about eight years ago, when his son was five, he brought in two other boys. He dyed all their faces blue, scarred their cheeks so no one can tell the difference between them, and has been raising all three as his sons so that no one knows which one's the real one."

Mala couldn't help her intake of breath. She pictured three five-year-old little boys crying as they were cut with knives and pierced with needles. *Who could do that to their own kid?*

Ein's reaction was slightly different. "That's pretty brilliant. Of course the kids know, right?"

Lowe shrugged. "So far they've either been too scared or too brainwashed to ever confess."

"Well don't you think that seeing Grandpa's ghost would get more of a reaction out of the real son than the others? What if we assassinate the real son instead?"

"Again. Not part of the mission."

"So we're supposed to go in as mindless drones to fulfill a mission that will most likely get us killed, even if I have an idea that might give us a better chance at getting out of there alive?"

"We're supposed to complete our mission as part of a greater strategy that you are not privileged to know. So despite your assumption that every thought flickering through your head is pure genius, we are NOT intentionally going to go outside the bounds of our mission."

Ein rolled his eyes and crossed his arms.

Lowe's lip curled up into a snarl. "This is why Typicals are nothing more than—"

"Target practice?" Ein interjected, taking a step toward Lowe.

Mala's eyes flickered between the two men, watching their battle of wills.

Neid put her hand on her brother's shoulder. He glanced down at her. Her eyes begged. Something passed between them.

Ein shrugged. "Fine. Assassination off the table. I still think the shock value of the melt outweighs everything else. Let's try it so we can get a few extra seconds to escape."

Lowe opened his mouth to argue but Mala interjected. "I can at least try it." She turned to Lowe. "If I can give you guys more time to get out, I'm for it."

Lowe's eyes clouded at that, but he stayed silent.

Ein moved toward her. "You've seen pictures of the old king, right?"

Mala nodded. Ein stood across from her, evaluating her. Unlike the beginning of the night, when he'd strode over to her confidently and dipped her into a deep kiss right in front of Lowe, he looked uncertain now.

Lowe piped in, "Are you going to kiss Mala or what? Get to it. She might not be able to turn back into a girl for your great escape."

Mala laughed. After all of the drama of the past day, combined with sleep deprivation, she found the idea that Ein didn't want to kiss her in her current man-form hilarious. "I'm glad I'm not the only one who has to suffer with this male body. Come on, Ein. Pucker up."

"I'm hoping it will still work," Ein responded. "We haven't tried when you're not in your natural form."

"Time to get started then," Mala winked at him. "Come on, get your motor running for me."

"Ugh. Stop talking," Ein said. "You make it worse."

"You don't like my pillow talk? But I've got this gravelly purr just for you honey. Because of you." Mala burst into girlish giggles and doubled over. She pounded her fist onto her knee. Tears came to her eyes. She was sure she'd broken just about every rule about Keptiker's posture that Ges had tried to beat into her over the past few days. But she didn't care. She laughed until tears came to her eyes. And then she wiped them away with a finger like a girl.

As she straightened, Mala found Ein's hand around her neck. "You have always been so insolent." And he mashed his lips into hers before she could respond.

This kiss started differently. She could feel his fear, feel his strain. But then she dropped her hand to one of his and stroked it softly. She kept her body back, aware that it would only make him more self-conscious. She pulled back from the kiss slowly, still stroking his hand. "It's still me underneath," she whispered. "Still the same little girl who hid all your crap in her hair. And who threw some very important gear of yours at Alba tonight, so you can't fix your plumbing. Still me."

Ein looked up at her. And to both of their shock, it worked. Mala felt herself begin to burn, felt her skin begin to bubble, felt herself shrinking. *But wait. No. The old King is bigger than Keptiker.*

Mala looked down. The General's clothing sagged on her frame, pants trailing inches across the floor. She lifted a hand. There was the scar from the hour hand on her palm. She'd melted back into herself. *Sludge.*

"What the muck happened?" Neid asked.

Mala looked at Ein, helplessly. He cocked his head, "It was working, right?"

Mala nodded. "I started to melt … but I just … couldn't."

Lowe came up to her and put a hand to her forehand. "Are you feeling okay? Maybe you're too tired."

Mala sagged into him. "Yeah, maybe."

But Ein didn't look convinced. His eyes were staring off into the distance, thoughts racing.

"Why don't we all turn in for a few hours?" Lowe suggested. "Let's stay here so we can wake up and just start working."

Everyone nodded, Ein rather vacantly, as he headed back to his map-making corner and dimmed the lanterns nearest him.

Lowe and Mala curled up together on the plush carpet. She brushed back a black curl.

"I don't know what happened. I'm sorry."

"Don't worry about it." Lowe gave her a peck on the forehead. "We'll try again in the morning."

He settled into sleep quickly, but it took Mala a few minutes to doze off. *Why couldn't I melt?* Her mind replayed that question until it became a dull chant that lulled her into dreams.

Her dream began as it always did: in the trees, at night, rushing away from the sound of the Erlender alarm. The dream had ceased to scare her: over the months it had become familiar. She waved at her mother, who was dancing with bare-bellied Barde among the saplings. Her mother spread her thumb and fingers in a victory sign. Mala passed the beach and all of the docked ships and waved at Sorgen, who jumped up from a boat deck and said "Mala – don't go!" She walked past rows and rows of empty grey faces, people she'd known in another lifetime. She marched on a road of gravel, and suddenly she was wearing boots. Big boots. And she was tall. That was new. She looked down. Kneeling in front of her on the gravel path was Verrat. The violet-eyed woman stared up at her with devotion.

"Move," Mala spat in Keptiker's voice.

"Yes sir," the girl scrambled to get out of his way. And she saluted as Mala passed her.

Shock flooded Mala's system. She sat straight up, instantly awake. "She called him sir."

Memory after memory fell into place, like a puzzle assembling before her eyes.

Sorgen had been near the abandoned mansion when the Erlenders had attacked. *He tried to warn me. Don't go. What else did he say? Lots of screaming. Lots of ayes and nos. Unless… he was trying to say I know. Like he'd found something out.*

What would he have known? Unless he'd seen the Erlenders. Unless he knew they were hunting Kreis. Unless he knew I was Kreis. Don't go. Was it don't go to the celebration?

Verrat had approached Mala the night of the celebration. Verrat had tried to give her something. *What if it was the necklace? What if she's been working with the Erlenders?*

And her mind flashed back to the video Ges had shown her. The General staring down at Verrat from his perch on his desk. *Keptiker said she'd had potential. As if he'd known her before …*

But Verrat had been with Bara's guard for years. Before Mala and her mother had joined them three years back. *So what is she? Another traitor like Blut? Or an Erlender plant? Does it matter? She had to have been in communication with Blut. Or he wouldn't have known to come looking for me. She has to be part of this spy ring Lowe's looking for.*

Her heart raced. She felt blood rushing to her head, as though she was suddenly upside down. But she wasn't upside down.

The world was. *Verrat is a traitor.*

CHAPTER THIRTY

A hand on her shoulder nearly made Mala jump out of her skin. She smacked it away.

Ein loomed over her and whispered, "Follow me."

He pulled Mala into the hall. He dragged her down three different corridors until they came to one with a wall of black windows: they were so deep under the lake that the moonlight couldn't pierce the water outside. Fish swimming past looked like smudges, or a trick of the eye. A single pillar candle burned in the hallway, telling her it was four in the morning.

Mala turned from the candle and pawed at her eyes, still half asleep. "What is it?"

"We need to test something," Ein muttered. He pushed her shoulders and practically slid her across the floor into a corner. "Stay put."

He reached up with his long arms and scraped the ceiling tiles with his fingertips. He pushed a tile aside. A small video camera with a blinking red light hung suspended. Ein pressed a button. The red light disappeared. He pushed the tile back into place.

"Okay, we have approximately half an hour before someone

comes to rectify that."

Mala raised her eyebrows. "What's with the secrecy?"

Ein's look was clear even in the shadows: exasperation. "Mala. There's a spy in here somewhere."

"I thought you said Alba was the spy."

"You think there's only one? Besides, the Ancients were awfully quick to accept that she was a spy. Without real evidence. Suspicious, isn't it? Anyway, that's off topic."

"What *is* the topic?" Mala's brain was slowly, reluctantly awakening.

"I suspect we may have discovered another limitation of your melts. But I'm not positive. I think there are two options. You might not be able to melt into someone you or the other person—your trigger person—haven't met."

"Or?"

Ein bit his lip. It was clear the other theory was worse. "Well, let's eliminate this option first. I'm going to kiss you. I want you to try to melt into the President. You've seen pictures—right?"

Mala nodded. She glanced down the hall and tried to pull the president's face into her mind's eye. Tall. Steel-grey hair. Ice-blue eyes. A marine wrench always hung from his neck as a symbol of his humble beginnings as a repairman's son. He wore a black vest. He pounded on a podium.

"There is no crime greater than invasion. The Gottermund River protected and sheltered us from destruction. While the rest of the world burned, she kept us safe. She gave us sustenance. She chose us."

"And then the invaders came. Day after day they violate her. Force her to submit. Try and change her with their voodoo and enchantments. But they are on the wrong side of destiny."

"We will NOT let these heathens pillage and rape and murder any longer. We will fight. We will pile their bodies until we stand on top of a mountain of dead. We will not stop until our children do not know the meaning or terror of the word Erlender. We will not stop until they are just a memory. We will defend our river. We will take back our home. Fire for fire. Blood for blood."

The old video feed had given Mala chills the first time she'd seen it. Even now, she had goosebumps on her arms as she turned to Ein.

"You've got a clear picture of him?" Ein asked.

Mala nodded. "I'm ready.

He hugged her to him and lifted her in his arms, wrapping her legs around his waist. Mala was disoriented by his gentle approach, but before she had time to say anything, he'd wrenched her hair back so hard her neck cracked. He body-slammed her against the wall. Air fled from her lungs. Then his lips devoured her.

Seconds later he dropped her. Mala heard the rip of fabric as heat stole over her.

"Mr. President," Ein dipped his head in mock servitude. Then he sighed. "That's what I was afraid of."

"What?" Mala didn't realize how powerful the President's voice was. That single word cracked in the dark like a whip. And stinging little echoes trailed behind it. She covered her mouth.

Ein took a small flask out of his pocket. He uncorked it and handed it to Mala. She took it, but didn't immediately pour the water over her hand as had become her custom.

"Shouldn't you be practicing kissing me when I don't look like me? Because that didn't work out so well last time. How do you know that's not the problem?"

Ein shook his head. "You started to melt. My amygdala somehow pushed through that issue. The problem came in when you tried to choose the subject for your melt. And this next melt … the one I'm going to ask you to do. It's going to be hard enough for me as it is. I didn't have time to remove the personal. We don't have time."

"What does that mean?"

Ein bit his lip. He almost looked vulnerable.

That's got to be a trick of the shadows, Mala thought. *Ein only has one emotion. Arrogance.*

He reached into his pocket again. He took out a small leather booklet and flipped it open. He handed it, wordlessly, to Mala.

She had to walk over to the pillared candle to see what he'd given her. It was a sketch. Neid laughing.

Mala looked up, confused. "I've already melted into your sister."

"It's not my sister. I want you to try and melt into my mother," Ein replied. A dozen emotions rippled across his face. Sadness, fear, pain, anger. He didn't try to hide them.

Mala glanced back at the sketch. If she looked closely, there were laugh lines. And the woman's mouth was a little thinner. "But why?" she whispered.

"I'll tell you afterward. I don't want to bias the results of the experiment any further," Ein muttered, resuming his normal voice.

Mala poured a few drops of water onto her palm. She watched as she melted and the thin little scar from the hour hand reappeared. She gave Ein back the flask and the booklet. She stared up at him docilely, trying to keep the pity from showing on her face.

A little voice in the back of her head reminded her that her clothes were shredded from melting into the President, who was bigger than Keptiker. But she ignored it. She wasn't completely indecent. *And Ein might need a little help getting into this melt,* she rationalized against her inhibitions. He was being hesitant.

Mala took his hand and guided it up to her face. She watched him steadily and gently guided his hand down her cheek, her neck, lower. Heat grew in his eyes.

He bent and kissed her. Normally his kisses were angry and hot, but this kiss had an edge to it. It was different. Violent. His hand snaked around her neck and started to squeeze.

Mala's eyes popped open in panic.

And in the dim light of the pillared candle she saw herself, her dark mass of curls and big lips, reflected in Ein's eyes. She stared, waiting for her face to bubble. She flexed her fingers, anticipating the burn.

Nothing happened. She and Ein continued to stare at one another long past the point they knew it was futile.

"I'd like to try one more time," Ein whispered. "Maybe that subject was too close for me. It may have skewed my amygdala's response. Too many other deep emotions firing."

Mala nodded.

"This time, I want you to try and melt into your mother."

It was like a knife to her chest. Suddenly Mala had trouble breathing. She tried hard not to think of Erinne. She shook her head desperately.

"Mala, please. Do you think I wanted to see my dead mother? Do you think what we just did was easy for me? The day she died—my sister was there. She saw it all. The... a... *someone* murdered my mother. He stabbed her through the stomach. Then he tossed her aside like she was a piece of garbage. I saw the body after. It was ... she used to work down in the ceremony department. My mom. Preparing rituals. Funerals. Initiations. Tests. You think I wanted to see her?"

Panic was stealing over Mala. She started counting out loud, still shaking her head furiously at Ein. "Nine, eighteen, twenty-seven ..." She doubled over. her stomach felt queasy.

Finally, Ein relented. "Okay. Too soon. How about your father?"

Though that wound still ached, it was not raw and pulsing. Mala had pretty much grown up without her father. She pictured him in her mind, a giant with a wide smile and eyes always crinkled from the sun or from laughter. The pain of Ein's earlier suggestion faded. Slowly she was able to stop counting. Her stomach calmed. She nodded.

"Okay."

Fast and quick, the next kiss led to another stare off. Mala realized Ein's eyes had tiny flecks of gold near the pupils.

"What does this mean?" she asked.

"It means you can't melt into someone who's dead. It means no dead king. No scare. But worse, it means we can't just kill Keptiker."

"What are we going to do? We can't just knock him out and leave him somewhere. He's good; he'll escape," Mala responded.

"We'll have to figure out a way to keep him subdued, keep him from escaping, and keep the King from recognizing him. It means our mission just got about twenty times more complicated."

"Muck and shit." For the first time since being given the assignment, Mala didn't feel the tug of destiny. Instead, she felt a tug that reminded her very much of a noose tightening around her neck.

CHAPTER THIRTY-ONE

Ein and Mala didn't speak as they returned to the meeting room. They both curled up in the dark and pretended to sleep as their thoughts whirled like storm clouds.

Eventually Mala must have drifted off, because a hand on her shoulder jerked her awake for a second time. "Ein, get away!" she muttered.

The shaking continued. Mala cracked an eye. She started. Someone's nose was almost touching hers. It was pitch black, but she could tell it wasn't Ein. Mala scrambled backward.

"Shh," Neid whispered. Mala's eyes struggled to adjust.

"What's going on?" Where are we? They weren't in the meeting room where they'd fallen asleep, they were in complete darkness. *Just like the rooms I was in for espionage training ... is this a lesson?* Mala peered around. The blackness so was thick, she could almost taste its bitterness.

"It's the final trial," Neid breathed. Her voice hitched as she spoke. "I don't want to do this. I don't think I can do this. Don't make me do this!" Neid grabbed Mala's shoulders. She started to shake her. "Don't make me. I can't!"

Is her breakdown my trial? Mala wondered. *Are they trying to get us to meltdown? What's going on?* She automatically put an arm around Neid, trying to comfort her, but the blond waived her off. Kept shaking her. Mala pushed her away, took a step back to protect herself. Neid was getting more frantic.

Above, a naked bulb flickered to life. Instantly, Mala returned to Neid and positioned herself so they were back-to-back. *What if the trial is a fight?* No one jumped out at them. No one else was in the room.

It was a black windowless room, like the one used during her initiation. Only this room had a reflective window, about five yards up. It wrapped the length of one wall. She watched it expectantly. Nothing.

What if we're supposed to fight each other? Mala whirled back around.

Neid stood still. Tear tracks made ugly pink paths down her cheeks.

What is this mucking trial? She stared at Neid, who was wracked by quiet sobs. *Why isn't she melting? Hasn't The Nimbo ever been sad* ... Ein's story about Neid witnessing their mother's death came to mind. *If she's not sad, what is this? What emotion could make her cry so much but not make her meltdown? What emotion hasn't she felt before?*

Fear tickled Mala's spine. *Whatever Neid's afraid of ... this can't be good.*

A dull clanking sounded. The floor began to tremble. A trap door slid open and a beam of light shot like a bullet to the ceiling.

Someone struggled to climb up through the opening.

A girl with a long brown braid emerged with a pack strapped to her back. She was a little chubby, definitely plain, but the determined look on her face gave her an air of strength. After the girl's eyes adjusted to the dimness, she marched resolutely to Neid. She wrapped the blond girl in a hug and began murmuring.

"It's alright, it's alright. Bests eternal. It's alright. I love you." Her words didn't seem to comfort Neid, who only sobbed harder.

Is it leaving home? Knowing it will never be the same? Mala watched them sadly, knowing that feeling all too well.

Suddenly, a second person appeared through the trap door. Someone short and gangly, with spiky hair, grinning ear-to-ear.

"Ges!" Mala rushed over to him. She tossed her arms around him. And inhaled a cloud of alcohol. "Whoa! What's going on? Why are you drunk?" Mala stepped out of the range of his breath.

"Self-medicating," Ges replied with a wink.

"What's going on?" Mala asked him.

His eyes widened. "No one told you?"

Mala shook her head.

The crackle of static rippled through the air. Immediately, the four teens grew silent. A speaker came to life somewhere above them. Tier's voice rang out. "Neid. Mala. It is time for your final trial."

Fell took over the microphone. "This trial takes the measure of your devotion to your vows. To the Kreis. To the Senebal nation."

Tier's voice scratched through the failing P.A. system. Mala struggled to make out the words. "A Senebal always promises to the death."

Yes. And you're sending us right to ours, aren't you? Mala's internal snipe fell short. She recognize the cold fear sprouting in her heart. It was the same kind of panic—that sucking, sinking sludge that the Erlenders had always engendered in her. It was unfurling, slowly, patiently, bit by bit, making her choke as she waited for the fear to completely take over. She felt sick. *I really hate that man.*

Fell's calm voice did little to reassure Mala. But Ges grabbed her hand. She smiled at him.

"Please repeat after me," Fell intoned. "I swear allegiance to the Senebal nation. I swear to complete this mission, all missions …"

Mala repeated the lines. Neid followed dully but only after a sharp jab in the ribs and a series of whispers from the girl with the brown braid.

"I swear to follow my orders … all orders. And I swear that the innocent life I take today will not be in vain."

Wait. What? Mala didn't finish saying the last line. Neither did Neid. "We have to kill someone? What is this?" *It's a joke. A practical joke.* She turned to Neid.

Neid didn't acknowledge Mala. But her hollow stare and tears spoke for themselves.

Mala turned to Ges. "What is this? Do we have to fight an Erlender to the death or something?" He didn't respond.

Tier's voice hissed through the speaker. "Repeat the line."

Ges and the girl with the braid both nodded encouragement to their charges. *No wonder they send our best friends. How else do you make it through the knowledge that you have to kill someone in order to become Kreis? Not just someone. An innocent life. An Erlender kid? A…* Her gut twisted. A stone dropped in Mala's stomach. The hair on her arms stood up. Bile rose in her throat.

"No," she whispered. She turned to Ges. "No." Her brain ran through a litany of memories. *Alba's warning to stay away, not to make friends; it wasn't just snobbery. Ein's jabs at Lowe. The funeral. The tension that day from the Typicals. All the Kreis up on the platform. Neid has always refused to pass the test. The only Typical ever to become Kreis has never passed the final test because, because …*

"They want me to kill you," Mala breathed. She felt like she'd been struck by lightning.

Ges gave her a tiny half smile. It didn't reach his eyes. "Don't think of it like …" he couldn't finish.

"I won't."

Ges tried again. He swallowed and stepped forward. "Mala, you are Kreis. You've sworn to put your allegiance above—"

"This is sick. This is insane. What good is killing them going to do?" Mala yelled at the window. Her voice reverberated throughout the empty room.

Tier's voice floated calmly down. "The weight of their sacrifice will carry you forward in your mission. It will be with you, pushing you forward. Ensuring you succeed."

"You mean our guilt won't let us quit," Neid's voice rang out, strong and angry. "Because if we fail, they aren't martyrs anymore. We aren't Kreis anymore. We're just murderers."

Tier's voice rose in anger. "If you select not to pass the final test, you will remain here. Lowe and Ein will attempt the mission alone."

Mala felt her heart stop. Freeze. *Lowe. A death sentence. Tier would do that? He would.*

Neid gasped. Mala turned her head to see the blond's skin bubbling. The thought of losing her brother had triggered a meltdown. Neid transformed into a little girl, no more than six. She swayed somewhat on her feet. Mala wasn't sure if Neid was going to pass out from shock.

Neid's friend steadied her, then slid the pack off her own back. "You can't leave Ein alone out there," she told Neid. She opened the pack and emptied it. Weapons scattered across the floor.

Neid started shaking, bowed forward as if a massive wind were bowling her over. The girl with the braid placed a gun in Neid's hand and trained it on herself.

"It's okay," the girl whispered calmly. "I volunteered. I know you. I know you'll go out there and make everything worth it."

Mala could only watch. She felt … light. As if she were floating. As if she weren't really here. *This has to be a dream. Wake up. Wake up.*

Tier's voice came through the loudspeaker once more. "Repeat after me: I swear that the innocent life I take today will not be in vain. I will honor this sacrifice. I will succeed."

Neid haltingly repeated the words. Her voice was little more than a scratch after all her tears.

Ges tapped Mala on the shoulder. "Not to rush you or anything, but it would be awesome if I didn't have to watch that before …"

"They want me to kill you," Mala was still stuck in shock. She didn't know if she had control over her limbs.

"Sacrifice," Ges corrected. "We are giving up our lives. It's different."

Mala stared at him. And something within her shifted. Out of the corner of her eye, she saw Neid's six-year-old self cock the gun.

"No!" Mala swung her arm and knocked the gun just as it went off. The bullet lodged in the wall.

"What are you doing?" Tier shouted.

Mala took the gun from Neid's quivering hand. She stared defiantly up at the window.

"The vow is to take their life. That doesn't mean we have to kill them."

Mala turned to Ges and the other girl. "I banish you from the Center. You have to leave. You can never return."

CHAPTER THIRTY-TWO

Mala and Neid stood on the deck of a speedboat, haloed by the sunset. Lowe steered through the choppy grey waves while Ein checked the map. As they approached a bend in the river, all eyes turned toward the Center, watching the reed huts shrink to pinpricks on the water. Mala pretended her eyes could see even beyond that, to where Ges and Neid's friend stood alone onshore. She bit her lip.

It's still really cold. Does he know how to hunt? Make a fire?

She felt a hand on her shoulder and turned. Neid smiled at her and softly asked, "How did you think of it?"

Mala shrugged. "I've had to leave a lot of places. And never go back."

Neid grabbed her hand. "Thank you."

Mala gave a curt nod. *Don't thank me until we know if I just sentenced them to a long brutal death, instead of a quick one. Damnit, Mala! Did you even think? I should have tried to slip him my necklace. One of my hooks. Something.* "Do … you happen to know if either of them hunts?"

"Nope," Neid responded. "They didn't get shore leave

often."

Horror swirled through Mala's stomach like a hurricane.

"But I made Verrukter vow he'd hunt for them until I get back." Neid patted Mala's shoulder and winked. "Don't worry. There are plenty of other Typicals who go to shore for oddball chores. Wood-chopping, herb-gathering. Little things. They'll be taken care of."

Mala took a deep breath and let Neid's reassurances wash away her fear. One worry settled, she turned to the next. She glanced at Lowe. He avoided eye contact. He'd been doing that ever since the impromptu hearing regarding her trial.

The Ancients had been summoned to the room. Black capes swirling, angry faces lit from below by lights from the trapdoors, it had been an unnerving sight. *I thought they'd kill me,* Mala reminisced. *But they voted.*

Mala's stomach had been in knots as first Fell and then her supporters, had one by one raised their hands to support Mala's choice of banishment. Their votes had straightened her spine, and she'd looked Tier in the eye even as he voted for her death. He'd been one vote shy of a bullet.

A grim smile tilted Mala's lips as she remembered how purple Tier had turned when he realized he'd lost. Again. The same shade was now creeping over the sky. Somehow, the shadows made her brave.

Mala walked to the boat's cockpit. Lowe didn't acknowledge her. She took a deep breath. "Can I talk to you?"

Ein's head swiveled between the two of them, then he

jumped up to take over steering. "Here, I can get that for a minute."

"I don't think—" Lowe started to protest.

"You can have this discussion in front of me, if you want," Ein countered. "But based on Mala's face, I don't think you'll want to …"

Lowe reluctantly gave up his post and followed her to an unoccupied portion of the deck. He still avoided looking directly into her eyes.

"What did I do?"

Lowe closed his eyes in frustration. "It's not—you don't even realize? What you did. Did you even think … what does that make the rest of us?"

"What are you talking about? The rest of you?"

"Yes. Us. The Kreis."

"The rest of you. As in, I'm not one? You think what I did means I'm not one?"

"You. It's all about you. You have no clue what you've done, do you?"

"If I recall, I started this conversation with, 'What did I do?' As in, what did I do wrong? Because, no, I don't know what the mudding hell I did that's so bad."

"You've turned us into murderers. Cold-blooded killers."

"You're a soldier, a spy," Mala seethed. "You've killed forty-three mucking Erlenders. How is that my fault?"

Lowe pulled his hair. "No, Mala —the ritual. The one where I had to shoot the dockhand I'd played poker with for two years. Point blank. Leaving his kid to grow up without a dad.

Those of us who actually went through with the final trial. You've turned *us* into monsters. So … there's the rest of us. And then there's you."

"So you wish I'd killed Ges? That I'd murdered an innocent person for no reason?"

"Damnit, Mala! There *is* a reason. Did your stupid assistant teach you nothing? His great grandfather was one of our flooding founders…"

"No one EVER told me anything about killing someone for the final test," Mala growled. "Not even you."

"Alba never told you to stay away from the Typicals? Not to get close to them? Not to make friends?"

"She never said I shouldn't do it because I'd have to kill one of them."

"Ges never told you about his great-grandfather's oath?"

Mala shook her head.

Lowe slammed his hand onto the side rail. "Well here's your damn history lesson then. Fifty-eight years ago, the first two Kreis found one another. Times were bad. Erlenders still had their jets. We almost lost the capital, DasWort. And the first two Kreis, Eigen and Urtu, vowed to do everything in their power to take out the jets. They snuck onto an airfield. Disabled a jet. But they ran into trouble. Urtu got out. Eigen had to fight off three Erlenders alone before he got away. Obviously, that led to trust issues. Until Urtu's wife told them she had a plan. She brought them to the edge of the airfield. She pointed at the jet she wanted them to take out. And then she slit her wrists. She made them vow on her death that neither man would rest until the airfield was stripped to nothing. Until a plane couldn't take flight. She bound them, by her blood, to their mission."

Mala swallowed. "How was I supposed to know if no one told me?"

"Innocent or not, you've now converted a tradition of *voluntary* sacrifice into a bloodthirsty ritual."

"I didn't mean—"

"Get over that. What you mean to do and what you do are totally different things. Mean to is NOTHING. Intent doesn't matter."

"How could I just accept what they wanted me to do at face value?"

"They're called orders, Mala. You follow them. You trust in them. You trust the fact that you're part of something bigger than yourself. That someone besides you knows what the hell is going on."

Mala's heart constricted. She felt like she was three years old again. She wrapped her arms around herself. *Did I do something bad?* She didn't have an answer. Timidly, she looked at Lowe, "What can I do?"

"There's nothing to do. You've just caused a huge rift. See them?" Lowe gestured back at Ein in the cockpit, Neid beside him. Both were stoically pretending they heard nothing. "She already looked at us like we were brutes. Other Typicals whispered it, too. Now … every Kreis who comes back from a mission … you've made their lives into hell. Every new Kreis that comes in and doesn't see the ritual the way you did … They'll be hated … we're all idiotic murderers. Can't see past our own bloodlust."

The tears started. Mala couldn't stop them. But she didn't make a sound. A waterfall raged inside her, but she remained silent as Lowe finally lowered his eyes to hers. They were dark, closed. "Now there's you. And us."

His boots made the deck shake as he stomped away.

Mala's heart shattered.

"Hey," a soft voice whispered.

Mala didn't respond.

Neid touched her arm. "He'll get over it. I promise."

Mala felt hollow, empty. Thoughts breezed through her head. *He's gone. He was all I had left. I'm alone.* She didn't acknowledge Neid. She hardly heard her. The emptiness inside felt so vast, so expansive. She just wanted to let it swallow her whole.

Neid squeezed her hand. "He'll come around. He will. Verrukter got over it when I couldn't take the test. And we fought about it a lot. I told him I wasn't okay with ritual sacrifice. I'm not an Erlender. I don't believe that killing someone will make the wind change or the crops grow or even that it will make me any more dedicated than I already am. I think it's shit. And I almost went through with it. You saved me from it. And I'm grateful. He's only mad because he wishes he'd never done it."

Mala didn't look at her, didn't move. She wasn't even sure she still existed.

"I'm pretty sure Keptiker doesn't cry in public," Ein leaned against the railing where Mala had stood, frozen in painful shock, for hours. He stared up at the moon, which was nearing its apex.

Mala turned away from him. The numbness had passed. Sorrow had since swallowed her up. She swiped at her eyes, anger flaring at him for interrupting her private mourning. "Shut it. I'm not melting into him until we capture him. So I get to be me for a minute."

"Uck. Are you sure you want to be you?" Ein wrinkled his nose.

Mala laughed hollowly. "No. I'm not."

He trailed a finger up her shoulder. "Well, we could turn you into a hot little blond and have some fun," Ein winked.

Mala gawked. "Are you actually trying to cheer me up?" She turned to face him.

In the moonlight, Ein's profile was as chiseled as a statue. Until he waggled his eyebrows. "You? No. I'm just looking to get some action. You know, since we've been sent off to our deaths and all. I was hoping we could wreck a bed, dance on the mattress, tangle toes, jazz, snizzle, rootle, doodle—"

Mala couldn't help it. "Snizzle? Doodle?" Her raw throat gave a bark that turned into a deep, lasting laugh.

"Thank goodness," Ein muttered. "I was running out of decent metaphors."

"You know more?"

"Please, I know everything."

Mala shook her head. "I know you're trying to be comforting but you are still so annoying."

"Annoying you is my greatest joy."

"So I've noticed. Why is that?" Mala leaned against the railing next to Ein.

"Let's call it a unique experience," he responded.

Mala turned to look at him, and a slow smile colored his face. "What's that supposed to mean?" she asked.

"Ever heard the saying, people in glass houses don't throw stones? Well there are other things people in glass houses don't do … particularly when those houses are underwater and rumors abound."

"Thanks for answering my question. I really appreciate it." Mala rolled her eyes. Despite herself, Ein was restoring a degree of normalcy. She both hated and was grateful for it.

"I'm answering your question."

"How about this one then? Why can I only melt with you?"

"You can melt with anyone," Ein replied.

She almost growled. "You know what I mean."

"I do know what you mean. And if your intellect weren't so microscopic, you'd realize I've already given you the answer to your question. But you don't know what I mean, do you?"

Mala smacked him.

He laughed.

They sat together for a moment in the dark, Mala mulling over his words. Neid steered the boat around a bend and the hills lapped up the moon, putting them into the shadows.

"Is it … the unique experience?" Mala asked.

Ein turned his face to her, but didn't answer. Mala punched

him.

"Hey, ow! I winked. Did you not see me winking?"

"No. Mudding jerk. Wait. Does a wink mean yes?"

Silence.

"Are you winking again?" Mala peered up at Ein, trying to tell. His shoulders shook. "Stop laughing."

"I love getting under your skin. In more ways than one. Sadly. Not the best way. Yet."

"I'm going to kill you."

"Well, that's just a few days earlier than I planned on dying, so go ahead." Ein swooped down and picked her up.

"Stop!" Mala smacked his shoulder but he didn't release her as he whirled her around the deck. "You're crazy!"

"About you," he whispered.

Mala immediately stilled in his arms. *He didn't say that. He didn't just say that. What am I supposed to say?*

"Ba-ha! Gotcha!" Ein dropped her on her butt. And he laughed so hard he snorted.

"I'm glad you were joking because there would be no easy way to let you down."

"No?"

Mala shook her head. "I don't know any nice way to say 'You're a pompous jerk-face who ruins my day every time I see you.'"

Ein came to crouch next to her. He put a hand on her shoulder and slowly slid it toward her neck. He gave the tiniest squeeze.

"Really?" His voice was harsh.

Immediately Mala's heart sped up. Her breathing quickened. She wasn't sure if he was serious or joking, if she should try to snap his wrist or just let it go. She tried to read his eyes.

They looked like pools of chocolate in the dark. He glanced at her lips, then back up.

"Lowe's wrong, you know," he whispered.

"About?" Mala tried to ignore the hand.

"Intentions do matter." Ein kissed her then, a soft brush of the lips, before making eye contact.

Mala melted immediately, and immediately knew she had no control. The melt was lightning fast. She felt her bones crack and shrink. She saw her hair go flat. Instead of looking at her new body, she stared straight at Ein, horrified. "What the hell just happened?" Her voice was high-pitched and whiny. Panic swirled. "Did you meet a girl? Are we broken? Is this broken? Am I gonna be able to melt into Keptiker?"

Ein stroked her arm. "Relax." He kissed her again, this time furiously. His hand clenched around her neck. Angrily. Hotly. He opened his eyes and they were blazing. Mala felt the familiar heat rise up. She chose to melt into Tier.

"What the mudding heck are you trying to do to me? If I could, I'd have you hanged." Fury boiled her stomach. *If I could kill him I would. I really would.*

"Fortunately for me, you're an impotent old Ancient who's about to be forcibly retired," Ein reclined his elbows on the deck, unworried.

Mala strode over to the side of the boat and stuck her hand into the spray. She melted back and righted her clothes. She took a deep breath to calm herself. “Alright. Explain.”

“Instead of thinking about you, I started bringing up memories of the first girl I kissed. A little young—eleven. Body didn’t really suit you. She was a sweet, giggly thing. Unlike you.”

“But I thought … when Lowe kissed me, I turned into the girl he first kissed. How are you an exception?”

“You thought I’d never been kissed?”

Mala didn’t know how to answer without insulting him. And she really wanted him to keep talking.

“When you melt, you tap into other people’s basic drives. Their desires. The desire they’re feeling at that moment. You melt into whomever is associated with intense emotions for them. But … what if you roam into uncharted territory?”

He stared at her while she struggled to catch up. “Unique experiences?” she asked. “Like what? Like you feel something new? Something different …” she trailed off. *Please don’t say love. Don’t say love.*

“Exactly.” Ein crossed his hands behind his neck and laid back on the deck, gazing up at the stars.

His failure to answer sent Mala into further panic. She didn’t want to hear the words, but she couldn’t help herself. It was almost as if leaving it unspoken was worse. Her heart did a tap-dance. She couldn’t hear her voice over its frantic patter. But she asked anyway. “Like?”

“Like the fact that I want to punch you and screw you in the same moment," Ein responded.

Insults. I can handle that. "Oh, is that why I can taste a little vomit with each kiss?"

She couldn't see it, but she could hear his grin in his voice. "Exactly. But, as you can see, when I concentrate really hard on another emotion, I can bring up that one instead: intention. It's all about the hypothesis. Nobody can control how everything turns out. Not all the time anyway."

"But why do I always melt into Stelle when Lowe kisses me?" Mala didn't mean to say it out loud. But it slipped out and hung in the shadows.

"Well. It could be the whole repression thing. I imagine it's not easy. Trying not to feel things so you don't meltdown and blow your cover. That might be the one emotion he remembers well. Or …"

Even Ein wasn't heartless enough to say it. But the words flitted through Mala's head anyway. *Or maybe he's still in love with her.*

CHAPTER THIRTY-THREE

Wilde was a port town. Or the disemboweled remains of one. Mala peered through Ein's binoculars to see a line of boats edging the shore, their reflections like finger smudges on the water. Behind the boats was a huge mass of rusting shipping containers. They were piled on one another like a mountain of blocks. That was where the Erlenders lived.

Blue noses scurried busily, stacking boxes and yelling orders. Kids swung from the roof of one container to jump to the one below like primates. Mala could see the dingy pallets and open fire pits littering the narrow patios created by the haphazard stack of shipping containers. Almost everyone wore animal hides instead of clothes. Clothes were a luxury, the sign of a good raid. And despite the massacre of Bara's guard, Wilde did not look like it was doing well on the raiding front. Two squabbles over food broke out before Ein snatched his binoculars back.

"Hey, I wasn't done looking!" she griped.

"Your slimy nose is coating my equipment," he chirped.

Mala gave Ein the evil eye. He grinned. Ein acted like he didn't care that Lowe had left them waiting across the river in a pile of dead brush while he went into Wilde to secure Keptiker by himself, using Neid as bait.

"No offense," Lowe had said to Ein, "But the fewer of us, the easier it'll be."

When Mala had begun to protest, Ein had sided with Lowe. "It's not like you have real field experience, anyway. You're more likely to meltdown at some kid crying than anything."

Mala had kicked him for that. She longed to kick Ein now. Even with the rift between her and Lowe, even with the silence she'd had to endure as she'd trained the last few days, she didn't want him to get hurt. She didn't like him going off without her.

He doesn't want you there, a snide little voice in her head said. *He hasn't so much as looked at you since the fight.*

Mala had been training with Ein and Neid, working to avoid meltdowns, to remain commanding, manly, to speak with an Erlender accent, to remember the layout of Troe's compound. Lowe hadn't stepped in once. He'd taken over as captain, steering the boat, breaking only to sleep. He hadn't spoken to any of them until he'd called them over to explain his plan. Even then, he'd carefully looked only at Neid and Ein.

"Wilde's a cramped little maze on the port. If Keptiker slips through my fingers, it will be easy for him to get away, easy for all of us to get caught. The fewer the better."

At this point, Mala had grown resigned to his indifference. It hadn't stopped hurting, but she had begun to cling to the tiny hope Neid had given her. *Maybe one day he'll get past this. Get past his anger. Get past his first love.* But he had to live long enough to get over anything. Which is why her heart churned in fear as she waited.

Ein gasped and Mala wrenched the binoculars out of his hands. "Where is he?"

"I can't believe they do that! It's disgusting!"

"Do what?" Mala asked.

"They're relieving themselves in the river. Who is in charge of sanitation here? This is why I insisted we boil the water last night."

Mala shoved the binoculars back into Ein's stomach. *It's been three mudding hours.* "I'm going for a walk."

Ein stood up. "We're supposed to wait."

"I just need … to pee," she lied. She just needed to do something. Anything. She'd never sat on her hands this long in her entire life. Even just walking and scouring the path for medicinal seeds, a chore she'd reviled when her mom was alive, sounded better than another hour with Ein.

"Don't pee in the river, pea-brain," Ein called, busying himself with the binoculars.

"Got it," she responded. Mala waded through dead brush. She spotted some moss at the base of an oak and bent to see if it had survived the winter. A twig cracked. She froze. *Ein, I'm gonna kill you. Or at least scare the shit out of you.* She slipped her revolver out of its holster.

She could hear someone stumbling through the underbrush. Chains clinked together. Mala tensed. *That's not Ein. Lowe?* She stood, gun at the ready. She froze. She blinked. *No! It can't be!* But it was. Mala cocked the gun. A woman stumbled at Mala's feet.

"Hey, Verrat. Running from your conscience?"

Verrat froze. Fear scarred her face, pooled in her violet eyes. Chains hung from her wrists. She'd clearly broken herself out of a cell.

There was a startled beat. Then Verrat snarled and jumped at Mala.

The gun went off before Mala fully registered it. Verrat fell sideways, clutching her thigh. Mala took a step back and trained the gun on her once more.

A second later, Ein smashed into the clearing. "Mala, what the muck does it take for your microscopic intel—oh!" He backed away from Verrat at Mala's signal.

"Verrat, Ein. Ein, Verrat. This is the woman that was working with Blut. She sold my guard to the Erlenders."

Verrat looked up. Indignation replaced pain. "I saved you. Blut would have given you to—"

Mala stared down at her. "Don't lie. You were supposed to mark me and you botched it. So you thought you could pawn that necklace off on Sari ..." The anger swirled. It howled between her ears. *You stole my mother.* She kicked Verrat's ribs.

Verrat grunted but didn't respond.

"Why?"

Verrat just curled into a fetal position.

A tornado raged through Mala's head. Reason blew away. She kicked and kicked and kicked again. Ein dragged Mala back.

"Okay, I hate to interrupt the revenge scenario that's about to play out here but ... We should move. They can't pinpoint the gunshot yet but I bet they're scrambling to try. Take her or leave her?"

"Take her."

"Fine. But rein it in."

"She killed my mom!"

"Time. And place. Not now. Not here."

Mala took a deep breath. Another. Her anger still swirled, but she held onto the calm in the midst of the storm. "Can you carry her?"

Ein nodded. He scooped up the once pristine warrior. She was barely more than a husk.

Verrat groaned in pain.

Mala smiled. "Don't worry. I'll patch up your leg. When I kill you, it won't be as easy as that."

Verrat turned her head. Her violet eyes flashed. "You won't kill me, Mala. Keptiker will. She's seen it."

"Who?"

But Verrat just smiled. She looped her arms around Ein's neck and said, "Where are we going, handsome?"

Mala seethed.

Ein laughed. "I hope all our hostages are as compliant—"

"Ein!" Before Mala could bark at him, another voice hissed.

He's safe! Mala's heart jumped.

"Get the hell out of here now!" Lowe's voice was quiet, but furious. "You idiots are gonna get us killed before we even get to the compound. Inland! We gotta put him outta sight. *Now.*" He turned. A limp form sagged over his shoulder. Lowe began marching inland.

Verrat was the first to speak. "Is that Keptiker?" Her face went white, and she began to struggle in Ein's arms. "No! No!"

Mala reached up to help. She wrapped an arm around Verrat's neck, and applied pressure to her carotid artery. Ein did his best to hold her, but Verrat was a trained soldier. Her leg swung around and caught Mala's side. She reached and wrenched at Ein's hair. A jab to the neck and he collapsed. Mala threw herself at the woman.

"No!" Mala pulled Verrat back, spurred by adrenaline. They fell to the ground, Mala atop Verrat. Mala tried to pin the woman down, but Verrat was bigger. The older woman quickly flipped Mala onto her back and scrambled on top of her.

"Don't," Mala gasped. But then Verrat's hands were at her throat, a wild gleam in the other woman's eyes.

"He wants you," Verrat muttered. "But he'll kill me. He. Will. Kill Me." Mala's struggles were growing more and more futile. Her eyelids flickered.

But that's when she felt it. A spark. Mala threw herself into the flame, forced her eyes open. She forced herself to stare at Verrat. The flames ate at her. And a vision suddenly replaced reality.

She saw a figure in a cloak standing before a canvas. The figure held a paintbrush and flicked it, splattering red paint onto the pale trunk of a tree.

Mala melted. She emerged, fierce, muscled. Male. She threw Verrat off her. The woman's eyes widened. Verrat began to shake. A solitary tear streaked down her cheek.

Mala retrieved her gun.

The gore that exploded from Verrat's head spattered the tree behind her. It looked exactly like the painting. The violet eyes stilled. Verrat's lifeless body fell to the ground.

"Muck!" The exact replica of a scene she'd just envisioned unnerved Mala. Goosebumps crept up her arms. She looked down at them. Huge and muscled. But familiar. Keptiker's arms. She had melted into Keptiker.

Verrat had said Keptiker would kill her. She had panicked when Lowe had walked up with him, Keptiker slung across his back. Verrat had believed Keptiker would kill her. Mala had thought it was simply because Verrat had betrayed him, because she'd escaped. *What was it she said? "She's seen it." A woman. Who? Someone was painting this tree. A blood-spattered tree. Just a coincidence. It's a tree. Maybe they were painting falling leaves. It's just ... not possible.*

Mala's mind flashed back to Lowe's scornful words when she'd first thought becoming Kreis was magic.

"Erlenders believe in that junk ... magic and fortune-telling. That's not real. It's a bunch of fairy dust and lies strung together for idiots."

Mala wanted to believe that. Part of her wished she did. But another little part of her whispered, *There's someone out there painting things. Things like this. How Verrat would die.* Her mind flashed to all of the paintings that Ges had been categorizing. All of those landscapes. Battles. But plenty of empty scenes, too. *What if they weren't just landscapes? What if they weren't just maps? What if they were predictions?* Mala's stomach dropped. She didn't want to think it, but the thought whispered through her head anyway. *Someone's painting the future. And getting it right.*

CHAPTER THIRTY-FOUR

Mala marched into Wilde, all swagger and dark confidence. She ignored the Erlender soldiers who moved aside as she swept past. She ignored the kids with distended bellies. She ignored her own desire to kill every Wilde soldier she saw in retribution for her mother. She kept her face forward.

Stay on mission. Remember: Keptiker's cold. Brutal. Lowe had made her repeat that all afternoon. He'd made her nearly hoarse, standing over the real Keptiker's body as she recited the plan. *Leave early for Troe's compound. Leave at night. Keep everyone exhausted and guessing so they don't notice if I do anything unusual. Un-Keptiker.* She'd recited it as she, Lowe, and Ein had taken turns kicking Keptiker in the face, hoping that some extreme swelling and a broken nose would hide his identity when he came to. Since they couldn't kill him if Mala was melting into him, they had to do what they could. They'd tied Keptiker's drugged and beaten body to a tree, and covered him in brush.

Mala had felt weak when she suggested they leave Keptiker a water jug. Starvation seemed like a cruel way to go. *If no one comes out this far to find him.* She couldn't think of her mother, but it seemed that the instinct to heal sometimes overpowered Mala, particularly when it shouldn't.

She'd been surprised when Lowe had agreed. "It might keep him alive a couple extra days, in case things go sideways on us. We might need the extra time." Mala wasn't sure why, but his answer had disappointed her.

As she strode through the Wilde complex, Mala hoped her cold attitude effectively distracted from Ein's shaking. For all that he stood tall and looked dismissive, his hands were a dead giveaway. She hoped no one would notice. Lowe, a lively six year old, kept up a constant chatter with soldiers, providing an effective diversion as their boots echoed through the hallways made of shipping containers. Lowe used his hands to subtly point and guide Mala through the maze of tunnels, until she came to a back room and desk that was Keptiker's office.

It was a dark room, lit only by natural light from a rough cutout in the wall. Wilde was too poor a compound to have candles. The desk held a rusted walkie and a few scraps of paper. Neid was chained to the floor in a spot Verrat had once occupied. Keptiker's chair was a wilting hunk of metal. Only the arsenal behind it was impressive: rack upon rack of weapons on the wall. Boxes of ammo on the floor. It all spoke of the Wilde's reputation as raiders. Of Keptiker's reputation as a ruthless killer.

It reminded Mala of her purpose.

"Change a' plans," Mala barked at a pair of soldiers who had slipped into the room behind him. The skeletal boy jumped at her words while the wizened old soldier merely grunted and leaned back against the wall, casually awaiting orders.

Mala leaned over the desk, grateful for the practice she had put in with Ges. She fastened her eyes on the kid's forehead, avoiding his direct gaze. "Heard summ'in dirty's in the water. Someone's been spreadin' lies 'bout us. Gonna head out ta Troe's tonight insteada' tomorra. Git everyone together now. Change out halfa' the group. New faces. Wanna smoke out or spook whoever's been flappin' lips. You git three hours. That's it. And I want dis new blondie on there for Troe." Mala jerked her head toward Neid, who rattled the chains in protest. "Keep'er clean. He don' want sloppy seconds. Oh—and these idgits from Stur township are comin' too." She gestured lazily at Lowe and Ein.

"A kid?" the older soldier looked skeptical.

"General Dummk got 'im some orders from Troe. Provide escort and check. Think he's tryin' to piss me off. Makin' me babysit."

Lowe looked indignant. "I's good with the numbers sir. That's why he sent me."

Mala appraised him coldly. "I think you'd be good for somethin' better than that."

Lowe gulped. The room went deadly quiet. Mala smiled harshly. "Don' speak outta turn again or you gonna learn jus' what it is I think you're good for boy." She barked out a laugh. The older soldier joined her.

"Sir?" The young soldier bit his lip. "Imma s'posed to tell you she's gone."

What? Who? Verrat? How am I supposed to react? Did

Keptiker know? Mala decided less was more. She raised an eyebrow, simply waiting.

"We had her stuff a'ready and packed for Troe like you said. But she just disappeared. Took one of dem boats, too."

A boat! Verrat didn't have a boat.

"Boy, you bein' as clear as mud right now. Spit it out."

"She's gone sir. The Chiara's gone. Left not five minutes past."

Mala froze, uncertain how to play this out. She knew the Chiara was an advisor. She knew that Keptiker had been meeting with her. She didn't know the significance of their relationship. *Mucking hell. I am totally unprepared for this mission. Ein was right.* She had to force herself not to look to Lowe for guidance. She locked eyes with the scrawny soldier. His grey eyes blinked rapidly. It was clear that he expected her to be upset. He was cringing. So Mala boomed out, "She's gone?"

"Yezzir," the blue nose continued, relieved now that he felt more confident of his commanding officer's reaction. "Said she hadda get them paintin's to Troe right quick. Important. She'd seen summin'."

Mala's heart froze. "Paintin's?"

The boy nodded.

"Of what?"

"She didn't say."

Paintings. The Chiara painted. And she'd left to show Troe a painting.

"Shit!" The words slipped out before Mala could contain

them. Everyone turned to stare at her. *Calm. Calm down. Cold. Control. Keptiker.*

She sat at the desk, though every instinct told her to send someone, everyone after the Chiara. But she couldn't. "Bring dese two to da prep room. Git 'em set up. Troe wants 'em overseeing. Makin' sure we ain't skimmin' him. Then roun' ev'rybody up. Three hours. We leavin' at nightfall."

Both soldiers saluted. They turned in the doorway, ready to head off.

"Wait!" Mala called out. "You," she gestured at the younger soldier. "Stay."

The boy visibly gulped. But he nodded. Ein and Lowe disappeared down the hall, but not before Lowe shot her a warning look. She ignored it.

"Take me to da' Chiara's rooms," she ordered the skinny Erlender.

Mala followed the young soldier, blatantly ignoring the curiosity radiating from him. She was deviating from the plan. She knew it. But her gut drove her forward. Somewhere at the Center, she'd shed the insecure girl who'd hidden behind her mother. Mala knew she was young and stupid and hardly trained, but her vow echoed in her head. *Blood for blood.* And Mala knew somehow this Chiara was the one who'd told Verrat about her death. *What does she know? What did she see?*

Scraps of paper littered the floor. Canvases stood stacked against the wall in a corner. A small fire burned in a tin trashcan that appeared filled to the brim. Mala ran to it and knocked it over, immediately stamping on the contents to salvage what she could.

When the fire was out, Mala squatted and scooped up the tiny shards of paper that remained. She felt eyes boring into her back. She whipped around and stared down at the young soldier. "Three hours! Git movin'."

He immediately left. She bent back over to the papers.

Lines. Mostly lines, incomprehensible pieces of much larger artworks. Faces. None recognizable. Mala flipped through page after burnt page, watching the paper disintegrate into under her fingertips.

Nothing. Nothing. Nothing. Wait. She stopped. She turned a sketch sideways. The lower half of the face was singed. Short curls. A straight brow. Eyes she would know anywhere. *Lowe.*

Her heart clenched. She stood, slowly, as if in a trance. She folded the paper, tucking it into her pocket. She glanced around the room, only half-seeing what was there. Stacks of canvases.

Numbly, Mala flipped through them. Dull landscape after dull landscape. *What do I do? What does it mean? What did she see? Why did the Chiara burn this sketch? Do I say anything?* She pictured trying to bring this to Ein or Lowe. They'd only scoff. But somewhere deep in her stomach, belief churned. Mala longed for Ges. *He would listen. He would say anything's possible.*

Verrat's dying words echoed in her head. *The Chiara draws things.* And she'd drawn Lowe. And now, that woman was headed for the King's compound. Ahead of them.

Mucking hell.

CHAPTER THIRTY-FIVE

The stars were cold pinpricks above. A full moon watched Mala and her ratty band of Erlenders march inland, down a dirt path that ran parallel to an old asphalt road that had long since deteriorated into a series of cracked black teeth. The wind whipped their skin, sending a stinging chill right to the bone.

But Mala hardly felt it. She was too busy turning her revelations over and over in her mind. She felt crazy. Felt like she hadn't in months. Like she was back in Bara's guard, the only idiot to ever possibly believe in the unbelievable. In magic.

The feeling made her claustrophobic. It made her count her breaths. It made it impossible to focus. Finally, she couldn't deal with it. And so she did something foolish.

"Unchain 'er," Mala gestured to Neid, who was attached to a long chain of prisoners snaking their way along the back of the procession.

Keptiker's soldiers looked at her questioningly. She flashed a grim smile. "Think I'mma paint her a little picture of what's comin' for her. Increase the anticipation. Troe likes 'em quiverin'. If ya know what I mean."

That earned a dark chuckle. She pulled her gun from her waistband and kept it trained on Neid, as the girl was re-cuffed into an individual pair of irons. "We'll take the rear, gentlemen. No needa' wait on our account."

Mala stood stock still, until she and Neid were several meters behind the last of the group.

"What are you doing?" Neid whispered venomously.

"I need to talk to you."

"You are an idiot. You're blowing my cover. *Our* cover."

"Ein and Lowe won't listen. I have to tell someone."

"What?"

Mala took a deep breath. "You hear that I killed Verrat?"

Neid nodded.

"Before she died, she told me Keptiker would kill her. She said the Chiara had seen it. And, well, I was me. But I had a meltdown. Into Keptiker. Right before I killed her."

There was a beat. Neid stopped moving. She stared at Mala, mouth gaping.

Mala gestured with her gun. "Keep moving." She gave Neid a little shove in case anyone was watching.

"You don't really believe—" Neid started.

"She believed. And it happened."

"But Verrat was his prisoner. We've been watching tape on Keptiker for days. He was gonna kill her anyway. It would be easy for her to believe that. Especially after she escaped. She had to know he'd come after her."

Mala paused. "Maybe." Neid had a point. But there was still

the vision when she'd melted. She felt uncomfortable mentioning it. *Visions aren't proof, right?* "But the thing is, Verrat believed, said the Chiara painted it. And what if Verrat's not the only one who believes? Erlenders believe in that stuff. So what if this Chiara working with Keptiker is painting things … that she tells people will happen?"

Neid's brow furrowed.

Mala hurried on, wanting to get the explanation out before Neid could pass judgement again. "I went to the Chiara's room. It was full of paintings. Drawings. Mostly landscapes. But there were sketches. She tried to burn some." Mala scanned carefully up the road. She didn't see anyone looking back. She dug the scrap of paper out of her pocket.

"I saved this. I don't know if you can see it very well, but it's Lowe. She drew Lowe."

Neid hissed. "How would she know what he looks like?"

"You mean other than having visions of the future?"

Neid rolled her eyes and handed back the scrap of paper. "Do you think Alba told her?"

Mala raised a brow. "Alba left before we got our mission."

"So either she's seen Lowe look like a kid on a past mission … or there's another mole."

Mala considered that. "Maybe. Maybe Alba wasn't one to begin with… who knows?"

"So Lowe's compromised."

"I dunno. But the Chiara left early to tell Troe something.

So it's likely."

"So we're walking into a trap."

Mala nodded. Her chest felt tight. "I think so. I think Lowe's in danger."

Neid leaned toward her. "Question is, what are we gonna do about it?"

CHAPTER THIRTY-SIX

"No!" Lowe protested, his six-year-old voice shrill and whiny. "You're sendin' me off so you gotta chance to skim offa Troe's—"

Mala punched his eye. Hard. "You wanna accuse me a' cheatin' my cousin? That's funny." Mala turned to the senior blue nose beside her. "Ain't that funny?"

The soldier nodded. His mouth gaped, showing a missing tooth. He looked shocked that she'd just leveled a kid.

Was that too much? No—don't second-guess. Mala clapped the soldier on his shoulder.

"Shave his head. And his eyebrows. Clowns otta look tha' part. Then take 'im with a group to get water. If you needa' – chain 'im up. Don' take no lip from a kid. Getta lotta water. I don' wanna run out. Our own supply. Don' trust no one inside."

Mala had to remind herself not to bite her lip as the soldier roughly manhandled Lowe. *It's for a good cause,* she told herself. It was the best she and Neid had been able to devise. Something that would delay Lowe's entry so they could scout out Troe's compound first. Something that would change his appearance. Something, anything to try to save him.

I'm sorry, Mala mentally called out after him.

Ein raised his eyebrows but kept his mouth shut. Either exhaustion or stress had tamed his arrogant streak. Mala was grateful; they'd marched through the night and she didn't think she could handle his protests, too.

The night sky lightened to grey around them and tendrils of fog unfurled over the next hill. As they reached the crest, Mala caught her first glance of Troe's compound.

It had been an urban downtown nearly a century before, a collection of skyscrapers clawing at the stars. But now, only one ominous black glass tower remained, surrounded by a jagged circle of debris. Troe's father had put explosives to every building for a three-kilometer radius. It gave him the advantage of a clear view, and a mound of rubble surrounding his compound like a glittering moat. Only two entrances had been carved through the mountains of steel and glass. And these were heavily guarded.

Mala heard guns cock as her group approached the main entrance. She stopped at the head of the group, next to Ein, waiting expectantly.

A gate lowered and a contingent of guards, looking much better fed than her Wilde soldiers, approached them, armed to the teeth. Knives, bows, axes, and guns were all strapped to them. Though some of them wore animal hides across their chest like the Wilde band, many had on actual pants or shorts raided from Senebal territory. The guards fanned out, blocking the entry.

"Weapons on the ground!" their leader called out. He was a

tall man, taller than Keptiker. His nose had been broken in several places so the blue lines now resembled jagged waves. He stopped directly in front of Mala, who handed him her gun.

He stared Mala down, his beady black eyes evaluating her. She didn't flinch. Didn't move. Didn't breathe.

He waited while his men collected their weapons. "Everyone on the ground. Hands behind your head!"

This isn't protocol. Mala's heart thrummed. *What would Keptiker do? Do I comply?* Instead of getting to the ground, Mala raised an eyebrow. The captain of the guard raised one in return. Mala waved a hand, indicating her people should follow the order. She remained standing.

The captain patted her down roughly. Then he kicked Ein in the ribs with a grating, "Git up," sounding in her ears. Ein struggled to his feet. The captain cuffed him.

Neid cried out. "Get off!" She struggled to her feet. Immediately a guard was on her.

Mala sucked in her breath as the captain of the guard stepped forward. He wrapped his hand in Neid's hair and pulled back until she screeched. He pulled until she dangled from her hair alone. He peered into her eyes. "Attached to your old master, little slave?"

Don't speak. Don't speak. Mala silently urged Neid to shut her mouth. She wasn't sure if her pleas did the trick, but Neid stared silently back at the captain.

A young soldier shuffled quickly over and shoved a crumpled piece of parchment at the captain. "It's her."

The captain studied the paper for a moment. Then he stared

at Neid. He held out his hand. The young soldier handed him a gun.

No! Mala didn't have time to scream before a shot rang out. Blood splattered across Mala's cheek. Ein stood frozen beside her. She felt shock. She knew horror was in there as well. But disbelief trumped her other emotions.

"Lil' vixen. Tried to git away."

She just tried to protect her brother.

"Chiara wuz right sir." The young soldier tossed down the blood splattered sheet of paper. It was thick paper, a type Mala recognized. She had a scrap of it in her pocket. She inhaled sharply.

The captain turned to her.

"Well now, Troe's gunna wanna talk to ya. About why you bringin' spies in here."

She forced herself to meet his eyes. "Careful captain. Las' man talked to me like that can' talk no more. Lemme see that paper."

The captain narrowed his eyes, but shrugged. "Dead now so dunno what good it's gonna do ya'."

Mala bent to scoop up the drawing at her feet. There, in charcoal, in the same style as Lowe's drawing, was Neid's smiling face.

Muck!

Next to her, Ein fell forward in a dead faint.

CHAPTER THIRTY-SEVEN

Mala stood rigid, defiant, in the small room. Five guards stood around her, guns casually pointed at different parts of her anatomy. She watched herself in the windows, Keptiker's body at attention. *His face looks calm at least,* she comforted herself. But anyone who laid a hand on Keptiker's chest would know Mala's heart was running a marathon.

Troe ignored her as he completed his ceremony. Kneeling at a wall full of broken clocks, he bowed. He cut his finger with a ceremonial knife. He whispered words under his breath. The king smeared his own blood over an emerald. And then he swallowed it.

Troe turned to Mala, a wall of windows at his back, curtains shoved aside. The sunrise painted a pink halo around him. A thin, sickly face. A long, pointed nose with faded stripes along the bridge. Salt-and-pepper hair. Everything was unattractive save his eyes. They were a light, nearly neon green. And his eyes were fixed on her. Troe stalked toward Mala, sweeping his tattered black cape behind him.

She didn't see the punch coming. Her head snapped to the side. Electric pain sizzled along her jaw. She righted herself and continued to stare at Troe, fighting the reactions Verrukter had ingrained. *Not yet. Timing. Surprise attacks are best.* She chanted lessons from Lowe in order to calm herself.

"Where didja' find 'er? Why'd you bring 'er?" Troe's voice rasped.

"My men found 'er in the woods near Wilde, tryin' to spy," Mala smoothly rattled off Neid's cover story. "We caught 'er, and I thought 'stead of selling 'er, she might appeal to ya. She was purty defiant." Troe watched her, cocking his head. She felt he wanted something further, so she tacked on, "If the Chiara had stuck aroun' lemme know what she saw, 'course I woudn'ta brought 'er."

Troe evaluated her for a moment. Mala maintained eye contact, counting each breath. *One, two, three ...* She exhaled. Troe waved at his guards and the guns dropped.

"That woman does havva flair fer drama," Troe acknowledged. "Coulda' saved us a lotta trouble. I'm meetin' 'er later. I'll give 'er a talkin' to."

"Good luck," Mala rolled her eyes.

Troe's eyes snapped back to hers, and Mala worried she'd gone too far. But a second later he barked out a laugh.

"Git outta here. I'll have my people count whatcha' brought. Send for ya then."

Mala gave a brisk nod, tapped her heels together, and exited the room. In the hall her legs felt like jelly, but she forced one foot in front of the other as two armed guards escorted her to Keptiker's room.

Inside, she barely had time to sink onto the cot before Lowe burst in, rage etched across his features.

"What the muck was that?" he seethed. "You think you should lead this mission? *You?* Tossed me in with that group and when we get here what's happened? You got Neid killed already? Five seconds in? What the mucking hell?"

Mala glanced at him. The rage radiating off him immediately sent heat to her stomach. She spiraled into a meltdown. Glancing down at herself, she realized she'd transformed into Fell. "Great. Where's Ein?"

"I don't know," Lowe seethed, child-size fists balled in anger. He glared at her, one eye a swollen purple knob from her punch.

"Well you better go get him before someone comes in here and sees me," Mala bit back.

"You haven't answered me." The rage in Lowe's face cut through Mala. Yes, he was angry. He was infuriated. But she thought she saw a glimmer of hurt underneath all that. It was the hurt that did her in.

"Here," Mala reached into her pocket and pulled out the scrap of paper. "They had a drawing of you. You were compromised. I found it in the Chiara's rooms. I should have told you." She hung her head. "I couldn't think of a way to talk to you. Or Ein. I'm supposed to be suspicious of you guys since you're from another township. But I thought Keptiker—I mean I—could get away with torturing Neid. With scaring her, I mean. And it was the best we could come up with to make you look different."

Lowe shook his head at her. "You don't get to pull shit like this, Mala. You don't get to change the rules. They had a drawing of me. So what?"

"So, they had a drawing of Neid and they shot her on sight!" Mala retorted.

Lowe took a deep, calming breath. "I understand you think what you did was for the best. But you have to run things like that by me. I'm point on this mission. You can't just send me off … even if you think you're protecting me."

Tears came into Mala's eyes. "I'm sorry," she whispered. "I just didn't want … I couldn't stand to see you get hurt."

Lowe cupped her cheek. He bit his lip. "It's really distracting when you look like my commanding Ancient."

"Yeah, well, sorry. You're the one who's mad at her, apparently," Mala retorted.

"For agreeing—sending us here," Lowe caressed her cheek. "When we are clearly not prepared enough."

"I'm sorry, Lowe," Mala repeated. She leaned her face into his hand.

"I know," he said. Then he gave a crooked grin. "Just don't do it again." He tossed her his small water bottle, so she could at least wait in her own skin.

"Aye aye," she retorted. For the first time since she'd set foot in Troe's compound, the tension in Mala's chest eased.

"Now I need to go find a man to kiss you," Lowe quipped.

"Wish it could be you," Mala pouted.

Lowe's sweet six-year-old grin widened as he slipped out the door. "Believe me, so do I."

CHAPTER THIRTY-EIGHT

Mala held her breath. She heard the scuffle of Lowe's feet as he raced down the hallway toward her, in six-year-old form. Behind him, the clunky footsteps of Troe's bodyguard drummed on the dusty floor tiles.

"Give it here' ya damned snake!" the guard bellowed.

Lowe laughed, and neatly jumped the tripwire he and Mala had set. He emptied the magazine of the bodyguard's gun. It clattered across the floor. Lowe tossed the weapon behind him, just as the guard approached the tripwire. The distraction was perfect: the man fell with a thud.

Mala grabbed a heavy binder off the shelf. She stepped out of an office and cracked the guard over the head. His eyes closed.

Lowe gestured to her. She tossed him a set of computer cords. "Close to rope as I saw in there."

He nodded. Mala knotted the cords over the man's legs and hands. Then Lowe reached into his shirt and brought out a small vial, just as he had the night he'd brought Mala to the Center. He smeared the contents across the guard's lips.

"That'll keep him sleeping for a good while," he said. He

stood. "Mala, meet your new body double: This is Kopf. Not the brightest star in the sky. But good enough. He's on duty tonight during Troe's meetings." He looked up. "You ready?"

Mala nodded. "Sure. Let me go get Ein."

Lowe had chosen well: the floor was abandoned. No one was around. No one was on the floor below, either, perhaps because they were forty-five stories high in the eighty-story building. Troe's force only occupied the first thirty stories and the underground parking structure. And if the dusty cubicles were any indication, no one from Troe's guard would be inspecting this floor for a long time.

Lowe had decided they needed to move quickly. With Neid gone, they'd lost reconnaissance opportunities in the prison, where guards tended to drink and get loose-lipped. They needed to listen in on Troe's strategy sessions. Find out his plans. They only had a few days before their cover was blown—if Keptiker survived. Lowe was a kid and therefore mobile, but he couldn't get into secure locations. Ein might have come up with something before … but he was listless. He hadn't said a word since Neid died.

Ein hadn't responded when Mala had hugged him. He hadn't responded when Lowe had yelled at him. He hadn't slept when they'd hunkered down in Keptiker's room a few hours ago. In a way, Mala understood. The unthinkable had happened: his sister had come on this mission to protect him. And she was gone.

So it all falls on my *untrained behind,* Mala's thoughts muttered as she dodged into a cubicle to grab Ein.

He sat on a desk, staring out at the landscape—a collection of houses and trees and trimmed grass so perfect and serene that you would never guess something was amiss. But just outside the mountain of rubble, there was a low rock wall. It marked the boundary before The Ice, as Erlenders called the tainted lands beyond the border. Everyone knew not to cross the wall. But the picture-perfect homes made for a tempting sight. They didn't look infected. But there was no movement, no life. Not a rabbit or deer, not a human in sight. The world outside the borders stayed frozen, untouched, because it still wasn't safe.

Rumors of poison gas and terrible fates still swirled through Senebal ears nearly a century after the explosion that changed everything. Troe's compound was just inside the bounds of safety, just beyond the fallout's fingers. But the windows had a clear view of how empty and desolate and beautiful the outside world really was.

Mala grabbed Ein's elbow. He didn't budge. He was too big to move, so rather than struggle against him, she sat next to him on a desk. "Hey handsome," she nudged his shoulder. "I came to see if you wanted to make out."

Ein's lip curled slightly, but he didn't respond.

"I know it sucks," Mala continued. "I know right now there's a hole in your chest. But I want you to know … I'll make sure it wasn't for nothing. I'll get everything I can on these stupid bluenoses. And then …" Mala choked up. She couldn't speak. Her mother's face flashed through her mind and sadness gripped her. "I know what it's like," she finished lamely. She reached for Ein's hand. She squeezed. To her surprise, he squeezed back.

"I know you know." His voice was raw. It tugged at Mala to

hear him so vulnerable. He'd never been vulnerable before. He'd always acted so superior. But the shield was down. A solitary tear made its way down his cheek. She had to resist the urge to wipe it away.

She waited a moment. And another. It was almost calming, to sit in grief together. But eventually she had to ask. "I know it's a lot. It's too soon, but I need to …."

Ein sighed. "I know. You need to melt. I just … I don't think I can … you know."

Mala nodded. She took a deep breath. She knew what she had to do. *I have to seduce Ein. Oh geez. Ein. I'm sorry in advance. I'm gonna be terrible. Here goes.* She leaned up to whisper innocently in his ear, "So, you don't think you could pull my hair and pin me down on the desk?"

Ein gasped. He looked over at her, shock etched across his face.

Mala raised an eyebrow and met his gaze head-on. "I know you like it rough." She leaned in further, so that her lips were just short of his. "I've actually started to like it rough, too."

And then his lips were on hers.

CHAPTER THIRTY-NINE

Mala edged toward King Troe, attempting to be inconspicuous as she and the bodyguard on duty traded out. She took up her stance and tried not to fidget with the sleeves of her olive flight suit. Troe's guard were stuffed ceremonially into pre-war flight suits, with no regard for fit. Mala's was more than snug. But she stood ramrod-straight anyway.

Troe hardly glanced at her as he shuffled through the paperwork at his desk. *That's a good sign, at least*, she tried to encourage herself. She avoided eye contact with the two other bodyguards posted in the room. Just in case.

Dull light trickled in from the filthy twentieth-story windows on the back wall. It caressed stacks of canvases Troe had shoved into the corners. The light couldn't quite reach the pictures he'd tacked up on the walls: Das Wort, the floating Senebal capital, shown from any number of angles; the canals; the president's sanctuary; the cheap houseboats of the poor that clustered around the buildings like fleas. The pictures looked just like Ges had described: surveillance. She couldn't see any indication of what Troe had planned.

Just as Mala was beginning to wonder if she'd have to stare

at paintings all day, an older woman slipped into the room.

"Yer sons to see you, yer majesty,"

Troe gave a brisk nod and shuffled some papers. "A'right."

The woman led three preteen boys into the room. It was all Mala could do not to flinch. Each of their faces was heavily scarred and tattooed. Scrawny and pubescent as they were, the boys gave off an air of danger. They stood at attention side by side.

"Well?" Troe asked.

"Haven't found 'er yet," the middle one replied. "But we will."

"When you do … be careful."

"Don' worry 'bout us. We can handle some girl."

Troe raised his eyebrows. "I meant, be careful with *'er*, you fool." He looked like he was about to continue his lecture, but another knock sounded at the door.

Again, the servant woman slipped in to announce the visitor. "The Chiara to see you, yer Majesty."

Troe waved to admit the chiara. "No, stay," he told the boys. "Lissen to what she gotta say."

A short woman dressed in grey entered. She wore a black veil over her hair. A paintbrush dangled from a string on her neck.

Mala felt a tingle, a sense of déjà vu. But she only got half a glance at the woman's pale profile, before the Chiara turned her back to Mala and faced Troe.

"She's here, yer Majesty," the Chiara intoned. She handed over a sketch.

Where have I seen her? Mala wondered.

"You sure?"

"I'm sure," the Chiara responded.

One of Troe's sons spoke up. "Well there's a lotta places here could be. Couldja' be more specific? I know it don' bother you none, but since you don' have to go lookin' and all …"

The Chiara cuffed the prince.

He retaliated by swiping her veil. And a lush mane of red hair fell across her shoulders as she reached for him.

Mala gasped. Red hair. Short, curvy figure. A woman Mala herself had melted into time and again. The woman who made Mala feel vulnerable, unsure of herself. The woman Lowe had loved. *The Chiara is Stelle.*

CHAPTER FORTY

Mala was drowning. She couldn't breathe. She remained at her post, unmoving, unhearing. If Troe and the Chiara mentioned any other grand plans to take over Das Wort and destroy the Senebals, she didn't hear it.

She's alive. The thought repeated in a long trailing echo. *She's alive. His first love. Of course she's alive; I can't melt into the dead. I'm an idiot. Of course.*

Once the initial shock and pain had died down, Mala's thoughts were able to follow a line of possibilities. But she kept circling back to one particular question. *Does Lowe know?* She'd transformed into Stelle so many times over the past few months, each time she and Lowe had gotten carried away. Part of her argued, *I turned into a younger version of her.* But another part was skeptical. Melts were about the first, most intense surge of emotion. Not present emotion. So he could know.

Lowe had always talked of Stelle in the past tense. *He said the Erlenders had stolen her.* Typically that meant slavery. Which was a short stop away from death. Most slaves were lucky to last two years. *Did she leave willingly? Was he covering for her? Is he working with her?*

Each new question felt like a cut. And unlike her mother's death, which had ripped her heart out, this felt like a thousand little cuts in her mind. On her judgement. On her choices. *Did I trust the wrong person?* Doubt bled her dry.

Mala was so involved in her internal dialogue that it took her a moment to realize Troe was standing before her.

"Glad I wuzzn't getting' attacked jus' now, or you and I'd both be dead," Troe commented sardonically.

"Sir, I'm sorry, night watch—" Mala fumbled for a reply.

"Don' wan' no excuses. Yer off the list for my office from here on out. But I'm hopin' yer still awake enough to carry something to the guard barracks downstairs?"

Mala nodded stiffly.

"Good. Give 'em this picture. Tell 'em to all be on the lookout. Lil girl here's gonna be my new queen."

Troe handed Mala the charcoal drawing the Chiara had handed him. Mala glanced down at it. She froze. It was a drawing of her face. *No.*

Troe tapped the drawing with a finger. "You sure you can handle this soldier? You lookin' kinda green …"

Mala glanced back up at him, willing an impassive look onto her face. Behind him, his sons were watching her closely. She couldn't see the Chiara's face. "Yessir."

"Good. Get outta here."

With that dismissal, Mala stumbled out of the room.

CHAPTER FORTY-ONE

Mala leaned against the wall near the stairs. She stared at nothing, her mind as blank as the wall. She counted for a second. But footsteps and a hushed argument reached her ears. She doubled over, clutching her stomach, intending to play up the part of the ill soldier.

Mala was startled to find out one of the voices belonged to the prince.

"—In an hour in the shrine. You'd better have more answers than that," the boy's voice threatened.

"I've told you—" the Chiara cut off as she spotted Mala.

The prince's cold voice rang out. "My father sent you to the barracks." He eyed Mala suspiciously.

Mala put a look of agony on her face. It wasn't hard. "I'm feelin' dizzy yer highness. I think I might be—" She dry heaved for good measure. That sent the prince and the Chiara scurrying downstairs.

Mala stared after them. *They're meeting in an hour.* The only shrine she could think of was the one with the clocks, where she'd met Troe as Keptiker. *Worth a try.*

Mala hurtled up the stairs. When she arrived at the top, panting, she headed toward the cubicles.

Lowe stepped out of one. "Well?" he asked.

Mala's heart nearly stopped. *Muck and shit.* She stared at him and swallowed. *I thought I knew you.*

"The Chiara showed up," Mala mentioned, gauging Lowe's reaction. His face didn't register anything. It was smooth, even. *But he's had years of practice hiding his emotions,* Mala reminded herself.

Mala held his gaze as she lied. "Nothing important happened."

Lowe raised an eyebrow. "Really? Nothing?"

"How many times have you gotten intel the first day into a mission?"

Lowe didn't respond.

Either he knows what the Chiara brought and he's working with her, or he can tell I'm lying. Which is it?

"Look, I need to check on Ein. I know he's having a hard time," Mala used her Erlender soldier's body to push past Lowe.

"Of course. Ein." Lowe couldn't keep the bitterness out of his tone.

"His sister just died," Mala retorted. *And guess what? I don't know if I can trust you and I can't stand lying any longer. So shut it.*

Lowe sighed, but didn't come after her.

She found Ein at the desk, still staring. Mala perched beside him. She waited for an eternity, until she heard Lowe walk away.

When Mala felt confident Lowe was gone, she held out a

hand. Ein took it. Silently, she led him back to the staircase and up another two floors.

"Kiss me," Mala ordered.

"Again?" Ein moaned.

"I'm starting to think kissing me is a burden, not your nightly fantasy."

"What gave it away?"

"It's your fault, you know."

"Oh, trust me. I'm aware."

"I need you to kiss me. It's important."

"Can you at least melt into you first? It's already hard enough …"

Mala rolled her eyes as she got out the tiny water bottle Lowe had given her earlier. "*You* better be hard enough …." She poured the water over her hands.

"Did you just make a dirty joke?"

"Surprised a mouth-breather like me is capable of one?"

"A little."

"Yes, let's talk about little …" Mala raised her brows, deliberately baiting him.

"You wouldn't know!" Ein said defensively.

"You slammed me half-naked into the wall of a submarine and pressed yourself against me. You think I didn't notice? I mean, there was hardly anything there *to* notice. But still …"

Ein grabbed her hair. "You're doing this on purpose."

"According to you, I'm not smart enough to do this on purpose."

Ein smiled. Almost laughed. Tears filled his eyes. "You always know just what to do."

"What?" *Tears? What did I do wrong?*

"You know exactly how to get under my skin."

Mala smiled. "I thought the point was that *you* wanted under my skin, sludge breath."

Then Ein did laugh. And he kissed her.

When she melted, Ein froze. "What's going on?"

Mala grabbed his hand. "Listen carefully Ein. I need you to keep Lowe busy for the next two hours. Barracks, inventory, taxes—I don't care. But don't tell him. Meet me on the sixtieth floor once he's eating. Have your best escape plan ready."

"You didn't answer me."

Mala took a deep breath. "I don't have time to explain. I've gotta get downstairs before … Ein I need you to trust me. There's a possibility that Lowe isn't on our side. And I have to find out. I'll give you five minutes to get him out of there. Then I'm coming down."

Mala turned to a window, straightening her baggy Erlender jumpsuit. Lowe's face stared impassively back at her. *Let's see what you've been up to, lover boy.*

CHAPTER FORTY-TWO

Mala waited in the shrine, curled uncomfortably into a corner. She was mashed between a grandfather clock and a gaudy red velvet curtain. Tingles traveled up her legs. *Hurry up and get here already.*

Her wish wasn't granted until after her left leg was asleep. The door creaked open. Mala peered around the curtain. The chiara entered hesitantly, a small book of drawings under her arm. She took a seat in one of the chairs, clearly expecting to wait.

Impulsively, Mala stepped out from behind the curtain.

"What?" Stelle dropped her book.

"I heard you were going to be here," Mala said.

"You have to leave. If he sees us together … If he thinks you and I are working together behind his back, he'll kill me."

Mala kept her face impassive. *You don't want Troe to realize you're conning him? So sad for you.* "I thought you'd be happy to see me. It's been awhile."

Stelle rolled her eyes. "Two months? Get out of here. I don't want you hurt, you stupid idiot."

The tone of Stelle's voice. The simultaneous frustration and affection clinched it. *They're together.*

"Maybe it's worth getting hurt," Mala retorted. *Whatever he's doing, Lowe thinks you're worth it. Betraying the Senebals. Betraying me.*

"Just hand over the girl already. And then Tier gets his Kreis. And then I'm free to leave."

Mala stood stock-still. Until she remembered she was already supposed to know all of this. "You really think they'll let you leave?"

Stelle's lip wavered. She stepped forward. Suddenly her lips were on Mala's. "We've had this discussion. Now get out of here." She pushed Lowe toward the door.

But the handle turned. Stelle froze. Mala scrambled back to her hiding spot.

The prince strode in, with a confidence too bright for a disfigured teenage boy. His smile was feral.

"So … whadja' see?"

"She needs the boy. What Tier said is true: this girl has limitations. She's not as powerful as you."

What?

The prince waved his hand dismissively. "A' course she's not. What I care about is how she got close. What'd she do?"

Stelle bowed her head. "I can't see the past."

The prince knocked her book out of her hands. "You'll need to give me somethin' more than excuses."

Stelle scrambled for her book and shuffled the pages. "Here, this is him: he's tall. Thin. He's there with her. Every time I see her. And I don't know what it is. But he's dangerous, I can feel it. He's dangerous."

Mala didn't need to see the picture to know Stelle was describing Ein.

"I think this boy came in with Keptiker. Let's go find yer danger, shall we?" He held out an arm. Stelle took it hesitantly. She pulled the door firmly shut as they left the room.

Mala almost fell out of her hiding spot. *They're going to get Ein! What do I do?*

CHAPTER FORTY-THREE

Mala slipped into the hallway. She grabbed the first unarmed Erlender that passed her. Slamming the girl into the wall, Mala grabbed her throat. And stared. She melted.

She let the girl run off screaming, as she continued down the hall. This time she didn't hide, assuming she'd melted into an Erlender. She did it again.

Grab a servant. Choke them. Melt. Let them run off screaming. Floor after floor she climbed, repeating the process. After three floors, she started to hear the thump of soldiers' boots. She grabbed her own neck hard and gave an ear splitting shriek.

Two blue noses came running. Mala pointed down the hall, breathing too hard to speak. The soldiers took off.

As fast as her legs would take her, Mala headed up to the sixtieth floor. Erlenders believed in demons. They believed in evil. *Hopefully they'll be spreading mud on every doorway and burning herbs in their cups. And those guards will be on a wild goose chase. Though the prince will know. He knew about me. He was looking for me. He'll be looking for me. I hope I bought us enough time.* As her thighs burned she tried to make decisions. She tried to weigh each option.

Mala had to catch her breath on the fortieth floor. She rounded a corner and saw a teenage Erlender couple struggling just beyond a stack of dusty cubicle walls near an open elevator shaft. The boy was wrapped head to toe, badly bandaged. The girl tugged at the boy, who froze when he saw Mala. The girl turned slowly. Mala started. *Alba!*

A second later Alba was on top of her, knife out.

"Alba!" Mala shrieked. "Don't!"

Alba froze, horror crossing her features. "How do you know me?"

Mala's eyes flickered between Alba and the bandaged boy, who'd crouched behind the cubicle stack. His face was grey, deathly ill. His blue tattoos were hardly visible. Red rims under his eyes … Alba was helping a dying Erlender. Mala felt pity rise up.

Sick of betrayal, two steps from death anyway, Mala decided to try trust. "It's really not gonna do much for your rep if you kill your roomie."

Alba froze. Her eyes narrowed. She climbed off Mala but kept the knife out.

For the first time, the boy came forward. He stood next to Alba staring down at whatever body Mala happened to be in. "Prove it."

Ges's voice nearly made Mala sob. She put her arms out to hug him but Alba stepped between them.

Mala stared past Alba, right into Ges's eyes. "It's not about what's probable. It's about what's possible."

Ges broke into a wide grin. He shouldered past Alba and enveloped Mala in a huge hug. "Here," he pulled out a flask and poured a little water onto her hand. Mala relaxed as she melted.

"Okay, what the hell is going on?" Mala asked, keeping an arm around Ges's waist. "Are you okay?"

"She didn't sell us out," Ges explained. "And I'm fine, I'm hero-ing. Apparently you need disguises and stuff. Which Alba is quite good at. Looking like a corpse makes people turn the other way. No one wants to look you in the eye."

"I came here to help," Alba said simply. "I thought the best way to prove to Tier and the Ancients that I wasn't with Blut … that I would never …. You know me. I want to help you."

Boots echoed up the stairwell.

Sludge. "Well, that help can start right now," Mala responded. "How the heck can we get outta here?"

Alba jerked her head. "Guess it's back to the elevator shaft."

Ges sighed. "If my arms don't fall off and I don't plummet to my death, I want it noted that I officially hate this. The anthill is so much better. I'll take boring dusty archives any day. Real heroics suck."

"Elevator was your idea, nerd-head," Alba boosted Mala onto one of the ropes, and then Ges, then swung aloft with one hand while she used the other to pull a lever that slid the elevator doors shut.

"What is that smell?" Mala tried not to gag.

"Elevator doesn't work. Guards turned the shaft into a latrine. Makes it an unpopular and dangerous way to travel."

"Yeah, don't ask us about any wet spots on our clothes," Ges muttered.

"Which way?" Alba asked.

"Up," Mala responded.

Ges groaned. "No!"

Mala grinned in the darkness. "It's only twenty more floors."

"Alba, hand me the knife. I'm pretty sure Mala wants us to kill her. Who other than a sadist would ever—"

"Ein should be meeting us at the top." Mala shimmied upward.

"Can't you climb any faster?"

A laugh bubbled up, but Mala swallowed it. She didn't want it to echo through the shaft. For the first time since she'd discovered she couldn't melt into the dead, she felt hope bouncing in her stomach, a tiny buoy in the midst of a terrible storm. *Thank you,* her mind whispered to the powers that be. As she heard Ges and Alba snipe at one another in whispers, she said it again: *Thank you.*

CHAPTER FORTY-FOUR

Mala's arms were screaming when Alba finally pried open the elevator doors on the sixtieth floor. The carpet was worn down to a grey moss. She collapsed onto it. Ges fell on top of her dramatically.

"You are going to have to spoon-feed me for the next two weeks," he groaned. "No, I take that back. Ein's going to have to do it."

Mala giggled.

Alba pushed the elevator doors shut. "Where is the brain-man?"

Mala froze. "On his way, I hope." She bit her lip, turning her head toward the stairwell, listening for sounds that weren't there. "He's been compromised. I tried to meltdown and freak out a bunch of servants. Tried to cause some chaos to give him a chance to get away. I dunno if it worked."

"What about Lowe and Neid?" Ges sat up.

"He's the mole." Saying it out loud made the hurt come back. Mala shoved it down. *There's no time for that, idiot. Focus. Focus.* She gave Ges and Alba the rundown.

"So Tier's in on it? He sold you?" Alba spit.

"Looks like it. Traded me for Kreis prisoners or something."

Ges nodded thoughtfully. "You die or disappear. Fell looks totally incompetent as your champion. He gets some Kreis prisoners of war back safe and sound… stays head of the Ancients. But wouldn't the King mind giving up prisoners? They never do that."

Mala shrugged a shoulder. "The prince didn't seem worried about it."

"The prince? Tier is working with some kid?" Alba scoffed.

"He could just be standing in for his dad. Easier for a kid to get around," Ges pointed out. "People don't notice kids."

Something Lowe had said months ago came rushing back to her. *People underestimate kids. 'Adults don't notice kids.' Maybe Lowe gave them the idea to use kids.*

"But, if Lowe is working with the Erlenders … why would he have killed Blut?" Alba asked. "That's messed up, if they're both on Troe's team."

Mala stared at the pair of them for a split second. *Why would he have made me kill Blut?*

"He's trying to save her. Get her out or something. Maybe Blut would have just handed me over to Troe. No trade."

Alba shrugged. "Kinda extreme."

"Look, you're talking about people who are all technically crazy," Ges reminded them. "Logic might not be their strong suit."

"Yeah, crazy," Mala repeated. *Lowe's crazy. For her. And I'm just some pawn …* a bitter taste filled her mouth. She let the bitterness harden into anger. *So he thinks.*

CHAPTER FORTY-FIVE

"We should just chain him up right away," Ges argued.

"That would blow Mala and Ein's cover, smarty," Alba retorted. "What are you gonna tell Troe? Oh, Keptiker just goes around tying up six-year-olds for no reason."

"Sh!" Mala stopped the bickering with a hand. *Shuffle. Scrape. Shuffle.* She heard gentle footsteps. Not Troe's soldier's boots, but the shuffle of worn shoes. *Ein?* She moved toward the stairs.

"Well, you caused some trouble," Ein muttered.

"Lowe?"

"Went to the kitchens to find out what the muck is going on. They're pulling everybody aside and questioning them. It's chaos. They're talking about a demon stealing people's skins. Hope it was worth—" He froze when he saw Alba and Ges.

"Um … we have some stowaways," Mala stammered. "Come to help." She pulled out a dusty office chair and gestured for Ein to sit. He did.

Ein cocked his head in silent question, but didn't speak. Alba and Ges jumped in, telling him how Alba had found Ges and

Neid's friend Bar, in the forest. Bar had run, but Ges had pounced.

"Like a kitten," Alba laughed. "But anyway, once it came out that everyone thought I was a traitor … and that Mala was here on this horribly understaffed under-planned mission … we just—"

"Decided to join forces. Little kitty and tiger mom to the rescue," Ges interjected.

Once their giggles subsided, it was Mala's turn. Slowly, she reached into her pocket and pulled out the drawing Troe had given her. She handed it to Ein.

"The chiara draws things. Troe thinks she draws the future. You heard Verrat before I killed her: she thought Keptiker was gonna kill her. And I melted into him. Technically, she was right."

Ein opened his mouth, sarcasm clearly written on his face. Alba and Ges kept silent. They had heard some of this. But Mala hadn't told them her plan. And she had to convince Ein that it was a good plan. Because she had the feeling he was the key to making it work.

She took a deep breath and continued, "The Chiara gave Troe a picture of your sister. Said she was dangerous. You saw that picture. The guards had it. When she saw them roughing you up, she got out of line. She was coming to help you. And they killed her."

"Troe's delusional and evil," Ein muttered.

"Even so … the Chiara gave him this drawing of me. She told Troe that I'll be his queen."

Ein's face contorted from shock to horror and then humor. "You can't be serious." He glanced at Alba and Ges, but they remained stoic.

Mala took a deep breath. "Ein, you've seen the girl I melt into when Lowe …" she couldn't finish.

"Yeah, the redhead," Ein supplied.

Mala forced herself to spit out the words. "His first love. The one you said he might not be over?"

"What does that—"

"She's the Chiara. Stelle. I saw her. She met with Troe. She's been feeding Troe all this information. All of these pictures." Mala ferreted around in her pocket. She pulled out the scrap in there. "But she burned the one of Lowe. This is from Wilde. She didn't bring it to Troe. She's drawn all the rest of us. But she hid his picture."

Ein's jaw dropped. "Lowe is the mole?"

Mala bit her lip. "Unless you think she's really predicting the future." *Come on, Ein. Possibilities. Not probabilities.*

Ein snorted.

Mala continued, "That's why I melted into him this afternoon. To be sure."

Ein stared, waiting, until Mala gave a solitary nod.

"Why? Why the hell would he do this? Why would he get my sister killed?"

"I know there's some kind of exchange—Stelle's freedom is worked into the deal for bringing me in—me for some Kreis prisoners. Tier and King Troe have some kind of deal. Troe and his sons… one of them is interested in how I melt. How I got the way I am."

"If Tier is trading you … we can't trust anyone at the Center."

Mala nodded. "We're alone." And she felt like she was treading water in the middle of a lake, in the midst of a storm. *Alone.*

Alba grabbed her hand. "Not quite alone. But not government guppies anymore. Bottom-feeding Ancient. But what are we going to actually *do*? Other than stop taking orders from people obviously out to kill us."

"Well …" Mala took a deep breath. "I have an idea. It's kind of out there. But you're gonna have to trust me and just do it. Do you trust me?" She stared straight at Ein.

He cocked his head. "Is it that bad?"

Mala bit her lip. She managed a small grin. "I don't think it's any worse than being paraded around in your underwear, shocked with electricity, forced to kiss an entire lineup of guys …"

"Okay, point taken," Ein smiled. "I'm evil. I'll do it."

Mala heaved a sigh of relief. "Good." She dug into the flight suit's front pocket. This time she pulled out the tiny item that she'd pocketed during her long wait for the Chiara. Slender and black, it sat like a tiny arrow on her palm.

"Yes!" Ges whispered. Alba chuckled.

Ein looked at it. "No!" He backed up.

"You promised!" Mala said. "Besides, if this doesn't work, who cares? Stupid Mala. Lowe's a traitor and I'm an idiot and Ein's right about everything. And the world goes back to normal. It's just a pinprick."

"Why the hell would you do this? I'm not even Kreis!" Ein retorted.

"I can't prove she can paint the future. But I can test whether magic exists," Mala replied slowly. "And I know you think this is crazy. But I've been thinking, since the prince asked this afternoon about me. About how I got the way I am. About what I did. He thinks I did something. That someone did something to make me what I am. And I was thinking about everything—this ceremony, Ges and blood sacrifice. We read a book. Ges and I. We thought it was the cut that was the blood sacrifice. But the final trial made me think—"

Ges sucked in a breath, the first to figure out where Mala was headed. Ein tried to interject, but Mala waved him off.

"My mom died to save me. The same night I did this stupid little ritual. And Neid tried to save you … Look I know that *this* is wishful thinking. Crazy talk. All of that. But we're partners, right? And I don't want to lose you. So I did some crazy things today. I melted down a couple times. Spread some chaos. People think demons are on the loose. But it won't be enough. Because Stelle drew you, too. Troe's looking for you."

Ein froze.

Mala grabbed his hand, "Ein, please please just do this for me. One little cut and then I'll know. I'll know that it's stupid, I just—I need this. If I can save you … Please. For me."

Ein gazed at her and she registered the pity in his look. But she didn't care. She had to know.

"Fine," he rolled his eyes.

Mala sucked in a breath. She held the hour hand like a knife. She turned Ein's palm faceup. She kissed it gently. "Thank you, Ein."

Alba took a spot near the stairs to keep watch. Ges stood back a respectful distance. Mala pulled Ein to his feet. She carved a line into his palm, waiting until the blood pooled on the surface. "Repeat after me."

Ein followed her, word for word: "Divine Spirit, split me open. Take what you need. In return, protect me. That no harm may look upon my face."

When it was done, Mala stretched up and kissed him. A soft grateful kiss, unlike those they'd shared before. A longer kiss, deeper and more passionate. And when she felt sure of herself and her emotions, Mala pulled back slightly and opened her eyes.

"Ein, look at me."

His hazel eyes were dazed. Until suddenly they wavered. And melted. They turned a brilliant blue. His hair curled and turned black. He shrunk several inches. His biceps ripped his worn grey jumpsuit.

Ges whooped. Alba abandoned her post.

"No mucking way," Ein stared down at Lowe's body. He held up his hands, Lowe's hands, turning them back and forth. He went to the window, staring at his reflection. "You poisoned me. I'm feverish. Delusional. This is not possible."

Mala smiled. Hope bubbled in her stomach. Ecstasy. *It's real.* She couldn't help herself. She spun around.

She grabbed Ges's hands. "It worked!" She forced him to

spin with her until they collapsed, dizzy on the floor.

As they lay sprawled, Mala asked, “Do you know how amazing this is?”

“Do you mean, how improbable?” Ein was still examining his reflection.

“Since I was four, I thought I was crazy. I thought I was cursed. I don’t know. I’ve just always thought … somewhere in the back of my mind … I’ve always believed. Do you know how good it feels to not be insane?”

Ein snorted, “Do you know how insane it is that this actually worked?”

Mala just grinned at the missing ceiling tiles.

Ges leaned over her. “Ok, I know it probably won’t work. But since it’s possible … me next.”

Alba chimed in. “Me, too.”

Mala grinned and got to her feet. Twice, they tried the ritual. Once, on Ges, nothing happened. When Mala planted a gentle kiss on Alba, the teen melted into a bony blond pre-teen. It appeared the blood sacrifice was essential to the magic. Alba stuck out a tongue at Ein. “Hate you.”

Ein raised an eyebrow. “Really? You wish your sister dead so that you could—”

“Gosh, you don’t have to get so morbidly literal. I’m just insanely jealous that you can melt into anyone you want, that’s all,” Alba rolled her eyes.

Ges cleared his throat. “So to break up this awkwardness, Ein I have a crush on you.”

Silence.

Then laughter.

"As if that hasn't been obvious since you were eight," Ein rolled his eyes. "Sorry. Other team."

Ges smiled, "I know. Just putting it out there. In case we die and all," he shrugged. "Plus, foot-in-mouth over there really knows how to put a damper on the fact that you're now our secret weapon."

"That's true. I'm kind of indispensable."

"Do not build his ego," Alba groaned as she melted back into her adult warrior goddess form. "Mala, please. Tell me the plan involves Ein melting into a dog."

Ein's eyes lit up. "We've never attempted cross-species—"

"Nope," Mala replied. "No dogs. But I was thinking about Troe. He sees himself on the throne with me as queen. He's trading people to get me. Or his son is. He must really want me for something."

"And we don't know why. Without knowing why we have no clue what you're walking into. It could be a trap," Ein argued.

She swung her gaze to Ein. "Normally, I'd agree. But, like Ges said, now that we have a secret weapon. Now that you're a potential substitute for a king … maybe we should make his dreams come true."

Alba sighed. "I always thought I'd look good in a crown. But I guess you won't be too bad either."

Ges punched her.

CHAPTER FORTY-SIX

They sat in a cross-legged circle on the floor of the abandoned conference room. "So, what's the plan?" Ges asked.

"We can't do much," Ein replied. "Lowe still has to think he's in control."

"True," Alba reflected. "But we could totally recon the princes. Figure out which one is the real son. Which one is meeting the chiara. And any other dirty little secrets they have."

Mala turned to Alba, impressed. "That's a great idea."

Alba shrugged. "You've got the hard job. How are you gonna pretend everything's normal with Lowe?"

Mala sighed. "Unfortunately, I've got years of practice to fall back on. When I thought I was crazy … it's not so different. Pretend to be happy. Normal."

"Yeah, except this backstabber broke your heart," Alba stated.

Mala swallowed. She tried to smile, to shake it off. But the truth echoed in her head. *He still loves her.*

"Alba, maybe you should talk about the job and only the job," Ges said. "Otherwise you and I need to sit down and have a chat about something called tact."

Alba stuck her tongue out at him. The distraction gave Mala a minute to recover her composure.

Ein rolled his eyes. "What about me?" he asked.

"Does she love you?" Alba snorted. "If you'd heard half the things she's said—"

"I meant, what's the plan for me? Mala falling for me is a given." Ein stretched his legs across the circle and kicked Mala with a foot. He winked.

Mala rolled her eyes. "Focus, everyone. We only have a couple more minutes before guards hit this floor. I'm sure they're mounting a full building search after my stunt." Her eyes studied Ein. He'd easily melted back to himself with a few drops of water. *He can't stay that way. Not with the prince and Stelle looking for him.* "We need to get you to melt. Into an Erlender. And fast. Ein needs to disappear right now."

Ein stared at her. "Well, just kiss me."

Mala gulped. Ein watched her expectantly. Alba and Ges studied their fingernails, the wall, anything other than Mala's tomato-red face. She stuttered, "I … I don't know if I can—"

"It's all about intentions, remember?"

She shrugged, "I get that intellectually—"

"Are you sure? Do you get *anything* intellectually?" Ein raised a brow.

Mala leaned across the circle and punched his arm. "I don't think it's as easy to control how I feel, particularly right now when my boyfriend just turned traitor—sludge-head."

"Just try."

Alba pulled Ges to his feet. "Ges and I are gonna split up prince duties and come up with some kinda rotation for spying on them. Then Mala needs to melt and get her Keptiker-looking butt downstairs. And we need to hide." They wandered into the hall.

"See I can be tactful," Alba pointed out.

"First time for everything," Ges's retort drifted back through the doorway.

Ein leaned close. "You act like kissing me is a chore."

"It kinda has been, hasn't it?"

"I know you're attracted to me," he whispered.

"Attraction isn't enough. I need to feel something unique right? Unfortunately, you're not the first cute muckhead to be a jerk to me." Mala retorted.

"I bet I'm the first genius you've ever met," Ein preened.

"Yes. I'm in awe of your ability to come up with evil torture to subject me to. Your creativity knows no bounds."

Ein gave a grumpy sigh. "Could you at least try to muster up something positive? Your entire plan is predicated on me being able to one day melt into Troe …"

Mala stared at him slowly. And an evil grin of her own spread across her face. "You know, *I* don't have unique feelings for you. But someone else here does."

Ein's jaw dropped. "You need to at least try—"

Mala cut him off. "Ges, could you come back in here?"

CHAPTER FORTY-SEVEN

No nerves. No nerves. Don't reach for your necklace. Don't touch your neck. It's your tell. He knows it. Mala, back in Keptiker's body, slipped into his assigned guest room. She glanced at the striped candle on the nightstand. Less than an hour until the official presentation of taxes and tributes. Then she'd be back on the road. Supposedly. Unless the handoff was first. But after much discussion, they'd agreed. Lowe was more likely to get rid of her on the road, when Keptiker's disappearance wouldn't cause such chaos. People died on the road all the time. It would be easier to explain than a disappearance in Troe's compound.

You can do this, she tried to pump herself up. *He's only an assassin.* She barked out a laugh at the bare room. *And I thought I was crazy before.*

Her door opened and she turned with a start. Lowe walked in, a six-year-old ball of energy and fluster.

"We have to leave," the words were out of Lowe's mouth before he shut the door behind him. His head barely surpassed the doorknob, but the tone of his voice was commanding. "Now."

"What? Why?" Mala's adrenaline kicked into high gear.

Leave now? But the tribute? The road. I'm supposed to have more time! Improvise, idiot. Improvise.

"We can't leave this second. It'll look suspicious." Mala reached for a blanket, only to have Lowe yank it out of her hands.

"It's dangerous. Too dangerous. We can't stay." He turned to the wall, where their belongings were piled. "Grab some weapons. And let's go." There was an edge to his voice, almost a tremor.

Feeling guilty? A tiny bit sad you're about to trade me? Mala ignored Lowe and kicked off her shoes, sitting on the bed. "We can't leave. There's too much chaos right now." She watched him strap an axe to his back.

"Yeah, I saw. There are exorcisms and crazy things going on in the kitchen. The servants are stringing up amulets like ornaments."

"They had a picture of Ein. They were gonna kill him. I had to do something so he could get out."

"He's gone?" Lowe's jaw dropped.

Mala nodded. She recited Alba's advice in her head.

"Half-truths are better than lies. He's been trained to spy on people. He's been trained to sniff out lies. Half-truths are harder to identify," Alba had talked Mala through this moment three times, while Ein had jimmied open an electrical access panel in the wall. It was a thin gap between two adjoining rooms, lined with wires that looked like limp, dead snakes. It was cramped, but the three of them could hide there. They could shuffle sideways from room to room and force their way out through another panel if necessary. And, as

Ein had pointed, out, most of the panels had rusted shut.

"I doubt anyone here even knows what the heck this panel's for. They clearly haven't had electricity in decades. Haven't opened it. We'll be fine."

Mala hoped he was right. She jerked herself out of her reverie and focused back on Lowe's shocked expression.

"Ein just left you?"

Mala shrugged, sticking to the script. "We're out of here in two hours. We just have to stand there for Troe while he does a ceremony—probably some ridiculous blood-letting, rain-dance thing."

"Why didn't you go with him?" Lowe strapped a knife to his ankle and dropped his pant leg. He stared at Mala, cocking his head like a bird. Piercing. Inquisitive.

Mala sat up in shock. *He knows! He knows I know! No... he doesn't. Don't be paranoid. Don't give it away.* "Why would I do that?"

"You need him."

"We need to complete our mission." Mala countered and stood.

Lowe's lips thinned. His fury was obvious. "And what if they have a picture of you too? You just put on a ridiculous demonstration of power. Erlenders are screaming their heads off about the devil, and a spell to end the world. You need protection. Mucking hell! This will leave you … we can't do this! We need to find him."

"No we don't."

"What if you meltdown? There's no way to reverse it. Without him you can't control your melts, Mala! You're in danger!"

A thought occurred to Mala and she smiled. *You want him because without him, I'm useless. A gun without a firing pin. An expensive doorstop. Not a very good trade.*

"You're insane!" Lowe roared.

Mala's eyes snapped back to Lowe's. Her hands acted of their own accord. Faster than she could blink, she smacked Lowe across the face and swiveled him into a chokehold.

"I am *not* crazy," she whispered. But, a second later, she wasn't so sure.

His skin shivered beneath her. It undulated in waves. And suddenly, she wasn't holding a six-year-old. Lowe had melted into his brawny mid-twenties—head still shaved, still sporting a black eye, and still far more lethal than Mala.

It only took another second before Lowe had Mala pinned to the ground, his knee at her throat. He took a deep breath. "I'm sorry. I shouldn't have said that. I didn't mean it. I know what those words mean to you…" Lowe paused, gathering his thoughts as he stared across the room. Then he looked down at her. His eyes were so full of tears it looked like the ocean was crashing inside them. "I would never hurt you—"

"Don't!" Mala snarled. Fire took over her skin. It crackled along her skin and thundered through her brain. Lowe let go of her, stumbling backward, a haunted expression on his face. And Mala knew, without looking, that her hair was a messy red.

She launched herself off the floor and flew at him. She

kneed him where it hurt most. *Now—even now, when you're about to sell me to men who'd skin me alive—you're thinking about her?*

"You'd never hurt me? But trading is okay? Selling me?" She dug her nails into his throat until she drew blood.

Lowe's eyes widened. He opened his mouth to retort, but she placed a freckled hand over it, muffling any excuses. He didn't block as she reared back her arm and punched his temple. She was shocked when he slumped to the floor.

"Father-mucking-sludge!" She checked his pulse. He was still alive. *Now what? I just ruined the plan. Just ruined it. Ruiner.* But the anger and adrenaline pumping through her system wouldn't let her regret her choice. *He deserved it. Mud-breathing traitor.*

She grabbed a pitcher and emptied it over her head, unable to stand being in Stelle's skin another second. *Damnit. Think. He's alive. Strip the weapons.* She removed his weapons and went to the window. Mala used his knife to cut the pull strings from the industrial blinds. She used the strings to bind his hands and feet.

The adrenaline started to make her shake. So she paced, deciding on her next move. *Do I kill him? But he was working with Tier. Tier made the deal. Tier sold me out. But Tier runs the Kreis. I kill him, I'm killing a Senebal soldier. It's an act of war. No turning back. But would they kill me at this point anyway? Not if I can go through with the trade. I want to go through with the trade. That was the plan. If we can take over the Erlenders and put Ein in as a false king, we can end the war... but without his handoff... Damn it. Maybe I should have stayed in that witch's body.*

Lowe started to stir. Mala kicked his head. He stilled.

Troe wants a queen. The Chiara told him she had a candidate. Mucking hell. Forget this. Mala ripped open the door and stomped down the hall, a brown-haired mess in men's oversized clothing. *Why make a plan when I'll just muck it up? I'll just make this up as I go.*

CHAPTER FORTY-EIGHT

Mala marched down to the first floor, ignoring the stares sent her way. She pushed through the double doors that led to the receiving area, where Troe met with his petitioners. She wove through the maze created by cubicle walls and clusters of guards that blocked any view of the throne. Mala by passed the line of starving Erlenders respectfully waiting their turn to plead their case for grain or sheep or shoes. No one stopped her.

Either I look intimidating, or I look like I'm reporting back after an attack. She grimaced at her own appearance. *Definitely an attack.*

Mala dodged around a family with unruly toddlers. *This not planning thing is working out—*

A hand closed around her neck. An Erlender soldier, with pock marked cheeks, a crooked nose, and a friendly smile stared at her. "Hey there—in a rush, darlin'?"

Mala met his eyes. They belied the friendly smile. They were so brown they were almost black, and they were as hard as stone. Behind her, she heard one of the toddlers cry.

"I don't talk to the help," she scoffed.

His smile widened. "Seems ya' jus' did." He let his fingers contract further around her neck. He lifted her, choking her. "Now, why you rushin' through here when all these good folks done waited their turn?"

Once he let her breathe, she gasped out her retort. "I'm special."

"And they're not?"

"Not like me." Mala gave him her most condescending look.

"You're better 'n them, then? How's that?"

"I'm a Senebal."

The guard dropped her. Mala latched onto his arms as she fell. He reached for a weapon. She wrapped her arms tight as a vice around him, so he couldn't lift his gun. She held his gaze as he tried to shake her off. She saw the flicker of surprise, of doubt, then anger. Anger turned into fury.

I can work with that, Mala thought as her stomach exploded in heat. Fire trailed up her limbs and danced over her eyelids. She melted down into a brawny beast of a man. The new body shredded even Keptiker's uniform. She slowly loosened her hold on the guard, who quaked in fear.

"I forgot to mention, I'm also a demon," Mala whispered in his ear. She heard a splattering sound. A smell wafted toward her. He'd pissed himself.

Mala grabbed his gun and shook her head, clucking her tongue at him. "I'm disappointed. I thought you were braver than that."

She gazed at him, then at everyone in the nearby vicinity.

"You will be silent," her baritone boomed down the hall. One of the toddlers cried again, cringing against his mother as he stared at her. Mala had to fight her instinctive need to comfort him. She needed these people afraid. She needed to remain untouchable. She needed to get to Troe.

Mala pointed at the boy but kept her eyes on his mother. "Silence it, before I eat it." The woman immediately scooped up her child and stepped back.

Mala turned to her guard. "You will escort me to Troe. You will do nothing foolish. Or I will wear the skins and eat the souls of everyone you've ever loved."

She wondered for a second if she'd laid it on too thick. But then the guard stumbled over his feet as he turned and led Mala through the slithering queue of petitioners. As Mala followed him a bubble rose in her chest. Full of adrenaline, full of giddiness, she had to bite back a laugh that people were taking her seriously. That she was almost to her goal. That her power made people wet themselves. She felt like a kid who'd stolen sweets and gotten away with it. *I'm just the mumbler's daughter everyone. Surprise. It's a hoax. Until they skin me.*

Mala bit her lip as the adrenaline bubble burst and fear came rushing back. She was treading in dangerous waters. The current could shift any moment, from fear to a mob mentality. She'd seen mob mentality at work …

She took a deep breath to steady herself as the last of the cubicle maze fell away to reveal a huge ballroom. The floors were white marble, but they were overshadowed by the walls. The walls were a blinding array of sparkling gemstones. Every Erlender for the last fifty years had been required to provide jewelry as part of their taxes. And Troe had decided that such magnificently useless trinkets shouldn't be left in his coffers. They should line the walls. Artists had been commissioned to create murals from the jewelry. *Murals of the time before the bomb—before the Freeze,* Mala corrected herself. She had to start using Erlender terms for things. Particularly since she was about to become their queen.

Mala tore her eyes from visions of diamond airplanes soaring like angels through a sky of sapphires and amethysts. She focused on Troe, who perched upon a cracked leather recliner, listening to a scrawny woman blabber in front of him.

"Then he got the spots. All ova'. And my otha' son. He gots 'em too. And then everyone wuz gettin' em. And fifteen youngin's already died. We got six more so bad right now, they can' see straight."

Mala strode up to the front. The guards surrounding Troe immediately drew their weapons. Mala held up her hands to show she was unarmed.

Troe turned in his seat. His electric green eyes seared her, taking in the state of her wet and shredded clothing. He glanced questioningly at the guard who had escorted her. But the guard merely trembled. His fear of a demon outranked his fear of his king.

"Your majesty," Mala swept into a bow. "Might I trouble you for a glass of water?"

Troe cocked his head. "All this way, an' that's all you want? You coulda' stopped at da' river."

“Please,” Mala made her tone respectful.

Troe nodded to a lackey, who ran out of the room, returning out of breath with a glass of water. The servant presented it to Mala.

“You have yer water,” Troe said. “Now I wancher name. An’ yer real purpose.”

“King Troe. I’m Mala. I’m here to be your queen.” Mala’s baritone echoed through the room. One of the guards cut off a laugh. Troe cracked a smile as he stared at her, eyebrows furrowed, trying to decipher her endgame.

Mala looked him in the eye as she saluted him with the cup. She suspected Troe would have had his servants add a little something ‘extra’ to her drink. *Might as well let them think I’m immune to poison, since I’m a demon and all.* Then she tipped the cup and let the water touch her closed lips. The melt took over. She returned to her own skin.

Shocked gasps erupted like geysers around the room. A hundred guns swiveled to face her.

Back in her own skin, Mala shook out her curls. She gave a small smile and folded her hands demurely in front of her. “I do believe you’ve been told to expect me. Well, here I am.”

Feedback

Please leave me a review. I want to see what you think probably as much as you want to club me right now for a cliffhanger. I am working on book 2. Promise.

Acknowledgements

To the big man, Rob, and Sarah: you have my unending gratitude.

A huge thank-you to all those people who picked and prodded and complained and cajoled until I revised the story to their liking: Cass, Stefan, Jenn and Jennie (my girls), Chip, Karen, Aubry, Marian the Librarian, Eric, and everyone else. I am also eternally grateful to my parents for their support and my children for their inspiration.

About the Author

I'm at Stay at Home Bookkeeper for my husband and Stay at Home Mom to two wonderfully mischievous children under age 5. I write after bedtime, so I suppose I should thank the creators of Melatonin for the ability to write this book. Just kidding. Sorta.

I love the arts: painting, theatre, and reading. I have an undergrad degree in Playwriting and a grad degree in Theatre History. Socrates rocks my socks.

I'm an INTJ. If you've never taken a Meyers Briggs personality test, I recommend them. I also recommend signing up for my email list. I will email to let you know when Book 2 is complete. If you're brave enough to contact me, I MIGHT let you read the first chapter of Book 2.

Be Social

Connect with Ann Denton via:

Facebook: Facebook.com/AuthorAnnDenton

Twitter: Twitter.com/AnnDentonAuthor

Instagram: Instagram.com/AnnDentonAuthor

Goodreads: Goodreads.com/AnnDenton

Her website: www.AnnDenton.com

59623295R00211

Made in the USA
Lexington, KY
10 January 2017